T-FLAC

GIDEON

BOOK TWO

NEW YORK TIMES BESTSELLING-AUTHOR

CHERRY-ADAIR

Have fun with Gideon and Riva
Cheers
Cherry Adair

GIDEON
Copyright © 2015 by Cherry Adair

ISBN-13: 978-1937774639
ISBN-10: 1937774635

www.cherryadair.com
shop.cherryadair.com

ACKNOWLEDGMENTS

For Mandi Beck because I promised.

ONE

The proverbial shit was about to hit the fan.

The *fan:* the vintage SE3160 Alouette helicopter carrying T-FLAC operative Riva Rimaldi.

The *shit*: a vision of a fiery explosion followed by the chopper hurtling toward the ground in flaming pieces.

Five out of the six people on board were about to die.

In lieu of a seatbelt, Riva gripped the cracked seat on either side of her hips as the chopper shimmied and rattled through pockets of turbulence. Whatever the cause of the explosion, she was sorry she couldn't forewarn the two operatives accompanying her of their impending death. A head's up would be useless. That was the bitch of her psychic ability. When she had a vision, she knew precisely *what* would happen, but not *when*.

Cheerful morning sunlight flooded the cabin, highlighting the hirsute, overweight pilot, Manny Ferrari. Anything less like a sleek, Italian sports car would be hard to find. A dirty wife-beater tank top showed hairy, beefy arms oily with sweat. His concentration was evident in the beetling of his Neanderthal brows and his white-knuckled grip on the throttle and cyclic control stick.

For a moment, she was downwind of him and her eyes watered at the smell. Garlic, sweat, and booze oozed out of his pores. Despite the chopper being doorless, he stank as badly as the two armed soldiers seated behind her.

She didn't need to read the microexpressions on his face to know what was going on in his head. He was shit-scared, and praying just as hard as any of his passengers.

Ferrari let out a string of obscenities as they bounced on a gust of air and he had to fight the controls. The cargo was too heavy; weapons, she knew. It was a damn miracle the bird had managed to lift off the ground in the first place.

"Are you capable of landing this piece of shit without killing us?" Riva demanded so that she had a reason to lean in and scan the controls. No GPS on this old chopper. Like the helicopter, the comm was crappy and crackled with feedback. His GPS was his watch, which she couldn't read from her position. Pilot error and antiquated equipment was not what was going to kill him, though.

Sweat ran from Ferrari's temple to the thick black shadow of his jaw. It took a full minute for him to respond. "Don't you *know*, Señorita Estigarribia?"

Riva settled back against the ripped plastic seat, cinching her arm more tightly around the bag on her lap.

"Would you like me to tell your future for you, Manny?" she asked sweetly.

With a shake of his head and muttering under his breath, the pilot crossed himself, then raised the fingers of his right hand to his lips. Then he was back white-knuckling the controls.

For the last-minute flight from Montana to Bogotá, she'd been given shots, pills, and the dossier and audio files of the woman she was impersonating—Psychic Graciela Estigarribia. Riva had spent every second in flight reading the intel on Maza and Graciela, and listening to recordings of their conversations. She was immersed in her role.

Now, it looked as though she might not need any of that intel.

The engine sounded asthmatic. The shitty condition of the chopper came as a surprise, because Escobar Maza had a fleet of high-tech planes at his disposal. As an added touch to throw off any observers, a faded red cross was visible on the fuselage. He was, quite literally, flying his psychic in under the radar.

The verdant canopy, whizzing by below, seemed dangerously close. Almost close enough to brush with her fingertips. As far as the eye could see, lush green. Jungle. Mountains. Trees. No signs of habitation, though Riva had no doubt there were plenty of dangerous humans, animals, and assorted other nasties lurking beneath the canopy.

One million three hundred thousand people lived in Cosio's two major cities, Abad and Santa de Porres, the capital. The small country, strategically placed between Ecuador, Colombia, and Peru, was just over six thousand square miles, consisting mostly of dense jungle, old emerald mines, and mountains.

How the hell would she find Maza if she was dropped in the middle of thousands of miles of jungle alone? Presuming her vision of one survivor was correct—she never saw her own future-and if *she* was the lone survivor, that didn't mean she'd be ambulatory. She might well live, but be incapacitated. In which case there was a big fat freaking *zero* chance of survival.

Riva had just nine days to find Escobar Maza, figure out his plan, then kill him. It would really screw up the plan if she ended up incapacitated.

Releasing her death grip on the seat, she unzipped the backpack strapped across the front of her body. As subtly as possible, she started removing things that could mean the difference between life and death should she and her pack part company. Small Mag light into her vest pocket, box of ammo for her SIG-Sauer P230SL into a pocket of her cargo pants.

While she waited to be blasted from the sky, Riva did a mental tally of what she knew. Superstitious Maza, head of the Sangre Y Puño, believed in the afterlife, psychics, and fortune tellers, so much so that he had his own clairvoyant on tap. He did *nothing* without consulting his psychic first. He spoke to Graciela on the phone daily. T-FLAC knew something was in the wind when those calls escalated to three, then four times a day.

Seven hours earlier, he'd insisted that Graciela join him in Cosio *immediately*. Cosio was *not* Maza's territory, Usually operating out of Europe, Maza always moved his base of operations one step ahead of the law. He was savvy as hell. Intel said he'd been in Cosio for five months, arriving with a huge, well-armed army, and shitloads of money provided by his massive drug enterprises.

To what end? Was the SYP trying to horn in on the ANLF, their biggest competitor?

The ANLF—the Abadinista National Liberation Front— wasn't based in the city of Abad. It had nothing to do with liberation, and everything to do with the drug trade, extortion, and arms dealing. Maybe back in the days of the group's inception it had stood for some politically charged endgame, but those roots were long forgotten. Now the

ANLF were international terrorists, extortionists, and killers, their global enterprises run by the mysterious, almost mythical, Sin Diaz.

Putting Diaz and Maza, two of the world's most wanted terrorists, in one very small, volatile country was like putting two high explosives in one tiny container. It was only a matter of time before the damn thing blew, and T-FLAC's intel indicated that time was running out. They knew that Maza had something big in the works. All they had to go on was an educated guess. And Graciela.

Speculation was currently centered on the possibility that Maza was planning some horrific surprise for the top-secret BRICS Summit being held in Santa de Porres in nine days. Clearly not a *secret* summit if Maza knew about it and was lying in wait. And if the BRICS Summit wasn't his target, what the hell was? The conference was all T-FLAC had to go on for now.

Whatever it was, it was imminent, and important enough that Maza wasn't content with the increased phone contact with his psychic. Since he insisted on having her on tap for minute-by-minute predictions on site, T-FLAC had switched out Riva for Graciela. Both women were five seven, with dark hair and brown eyes. Riva was in her late twenties to Estigarribia's mid-thirties. Close enough.

As far as T-FLAC knew, Maza and his psychic had never met. Sending Riva in was a risk worth taking. It would be easy enough to modulate her voice to match Graciela's.

Maza's soldiers had been waiting at the private strip in Bogotá to pick up Estigarribia and her two bodyguards, all of whom had been whisked off by T-FLAC before they made it to the airfield, leaving Rimaldi, Sanchez, and Castro to take their places.

Riva dug in her backpack again, then stuffed two protein bars into her hip pocket. More from anticipation than fear, her heartbeat was slightly elevated, yet she felt amazingly calm considering the approaching disaster. She thrived on danger and excitement, but dying before the op even got started wasn't in her plans.

Seated beside her, replacing Graciela's bodyguards, were fellow T-FLAC operatives Steve Sanchez and Ruiz Castro. As indicated by the sheen on his tanned skin, and his convulsive swallowing, Castro was about to puke. Fortunately, he sat on the other side of their commanding officer Sanchez, beside the open door.

"What's our estimated time of arrival in Santa de Porres?" Riva shouted in Spanish. She kept her tone cool, pretending a crash wasn't imminent as she tried like hell to get a fix on where in the damn jungle they were.

"We're not going to Santa de Porres, señorita," Luiz Vidal leaned in to shout directly in her ear. His breath suggested the recent death of a rodent. Maybe not so recent.

Mierda. "We can't deviate." The wind whipped the words away. "Señor Maza expects me."

"Do not concern yourself, Señorita Estigarribia. *Jefe* knows where you will be."

She made sure her GPS was safely tucked into the corner of her bag so *she'd* know where the hell she was.

The rest of the T-FLAC team expected them in Santa de Porres in a couple of hours. Control constantly tracked their position via satellite so they'd know where and when the chopper went down. The rest was up to Riva to figure out how to navigate six thousand miles of jungle to find her target.

Sweat trickled down the side of her neck to soak into her already damp T-shirt. It was insanity to travel in this part of the world practically unarmed, yet arriving in all-out combat gear would have created suspicion. That had been the subject of debate at the briefing. Some weapons would be expected. That didn't mean MP7s, Uzis, or handheld rocket launchers. Riva felt naked with only her SIG in the small of her sweaty back, the fighting knife in an ankle holster, and the mini boot knife hanging on a lanyard between her breasts. No one had blinked at the KA-BAR knife in the thigh holster.

The heavy backpack on her lap held a few more surprises. To ensure it went where she went, she'd angled and cinched the strap tight across her body. It was uncomfortable as hell, but was the least of her problems.

The chopper bucked high, then shuddered and dropped. One of the men behind her groaned. Taking a plastic dispenser of Tic Tacs out of her breast pocket, Riva popped several in her mouth. As she returned the container to her pocket she observed the blurred rush of the tree canopy. Three brightly colored macaws flew by the open door in a flash of blue and yellow, then disappeared high into the cloudless sky, indicating just how damned low the chopper flew.

She freed one hand from the seat to swat away a fist-sized black, buzzing insect, then resignedly addressed her fraying braid that had started to lash her face with loose strands. Given that her hair had a life of its own, and any braid was only a temporary fix, she found a ball cap in a side pocket of the backpack and crammed it onto her head.

Vidal, a tall, thin Cosian, tapped her on the shoulder. The fact that he'd been sent to pick her up showed how important Graciela was to the Sangre Y Puño. "You have everything you need in there, señorita?" he yelled, six inches from her ear.

"Of course," she said coldly, putting her hand on his forehead and giving him a less than gentle shove to get him out of her face just as the helicopter shook. "I don't ne—" The words cut off as the engine hiccoughed.

Riva's tightened her grip on her backpack with one hand, clinging to the seat with the other as she bounced up, then down, then up once more before landing on her tailbone on the hard seat. Biting her tongue, she tasted blood and annoyance. In a few minutes, biting her own tongue was going to be the very least of her problems.

A glance at Ferrari showed him leaning forward, all his concentration on flying the doomed chopper. "What's our ETA?"

"¡Cuarenta y siete minu- Qué chingados?"

She saw it as the pilot did. A bright, swiftly moving light headed up at them from the trees below.

"SAM." Surface-to-air missile? Out here? In the middle of nowhere? That answered the *shit* question.

Curling into a ball around her bag, one hand wrapped in the straps, Riva braced for impact. She might as well kiss her ass good-bye. Despite what she'd seen, no one would survive the hit, and if she did, she'd wish she hadn't.

Between one heartbeat and the next, the missile slammed the tail with a loud, fiery explosion, spinning what was left of the chopper end over end. A blast furnace of heat engulfed her as she was thrown around the cabin like a rag doll. Everything gyrated like a kaleidoscope around her, as if she were separate from the event. In the split second when rational thought was possible, Riva knew she couldn't jump out. Even if she had a chute, which she didn't, she'd be sliced and diced like chopped salad by the swiftly spinning blades if she attempted it.

I'm screwed.

Death wasn't the worst thing that could happen to her. At the age of five, Riva had taught herself, out of necessity, to block out fear. T-FLAC training had reinforced her self-taught ability to remain calm when the world turned to chaotic shit. Yet having never been in a helicopter crash before, she couldn't draw upon the cast-iron will she had created for herself, because reality was nothing like the simulated airplane crashes she'd endured. Things went crazy in ways she hadn't anticipated.

One of the men crashed into her and held her in a momentary death grip of flailing, fat arms, before metal flew through the air and partially decapitated him. Then her feet were over her head, as another man with burning fuel on his clothes flew past her. His mouth was open in a shriek she couldn't hear, temporarily deafened by the explosion.

Primal fear set in and all she could do was scream as she, and what was left of the burning chopper, hurtled uncontrollably toward the trees.

TWO

The acrid stink of burning Jet A fuel hung on the still, muggy air as Sin Diaz and a small group of his men hacked through thick vegetation to reach the crash site. There might be something they could learn from the wreckage. Even better if they found something to use against Escobar Maza.

Anything to even the battlefield.

It was a grueling three-hour hike up the mountain, through dense jungle filled with hungry animals and other assorted dangers. Always on the lookout for Maza's men, they were ever vigilant. They sliced a path with razor-sharp machetes in the direction of the giant fireball and thick plume of black smoke rising high over the tree canopy.

"This is no way for a man to spend his birthday, *amigo*," Sin's friend and first lieutenant, Andrés Garzon, teased him as they walked abreast. "We should be over at Ascencion's place. She has two new girls. I'll give them both to you for your natal day. You'll like Noely. She has big tits like pillows, and a tight—"

"Bringing down Maza's chopper is gift enough for me, *mi amigo*." Sin didn't want to discuss his lack of a sex life, even with his best friend. He forged slightly ahead as a thick tree trunk narrowed the path Tomás was cutting up head of them. "Perhaps I'll take you up on your offer to-morrow, my true birthday. Is that what we usually do for special occasions? Go to the local *putas*?"

"You forget even *this*?" Andrés muttered incredulously. "I'm disappointed, my friend. But not as much as I'm sure you are. Ah, to not remember the pleasure taken in a woman's arms? It's time to make new memories then. It will be like your first time, no?"

"I haven't forgotten *how* to do it," Sin told him dryly, hacking off a low-hanging branch that had whipped up be-tween his head and Tomás' machete ahead of him. "Have you forgotten Saturday night?"

"That was a month ago, my friend."

"A month. A week." Sin had other things on his mind. "What does it matter?"

"It matters very much to your *pollo,* I think. We will visit the ladies tomorrow. Then you'll remember what that tail is for."

Rain came intermittently, often in hard brief downpours they were used to. Sin ignored the water sluicing his skin and the wet cling of his shirt and pants. They'd dry soon enough in this heat. He kept slicing his way through the dense understory of vegetation, the vines as thick as his thigh, and as hard to sever as a steel cable. What they couldn't cut through, they circumvented.

The harsh drumbeat of water pounding the foliage made further conversation impossible. Just the way Sin liked it. His lack of recall bothered him more than he let on. In five months he hadn't regained any memory of his life before Maza himself had gunned him down in a battle Sin didn't remember.

It was annoying. What's more, it was dangerous as hell not to recall his own fucking life. Having his family and friends tell him who, what, and when, made him appear weak. Vulnerable. He needed those damned memories for himself. After almost half a year, Sin doubted that he'd regain more than the fragments he had now. Thirty-six years wiped out. Gone. It was disconcerting to know that everyone in the fucking camp knew more about him than he did himself.

The harsh stink of kerosene became more powerful the higher they climbed. Most of the animals, afraid of the humans and lights, kept their distance, but a bold monkey chattered from high in a giant mahogany tree, then swung off to join his tribe, yelling all the way. Flying insects stuck to Sin's damp skin, or swarmed in front of his face. Even the vegetation was dangerous. Lashed by sharp leaves and snaking vines, and tripped up by roots and thick foliage, their progress was slow. Cuts and scratches on his arms, some deep and long, burned and itched, but were ignored.

Keeping conversation to a minimum, and alert to any sounds of other humans on their ass, he and his men hacked and chopped. Everything in the jungle grew so rapidly that in days their path would once again be overgrown, hiding that they'd ever been there.

The rain stopped when they reached the smoldering wreck by midafternoon. Pockets of fire still burned orange, leaping into the air to cast dancing coppery reflections on the surrounding wet foliage.

Twists of blackened metal protruded from the trees, and a shredded seat, caught by a heavy branch, hung twenty feet above his head.

Sin surveyed the scene through watering eyes. Thick kerosene-oxide-scented smoke wove through the foliage and tree trunks like a noxious, ghostly, dark gray veil. "Tomás and Cesar keep watch," he said over the crackling of flames that fed on materials from the downed helicopter. The vegetation was too green and wet to burn, but leaves curled and turned black in retreat from the dozens of small and large fires.

"Just because Maza's people aren't on top of us now, doesn't mean they aren't on their way. Eduardo, Vincente, see if you can find anything useful."

The men went to do as instructed.

Andrés wandered into the clearing for a closer look at some of the smoldering debris, then returned to Sin. "You were right." His satisfied smile held a glint of gold in the flickering glow as he surveyed what they had wrought, using their enemy's own weapon against them.

Poetic justice, Sin thought, pleased. They lived in a feral dog-eat-savage-dog world. The ANLF and the Sangre Y Puño were constantly at odds. One group advancing, then falling back as the other got the upper hand. It was fucking exhausting. Frustrating. Sometimes Sin thought he'd just leave the jungle. Would it make a difference? He could go to a big city where he could lose himself. The bloodstains on his hands were harder to wash off these days, though. Killing and extortion were becoming a fucking drag, his newly awakened conscience, even more so. Had he always been this conflicted, or were his shooting and weeks-long coma, and mind-numbing recuperation, responsible? Hell if he knew. Hell if he could remember.

Where the fuck could he go and what would he do? The jungles of Cosio had been his home his entire life. And while he didn't remember most of his past, his mother and best friend did, and they, in their own warped, sick way, he supposed, cared about him. Yet something didn't seem right about the attention they gave him. Something was... off. Son of a bitch. His mind was playing games with him. He was becoming more paranoid by the day.

"That SAM *has* come in handy." Andrés, who'd secured it from the SYP, was proud of his grab. "Now we should be lucky enough to find Maza fried to a crisp, and our job will be done."

"From the flight path, they weren't heading directly into Santa de Porres," Sin pointed out, eyes scanning the shadowy area and the orange sparks dancing in the air like fireflies. "It looks like they were going farther into the higher elevations."

Sin had long suspected Maza had a camp up there. This could be the confirmation needed. If they could figure out the final destination of the flight, he and his men could do a night raid and take out the entire camp. That wouldn't defeat Maza, God only knew, but it might put a crimp in whatever he was planning next.

"With something of value being delivered, I hope." Andrés took out a bandana and swiped at his streaming eyes. "His loss is our gain."

They'd taken the surface-to-air missile from one of Maza's groups three months earlier. The son of a bitch had pockets of men training in hidden camps in the jungle. *Sin*'s jungle. Other than that night, when Maza had shot Sin, the two men hadn't met again. Sin had absolutely no recollection of that meeting. Just third-hand accounts and the scars to prove it had ever happened.

"What the hell is he up to?" It was a rhetorical question. They had no idea. The son of a bitch had shown up out of the blue right before Sin had been found, and had created mayhem while he'd been in a fucking coma. Well, he was awake now. Maza was determined to cut into ANLF's thriving business. Hell, he wanted all of it. Unacceptable. Sin and his ANLF soldiers pushed back. Maza and his soldiers retaliated.

By the sudden flurry of communications, and the influx of more and more weapons, they knew that whatever Maza was up to, it was big and it was coming *soon*.

Sin's eyes strafed the area as he peered into the darker pockets for movement or anything untoward. He motioned with his MP7A1 to keep walking.

"With any luck he was bringing in more weapons and ammo. We can use whatever we fin—" Sin raised the compact, lightweight submachine gun and stopped as a shadowed form emerged from the trees. He relaxed when he saw Tomás Saldana, but didn't lower the weapon. He was always ready to shoot something. "Find anything of value?"

"Ortiz and Vidal. Dead and partially burned, but Vincente recognized them. Found a third guy, probably the pilot. Another two guys we don't recognize. New recruits possibly. We hit the jackpot tonight. Several crates of submachine guns broke open. They're scattered all over hell and gone."

"Ammo?" Sin asked. Guns were only of use if there was ammunition to go with them.

Tomás grinned, showed his missing lateral incisors, making him look a little like a feral rabbit. "*Sí*. 9×19mm Parabellum cartridges. Looks like five, six crates. Also, 120mm mortar shells and MPT-9's."

The cartridges were business as usual, just in greater number than before, but the mortar shells indicated serious firepower, as did the Tondar submachine guns, Iran's answer to H&K's MP5s. Maza was gearing up for war. This had been in the air for months by the time Sin figured out that Maza was done with small skirmishes and was planning to take out the ANLF in its entirety. He had something bigger up his sleeve.

What, Sin had no idea.

He mentally cursed that he'd been incapacitated for so long, and now had to play catch up. "Radio Mama our coordinates, tell her to send up more men. Have them bring tools and those wood pallets behind the mess hall. They can make crates when they get here. Tell them *que se apuren*. Maza's people might not give a shit his top men are dead, but they *will* come for these weapons. We'll take what we can, come back later. Go get the others."

"We need to go into town, see if we can find out what he has planned," Sin said quietly, spotting something in the undergrowth a few yards away as they walked. Another broken crate of guns would be good. The howl of a puma reminded him they weren't alone, and predatory eyes watched their every move, just waiting for an opportunity to attack.

"What do we hear from Loza? Is he still feeding us intel?" Loza, a mole for the ANLF, and low on Maza's totem pole, was a mine of useful information. If and when they could contact him.

"For a hefty fee? *Sí.* I'll see if I can get hold of him; he's a slippery asshole. I'll leave a message with his sister."

Since Loza refused to deal with anyone other than Andrés, Sin merely said, "Good," as he used his machete to brush aside a dense clump of ferns growing amidst a tangle of leafy vines to see what had caught his eye. "Set it u— "

A pale, slender arm protruded from beneath the crushed branches. He pushed aside the concealing fronds to reveal the body of a young woman. "What the fuck?" Sprawled on her back, nestled on a bed of broken foliage, she gave the appearance of a sleeping woodland creature.

What a fucking waste that she was dead like the others.

As he straightened, he caught the flutter of her long eyelashes. Impossible. A trick of the light— No. There it was again. Her eyes didn't open, but her lids twitched as though she was dreaming.

Pretty sure it was his imagination he crouched beside her to feel for a pulse as Andrés said, "The animals will feed well tonight."

"She's *alive.*" Impossible, but Sin felt a faint pulse throbbing beneath her ear.

"No, *amigo.* It is wishful thinking." His friend reached down to peer at the woman's face. Other than smudges of black dirt, and leaves in her hair, she seemed blissfully asleep. "Too bad. She's a fox." Andrés laid his hand on Sin's shoulder. "Come, we need to make haste before Maza's men get here."

Was he mistaken? Sin repositioned his fingers to make sure it was her pulse he felt, and not the throb of his own heartbeat in his fingertips... No. A faint, but unmistakable pulse beat beneath her damp skin. "She's alive. Give me a minute to see what's broken. We'll take her back to camp. If she lives, she might have wealthy friends who'll pay ransom. Christ, wouldn't it be sweet if *Maza* pays the ransom?"

Andrés stood there shifting impatiently as Sin felt for broken bones. "Mama has good medical skills, but even she won't be able to knit every bone in this woman's body." Everyone in the ANLF referred to Sin's mother as Mama. From his tone, Andrés was clearly not happy about the new turn of events, no doubt thinking through the logistics of how they were going to get the woman down to camp. "Besides, she'll die on the way back, and you will have exerted yourself for nothing. Let Maza find his dead *puta* for himself."

Stunned to find anyone alive in the debris, Sin barely listened to Andrés as he ran his hands over her from head to booted feet. To survive such a fall meant she had extraordinary luck. And the ability to bounce, since she was the only passenger alive. She didn't react to his touch.

"Don't appear to be any bones broken, but God only knows what kind of internal injuries she's suffered. Here, hold this for a minute." Sin handed over his gun, then carefully lifted the woman in his arms. Her head flopped against his chest, and the long skein of a dark braid fell over his arm. She was light but solid in his arms, and smelled faintly of apricots and sweet mint.

"*Eres un idiota.*" Andrés shook his head. "How will you carry your—"

Sin maneuvered her limp body over his left shoulder in a fireman's lift, then held out his hand for his weapon.

"*Sí*, that will work." Andrés grinned as he handed back the submachine gun. "Ah, it looks like you got two birthday presents when the *helicóptero* was shot down."

"Well, don't light my birthday candles just yet. She might be dead before we get back to camp."

THREE

S in's birthday gift was all fucking kinds of inappropriate. Mama, not known for either her benevolence or generosity, had tended the woman's wounds, then returned her to him as a *regalo de cumpleaños.*

An unwrapped birthday gift.

As in naked.

And tied to his bed.

He entered his small cabin, eyes riveted to the offering Mama had provided. The sight shouldn't bother him, but considering that it was his mother making the offering, it sure as shit did. His cock paid attention, nonetheless, and he adjusted his fatigue pants to accommodate the restriction. He wasn't dead, after all.

Mama was the only other female in camp. Once there, he'd left the woman to be tended by her. She, in turn, had given him carte blanche to do with the woman as he wanted when she was done.

Sin wanted.

His dick twitched with anticipation, and his mouth watered at the thought of taking one of those tight little pale brown nipples between his lips to roll on his tongue. Sin allowed himself the luxury of letting his gaze play down the streamlined length of her, from shoulders to slender ankles, pausing now and then to admire the landscape.

Bruises, small cuts, and that long scratch on her thigh. A miracle, really.

The patch of hair between her legs was as black and silky as the loose strands of wavy, dark hair hanging wildly around her face and shoulders. Thick and glossy—freed from the long braid down her back—strands clung to her damp skin, concealing absolutely nothing.

Yeah. He wanted. But he doubted there'd be enough time between now and when she was interrogated to fully enjoy her and he didn't want to be on top of her when Mama walked back in. Whoever she was, the woman would soon wish she'd been killed in the crash. Mama wouldn't give her up to the Sangre Y Puño until she knew her value to the last *bolo*.

The SYP had nothing on his mother's interrogation techniques. She would extract, without mercy and with sadistic alacrity, anything the woman knew, at first light.

Sin almost felt sorry for his enemy's toy. Almost.

He dragged a straight-backed chair up beside the bed. Three questions needed to be answered: "Who are you?" he murmured. "What were you doing on Maza's chopper?" *And, most importantly, how can I use you against him?*

Because if she had *anything* to do with Escobar Maza, no matter how tangential the association, Sin *would* use her. He could hold her for ransom, either to Maza or her family. Someone would pay dearly for this one, he knew. Women this clean and pretty were valued for all kinds of reasons. Hell. He could use her as a *puta* until she bored him. Or he could just kill her and not be bothered.

With her wrists manacled to the rusted headboard, she lay stretched out in invitation like some fantasy pagan goddess. Sin could think of all kinds of ways to partake in her bounty.

Fascinated by the possibilities of his gift, he stacked his hands beneath his head, tilting the chair back on two legs. She had the body of an athlete. Long, taut lines, sleek toned legs, and small, high breasts, tip-tilted by her raised arms. Her nipples, soft and a pale pinkish-brown, drew his gaze before he dragged it back to her face.

Golden light from a simple oil lantern draped over her sweat-dampened, pale olive-colored skin like a glistening diaphanous blanket. Despite how and where she'd been found, and subsequent time spent on a bed of ferns, she smelled damn good. Flowers? Mint? His sex-starved imagination?

Christ. Andrés was right. It had been too long since he'd had a good fuck. Ascencion's whorehouse was only a few miles away in the village of San Mateo...

Except there was some serious crap brewing. He couldn't leave now. Which was just an excuse, no matter how valid. It showed him how unimportant sex had been to him lately. His gaze drifted for a moment to her wide mouth, the lower lip plump and the same color as her nipples. What had been unimportant was suddenly a paramount need. He liked the pillowy look of her mouth, liked that it matched her nipples. He thought of the things she could do with that wide, lush mouth and his cock stirred eagerly at the mental foreplay.

Forgetting sex was no easy task, considering what filled his vision, yet his head with a brain in it demanded that he think about something other than satisfying the smaller head that was yearning for release. If this woman was on that chopper because Escobar Maza *had* sent for her, then she was of value beyond just a satisfying fuck. Who was she to Maza, and why had she been sent for? He'd find out. One way or another. His enemy's loss was Sin's gain.

If Maza got wind she was still alive, was she important enough for him to try to retrieve her? A girlfriend? No, this was too odd a time to bring in a woman just for sex. A colleague? A specialist? Specializing in what, exactly?

Dropping the chair to all four legs, he traced the length of her legs, up, to her mound. What was this woman's skill? Unlike many of the men who lived in the jungle, he wasn't so much of a chauvinist to think that a good-looking woman couldn't be skilled in something other than pleasing a man. Not all females with power looked like his mother.

He'd seen the red cross through his sights in the instant before he fired the SAM. Still, he hadn't hesitated. He'd recognized Maza's chopper and knew the man wasn't flying in relief workers. Aid wasn't Maza's style. She and Maza's crew were as far away from international aid workers as he was from priesthood. Given what he'd been told of his life, that was pretty goddamn far.

An image of himself running through the jungle transposed itself over what he'd just been thinking about. It was him, but not. People yelling, shots fired, he was afraid—but not for himself... A blond woman? Jesus. He didn't *know* any blondes. A memory? But not? The flashing images felt like a long-forgotten movie with unfamiliar actors. Pain hazed the edges of his vision.

That was a memory, right? That was good. His memories were returning, but in a disjointed jumble of images that were hard to unscramble because of the pain. His mind required defragging. He wanted something better than a notebook and pen to keep track of these fleeting thoughts. What he needed was a high-powered computer, with Internet access.

How he knew anything about high-powered computers, he had no idea, especially since they'd never had any such equipment at the compound. Also, he sought continued, unfettered access to a powerful search engine like ZAG, so he could correlate memories with hard data. He stopped and shook his head; what the hell was a ZAG search and why did that term come to mind so easily? Just another mystery, to pile on to the others. His father, Carlos, had run the Abadinista National Liberation Front until his death seven years ago. Sin had worked closely with him as his first lieutenant until his death, when he'd taken over as *jefe,* according to Mama and the others.

Too bad he didn't remember any of it.

And he had absolutely no memories of his father.

He carried around a torn-out page from an old magazine he'd flipped through when he'd gone to the dentist in Abad a couple of months earlier. A couple of guys looking hale and hearty, healthy and happy. They looked...not *unfamiliar.* He had no idea who the guys were, but there was something about their obvious connection to one another that made him want to know more—and that was just plain damn weird. Yet he kept the page so he could do a ZAG search on the image or at least on the magazine, which had most of the pages missing, and no front cover. Still, he'd track down the publication, and ID the men. See if there was anything there to jog some real memories.

Sin massaged his temple where the months-long headache throbbed. Mama's home-brewed medicine helped
some, but it also made him feel distanced and foggy, as
though he were viewing things through a shifting, smoky
pall. He'd secretly stopped taking it a few weeks earlier,
preferring to have his brain clear, even if it did hurt like
hell. Weird dreams came with the pain. He'd give his left
nut for the chance to sleep dream and pain-free.

He had questions, and no one he trusted enough to give
him answers. Not even Andrés. And certainly not Mama.
Which was disconcerting. He didn't have any basis for not
trusting them, but his gut now said not to and in the jungle,
he'd learned to trust his gut. Always.

There was so much in his life he was uncertain about. At
least he was sure he'd get some answers from the mystery
woman.

"Might as well open your eyes, *querida*," he murmured
in Spanish. "I know you're awake."

Not so much as an eyelash flickered. Rising from the
chair, Sin leaned over her, his long hair obscuring his features. Inhaling the feminine scent of apricot soap and
shampoo and female, he skimmed his fingers down her
cheek. Warm, damp silk. He paused for a reaction. *Nada.*

He was pretty sure she'd returned to consciousness five
minutes earlier, right after he walked in. But surely to God,
if she *was* awake, wouldn't she be screaming the parrots
out of the trees by now? Yet she remained limp and unre-
sponsive. He hadn't gotten where he was now, nor stayed
alive, by not being able to read people. Whoever she was,
she had remarkable control over her body. The woman had
nerves of steel, he'd give her that.

He stroked her eyelids, brushing his thumb across her long lashes. She didn't so much as quiver at the contact. *How far will you let me go, before you react?* With the tip of his thumb, he explored her features, climbed the short jut of her nose. He bent his face to her as his thumb skated down to lips like dewy petals, soft. He inhaled deeply as he hovered over her slightly parted lips. Her breath smelled sweet.

An old memory, his imagination maybe, surfaced. *Tic Tac.* Yet Sin knew he'd never seen the candy, let alone tasted it. How could he know the smell, or even the name, for that matter? The steel band of the headache tightened around his temples. He wanted to taste her mouth to see if that would jog his memory.

Her features were maddeningly enigmatic in sensual repose. By the slight elevation of her heartbeat beneath his fingertips, he knew she was conscious, but she gave every appearance of deep sleep.

He wanted to fuck her.

Balls-deep.

Wanted to get naked himself, spread her legs, and take her. After he had his fill, he'd lie beside her on the narrow cot, skin to skin. Imagining how it would feel to come inside of her and the sweat that would bind them together, he groaned. But having sex with a comatose prisoner—even when encouraged to do so by Mama—was grossly unappealing. *Especially* when encouraged to do so by Mama.

Yeah, he wanted her. But awake, responsive, and receptive.

Another goddamn mystery to him was why he hesitated. Why awake meant anything in this context, and why responsive and receptive were even words in his vocabulary, when it came to this woman and fucking her, was beyond him. Because if he was half the man Mama said he was, with a woman this gorgeous he should be on his second time by now, even if she was comatose and knocking on death's door, and even if Mama walked in for the show.

Well, she *was* awake...

Damn, he was hornier than he realized. Sin splayed his fingers against her throat. The contrast of his large and dark hand against her pale gold skin made his heart hammer and his mouth go dry. He stroked his palm up the tight cords of her arched neck. Lowering his head, Sin brushed his mouth to the dark bruise just below her collarbone. Her warm skin felt tantalizingly smooth as he lingered over the flub-dub-flub-dub of her heartbeat at the base of her throat

Definitely awake.

Savoring the tension, he slowly explored her satiny skin with his lips while he skimmed his fingers down the taut plane of stomach. Stroking his parted lips across the plumped swell of her breasts, he painted her skin with his tongue as his pinkie ventured into the crisp dark hair at the juncture of her thighs. Her nipples beaded against his tongue. A glance at her face showed her eyes still closed.

"Open your eyes," he repeated, this time in English, voice implacable. "I know you're awake."

A shudder racked her body.

When he lifted his face from her breast it was to see brown eyes, large and long-lashed, pop open to give him a cold look. "Are you done groping me, you son of a bitch?"

Four

Irises so dark brown as to be almost indistinguishable from the pupil telegraphed her anger. She tugged at the ropes binding her wrists to the rusted, paint-chipped headboard. The metal rattled against the wall. Mama had tied those ropes. They held.

Coiling a long tendril of her hair around his fingers, he absently rubbed the silky strands between the rough pads of his thumb and index finger. "For now."

"Then you can let go of my hair."

He slowly uncoiled the hair and pushed the dark skein behind her damp, bruised shoulder, letting his fingers linger on her soft skin.

She shrugged as if that would shove his hand off her. "Did you rape me while I was unconscious?" she demanded, a faint tremor in her husky voice. There was no such hesitation in her eyes before she dropped her lashes, however. After a moment she dragged in another breath, then returned her wary gaze to his face.

"No. I was waiting until you decided to wake up." He gave her a thin smile. He liked her awake, naked, and helpless. Every male predatory instinct urged him to crush that sweet-scented mouth under his own, as he lay on top of her supple body and plunged into her wet heat.

He knew his reputation. Knew that he raped women for sport. Didn't have a memory of doing that, but the way people looked at him with fear in their eyes told him the stories had to be true. God only knew he was a badass, and had living proof of just how far he'd go.

But he wasn't going to rape this woman.

All things considered, that could change on a dime, however. He went back to the chair and planted his ass four feet away from her enticing body.

She had cause to be afraid, yet she didn't draw up her long legs in a show of maidenly modesty. She didn't hide behind lowered lids. In fact, she acted as though she were fully clothed. He studied her mouth, eyes, the calm pace of her respiration. Her cheeks had no flush of pink, angry defiance. If anything, as she watched him let his gaze do the touching his fingers craved, she looked...bored.

Absolutely fucking amazing.

"Do you hurt anywhere?"

She gave him a cool, steady look. "Do you really give a damn?"

"Only if you're bleeding internally and die before I get some answers."

Her lashes fluttered as she looked up at him without expression. "Maybe it's a slow bleed."

"If it's a slow bleed, you still have time to answer my questions," he said, tone wry as he bit back a smile of admiration at her cool cockiness. She was acting as though she had the fucking advantage. Such bravado in such a desperate situation either came with serious training or inbred stupidity. This woman certainly didn't look inbred or stupid. "Who are you?"

If Sin hadn't been watching so closely, he would've missed the infinitesimal hesitation before she said, "Riva Rimaldi. Who are you?" *Now* she sounded nervous.

Was that her real name? And if not, why lie? "Sin Diaz."

Long lashes fluttered and her facial muscles flinched, then smoothed out almost instantly. She recognized his name and he guessed that Maza's enemy wasn't who she'd been hoping for.

Tough shit.

Between himself and Maza, Sin was the lesser of the two evils. But not, he acknowledged, by much. Both he and his nemesis were at the top of the bad guys list from Argentina to Venezuela and well beyond. The United States of America shit their pants every time there was an uprising in Cosio. The control they thought they had over his country was about to come to an abrupt and bloody end. *Whichever* side won, it would be extremely bad for the free world.

Unfortunately, for the moment, Maza had the upper hand. More men. More weapons. More contacts worldwide funneling money directly into his coffers. Sin, though, had something Maza wanted. Sin and the ANLF had the jungle with its emerald mines. The mines were largely untapped, a resource just waiting to be exploited. Right now they were distributing samples on the international market, testing demand. For the color and clarity of the samples they had sold, the demand was bigger than huge. Another reason the SYP wanted in. Maza couldn't know where all the mines were; he might be trying to figure it out, but he didn't know. Yet.

The SYP was a well-oiled machine. Maza's people were well trained. But they didn't know Cosio's jungles like Sin and his men did. They didn't understand the lore and the people. What the fuck were they doing in Cosio? For fuck-sake, the SYP had control of drug distribution for half the free world. The ANLF was slowly but surely gaining ground in the other.

Maza apparently wanted it all. Too fucking bad; so did Sin.

And since it looked as though the SYP was in Cosio to stay, the only way to rid himself of the problem, Sin knew, was to kill Maza and assume control of his army.

Easier said than fucking done and he was goddamn tired of saying it without doing it.

All he had to do was find the man. And while the woman was enticing and certainly intriguing, unless she drew Maza to him, Sin didn't plan on wasting time with her. The ANLF had a prison where they kept kidnap victims await-ing ransom payments. He could toss her in there, broadcast some photos of her, and see if Maza took the bait.

The woman's biceps flexed as she shifted slightly, her weight on her wrists. Bruises marred the smooth skin of her hip, and an ugly scrape streaked down her thigh. Didn't look as if stitches were necessary, but it must hurt like hell. Mama had slapped some noxious yellow salve on it to stave off infection. Out here in the jungle, even the smallest cut could lead to blood poisoning if untreated.

Every muscle and bone in her body must be bruised from the long drop, but she had yet to complain.

"What kind of name is Sin?" she asked in English. "Is that short for something, or your predilection?"

"What are you doing in the middle of the jungle, Riva Rimaldi?"

She still didn't try to draw up her long legs to partially cover her nakedness, or tug at the binding. Merely laid there, watching him warily from dark, steady eyes. "It's hardly fair that I'm trussed up like a Thanksgiving turkey and you're..." Dark eyes ran up his naked chest. "Almost dressed. Return my clothes and untie me. This is a ridiculous way to have a conversation."

With her long dark hair, dark eyes, and pale olive skin she looked more Hispanic than he did. Thanksgiving turkey indicated *American*. No discernable accent, however. She could be anything. Spanish, Italian, Iranian... "I guess when it's your party, you can designate a dress code. Here, you're attired exactly as I want you. I repeat, what are you doing hundreds of miles from civilization?"

She looked at him blankly. "I don't speak Spanish."

Sin switched to English. "You visit my country and don't speak the language? How rude." He repeated what he'd said.

"The helicopter I was in was shot down," she answered. "Did anyone else make it?"

"No. Who were the others, and where were you headed?"

"To Santa de Porres with fellow aid workers." She rubbed her cheek on the mattress to get a strand of hair off her face. Her breasts shifted enticingly. He dragged his gaze back to her face as she asked, "Did you do the shooting?"

"What makes you think the chopper was shot down?" Not something the average person would even think of. Sin suspected she was far from average. And considering Mama had set aside a SIG and utility knife among other things found on her person, he doubted she was who she said she was. Which left him with a few intriguing possibilities. "Maybe it was an engine malfunction."

"Sure." Her tone was dry. "That makes more sense than seeing a projectile strike the tail, feeling it hit, and then the helicopter exploding. Why didn't I think of that?"

Pretty damned confident when both bare-assed naked and physically restrained. Her sass both worried and amused him. In this neck of the woods her attitude would get her killed. Why that mattered bothered him, but within a second of becoming aware that he was bothered by that possibility, he became bothered by the fact that he was bothered. He immediately repressed the thought, because it was very likely he was going to be the one doing the killing.

Sin kept his features even. Hell, maybe he didn't know how to smile. He didn't remember when last he'd felt anything as benign as amusement. Her presence in camp was a dangerous minefield, with opportunities for disaster too numerous to count.

"If you're holding out for your white knight to swoop in to save your tight little ass, I'll disabuse you of the notion. First, Maza-"

"Who?"

"Escobar Maza won't step foot in my compound unless he has a death wish. Second, don't pretend you don't know who he is, because you were onboard his chopper." He smiled. "Which I took down. There'll be no rescuing or help from him. He'll think you died. The animals make short work of fresh meat, there won't be a trace of his people, and he wouldn't expect it. Third, if you think Maza is a white knight, I can disprove that theory by showing you the bones of villagers in the last mass grave he populated."

Her stony look told him fuck all.

"You're damn lucky to be alive—it's a fucking miracle, really. You dropped a hundred feet and not a broken bone."

She gave a small shrug. "I'm fortunate I'm not chopped salad right now. I took a chance." She glanced down her body. "Are you sure I didn't break anything?"

The tree canopy had been kind, breaking her fall and saving her from the final fate of her associates. "The day's still young."

"Ah. A professional comedian. How long do you plan to keep me tied up?"

Until I decide what the hell to do with you.

He'd prefer to get what he wanted out of her before Mama expected a different kind of interrogation. In his aching head, he heard the metronome ticking. "What is it Maza wants of you?"

"No matter how many times you ask me, I still don't know who that is."

Perhaps she was a spy of some sort. Or from some obscure and useless branch of Cosio's puppet government. *El presidente* was scared shitless of a coup. If the president of Cosio was stupid enough to send a spy in to see what he was hatching, he was playing a dangerous game.

Maza was a lot stronger, his army considerably bigger and better armed than the one controlled by the Cosio's leader. No, he didn't think *el presidente* was that foolhardy. Attacking Maza—and he would see that kind of move as an attack—was the equivalent of kicking over an anthill filled with fire ants, just to see what would happen. Not a great idea.

The logical deduction was she was here to do something for Maza. Which meant she was bringing a special skill to the table. She was no *puta*. Maza was no fool. No ordinary woman was worth this effort, when the country was full of beautiful women who would gladly spread their legs for a man as powerful as Maza.

Which meant that whatever that skill was, Sin wanted her. *It.*

Night blackened the single window. Without cross ventilation, the air felt thick. Inhaling the humid air was second nature to him, but her labored breathing indicated she was having difficulty sucking in oxygen at this high altitude.

"Delightful as it is to look at your tits, I feel it my duty as your host to lay out the rules of the house."

Her eyes flickered to the bare room, the vines growing through the cracks in the cement block walls, the dirt floor. The narrow cot on which she lay had a thin pad for a mattress—it was as uncomfortable as hell. The metal slats beneath her would be digging into her shoulder blades and pelvis. He knew. It was his bed.

Not that he did a lot of sleeping. Mostly he lay awake. Waiting.

She opened her eyes wide. "This house has rules?" she murmured in a light, innocent voice that didn't fool him for a second. She was summing him up and checking out her surroundings. "Fascinating. I must get the name of your decorator. Go ahead. I'm hanging on your every word."

Sin shoved the chair back to take the few steps necessary to tower over her. Her head swiveled to take in the length of his body, then came to rest at eye level with the bulge in his jeans.

He leaned over to take her stubborn chin in his palm so he could draw her attention back to his face. *Mistake.* Her damp skin was impossibly soft. Insects would love feasting on her, once he was through. Once again, he mentally flinched from the idea of her death, and couldn't understand why.

"You're not afraid, and that's a very bad thing. You were headed for Maza's camp and you wound up here, and both places are extremely dangerous for anyone—especially a woman—to be right now. And knowing the people residing here, I would venture to say you're shit out of luck as far as hospitality goes." He released her, because if he didn't, he knew he'd drop down on top of her, shove her knees apart, and take her.

Instead, Sin took a step back and pushed his fingers deep into his back pockets to prevent himself from touching her. The scent of her skin, even more so than the sight of her nakedness, made him so horny his back teeth ached. One more touch and he'd be doomed. There'd be no control.

"This is going to be one hell of a crappy day for you, Miss Rimaldi. If I'm not enough to terrify you, wait until you meet Mama. There isn't a civilized bone in her body. If you won't tell me what you've come here to do for Maza, you'll give it up to my mother in five seconds flat."

"She sounds charming, and it's warming to hear a man speak so affectionately about his mother. Ask her to bring me my clothes when she drops by for that visit." And the batshit crazy woman closed her eyes.

Sin had to admire her sangfroid. It wouldn't last, of course, but he enjoyed the moment.

FIVE

As soon as Sin Diaz left, Riva opened her eyes. *Ow, mierda.* She felt the pulse of her heartbeat in every bruise and laceration. *Everything* hurt, from her toes to the back of her head. But she didn't consider the throbbing pain anything more than a countdown clock warning her she had to get the hell out of there. ASAP.

First she needed at least a minute to get herself centered on the now. Sucking in a shaky breath, she took stock of the situation.

In all her years as a T-FLAC operative, Ria had avoided capture. But swimming slowly back to consciousness, aware at an animal level that she was bound and helpless, had thrown her into the nightmare of the bad old days.

For a few hellacious moments she waited for the slash of that fiery little whip from hell to come down on her back. Joe giving it his all to beat the "crazy" out of her. Nothing sexual there.

For a few seconds she'd been puzzled and repulsed as the man's mouth crawled over her skin. Then she was neither puzzled, nor, damn her, repulsed.

The latter scared the living shit out of her.

With annoyance and yes, damn it, humiliation, Riva acknowledged she'd been sexually aroused by a tango. *Dammit.*

Diaz was a big guy. Six three or four at least. Not conventionally handsome, but arresting despite looking as though he was three days past his last shave. Dark brows slashed over dark eyes. Long chocolate-brown hair brushed broad shoulders thick with well-honed muscle. Deeply tanned—he must go half naked a lot—he had a light mat of dark hair on his broad chest which arrowed down chiseled abs she bet she could bounce a coin off. God, she'd lost her ever-loving mind.

His gaze had poured over her like heated quicksilver. His deep voice had stroked her nerve endings like smooth, supple leather, and when he'd bent over her she'd sucked in the smell of his skin and drowned in that fiercely male scent. He was so male it made her blood race through her veins like a schoolgirl with her first crush.

How had a man like *that* managed to skate under the radar for all these years? He was larger than life. Virile. A force to be reckoned with.

It hadn't then, but now her heart pounded wildly.

To her immense relief, he'd left. She took in a shuddering breath.

Lying still, she estimated the extent of her wounds as she mentally shook off the burn of bruised muscles and the burning streak of pain down her thigh. All she cared about right now was if she was ambulatory or not.

If she couldn't walk, she was a dead woman.

She shifted her legs. She'd be able to walk/run/escape. Good enough. The rest would heal.

She breathed carefully into lungs aching from being deflated for so long, gladly taking the aches and pains over the alternative.

Craphelldamn.

First things first-she activated the locator chip in her molar with the tip of her tongue. This scenario had already been discussed in flight from Montana. Intel indicated that radio frequencies in the jungle were jammed. That, coupled with the dense tree cover, made Riva's ability to communicate with either Control, or her fellow operatives making a base in Santa de Porres, unlikely.

There was a chance—a slim one—that T-FLAC's satellites could penetrate the tree cover, override the block, and find her position through the locator chip. Certainly they'd send in drones to search for her when the chopper disappeared from their readings. If they thought she'd died in the crash, her team would come to retrieve her body. Or parts thereof.

Didn't matter. Right now she was here, alone, definitely not dead, and the more chances she gave someone to find her, the better.

Each operative carried a booster to enhance a wireless connection. Either to the satellite, or phone and computer connections. If there was *any* juice available, the booster would grab it and intensify the link to T-FLAC's satellite. But since she was naked, and hadn't seen her clothes, or her go-bag, she was screwed there. And talk about being screwed—

Mio Dios, Sin Diaz? The Ghost? The man people believed was part human, part demon, because so few had ever seen him, yet half the world knew his name? Whose exploits were legend across not only South America, but North America and Europe as well?

Wrong damned terrorist, Rimaldi!

This was bad. Really, really bad.

When she'd realized who had her, it had taken every bit of her training to keep her heartbeat even, and not to break out in a nervous sweat. *He* didn't scare her—well, yeah—of course he scared the hell out of her. He was Sin Diaz, for crapsake.

It was her own reaction to him that terrified her. Turned on by a tango? Should be the lyrics of an obscene rap song, not the anthem for this damned op. She'd better shake off the fell-on-her-head-lust and unscramble her brain. No slipups. No wrong moves. No showing her hand.

No being turned on by the tango.

Mama was, of course, Angélica Diaz, known as *Angel de la Muerte*. Angel of Death. Mother and son were both in the same criminal hall of fame as Escobar Maza. All of them evil, corrupt, and dangerous as hell. Terrorists on the top of every agency's watch lists. Including T-FLAC's.

When the Sangre Y Puño had swooped in out of nowhere five months earlier, the ANLF had gone from king of the jungle to feral underdog. Diaz and his people were in a fight for their lives as they struggled to maintain supremacy in Cosio, Colombia, Peru, and Ecuador, their stronghold on the European drug markets, and control of the region's emerald mines.

Had the Sangre Y Puño arrived in Cosio because this was the seat of Abadinista National Liberation Front's enormous power? *Was* the SYP here to wrest the power from the ANLF?

Was that what Escobar Maza needed Graciela to tell him? Nothing to do with the BRICS Summit being held in nine days, but instead the right timing to take control of the ANLF?

Made sense. Two dogs, one lucrative bone.

Nobody had known the location of ANLF's seat of operations. Thousands of miles of dense, mountainous jungle hid them more effectively than any stealth technology available. Now *she* knew. Not that she knew *exactly* where the hell she was, between the crash and being transported to this room. Judging by the darkness, several hours had passed; she could be anywhere.

Still, T-FLAC would know where the chopper went down, and if she was able to contact them, they'd at least be able to narrow down the search for the ANLF camp. She could only have gone so far in the dense jungle in that limited period of time. Every bit of information was valuable.

With two fighting groups of tangos vying for supremacy, and the astronomical amounts of money funneling through the tiny country, Cosio was a powder keg of instability just waiting to explode and light the world on fire.

Wrong damn place, wrong damned time. Her situation in Cosio was dangerous in and of itself. But if the Diazes discovered her value to Maza, her life wouldn't be worth shit.

She hadn't been tasked with killing the Diazes. But she added their deaths to her rapidly growing to-do list. She was here, why not? Weren't her superiors at T-FLAC always preaching about the importance of operatives being flexible and opportunistic?

There was a possibility that Maza and his men would search the wreckage for survivors, and when they found her body missing, come after Diaz. The ensuing bloodbath might make that possibility more attractive if she wasn't damned sure that Diaz and his scary mommy would tear her limb from limb just to piss off Maza even more. Ensuring that if one side couldn't have her, neither could the other.

If Diaz knew she was here at Maza's request, he would use her in any way to his advantage. Knowing who and what he was, that way would consist of mental and physical torture.

She'd resisted both before. But never had there been this added layer of inappropriate and intense physical attraction to one of her captors.

Had the Diazes given her something while she was unconscious? One of their designer drugs to make her more complacent? The thought would scare the shit out of her if that was the case. But Riva was a realist. They hadn't given her anything, she was pretty sure. In a way she wished they had, because a drug wore off. Her intense physical reaction might not, and that was a problem.

Fortunately, she was about to put a jungle between them.

Get to Escobar Maza. He'd be her protection against Diaz. Until she killed him. Then she'd be on her own until she could make it back to civilization and the rest of the team waiting in Santa de Porres, or figure out a way to make contact for exfil.

She either needed to kill both Diazes or get the hell out of there ASAP. If she had time, she'd do both.

Diaz's eyes had glittered in the semidarkness, and there was a moment there when she was damn sure he was contemplating snapping her neck to save himself the aggravation of questioning her.

She'd fallen from the frying pan into an active volcano. Fire didn't seem to cover the kind of shitstorm that was brewing deep in the jungles of Cosio.

She'd come to, knowing she was being watched, but needing a few minutes to assess just how much danger she was in. She'd *thought* she'd been retrieved by Sangre Y Puño. Felt relatively sure the guy wouldn't harm her knowing she was under Maza's protection.

Sneaky bastard feeling her up. She didn't like being touched, had never developed a need for it. There'd been no one to touch her with love growing up, and she'd learned she didn't need to be soothed and told she was safe by anyone other than herself. The lie would be nothing but an illusion. Touching meant pain, shame, guilt, and blame. So while his hands explored her, Riva hid inside her mind until he stepped away.

Too late.

She didn't like that she'd *liked* his touch. Didn't damnwell like it *at all*. Erotic images of their bodies entwined, hands exploring, mouths wet and avid, provided a sensual pulse she didn't want or need right now. It was *not* a physic vision, but purely an aberration brought on by the stress of capture.

God Almighty, Sin Diaz was a potent package. She wished he hadn't touched her. Having his attention on her when she was vulnerable and naked was bad enough. The feel of his calloused fingers on her body had—

Nothing. She'd felt *nothing*. Just a toxic cocktail of endorphins mixed with adrenaline, that was all.

Riva liked sex just fine, she just didn't internalize it. And the last person she wanted scratching her itch was Sin Diaz.

Diaz was bigger than she'd been led to believe, but then no one had a clear picture of him. No pictures, and the physical descriptions varied wildly. He was a ghost. A dangerous, predatory, evil urban legend. Seeing him up close and personal made her wonder why no one had ever gotten a picture of him.

He'd watched her from dark, cynical eyes, with the intention of intimidating her, but holy crap! His killer good looks were a minus as far as she was concerned. And damn, his toned, ripped, half-naked body made her tongue stick to the roof of her mouth.

Snap the hell out of your sensual haze, operative!

The bastard had taken the lamp with him. Being in the dark, *naked,* was the least of Riva's problems. The lamp hadn't shown her much, other than the width of his broad shoulders, the solid chiseled steps of his abs, and the crisp dark hair on his chest arrowing down his belly to disappear into the low-slung band of his camo pants.

Groping her had turned him on, as indicated by the sizable bulge in those pants. His long dark hair had brushed her face as he'd leaned over her, causing her nerve endings to send out mixed signals she had no intention of analyzing. The smell of his musky skin was part animal, part virile male, and her body had reacted to the stimulus whether she liked it or not.

Big frigging mistake to meet the intensity of his potent, focused stare, especially at such close quarters. She'd lowered her lashes and gotten her shit together before looking at him again.

Scared woman. That might keep her alive a little while longer if she tried using that approach. If and when that didn't work, she'd go back into her bag of tricks. Even without a weapon, she wasn't weaponless.

Riva had to sip air slowly into the painful clench in her lungs for several minutes.

Had the fall done more damage than she realized? She'd fallen out of the sky, for God's sake. Concussion at the least. How would she know until she dropped dead? A decent night's sleep and some damned water would've been nice, and she'd be back to running on all cylinders again. She hoped.

She tried to summons a vision. Of course, that had never worked for herself before, but she gave it a shot anyway. Of course nothing came. Her damned life was a closed book to her. Closed and locked. Unless she saw her future through someone else's eyes. Still, the absence of a vision—anybody's damn future—made her feel a shitload more vulnerable than lying here naked. It had defined her for her entire life. It gave her an edge most other T-FLAC operatives didn't have. She needed that damned edge *now*.

SIX

Bright lights burned into Sin's skull, sharpening his ever-present headache. Mama was circling the room, puffing away on one of the Russian cigarettes she favored. The noxious cloud of smoke only exacerbated the pain.

Generator-powered lights turned the inside of the armory bright as day, even at night. The small metal building had no windows, and a heavy steel door. Weapons of every description were piled on shelves and gun racks, in drawers, and layered inside heavy wooden boxes. Mama knew to the last box of bullets how many of everything was in inventory. She kept a tally in her head. No one came in or out without her.

She'd taken her job of stand-in *jefe* seriously when Sin had been injured. But he was well now, and wrestling control back from her was proving to be a pain in his ass. She gave him nothing but lip service and aggravation.

She pretty much ruled everyone by the short and curlies, minus the velvet glove. It wasn't his imagination. Her deference to him seemed to be eroding daily. *That* had to be nipped in the bud. If his men thought him pussy-whipped, he might as well sign his own death warrant.

Dressed head to toe in camo, wearing heavy combat boots, and a scowl, Mama, was, to put it mildly, not an attractive woman. Her lined face looked as parched as untreated leather. A pugnacious, jutting jaw and thin mouth, perpetually turned downward, made her appear permanently angry and about to erupt. Not far from the truth.

She had an irrational, hair-trigger temper and a psychopathic mean streak a mile wide. Stocky and solid, she was barely five feet tall, so that at six three, Sin towered over her. Occasionally she cut her chin-length, harsh black hair with what she called her "Rambo knife"—the Aitor Jungle King she kept in her boot.

Blunt, cruel, and impatient; those were some of her good qualities. Everyone in camp was shit-scared of Mama, even more so than they feared him. And they all had a healthy fear of Sin, because he brooked no bullshit and meted out punishment accordingly.

Mama didn't work on logic. She'd sliced a man's throat because he looked at her with disrespect.

Sin felt disassociated from her. Ever since he'd woken from his coma months ago, he'd felt no connection with his mother. And since everyone in camp called Angélica Diaz "Mama," that's what he called her, too. Imagining the woman cradling an infant was impossible. There wasn't a warm or nurturing bone in her body.

He might've been flat on his back and recuperating for months, but he was in top form now. She needed to step the hell back and let him do his job. "All I'm saying is we need to utilize social media," Sin told her tightly, checking his weapon and grabbing an extra clip for another trip up the mountain.

"Facebook, Twitter. Instagram. It's the quickest way to recruit more followers, as well as supporters, not to mention getting our product out to new customers and forming alliances worldwide, not just in the markets we have now."

Shit. Same argument, just a different day. He needed to get the hell away from camp; that's why he was joining the dawn patrol for a few hours. At the same time, he'd go back to the crash site to make sure every weapon and box of ammo had been taken. And yeah, a small skirmish with a few members of the SYP would go a long way in mitigating his lust for the woman who was staked and naked on his bed.

"*Social media*? Ridiculous." Mama's black eyes tracked him as he moved about. Folding her arms over her chest, she narrowed her eyes. "Your father had no need of this rubbish."

Sin had absolutely no memory of his father. He must've been a saint or the very devil himself to have put up with Mama. "He died before social media became as massive and powerful as it is now. These are new times. Drastic measures *must* be taken. The SYP has a strong social media presence. They're on the Dark Web, taking payment in bitcoin."

She gave him a look, part blank and part hostile.

"They have a *website,* for God's sake! They have five times more followers than we do. If we don't get with the times immediately, in the blink of an eye they'll own this mountain, Cosio, and everywhere else we do business. When I go to Santa de Porres, I'll look for a media expert. Better yet, I'll go to Bogotá and find an expert there." As powerful as the Abadinista National Liberation Front was, they were in a small, poor country with few sophisticated resources.

Sin absently slapped a buzzing insect on his neck. He should probably have rubbed insect repellent on his prisoner. The bugs were going to feast on her. But if he'd done that, he wouldn't be standing in the armory fighting with Mama on a subject that was, as far as he was concerned, a done deal. He'd be back there fucking Miss Rimaldi's brains out.

It had never occurred to him to administer insect repellent to the five *other* prisoners across the compound, waiting for their ransom demands to be met. Mama had already sent two families a finger apiece.

Her thick eyebrows disappeared incredulously beneath her heavy bangs. "Are you saying you are too weak to beat Escobar Maza away from our door?"

Sin's jaw clenched as he strapped a hunting knife to his thigh, then reached for a flak vest and pulled it on over his naked chest. "He has more manpower, more fucking *firepower,* and a larger online footprint than we do. We *have* to get our shit together. Go global."

She looked as confrontational as an attack dog, yet not nearly as friendly, and the flare of her nostrils told Sin she was furious. "Our products *are* global."

"On a small scale. South and North America, yes. But we need better distribution in Europe. Russia. Asia. That means more people. In the manufacturing plants, in sales, in marketing. Manufacturing employment has fallen as our people go to work for the Sangre Y Puño. Production is critically important if we want to stay competitive in the market. We can't do that if we're understaffed and have shit distribution."

"*We* made that market and built it up. It's not going to disappear overnight."

Sin gathered his shoulder-length hair and tied it with a thin leather cord at his nape to get it off his face. Without ventilation, the room was stifling hot. "No, not overnight, but in six months it might. We've lost twenty-six percent of our sales in the five months Maza has been around and the loss is growing exponentially. We can't afford to lose any more. He's not going away. He's here to stay. He wants what we have, and he'll get it unless we fight back and be smarter about it. And I don't mean small skirmishes between the fucking trees, or charging less for protection to the miners so they'll come back to us.

"I mean taking this seriously, and fighting back where it'll hurt them the most." He grabbed a box of shells and stuck them in one of the pockets down his pant leg. "*Financially*. We have to implement global growth with innovation. We have to get on social media at an accelerated rate. We need media experts, public relations and marketing professionals." None of whom hung thick on jungle vines. He needed to go to a major city to find those resources.

"Who have you been talking to?" She blew a cloud of smoke in his direction. "Where does this nonsense come from?"

Research, but she wouldn't want to hear that. And for some reason he didn't want Mama to know he had a computer stashed in one of his hideouts in the jungle. The only computer in the compound was the one she had locked away. Not that it worked due to Maza keeping the signals blocked.

Last time he'd been in Santa de Porres, and right after he'd stopped taking Mama's powerful headache potion and the fogginess started to dissipate, he'd ZAGed the Sangre Y Puño, The search engine had given him more than he needed to know about his powerful, and savvy, enemy. Enough to chill Sin's very marrow.

Fighting Escobar Maza was like holding up a paper napkin to staunch a flood. Sin tried to figure out how the hell he'd let things slip out of his fingers for so long? Surely his father must have left the business in good shape prior to his death seven years earlier? Or had he been left with a crumbling business, weak and sickly enough that Maza thought he could just stroll in and administer the death blow?

Still, Sin couldn't imagine allowing a thriving, multi-billion dollar business fall into ruins. What the fuck had *he* been doing for the past seven years? Not running the business the way it was supposed to be run, obviously.

Time to change things up.

"We run a *business*," he reminded Mama, squeezing the bridge of his nose. "We have to treat it as such. Tomorrow I'm heading to Santa de Porres to hire the people we need. I'm done talking. We have to take action or be prepared to lose, and/or die. Andrés is waiting outside. I have to go. It'll be light soon."

He opened the steel door, but Mama halted him by grabbing his forearm, short sharp nails digging into his skin. "You won't do anything until we've discussed this, Sin!"

"We just did." He shook off her tight grip. "Now it's time for action."

SEVEN

Riva had easily read Diaz's microexpressions, even in the flickering light. It's what had made her an invaluable juror selector, which was what she'd been doing when she'd been recruited by T-FLAC six years ago. The face had the most complex system of muscles in the body, making it almost impossible to hide micro changes if one was looking for them. And since Riva's life depended on her reading both body language and facial expressions before she ended up with a machete bisecting her skull, or a bullet in the back of her head, she read him.

The human face was capable of displaying tens of thousands of different expressions without the person even being aware of them. Riva read Sin Diaz's face like an open book.

Desire had dilated his pupils and tightened the muscles around his eyes and mouth. Anger was responsible for the tightness around his jaw, and lowered eyebrows...

He wanted her. He was conflicted. And he was pissed.

The *conflicted* was intriguing. When push came to shove, she could use her knowledge to her advantage. But she'd be even happier with the weight of her SIG in her hand. Her boot knife was, of course, gone with her boots. The small boot knife on a cord around her neck had been taken, too.

Hands, teeth, feet, smarts, and her special skills. That was it for weapons. For now. That should be enough.

He'd touched her with callused, warrior hands, and she'd reacted like a girl, not a fellow warrior. She even forgot to act scared. A man like him would expect a bound and naked woman to be terrified out of her mind. Riva wasn't terrified out of her mind. But she had a healthy respect for the danger she was in. At least she'd made sure he thought that she didn't speak the language. Pretending not to speak Spanish might very well save her life. The less the enemy thought she knew, the better her advantage.

Tied up like a sacrificial lamb, she tested the hemp binding her wrists over her head the moment she heard his footsteps crunch on the vegetation outside. Everything hurt as though a herd of elephants had used her body as a trampoline. Or she'd done a long free fall out of the sky.

The aches and pains she'd work out once she was free, but right now there was no use dwelling on them. She'd learned early that no one was going to kiss her booboos better. That no one, in actual fact, gave a flying fuck about her physical well-being. It made life a whole lot simpler when her expectations were zero. The only place left to go from ground zero was up.

She liked being on her own. She played just fine with others, but she preferred depending on herself, her own unique skill set. Add a detonator or an AK-47, and she was happy as a clam.

Ignoring the fire of the rope burn around her wrists, and the incredible discomfort of having her arms cruelly twisted above her head, Riva swiped her cheek against her upper arm as sweat trickled down her temple. Time was of the essence.

Pulling her knees up to her chest, she twisted and turned until she was on her knees, practically dislocating her shoulders in the process. Excruciating enough to make her eyes sting, but it made things easier and took some of the torque off her wrists. Panting, she had to pause a moment to catch her breath. The heat and humidity of the jungle combined with the high altitude made breathing feel more like sucking air through a wet blanket.

Go. Go. Go.

The hemp was heavy and thick. The only thing she had to slice through her bindings were her teeth. She got started.

The rough rope tore into her lips, shredding the tender membrane of her inner lips and tongue, and dug into the side of her mouth. Since there was no alternative, she continued gnawing, letting her mind drift as she worked. She needed the distraction so as not to focus on the pain. Concentrating on the mission and what she had to do was better.

One unraveled strand scratched her cheek, and she lifted her head to try and lubricate her dry mouth, but there was no moisture to be found; the taste of that Tic Tac was a distant memory. One down, and God only knew how many to go. Bending her head, she went back to work.

Somewhere in that wreckage was her backpack, with everything she needed for the op. She'd have to figure out where the chopper had gone down, get to that location, retrieve her bag, then find Maza. If Diaz hadn't blown the chopper to hell, it would probably have fallen out of the sky at some point. It had just been a matter of time. She'd kinda hoped it would be on some other flight.

It was only the weight of the cargo, which had forced them to fly low, that had saved her bacon. She'd escaped certain death-miraculously *somehow*managing to autorotate to the ground, forcing herself to stay limp as she went, so that her body absorbed the impact from the branches she hit, instead of being broken by them. It had all passed in a blur of fear and motion. There were several blank spots, and then she'd woken, tied and alive, to find the tall, half-naked tango watching her as if she held the secrets to the universe.

She'd been trained to outwit the bad guys, tangle with terrorists and win, and survive in nearly any environment, and T-FLAC had given her the tools to resist just about anything. No one had anticipated that Maza's enemy would shoot down the damn chopper, though. So much for Plan A.

In spite of the tragic deaths of fellow operatives Sanchez and Castro, Riva still had her mission to complete. Connect with Escobar Maza. If he needed reassurance to do whatever the hell he planned for the summit, then she had *nine* days. Eight, really; surely it was past midnight. She was losing time, dammit.

If what he had planned had nothing to do with the summit, then she had no damn idea *how* long she had to make contact. That was if she'd only been out of commission for a day. In truth, she didn't know how much time had passed since the chopper dropped out of the sky, or how long they'd had her tied up in this hovel in the middle of jungle hell. Her usually reliable inner clock had been shaken up by the crash.

Shitcrapdamn.

For all she knew, they could have drugged her for days and whatever Maza had planned might have already happened. The ANLF was famous, or infamous, worldwide for *El aliento de demonio*, Demon's Breath, their brand of the drug Scopolamine. Being both colorless and odorless, they could've fed it to her, or even blown it in her face while she lay unconscious. The drug acted on the brain, blocking the formation of memories. The chilling thought that they could've done anything, made her do anything, while she was unaware gave her impetus to chew a whole hell of a lot faster.

Riva put an eight-day time clock in her mind, determined to think positively. She was a pro, and she had work to do.

But first she had to get the hell out of Diaz's compound.

Tasting blood from her abraded lips and tongue, she paused, breathing hard. Two twisted threads waved triumphantly inches from her nose. All right! Licking her lips to get the stinging sweat-salt out of the multiple small cuts, she went back to work.

One more twist gnawed free. Her lips were numb, which was a blessing.

Being in a dangerous situation like this was both terrifying and exhilarating. She had all the skill, all the experience necessary for this mission, she just lacked some critical pieces of information. And for all intents and purposes, she lacked backup. Control had been tracking her via satellite, until the crash.

Now? Hell if she knew what they knew. Did they have even a clue where she was? They knew where the chopper went down and that was all. She thought again about the locator signal on her molar, about the signal jamming that she'd been briefed on, about being a needle in a very, very large haystack.

Sweat trickled down the side of her neck to soak into her hair. Her breathing became so labored she was afraid she'd pass out, and she stopped gnawing for a second or two to regulate her breath and slow down her heartbeat. Passing out from lack of oxygen would be a rookie mistake. And a rookie mistake out here would be deadly.

Closing her eyes, she imagined cool lake water swirling around her heated body in a soothing caress. But that soothing caress turned into the rough, hot stroke of Sin Diaz's hands on her. Every cell in her body went on red alert.

Not just no. But *hell no.*

A quick glance at the window set into the thick cement block wall showed nothing but darkness; no hint of exterior lights. She took stock of her situation as she gathered herself for the next round of gnawing on the damned rope.

The alive part was good. The impending arrival of Mama was extremely motivational. How the hell was she going to get from Diaz's hideout to Maza's camp when she had no clue where she was? And she desperately wanted to get away from Diaz. While Maza was the target, Diaz wasn't far behind. In some ways, he was considered a much more dangerous adversary than Maza.

Ruthless, relentless, and vengeful. And those were his good qualities.

How many miles would she have to travel, through dense jungle, without so much as a compass, weapon, or clothes, at night? Would she be *able* to find Maza in thousands of miles of jungle, in the eight-day time frame? If she truly still *had* eight days.

Because if she *didn't* find him, what and when he was doing whatever would be moot because he'd still be very much alive. And that was assuming he hadn't already carried out whatever the hell he was planning.

Dammit.

She *had* to get the hell out of here. Now!

No weapon, but she'd improvise until she found something. A gun would fit the bill, but in a pinch anything she found lying around could be used as a weapon.

T-FLAC had coordinates for some of ANLF's various jungle locations. They not only picked up and moved camp regularly, from satellite images they appeared to have structures deep within the jungle. Safe houses, they suspected. Made sense. Now she suspected that many of those locations actually belonged to the SYP.

Damn jungle was riddled with tangos. They'd always be fighting. Always in hiding from each other and the authorities. They'd have bolt holes. She mentally brought up a map of the terrain and pinpointed as many of those locations as she could remember from the briefing.

Those caches of weapons and provisions could save her ass if she could find them. Fine and dandy, once she ascertained just where the hell she was *now*.

She needed a plan.

First. Get free.

Second. Obtain a weapon.

Third. Clothes.

Fourth. Figure out her exact location and how much time she had left on the clock until Maza acted.

Another strand popped free. Great. Progress. Only about thirty more to go.

She licked blood off her upper lip, ignoring the sting in the abrasions. Almost home free. Riva went back to gnawing on the thick hemp rope tethering her to the bed.

Her heartbeat picked up the rapid beat of the countdown timer in her head.

EIGHT

"If Loza is correct, Maza is here now," Andrés whispered. They'd taken a small group, Cesar, Vincente, and Giosue, letting the others go a different route up the mountain to the crash site.

"He's correct, what? Forty percent of the time?" Sin scanned the small enclave with the NV scope on his rifle. Six men in varying stages of undress, with bottles of booze in hand, were gathered around a small fire. Three naked women writhed on a blanket, putting on a show for the men as they toyed with each other's breasts, lolled their heads back, and spread their legs in open invitation. There was laughter, giggles, and, from the men, sensuous groans. All the eyes of the men and women were glazed, due no doubt to booze and pot. None of the men were familiar to Sin, and he didn't expect to recognize the women.

As he watched, one of the women reached between her legs, moaning as she slid her fingers through her folds. One of the men dropped to his knees on the blanket, unzipped the fly on his fatigues, and mounted her. Another man approached the blanket, eyeing one of the other of the women. Unbuckling his belt, he dropped his trousers as he walked.

Sin turned his back on the group. "Maza's not here."

"Loza—"

"Was mistaken. His men wouldn't be smoking *mota* and having an orgy if Maza was in camp. Let's go."

"We take out the men who are here, then. You know it's what we do."

"Not when the men are stoned out of their minds and unarmed. Not when innocent women are present and all they're doing is fucking each other. Nothing feels right about this."

"Nothing seems right with you lately, *tio*. You got a headache? Take Mama's bug juice for crapsake! It'll get rid of that headache and with it your sudden burst of morals. These are our enemies. We eliminate our enemies, right?"

"Not tonight. I have a prisoner to interrogate. No point alerting Maza to us when there's no need. We head back."

Andrés glanced at the other two men, who nodded in agreement. He turned his head to look at Sin. "We kill them before we go."

It was, Sin, thought, *murder*. The people in the clearing were having a good time. There wasn't a weapon in sight, and they were too impaired to use one even if it was close at hand. Maza wasn't anywhere near. He stood his ground. "You coming?"

Andrés indicated he should take the others with him. "Go ahead. I'll catch up."

Sin stopped. "We don't have time to kill them. Let's go."

"You never feel more fucking alive than the moment that you're killing another human being."

No. That was how Andrés felt, not him. "This isn't warranted," Sin told him, voice tight.

"Mama says you have a conscience that makes you weak. You have a moral compass that won't let you kill someone because it isn't personal. Is she right, amigo?" Andrés shrugged. "No *importa*. I have to piss."

"Andrés—"

"*Jesús Cristo,* Sin. When did you become such a pussy? I liked you better before."

"I probably liked me better before, too." At least his friend was walking with him. Giosue went ahead to use the machete, and they had to walk in single file.

"What was that about at the armory?" Andrés was directly behind him. "Fighting with Mama again?"

"She doesn't listen. I was explaining how we have to update our computers, figure out exactly what our margins are so we can perhaps undersell the SYP. We have to expand our markets."

Andrés gave Sin a sympathetic glance. "She's old-school."

"*Windows Ninety-eight,* for crapsake? Haven't you wondered how the Sangre Y Puño amassed such power in such a short time?" Sin asked, frustrated. "Five fucking *months,* Andrés. Plus or minus. *A hundred and fifty days.* Where did Maza *come* from?" Of course, the same could be said of Sin Diaz. He'd emerged from his months-long coma at about the same time. "Where did he start? He wants our Demon's Breath and cocaine market, he certainly wants our emerald mines. Does he fucking think he can just show up and take charge of the ANLF, too?

"Everything I've been trying to do for months, he's *already* doing! He's way ahead of the game, and we're eating his dust. We should be much bigger in Europe, and have a presence in developing nations. Cheap labor, and an endless supply of consumers. Customers already have plenty of options for product. The Sangre Y Puño is selling their wholesale cocaine cheaper than we are, to get our customers.

"Product demand is shifting. And so far, almost a quarter of the mines are now paying protection to them instead of us. How much longer before we lose tens of millions of dollars annually because we were too apathetic to take control?"

"I don't understand anything you're saying, my friend. Computers, and margins, and expanding markets? *¿Qué quiere decir eso?* I like the way we've always done things. The way *you've* always done things. We can beat them. We know the terrain in our mountains better than anyone." Andrés lowered his voice. "Mama wants you to find out what the woman is to our friend."

Andrés didn't want to hear about expansion and innovation any more than Mama did. Sin was on his own in this. So be it. He'd drag the ANLF into the twenty-first century whether they wanted to go along for the ride or not.

Mama and Andrés clung to the old way of life. Clung to what his father had done, and Sin, apparently, had done before Maza shot him. But since Sin didn't remember *any* of that, he was going with what he knew *today.*

"I can't be in two places at once," he said, considering the best time to leave camp and take the two-day trip down the mountain to Santa de Porres. The sooner the better. Things seemed to be escalating with Maza. He had no idea why. But he was ever vigilant to the pulse and activities of his enemy.

"She's secure," he said easily. "I'll question her again when we return."

"Unless Mama interrogates her while we're gone."

"Right. Unless." Sin hoped that wasn't the case. He'd hate to see that bright spirit broken. "Let's see how pissed Maza was to find most of his toys gone." Sin's voice was pitched low as they reached the edge of unsecured trees beyond the borders of the compound.

Two groups of his men had been up, then down the mountain in the last few hours. They'd retrieved almost all of the weapons. He'd increased the security patrols around camp. Maza's people would've counted the bodies—or parts of them, anyway. It wouldn't take a genius for them to realize someone was missing. With the weapons cache gone, too, he'd put two and two together.

Sin doubted that anyone would even consider that she was *alive*. But he wasn't taking any chances. Capturing the two latest weapons shipments of Maza's put Sin ahead of the game they played.

He had one more thing Maza didn't have. Riva Rimaldi. Whoever, or whatever, she was.

Taking a seven-man team with him, Sin split off from the regular patrols and headed east. Back to the crash site.

"You've got that look on your face again, *amigo*." Andrés came alongside him as the cleared path widened so they could walk two abreast. "What's bothering you?"

"The woman had a SIG Pro, a hunting knife in her boot, another under her clothing."

Andrés raised a brow. "So?"

"Does that say civilian to you?"

"You'd rather go on patrol than bounce on your prisoner?" Speaking softly, Andrés nudged his arm with his shoulder. "Are you sick, man?"

"She's not going anywhere. I'll have another opportunity, if I want." He wanted. Badly. But the circumstances weren't right, and God only knew why that was, because he sure as fucking hell didn't. When he had reluctantly left her, she'd been pretending to be asleep and was securely tied to his bed. He'd taken the lamp, leaving her in darkness. A generator powered lights in camp; the lantern had been for show. No reason to attract more bugs, though; she was uncomfortable enough as it was.

Her bravado under the circumstances intrigued him. Civilians weren't that contained unless they were trained, or, like Mama, had endured unimaginable things that had warped them past the point of caring or common decency.

"Mama patched her up, then secured her to my bed." Sin's voice was dry as he rotated stiff shoulders, scanning the dark foliage. A pair of red eyes flashed, then were gone in a flurry of leaves. "She's okay for a few hours."

He put the woman from his mind and thought about the crash site. He could still smell harsh, acrid stink of smoke. The weapons would already have been removed, but maybe he could find something else of interest. Or nothing at all. Andrés was his first lieutenant, he could handle the patrol. But Sin wanted to face more realistic dangers than a smart-mouthed, naked woman or his mother who couldn't decide who was boss.

Dense vegetation, and a narrow but swiftly moving river to ford made it a three-hour round-trip. Not the route they'd used earlier. This time he took a different route to come in from an unexpected direction.

A six-hour trek through the jungle, his second such trip within twenty-four hours, would do the job of easing his frustration. And if he encountered Maza's men en route, that would be a bonus. He was itching for a... *fight*. Not a *fuck*. If he didn't get one, he'd take the other.

He stepped up the pace to one that was more of a workout than a meander. Andrés walked several yards behind him. The men were intentionally spread out, weapons in hand, anticipating an attack at all times.

They maintained verbal silence as they moved through the thick understory, any noise they made covered by the activity of the nocturnal denizens in search of their next meal. The jungle was never quiet.

He'd seen a sleek black jaguar in this area on an earlier patrol, and he heard it now, crying for its mate. Its howl carried on the rustle of leaves. Monkeys and other small animals used thick vines and entwined branches overhead as a superhighway between the trees. His flashlight revealed bright yellow orchids, as small as his thumbnail and as delicate as butterflies, draped like intricate lace from a nearby branch as he used the machete to hack a path through waxy, wrist-thick vines.

A succession of rapid-fire gunshots broke the stillness. Sin spun on his friend. "Damn it, Andrés—"

Andrés raised his hands. "I'm here with you, *amigo*."

Sin turned around and continued walking. His friend had sent Giosue back to deal with Maza's men. The women, too, he supposed. Sick to his stomach at the senseless—unnecessary, God damn it—killing, he gritted his teeth and kept going.

Two miles in, they passed one of Sin's secret hideaways. Large-leafed vines, tangled with giant philodendrons, effectively concealed the entrance. If he hadn't known exactly where it was, he'd have missed it. He'd stashed his com-puter there, although he still had to get into town to use it. And even then he used strong encryption, and a long, 67-character random, ASCII key/password/ passphrase.

Sin wanted no eyes on what he was looking at. He'd set up installations to block all signals for a hundred mile radius. If Maza wanted Internet connection, satellite connection, or even sophisticated comm systems to communicate, he was SOL. Now Maza was doing the same fucking thing. Blocking their communication to the outside world.

The ANLF had camouflaged shelters, both above and under the ground, throughout the forest. Small, well-hidden structures holding weapons, ammo, and basic supplies. Places where several men could lie in wait for their enemy, or duck out of sight to avoid them when necessary.

He'd personally hacked this one out by himself, for himself, three months ago. Equipped with weapons, ammo, and basic supplies, it was a place to get away to try to quiet the noises in his head without interference from Mama or anyone else. It was his attempt to make some sense of images and half memories that twisted and turned like a kaleidoscope in his mind. Didn't matter whether he was asleep or awake; the nonsensical images constantly assaulted him, along with the pain. The harder he tried to piece them into whole cloth, the less sense they made. Maybe he was losing his mind? Something Sin didn't completely rule out.

Even Andrés didn't know about his hidey-holes, scattered between camp, Santa de Porres, Abad, and the river. He'd trusted Andrés implicitly, but with this latest insubordination, that trust was rapidly eroding. Now he didn't know who the fuck to trust. Everyone else under his command? No. They did as ordered, showed a veneer of respect, but there was something—

Fuck. Were his own men planning a coup?

Did someone want to overthrow him to rule the roost? He almost laughed. They'd have to get rid of Mama, too.

Did he give a rat's ass if Maza wanted ANLF territories? Honestly? More than once he'd contemplated what it would be like to just walk away, start over as someone with a different identity who didn't run a cartel deep in the jungle and instead drove a sweet car to a sleek office in a high-rise somewhere.

He'd clearly been satisfied with raids on *politicos* in Santa de Porres, kidnapping tourists for ransom, moving huge quantities of drugs and weapons, before he was brought back from the dead. But now? Not so fucking much.

Dammit to hell. Not for the first, or even thousandth time, he wondered if being shot and concussed was responsible for a complete change of personality. Maybe he was just bored by the violence and senselessness of it all. Hell if he knew. All Sin knew was that something had to give.

He just didn't fucking know *what*.

What he did know was he had to keep these thoughts to himself if he wanted to stay alive. The merest hint of doubt sent Mama into a full-blown rant, followed by homicidal rage.

Andrés claimed he didn't want or need a leadership role, that he was more than happy to be Sin's right hand. But was that true? If Sin asked, would he answer honestly? Could he, hell, *should* he, just hand the reins over to his friend and walk away?

He'd ask Andrés when they returned. Change was necessary. But before he presented questions and options to Andrés, he had to think through his *own* fucking options.

Back at camp, sentries patrolling the narrow dirt track between the buildings would pass his hut every ten minutes. His prisoner wasn't going anywhere, unless someone untied her, or she took the bed frame with her.

The compound was several days' hike from the capitol, and well hidden in the jungle. It was a good central point for their vast operation. A few dozen small houses, and two long barracks for the men, all surrounded by dense, booby-trapped jungle that hummed with insects in the humid heat. Early-warning systems on the perimeter of the compound would warn of Maza's approach before he and his men returned.

"Did you screw her brains out? Will she be able to walk when we get back?" Andrés gave him a licentious smile, his gold tooth gleaming.

Sin merely made eye contact with his friend. Not for him to know one way or the other. And as *jefe,* it was Sin's right to claim her. Until he gave her up, she was his to do with whatever he wished.

"She wouldn't have been on the helicopter if Maza didn't send for her. And if she wasn't important enough to hide, he wouldn't have used that pile of shit Red Cross helicopter. She's here for whatever he has planned." Sin couldn't imagine *what.*

"Or she is a *puta,*" Andrés whispered as vegetation flew under the swings of their machetes. A swarm of clicking insects swirled around his head, and he absently waved them away from his face. "Here to service him before the big event. Instead she can service *you.* Unless, if she isn't to your liking, I'd be happy…" He let the words trail off hopefully.

Sin shook his head.

She didn't speak Spanish, which was a bonus. A silent woman with skills. But he'd never encountered a *puta* with that kind of fire in their eyes. Most were broken toys, their spirit taken by the men they serviced. "I'll let you know when I'm finished with her. Until then, keep the others away from her. A few hours of being vulnerable and afraid should pry some information out of her. If not... Shh—" He froze, listening to the crunch of vegetation underfoot and the brush of something solid passing between the leaves.

A puma. Too bad. He was in the mood for a fight. He squeezed the fingers of his free hand around his temples as he walked.

"Need to go back for one of Mama's potions?" Andrés asked.

"Hell, no." The cure was worse than the ailment.

Illuminated by dappled moonlight, his friend shot him a concerned glance. "When last did you sleep?"

Now that he was no longer taking the pain medication, he rarely slept. When he did somehow fall asleep, he always woke with clear memories of his dreams. Of snow. Of the Eiffel Tower. BASE jumping the Burj Khalifa in Dubai, for fucksake.

Of...fucking hell. Places he'd never *been* to. Things he'd never done. Maybe he'd seen pictures in the newspaper, or one of the magazines Mama favored. Maybe he was just in-corporating what he read into dreams that featured him as the hero. Wherever he'd seen the images, in his mind they were real, but as one-dimensional as a snapshot, because his brain provided no context. The images looked familiar, yet he didn't remember being in any of those places or do-ing any of those things. His inability to connect the scenes or ground them in any kind of reality was driving him absolutely batshit crazy.

"Before my accident, how often did I travel?" Sin asked, wielding the heavy machete in a precise arc to sever a clump of thick new growth.

"We were in Bogotá—when was that? The month before Maza tried to kill your ass? Trujillo the same time—" Andrés raised a brow under his bandana. "Now you still don't remember?"

"I remember a few weeks ago." Hell, he remembered three/four months ago. Before that was the blank space where his memories should be. "North America, Europe, China..."

Andrés laughed. "*Mi hermano,* we were born on this mountain, and other than the trips to procure or sell our products, we haven't been anywhere that exotic. Never will. We'll die here."

"No doubt about that." A howler monkey yelled, then fell silent, his whoops echoing in the jungle. Leaves rustled, stirred by a faint breeze that didn't reach the understory.

For some reason, the American woman had stirred up more than sexual interest. Sin hadn't heard American English spoken since they'd held that journalist for ransom a few months earlier. When her ex-husband had refused to pay the ransom, Mama had given the woman to the men as a bonus.

Annoyingly elusive thoughts skirted the very periphery of Sin's mind, stirred up like dust from the dark corners where he'd pushed them as mere fancies. They were maddening, frustrating, and unwelcome. Especially now, when he needed his mind to be clear and fully functioning, if he was to beat his enemies who were already at the gate. "Was I...different before the accident?"

"Different how? You've always been ugly and surly."

"So, no changes you've noticed?"

"Why the sudden questions? You *never* talk about before the attack."

One of Sin's many problems was that while he knew Andrés was his best friend, that they went everywhere together, that they'd been raised together, he didn't *feel* it. Not feeling that bond, that closeness he knew he *should* feel, was like observing some else's life through the bottom of a glass. Disconcerting? Fuck yeah. To say the least.

"That's because I don't *remember* before the shooting," Sin snapped, squeezing his temple. He didn't remember much about the incident either. Pain was a big part of it. Falling. Yelling. Desperation. Mama and Andrés had filled in the rest, describing how she'd found him after Maza's men had shot him, then beaten him to a pulp and left him for dead. It had been touch and go. He certainly had the scars to prove he'd been in a life-and-death struggle for survival.

He'd heard so many stories about his life prior to the attack, and about the aftermath of the attack itself, that he thought he might be remembering. Grainy images in yellowed press clippings Mama had saved in an odd show of sentimental pride.

He'd read them and reread them, looked at the worn pieces of newsprint. Himself and his father. The start of the myth of Sin Diaz. Rarely seen, but his power growing and expanding over the years. The indistinct figures in those pictures could have been fucking *anybody*.

Even if his life felt as though he'd been shoved into an ill-fitting suit, and he'd been placed onstage without a script, this was his life. Sin Diaz was who he was.

He'd murdered numerous men and kidnapped countless others. Extortion. Weapons brokering. Drug trafficking and prostitution. They used the profits from narco-trafficking to buy weapons and other necessities to fund their insurrection. The ANLF was a veritable smorgasbord of terrorism.

Sin knew most of the past from anecdotes from his men, Mama's bragging, and the press clippings she treasured. He remembered none of it. Not if it had happened more than five months ago.

He had a son he'd never met. Product of a rape he didn't remember.

Sin slid his hand into his front pocket and fingered the slick, folded piece of paper he'd torn out of a magazine and carried everywhere. He should probably toss it. But for now he'd hang on to it. Maybe something in the image would jog his memory. His dreams spelled out a completely different life. Someone *else's* life. None of it made any fucking sense. Because his friend was right. They'd been born and raised right here on the mountain.

Mama had found Andrés at an orphanage in Santa de Porres and brought him home as a playmate for her son. Best friends from the age of six, they'd played together, been raised as hellions together, gone whoring together, and fought side by side. Closer than brothers, they'd shared almost thirty years. Twenty-nine of which Sin didn't remember.

He wasn't sure if what he *thought* were memories were just images implanted from hearing the story so many times. It was maddening, frustrating, and now he'd exacerbated his constant fucking headache just by *talking* about it.

"Well, everyone in camp remembers before the attack. You were a pain in the ass then, and you're the same way now. *You* haven't changed. You're the best friend a man could ask for, and a hell of a fighter. There's never been another man I'd follow this blindly. So whatever kind of man you think you were or weren't before the accident, you're still my blood brother."

"It doesn't bother you that I don't remember?"

Andrés shrugged off his question. "You remember bits and pieces, right? It'll all come back one of these days."

"Showing me those old newspaper clippings is pointless." The piercing headache stabbed behind his left eye like a sharp, throbbing dagger. "I tell her I remember once in a while because I can tell she gets frustrated. But honestly, Andrés? I could be looking at reports and pictures of some other guy."

"Well, it *wasn't* some other guy. You're you."

That wasn't an answer. He shouldn't have bothered. Sin pressed two fingers into his temple where the severity of the headache made nausea well in his throat, but his concern had shifted from himself to Riva. He'd warned the guards to leave her alone, but the guards at the compound were the same caliber of men who had just broken an order and killed stoned, defenseless soldiers who were having fun with prostitutes.

He'd left Riva tethered to the bed, naked, like a sacrificial goat in a compound where men had higher testosterone levels than IQ scores.

NINE

The last strands of rope frayed between Riva's teeth, allowing her bound wrists to drop to the thin mattress. For a moment she lay there panting, as out of breath as if she'd run a marathon. Who knew the frantic, gnawing movements of jaw and mouth to saw through the rope over the last hour would be so exhausting?

God, her mouth hurt. Her tongue hurt, her cheeks frigging hurt. Sweat ran into her eyes, making them smart. Salty blood in the numerous small and large lacerations caused by chewing through the rough rope made her want to gag. *Hell.* The act of touching the rope with her mouth made her want to gag, because God knew who, or what, else Sin Diaz might have tied to his bed.

The metallic taste of blood on her tongue and the musty flavor from the rope made her thirst even more intense. She lay still for a second, trying to figure out if there was any part of her body that didn't hurt. Thanks to the injuries from her death-defying fall, the answer was no.

But, damn it, she was finally free. Whoopdedoo.

Still breathing hard from the exertion, she went down her mental checklist as she swung her legs off the lumpy, rock-hard mattress that smelled of Sin Diaz. Looking around, she noted it was still dark outside. Good. She made out a tall, narrow metal locker across the room, the kind kids used in school. Whatever it held, she'd use.

The floor felt cold and smooth beneath her bare feet. Tile? Cement? Blocking the pain in her shoulders, and the pull and twinge of a long gash on her thigh, Riva hotfooted it to the locker.

Locked? *No!* She gave a sigh of relief. She pulled the narrow door open, cautiously because she didn't want it to creak. Thankfully, it didn't. That made two things that had gone right in a mission gone to complete shit. Feeling around she encountered cloth. *Clothes.*

Hell, she didn't care if anything fit or not. All it had to do was cover her nakedness. She'd had enough of being an all-you-can-eat buffet for the local insects. Pulling on a soft T-shirt made her feel 80 percent better. It smelled of hot male, sun, and greenery.

She was surrounded by Sin. Riva dismissed her ridiculous urge to bury her nose in the much-washed cotton. Instead, she found a pair of cotton pants by touch. Anticipating they'd be about a foot too long, she rolled the hems before dragging the pants up over her bare butt. There was a good chance they'd fall around her ankles, because his waist was as big as her hips.

But they had belt loops to hang things on, and half a dozen pockets to stuff with whatever she could get her hands on. The man didn't have many clothes, and a quick search at the bottom of the shoulder-wide locker didn't net any shoes or a belt. And certainly nothing she could use as a weapon. Makeshift or otherwise. She glanced back at the hated rope tied to the bedpost and decided to make do. Unknotting and pulling a length of it out from the headboard, she threaded it quickly through the belt loops only to find it wasn't quite long enough to tie together around her waist. Damn. So much for that idea. She stuffed the length of rope into one of the pockets in case she needed it later.

As she searched for shoes and socks, a weapon, she kept her ears pricked for any unusual sounds from outside. She wiped sweat off her cheek on the shoulder of his shirt. Where was he? Probably sleeping. He'd been a busy boy all night. She presumed *he'd* presume she couldn't budge from where he'd left her. Frightened woman left alone, God only knew where, tied up in the middle of the jungle, bare-assed naked and being eaten by mosquitoes, gnats, and whatever.

She shuddered to think of what else could be crawling in that bed of his. Fleas? Oh God, crabs? Lice? Damn. She'd need to be deloused when she got home. She shrugged. Wouldn't be the first time.

"Nice try, buddy. Enjoy your nap. I won't be anywhere near here by the time you wake up." She had a flash-image of a rumpled Sin, sleepy-eyed, and naked. "Idiot," she chastised herself. Her brain had clearly been shaken up by the fall.

Assuming the large square outline of charcoal-black indicated a door, she headed there and cautiously pulled. Surprise, surprise. Not locked either. Perhaps, isolated in the middle of their compound and surrounded by his men, Diaz didn't feel the need to lock his property. Goody for him. Better for her. Finding the handle in the dark by feel, Riva cautiously opened the heavy door inch by slow inch.

Standing dead still in the darkness, she counted her own heavy heartbeats as she waited for her captor or a guard to come charging in, guns blazing. God, she just loved being underestimated.

Luck was on her side, because other than her own heartbeat, it was relatively quiet as the jungle slept. The quiet was broken occasionally by the hum of the insects, a lonely bird call, or something substantial rustling the foliage. While she had a healthy respect for spiders, snakes, and other creepy crawlies, nothing even came close to the danger of her mother's husband. Give her a jaguar or boa constrictor any day. Fear simply wasn't an issue for her. Or an option.

Adrenaline surging through her veins, Riva eased through the open door, stepping outside barefoot. Braced and ready for attack she half—no, three quarters—expected someone to grab her. No one did.

Fellow operative Sebastian Tremaine had taught her how to move as silently as a ghost, using whatever was around to conceal herself. It was dark, but the shadows cast by trees, shrubs, and various buildings provided even denser black. She ran lightly from one deep shadow to the next on a narrow, dirt strip that could hardly be called a road, ignoring the damp ground.

The muggy air smelled of wet earth, vegetation, and cooked meat from a recent meal. Her stomach rumbled; she hadn't eaten anything on the chopper, or since. She wished briefly for one of the protein bars she'd stuffed in her pocket before the crash, then resolutely ignored her hunger. She'd deal with it later.

She paused in one of the shadows, listening. The dark jungle pressed in on all sides like a living wall. Everything was made even darker by what appeared to be a net covering draped overhead between the trees. Camouflage for spy satellites, drones, planes. Clever, but claustrophobic now

that she knew it was there. It blocked out the possible sight-
ing of moon, stars, and passing aircraft completely.

Focus. Breathe. Move.

The ground, cool and slimy-damp, oozed up around her
bare feet and between her toes. Once she ventured deep
into the trees she'd encounter snakes, spiders, and various
insects, not to mention spiny vegetation she'd need to walk
through or over, and that couldn't be done barefoot. Her
own waterproof boots, SIG Pro SP 2340, KA-BAR knife,
and the small knife she'd worn on a lanyard would be ideal
right now. If she knew where they were. Which she didn't.
She'd take whatever she could lay her hands on.

Hitching up the pants, she rolled the waistband down
three times to keep them at least marginally at her hips.
Riva crowded against the dense black tree line, blending
into the darkness as she allowed her gaze to strafe the area
for danger.

Sin's shack was separate from a group of other buildings
several hundred yards across the clearing. Another stood
even farther apart. Thick vegetation encroached on all
sides of the small enclave as she ran lightly across the open
space.

Riva had an excellent sense of direction. Unfortunately,
she had no idea where she was, since she'd blacked out after the helicopter crashed. While there were some stars visible between the branches of the tree canopy, once she was
out from under the camouflage netting, there weren't
enough to ID her relative position and give her a sense of
direction. And even if she knew north from south, she still
wouldn't know where she was, relative to the crash site.

Focus. Shoes. Weapon.

In the distance, someone snored unevenly. *Get a C-PAP, el pendejo.* Other than that, no unexpected sounds, no movement. The birds and animals wouldn't be silent if there was a predator—animal or human—nearby.

Riva stopped and listened, senses attuned to her surroundings. Moving with deliberate caution toward the group of low buildings, she sketched mental quadrants, sectioning off each area, making sure her way was clear. No lights showed, and other than the erratic snorer, all was dead-of-night jungle quiet. Leaves rustled, small claws skittered on branches, and insects buzzed, and an occasional bird cried out, sounding chillingly like a woman shrieking in pain.

All of which masked her own footsteps.

So far, so good.

What *wasn't* good was that she suddenly "saw" hostages nearby. Her vision was crystal clear, as if she was watching a television. Five—maybe four—of them. And not in good shape. Some had been in captivity for months. In two days, they'd all be dead and there was not a damn thing she could do about it. They'd definitely die if she'd left them where they were. At least she could give them a shot. And damn it, her visions weren't always pinpoint accurate...*Shit shit shit.*

Riva hesitated. Okay. *How* nearby? Close enough to rescue them? And then what? She couldn't take half a dozen people with her while on the run *and* looking for Maza.

Was it fair to give them hope and then just as quickly rescind it? *Crapshitdamn.* Even if she got their info to take back with her—*whenever*—it could very well be too late for them. Riva mentally swore. She couldn't take them with her, and she couldn't leave them here. She sucked a breath into her still-sore lungs and kept moving. Now, more than before, she needed weapons.

The compound appeared to be about the size of a football field. Long, barracks-type cinder block buildings with galvanized corrugated iron roofs were covered with what looked like short grass or moss. More camo protection from scout planes above. A couple of small shacks stood slightly separated from the motel-type buildings. Sin's was one of them. The hazy glow of the moon gave some illumination, painting the scene in stark black and gray. The dense jungle on either side seemed like a living, breathing entity.

Riva slapped a bug off her cheek, then stumbled over an exposed root, stubbing her toe painfully. She sucked in a breath, pausing to allow the smarting to abate. She needed shoes.

People would be up and about soon. She sped up. While stealth was necessary, speed was even more so if she had a hope in hell of finding the prisoners, then escaping while everyone still slept.

She had no idea how many people lived here. A dozen, two dozen? A hundred? It was hard to tell how many buildings were clustered together.

Damn, she needed to get out of there, and fast. If Sin realized she was Maza's psychic, idle curiosity would become a power play. He'd come after her for sure. She'd be a damn good bargaining chip. One more valuable to the Abadinista National Liberation Front alive than dead at this point. But Riva had no intention of being captured. Again.

Safety lay with Maza, and since there was no way to contact him, she had to *get* to him. He needed her. At least with him she knew she'd stay alive until she'd done what he'd hired her to do, or she killed him. Here, who the hell knew what her odds were?

The first building she came to was the snorer's. His sounds of a water buffalo in heat covered her helping herself to the thickly caked, muddy boots he'd conveniently left outside his door. They were damp with sweat and dew and probably stank, but who the hell cared as long as they prevented her from puncturing her feet.

Hello, what do we have here? The kWh-meter on the wall near the front door indicated a power source in the settlement. Diesel, probably. With the covering overhead, not solar. Whatever the source, it would provide energy and probably communications. Finding and disabling it would be a nice going-away present. To delay them, it would be worth taking a few extra minutes to disable whatever comms they had.

Backtracking out of sight, she crouched to put the boots on. Way too big, so not conducive to running, but better than her bare feet. Now, if only someone had conveniently left an Uzi or handgun for her...

Hidden from view, she observed a two-man patrol heading her way. Ducking into the thick undergrowth, she hunkered down as the men walked past her hiding place. Something tickled, or rather *crawled* up her pant leg. Riva didn't move so much as a muscle until the men passed ten feet from her.

Moving cautiously she checked their position, then turned to see where the other two men from the second team were. Opposite direction. Not two. One. So there was a man on the loose. *Mierda.* Where the hell— Yes, *there.* Ducking between two buildings.

Bad boy.

Riva darted behind the row of buildings to follow him, jogging alongside Water Buffalo's hut. The buildings on this stretch were cinder block, built in a long row, like a cheap motel.

She sped up, then came to an abrupt halt as the soldier emerged into the clearing between the back of the building, and the trees. "It's my lucky frigging day." Not only could she see the bulky shape of a gun in the small of his back, but he leaned what could be an Uzi or Mk47 against the wall.

"*Muchas gracias, amigo,*" she said under her breath.

The sound of him peeing masked her rapid footsteps as she lightly ran up beside him. A good pee, apparently, as he gave a groan of satisfaction and kept going.

A soundless neck lock.

He crumpled to the ground.

Riva went through his pockets lightning-fast. Two weapons, shoes, and a smart cellphone. A trifecta.

Except the phone had no signal. So, no GPS. A quick scroll showed her the guy had saved a few routes. One to Santa de Porres. Riva quickly memorized that. One to Abad, ditto, and a couple more places located in the jungle. Girlfriend? Bars? Brothels? Who knew. She committed them all to memory in case she needed them later.

Rolling the dead guy beneath the concealing branches, she went back to the deep shadows of the building. The hostages were nearby.

The phone was now a liability. Once the body was found, they'd ping it. Riva removed the battery and shoved it and the phone in her back pockets. Might be useful later.

At the end of the row of conjoined block buildings stood several, freestanding smaller structures separated by narrow swaths of cleared land. All camouflaged with paint, and artfully placed vegetation.

"Please," a man begged, voice thick and hoarse. "We need water, *por favor*. Water."

"You don't even know if they're out there, Sol," a woman said hopelessly. "They won't give it to us even if they are. Save your breath."

Good news: She'd found the hostages. Bad news: She'd found the hostages.

A large metal key hung off a nail pounded into the cement block a few feet from the metal door. That was nice of the kidnappers. Riva unhooked it and slid it into her front pocket. With her back flattened against the wall, she considered her slim options. They'd need weapons, supplies. Oh, for crapsake! Like herself, they probably needed *shoes*. Where the hell was she going to find *any* of that before dawn broke and everyone rose and shone?

For a nanosecond she considered alerting the hostages she was there, or letting them out to find their own way... Couldn't do it. They'd be just as dead out there as they would be if they stayed put. She decided she'd release them when she was ready to actually *do* something. Civilians were notoriously unpredictable, and she couldn't allow anything to jeopardize her op.

Weapons, food, water, medical supplies, shoes. Any and all of the above. She mentally gave herself ten minutes to hunt and gather. After that, they were on their own.

Riva went hunting.

In the end, the weapons were the easiest to come by. She overpowered three guards, one by strangling and breaking his neck, another by stabbing him in the jugular before cutting his throat, the third with a swift thrust between the ribs as her hand came over his mouth.

She dragged the bodies into the concealing shrubbery just as the third sentry came at her from the side as she was dragging his buddy into the shrubbery. Deflecting a punch to the side of her head, Riva grabbed him by the muzzle of his sub machine gun, surprising the hell out of him as she used it as a fulcrum and swung him around. The minute he went down, she was on him. A knee to the temple, and on her feet to punch down with her heel on his balls. When he doubled over, she grabbed his hair, and used her newly ac-quired knife to cut his throat.

Sweating, breath heaving, she dragged his dead ass into the thicket as well.

She made good on a small haul of weapons. Two AKs, three ankle knives, thank you very much, and a hybrid semi-iauto Riva figured would be risky to attempt firing while she was in camp. She wasn't about to make any noise to attract attention.

With weapons came three pairs of boots. Riva immediately kicked off the too big boots and shoved her feet into a better fitting pair. She also scored three large canteens filled with water.

She had to kill the cook in the mess hall when he showed up too soon and spotted her in his storeroom grabbing what she considered food to go. Employing the small knife she'd used on the sentry just minutes earlier, she stabbed him up high in the kidneys. He didn't make a sound as he dropped. Riva hauled him into the storeroom.

Another pair of boots. Crouching, she swore under her breath as she struggled to quickly untie the stiff, wet laces.

Buzzing, high on adrenaline, Riva grabbed protein bars, ripping one open and shoving it in her mouth as she grabbed apples and some unpleasant-smelling cake thing that was rock hard. Whatever it was, she snagged a lot of it, and stuffed everything—weapons and shoes included—in a filthy, mud-colored knapsack she found by the back door. Under the backpack, quite conveniently, hung a small, metal first-aid box. She rattled it. Whatever was inside was what she had. It would have to do.

She had no idea how long she had before the darkness gave way to dawn, and decided to take no more than fifteen minutes to break the hostages free and send them on their way if any of them had a prayer of not getting caught.

She made her way back to the prisoners' building and unlocked the door.

"*Por favor*. Water."

Riva pulled the door almost closed behind her in case anyone wandered by. "Shut up, Sol, and listen up. Here, drink this while I talk." She shoved a flask at an elderly man leaning against the wall by the door. He grabbed it. "I know you're thirsty, but sip it slowly or you'll just puke it up." He was pretty much just a vague outline; she could only tell he was elderly by his voice.

In the far eastern corner of the hut, a young woman whimpered quietly. She'd been doing it a long time. Months in fact.

Riva waited while her eyes adjusted to the darkness. "How many of you are in here?" *There should be five.* She saw four figures. Two men, and two women.

"Fi— Four," the woman who'd spoken early said quietly. "Sonia Henderson died half an hour ago."

"Sol," Riva said firmly, "hand the lady your flask, you're done for now. Who's in charge here?"

A younger male answered rapidly. "No one. Some of us have been here for months, Sol and Denise were delivered three weeks ago."

"Pick *someone* to be your leader, because once you're out there, someone's word better be law. I have some supplies, protein bars, fruit. Guns, some ammo, and one water flask. Everyone come over here and grab a pair of boots. I don't care if you have to cut off your toes, or stuff leaves in them to make them fit. Everyone needs something on their feet out there." She took out the boots and handed them over. If they had mismatched pairs, they could figure it out on the run. "Is everyone ambulatory? Say yes, because whoever isn't, if the rest of you can't carry them, will be staying behind."

"We can all walk," the woman, Denise, told her firmly.

"Good." Riva shoved the heavy sack at the woman's chest. "You're in charge. Santa de Porres is due south from here." Unfortunately, Riva had no idea how damn far away it was. "The jungle is filled with armed guerrillas. There's a flashlight in there. Try to hide during the day and walk at night. Fill the canteen wherever you find running water, and keep moving until you hit the city."

"Who are you?" the younger man asked.

"The person getting you out of here." Riva could practically hear the clock ticking in her head. Every second she spent chit-chatting with the hostages was another second closer to getting caught herself. "When I open the door, *run*, don't walk, across to the other side of the road, and get into the trees. You'll be heading south. That way." Riva pointed in the general direction. The best she could do. "Move as quickly and quietly as you can and put as much space between this camp and yourself as you can. It'll be scary as hell out there. Don't think about it. Just think about being home, sleeping in your own beds after a hot shower, and enjoying a thick juicy steak. Give me your names. If I can, I'll contact your families to let them know I saw you alive, so they can come and look for you."

Denise Karlins, Sol Bergman, Eric Reiman, and the crier was Eric's wife Tonya. As they each called out their name, Riva knew the chances of the four making it through a predator-infested jungle alive were pretty much slim to none. But she couldn't leave them here. At least out there they had a chance. Some of them would make it.

"Oh, God..." Denise's voice cracked. "Come with us. At least you know how—"

"I'm opening the door now. Run as if your lives depend on it, because they do. And for God's sake, shut the fuck up. Be quiet. Go!"

Riva slipped out after them, locked the door, then re-pocketed the key as she watched for a moment. She didn't have time to make sure they were safely tucked into the jungle before she darted around the back of their little prison. She'd sent them south, and high above the black treetops off to the east, a flickering spiral of sparks and smoke indicated where the chopper had crashed.

That was her first stop. Hopefully somewhere in the wreckage she'd find one of the booster tracking devices. Contact with her team was imperative.

She had to move fast, and— *Hello. What do we have here?*

She'd almost slammed into a large metal structure. Five feet high, by five wide, it appeared to be a large generator/electrical box.

Perhaps today was her lucky day after all. Which would only be justice because yesterday sure as hell hadn't been. Circling it, and keeping her eyes moving for imminent danger, Riva found the door. Yanking it open, she saw wires and circuits. Not giving a damn what anything was, she reached in to disconnect whatever she could. If nothing else, it would slow them down or disable whatever warning system they had in place.

"I wouldn't do that if I were you." The silky, annoyingly familiar voice came from directly behind her, stopping her with a fistful of wires clutched in her hands. "Shouldn't you be running away rather than playing electrician?"

TEN

Riva spun around to see Sin Diaz leaning against a nearby tree, a small submachine gun pointed at her heart. He was as stealthy, sneaky, and lethal as a jaguar. There was just enough light from the pilot light on the electrical unit to see him. Which she'd prefer not doing. He should be somewhere else. Somewhere far the hell away from her when she was this freaking close to escape.

He'd pulled a camo flak vest over his impressive naked chest and tied his hair back in a stubby tail. Booted feet spread, he held the weapon with familiar ease. She read his face and body language. He wouldn't hesitate to shoot.

"I see you've helped yourself to my clothes. Too bad, I like you better out of them." He gave her a steely look. "Take out the gun. Slowly, and with two fingers."

Arrogant, reptilian slimebucket, was enjoying this. See how you like the blade of my hand slicing your trachea, asshole. A bullet directly into his eye would be faster... Heart tripping, Riva calculated her chances of getting off a shot before he did. Not great. Her pilfered weapon was tucked down the too-big pants in the small of her back. Did he have X-ray eyes, for God's sake? How did he know she had a gun?

His was firmly in his large, rock-steady hands. At this range, seventy-five percent chance he'd shoot her before she could fish out her weapon. Ninety-eight percent odds his shot, wherever it hit, would be fatal, especially out here hell and gone from decent medical care.

She wasn't going to do T-FLAC any good dead, and she wasn't stupid enough to underestimate Diaz. With one hand up so he could see it was weapon-free, she put her other hand down the back of the loose pants. She was lucky the damn gun was still there. Taking it out between two fingers, she palmed out the clip and tossed both it and the weapon to the ground between them, keeping her hands where he could see them. Wishing for more light so she could read the microexpressions on his face was a waste of time. His body language said he was not dicking around. He was big, bad, and annoyed as hell that she wasn't where he'd left her.

"Now my clothes."

Riva grit her teeth. Bastard. She toed off the too big boots.

"And the pants."

No way out of it. Stoically, she yanked the utility pants off her hips and let them drop to her ankles. Not like much had been there to hold them in place anyway. At least the T-shirt was long enough to skim midway down her thighs.

The sneaky, self-satisfied look on his face irritated the hell out of her. The pistol in his hand didn't waver. "Now the shirt."

"Absolutely *not*." Riva folded her arms over her chest and glared at him as a large, winged insect dive-bombed her head, then circled her face like a plane coming into LaGuardia. Spreading her feet to center herself, she gave him a stony look. She was *not* stripping down to nothing and *not* going back to his hovel. Not going to freaking happen.

"Haven't you heard of the Geneva convention?" she asked. "Let me paraphrase the protocols for you. They're at the core of *international* humanitarian law, the body of international law that regulates the conduct of armed conflict and seeks to limit its effects. It specifically protects people who are not taking part in the hostilities. You know, like civilians, health workers, and *aid workers*? *Of which I'm one.* If you want me naked again, you'll have to shoot me."

"You think I won't?" His eyes grew dark and intense. "I left you naked and tied up earlier, and you still escaped. I underestimated you." His gaze dropped to her swollen lips, then back to meet hers. Not a jot of sympathy for her poor abused mouth to be seen. "I won't make that mistake twice. And I don't give a fuck about the Geneva convention. Shirt. Off."

And just like that, her lucky day took a nosedive.

Riva pulled at the hem of the shirt and yanked it up and over her head, the smell of him invading her airspace as she did so. Her skin, already adjusted to the meager warmth of the clothing, tightened, her nipples turning hard.

"There's your damn shirt." Bare-assed naked again, she flung the wadded cloth in his general direction, taking the huge bug with it. The corner of his mouth lifted as he caught the shirt out of the air one-handed.

A shuffle of feet approaching made him frown, his penetrating gaze darting for a moment to the source of the sound before landing squarely back on her. "On second thought, perhaps for the moment, the shirt might be a good idea." He chucked his shirt back at her. Riva didn't ask questions. Pulling it over her head, she covered her body just before a group of armed men rounded the nearby building.

She was doubly screwed.

Stepping into her, Sin grabbed her upper arm, fingers like steel bands on her bare skin. "Don't do or say anything stupid. Understand?" he whispered almost soundlessly in her ear, his breath hot on her cheek. He spoke English.

The tone of his voice, urgent, commanding, but with a note of oh-fuck *worry* that seemed out of place, given everything she knew about him, made Riva wonder who was the bigger threat—Sin Diaz or whoever was coming around that corner.

ELEVEN

ccompanied by four of her lieutenants, Mama came into view, fire in her eyes. *Shit*. Barely five feet in heavy boots, she put the fear of God into every man in camp with just a single glance from those soulless black eyes. Any one of his men could physically crush her with one hand, yet they didn't dare. Tiny of stature, she wielded her power like a titanium hand in a graphene glove.

A cigarette, the end glowing red, hung from her mouth and her favorite AK-47 was cradled like a beloved child in her arms. She was damn good with a gun, and at this range, she wouldn't miss.

Sin's gut tightened and his heartbeat accelerated.

Beside him, Riva whispered, "Crap."

She had no fucking idea.

"No time to sleep?" he asked his mother when she stopped several yards in front of them. He'd left her not six hours earlier; what the hell was she doing up and patrolling now?

With an irrational need to protect his prisoner from his mother, he instinctively stepped between the two women. He was fucking done with Mama barging in.

By the way her dark eyes flashed with annoyance, it was clear his presence irritated her as much as hers pissed him off. There was a massive disconnect. Since Sin had stopped taking the vile concoction she made for him in the hope it would restore his full memories, Mama was becoming more and more of a pain in his ass. Even when he'd been taking the nasty-tasting brew, he'd sensed no maternal warmth from her and none of the love that a son should have for his mother.

He had zero familial sentiment for her. Honest to God, for all the connection he felt, he could just as easily have crossed paths with her going into the mail room.

What mail room?

How the hell did he even know what a goddamned mail room *was*? He had memories of things he couldn't know anything about, and knew nothing about things he should remember. He started to lift his hand to rub at the sharp pain at his temples, then dropped it. Mama was the last person to whom he wanted to show any weakness.

The possibility that she'd been drugging him had crossed his mind more than once. Another reason for the solo trip into town. He had a flask of the shit she'd been giving him. He wanted it analyzed.

Cold and calculating, and far from rash, he never turned his back on his mother. He didn't now. He knew she wanted to interrogate the young woman he'd rescued. She couldn't have her. He wouldn't back down. Neither would she. They were at an impasse. There was a strong possibility that one of them would end up dead.

Mama spread her feet.

"*Don't,*" he warned his prisoner under his breath as she shifted beside him.

He'd tossed the *get out of my clothes* dare to see how far she was willing to go, and test her level of fear. She had none. Her eyes had shouted *fuck you* as clearly as if she'd said it out loud. Too fucking bad Mama had almost caught her naked out here in the middle of the clearing. This was a dangerous situation. Like Mama, he had to discover Riva Rimaldi's purpose, yet more time to convince her to talk had just been yanked from his control.

Taking a drag of her cigarette, Mama gave him a hard look. "Why did you not send for me when you returned?" She exhaled a plume of smoke, then spat in the dirt.

"Jesus. I just got here. And there was no need anyway. I have the situation under control."

"What is the *perra* doing out here?" she snapped, as she gave him an accusatory glare. "It's too soon to give her to the men. Bring her to my quarters. I'll interrogate her myself."

Yeah, Sin knew how that would go. Mama would crush the young woman with the fuck-you eyes beneath her boot heel until there was nothing left. He gave her a cold look. "Do not question my authority, woman. I questioned her already. She has nothing to offer. She's an aid worker. That's it. She's no use to us. I'll send her to Santa de Porres, and we'll be rid of her."

"Are you mad?" she snapped. "She's of value to *someone*. Who is that someone if not Maza? We first need to know who she is to know her value. Can you tell me that? No, I think you cannot. And if you're thinking of jeopardizing our safety by using the helicopter to get her there, while our enemy's men patrol *our* turf, you're a fool."

Hidden four clicks away was a small four-seater helicopter. They hadn't taken the Hummingbird up to go to the city in weeks because they didn't want what had happened to Maza's chopper to happen to theirs.

"Who said anything about using the chopper? I'll have her walked in." Two or three days. She'd be lucky to make it, in the already hostile environment. Sin reminded himself he wasn't responsible for her safety or well-being. And just because he felt an unaccustomed need to assume such, didn't mean he wouldn't interrogate her, then drop her lifeless body somewhere conspicuous for Maza to find later. She wasn't his responsibility.

"She was on Maza's chopper." Mama kept her eyes fixed on Riva, exhaling a cloud of noxious cigarette smoke as she stepped closer. She gave the barrel of her gun a hard jerk, indicating he should move aside. "She works for him. Since when has he ever brought in an *aid worker*? He does nothing that doesn't directly benefit himself."

As did the ANLF, Sin acknowledged, standing his ground. If he were Maza, why would *he* bring in an aid worker? He wouldn't. He felt the prisoner's hot breath on the back of his arm, felt the heat of her body down the length of his back. "If he brought her here for another purpose, I'll find out what that is."

Yeah, Sin was pretty damn well positive Riva Rimaldi worked for his enemy. He didn't want Mama to interrogate her with that assumption. "She doesn't speak Spanish, and she doesn't know anything useful. *Martillar en hierro frio.*" Pretty much stop flogging a dead horse.

"You're acting the fool over a fuck."

He gave Mama a steely look. "That's enough. She is my business. Not yours. She's going to town, if I have to take her myself."

"At such a crucial time? No. Ask her what she is here to do." Mama fondled the stock of her gun with stubby fingers, nails bitten to the quick. "It will give us an advantage over the *Pijo*."

The "prick" was Escobar Maza.

Hell. Sin knew that look. Mama was digging in her heels. Her instinct wasn't wrong. It rarely was. She knew it and the men at her side knew it. No matter how much he preferred it otherwise. He'd known the second he'd found her that the woman was going to be trouble. "I already—"

"*Ask.*"

He half turned to Riva. Her cheeks were flushed, not, he suspected, by embarrassment, but by anger. She stared up at him with furious eyes and a raw mouth, and the look she gave him was a promise of retribution. Jesus. She was all but naked, surrounded by danger on every side, and she was still defiant.

"Mama wants to know what you're here to do for Escobar Maza," he said harshly in English.

She gave him a blank look. "I told you. I have no idea who that is."

Seeing Mama raise her hand to strike out of the corner of his eye, Sin spun around. Riva hastily backed up. He stepped into her. "Gonna hit you," he said under his breath, keeping his eyes locked on hers as he drew his fist back. "*Drop.*"

"Fuck you," she said just as softly. Chin raised, eyes shooting sparks at him, she planted her bare feet in the spongy ground and stood like a rock.

Sin punched her on the jaw, expecting her to anticipate the blow, and to fall backward. Instead she took the full force of the punch, and even though he'd held back, it was still hard enough to knock her back several staggering steps.

He walked over, grabbed her upper arm to prevent her from crashing to the ground, and hissed, "You don't follow instructions worth a damn, lady."

"Get out of the way." Mama grabbed the back of his flak vest and yanked.

No. Fuck no. Furious, he spun around and knocked her hand away. "She's mine to do with as I please. I *please* not to have my property broken by you before I'm finished with her. I'll do what's necessary without your interference."

Mama's cigarette, smoked down to almost nothing, glowed as she sucked in a breath, holding the smoke in her lungs as if it were a joint. "You challenge my authority?" She exhaled in two jerky huffs as she fieldstripped the burning nub.

"*Your* authority? You forget your place, woman. *Soy jefe.* There is no room for two of us. Make a choice." It was a battle of wills he'd win. Perhaps he'd been physically impaired and disoriented by his injuries and she'd had to be his representative with his men for a few months. But he was well now, stronger than she could ever hope to be, and he'd brook no interference with this business, especially from his mother.

"Get the information. If you can't, I will. You have one hour."

"It's not for you to give me an ultimatum. Challenge me again on this and your punishment will be swift. Do I make myself clear?"

Her black eyes flashed anger before she backed up, head bowed. "*Sí, Jefe.*"

In the second before Mama turned away, he saw a glance filled with hard, pure evil. Her compliance was a sham. Mama was plotting against him. She'd have watchers on him from here on out, men who would be reporting his every move to her. Great. He'd have enemies within and enemies without. He had no idea why he'd chosen this morning to draw the line in the sand with Mama, but he had.

He glanced at Riva Rimaldi, into the fire that burned deep within those angry brown eyes. Something told him she was worth it. Why? He had no fucking clue.

TWELVE

Agitated, furious, and yeah-*scared,* Riva breathed hard. Thank God the missing hostages and dead guards hadn't been discovered. Yet. It was only a matter of time, however. She was sick of being manhandled, and damn sick of being practically naked. All she wore was his—thankfully too big—T-shirt. Being this close to naked, and aware of the high adrenaline and testosterone pumping through Sin Diaz's veins, made Riva acutely conscious of her vulnerability. She wasn't sure which need was more critical: underwear or a weapon.

She tried to jerk free as Sin shoved her ahead of him across the clearing, his iron-hard fingers like manacles around her upper arm. She tried, "You're hurting me," pretty sure it wouldn't work.

It didn't.

"What's your point?" He gave her a little shove to reactivate her feet, which she'd dug into the mush. "Shut the fuck up and keep walking."

Hating Sin Diaz's guts, she resumed walking. Killing him would be her pleasure. Riva's jaw throbbed, and she'd bitten her tongue when he'd slugged her. Bastard. It wasn't the first time she'd been hit, and in her line of work it wouldn't be the last, but for some annoying reason, she considered *this* man striking her as personal.

Tilting up her chin, which she hoped was already turning black and blue so he'd feel guilty as hell for hitting what he thought was a defenseless woman, Riva fixed him with what she was certain was the most speaking look she'd ever given anyone in her life. Projecting *vulnerable,* hurt, and wobbly on her feet, she said with fake bravado and a faint quiver in her voice, "Nice to know I'm not singled out."

Mud oozed between her bare toes, and when something large and slimy landed with a faint wet plop on her thigh, she let out a little, very girly shriek. She swiped at it with her free hand. "You even bully your mother."

His mother and her goons had shown up and he'd gone from mocking to absolutely furious. Cold, calculated, and vicious. She didn't need her training to read those expressions, and they were far from micro.

Mother and son hated one another. The mother hated that the son was stronger. She didn't respect him and didn't like stepping back from the confrontation. She considered herself stronger, more powerful. In charge.

So did he.

Interesting.

If necessary, she'd use their hatred of each other to get the upper hand. A cheerful thought when she was practically being dragged down the narrow street back to his hovel.

In her line of work, she'd seen man's inhumanity to man, and Diaz was no exception. The things he'd done in his checkered past made her blood congeal. She was lucky he'd only punched her. But the day was still young.

At least the missing prisoners hadn't been discovered yet. More time for them to disappear into the jungle without being caught. How far had they run? She got a brief flash of them in her mind's eye. Not far enough. She'd done all she could. The rest was up to them.

She cast a quick glance at Diaz's face. Jaw tight, eyes intense. Royally pissed. Too freaking bad. She'd pit his anger against her righteous indignation any day. "Give me back my clothes, and I'll get out of your way. I hate to come between a loving son and his mommy."

Hard fingers clamped more tightly around her upper arm as he shoved her ahead of him. "I said, shut up and keep walking."

"Or what? You'll hit me again?" He'd mumbled something under his breath before hitting her, but Riva had been too busy watching the interplay between Sin and his equally scary mother to listen.

"That was a tap."

"I've been tapped harder." She'd mitigated the blow slightly by staggering backward just in time, but his fist had still made contact, and her jaw throbbed. Her fury was white-hot. Riva knew she had to get a grip on that anger, and fast. Her mouth had always gotten her into trouble. She knew better. Being a smart-ass was not in her best interest. It never had been. And now was no exception. She was freaking aware, damn it, but sometimes her smart-assness just got away from her. A coping mechanism brought out by her stepfather's abuse. Usually, her rigorous training and some serious psych counseling kicked in in time for her to rein it in.

Zip it.

No missteps. No flying off the handle. Control and guile were the names of this game. In fact, she had no idea why she was so pissed. She'd had a lot worse, and lot more unexpectedly.

It seemed as if she'd anticipated physical violence from the time her flighty mother married Joe when she was five. And she certainly anticipated it every day when she was in the field. The jungles of Cosio and the charming Diazes were no exception.

The lessons Joe had inadvertently taught her had stood her in good stead for her work as a T-FLAC operative. Bones eventually healed, but stupidity could get one killed. Keep cool. Stay focused. Remember the mission. And don't let your emotions rule your actions.

Now that he'd caught her escaping, he wouldn't give her another chance. He'd secure her better the next time. There couldn't be a next time. Next time he'd kill her. Her only hope was to kill him before he got her back to his hut.

She had to back up. *Act afraid. Act hurt.*

She gritted her teeth and said sweetly, "I hope you and your mother weren't fighting over me."

"I should've let you keep running," he said sourly. Oh yeah. He was truly pissed. Like she gave a damn. His fingers bit into her upper arm as he gave her another shove. "The hungry animals would have saved me the hassle, not to mention the time."

He had no accent when he spoke English. Damn good English. "Do you pull wings off innocent butterflies, too?" *Shut the hell up Riva. Shut. Up. Do. Not. Engage. The enemy.*

His cinder block shack was about three hundred feet ahead. Once there, he'd tie her up. And this time he wouldn't underestimate her and leave her alone.

The fact that she was all but naked, and barefoot, wouldn't deter her. She had to put him out of action, make a run for it, and find Maza. Had. To. *Now.*

Riva slowed her steps and he bumped into her. The contact jolted her from the top of her head to her muddy toes as if she'd been given a powerful electrical shock. His body was rock-hard, and *hot*.

He gave her the evil eye. Those eyes weren't the black pits of hell like his mother's, but a deep, stormy hazel green. "Want me to knock you out and carry your sorry ass?"

She'd take care of *his* sorry ass and enjoy doing it. But first... Putting a hand to her face, she sagged a little in his hold. "I don't feel so h—" Rolling back her eyes, she let her legs fold.

Without missing a beat, Sin scooped her up against his broad chest, arms like two steel bands pinning her there. The same vision—their naked, sweating bodies twined in shockingly intimate embrace—flashed through her mind. Riva remained limp, fighting the sudden, inexplicable urge to curl into him.

Her head flopped onto his hard chest. He smelled faintly of soap and delectable sweaty male. Arousal swamped her in a shocking flood of inappropriate and unwanted need. A new sensation. It baffled Riva and yes, dammit, frightened her.

This was something new, something she had no time to analyze as the images slammed into her brain in three-dimensional technicolor. She fought to bring up an image of the just-released captives instead, but his stimulating smell surrounded her, making it hard to pull up the other vision. Closing her eyes, something she normally didn't have to do, she tried again.

Her life depended on keeping a cool head, and trying to figure out why Sin Diaz turned her on so powerfully was far too distracting.

He adjusted her dead weight, supporting her back with one arm while he draped her legs over the other. When she sagged between the two, he shifted one large, splayed hand to cup her bare butt, holding her up as he walked. It annoyed the living bejesus out of her that, despite the rope burns, her sore jaw from his punch, her lacerated lips, and her additional scrapes, she *liked* the feel of his rough hand on her skin. Since she couldn't talk, being unconscious and all, she kept her thoughts to herself as she called herself all kinds of fool.

It was too damn early for Stockholm Syndrome to set in. Whatever this was about, it was something else. She wished to hell she could block out the image of the two of them, naked and sweaty, her knees bent over his shoulders as he pounded into her. They were in a...tent? A tent for godsake! and she was screaming while having a violent orgasm.

Dammit, she was never that creative in her lovemaking, and no one had ever made her scream like that. Damn him.

Not a prediction. The images had nothing—absolutely not a damn thing—to do with her psychic ability. What woman *wouldn't* have thoughts of hot sweaty sex when three quarters naked and in close proximity to a virile specimen like Sin Diaz? His hand was cupping her naked butt for God's sake, his fingers almost in her mound. Sex? No wonder. She could just as easily picture shooting the son of a bitch between the eyes. Except that wasn't the visceral image she was seeing in her mind's eye as he cradled her against the hard wall of his chest and carried her rapidly toward his home.

"Little fool," he snarled as he kicked open the door, stepping from dirt onto concrete. "Fucking hell. I do *not* have time for this complication."

No shit, Sherlock.

THIRTEEN

Conflicted as hell, Sin kicked open the door and carried her inside his hut. Fucking, fucking, *fucking* hell. Goddamn *pequeña hembra* was more trouble than she was worth.

He didn't hit women, a weird code of ethics considering everything else he *did* do. He'd held back as much as possible to mitigate the blow. Stubborn little witch had stood her ground, eyes glaring death and dismemberment until he'd practically knocked her on her ass.

She hadn't passed out from that punch, he didn't think. What he *did* think was maybe internal injuries from the crash. *Dios.* There wasn't a hospital, or even a clinic, in hundreds of jungle miles. Because of Maza, Sin had a moratorium on taking up the Hummingbird, which was kept hidden and well-camouflaged deep in the jungle.

If her injuries were serious, she'd die right here in his camp. While that would solve the problem her presence presented, the thought was supremely unappealing. "Besides, you're just too damn pretty to die," he told her, not realizing he'd said it out loud. And the millisecond he thought *that* illogical sentiment, he remembered he didn't do soft.

No. Not unappealing. "*Inconvenient.* If I'm going to know what the hell Maza's got up his sleeve, you have to tell me what the fuck *you're* doing here." If she died, he wasn't going to get a damn thing.

Laying her carefully on the bed, Sin swept aside strands of telltale bloodstained rope. "You *chewed* your way free? Christ, woman..." He gritted his teeth with fury. The corners of her mouth were bloody and raw from gnawing through her bindings, her lush lips, slightly parted, were swollen and red. She didn't move. Eyes closed, she looked serene and dick-pulsingly beautiful.

Sin pulled down the T-shirt to cover her exposed lower body. Everything about her turned him on. The creamy tawniness of her smooth skin, the long sweep of her lashes, the swell of her breasts, and the long delectable lines of her smooth legs. He wanted it all.

He was damned sick of being turned on by a comatose woman.

He made a decision as he curved his fingers over the warm skin of her thigh. If she didn't die, he'd walk her into Santa de Porres himself. Kill several birds with one stone as it were. Get the sedating, brain-deadening brew analyzed, then go and look up Luisa, an accommodating young widow he had a loose arrangement with in town. And if she did die? Fuck. He couldn't let that happen. Because what took precedence over all of the above was discovering what Maza had up his sleeve for him, and she was the key to that.

The ANLF had to take action before the SYP struck.

So, no time for dicking around. No time for sex...

Pushing aside the thought of sex—because God only knew, it wasn't the buxom Luisa he was visualizing—Sin went to his locker to find the first-aid kit he kept well stocked with everything he could possibly need up here, so far from help. It was in a secret section at the foot of the locker, under his folded pants.

He had her SIG there, as well as a compact, lightweight 4.6mm MP7A1 submachine gun. Sin was well aware that someone, or someone's flunky, periodically went through his shit when he was away. He'd made the locker himself to hide crap he wanted quick to hand, and to have somewhere to hang what few clothes he retained in camp. He'd already decided, before this clusterfuck, that he'd get to the city this week. See what he could piece together from this mismatched patchwork that was his memory. Or lack thereof.

He went back to the bed, put the metal box on the floor, then picked up her wrist to check her pulse. Seemed to be fine. Sin wasn't a doctor, but he knew she'd shown no signs of weakness, or confusion; just the opposite in fact. Instead of a faint, this could be a coma, in which case she was shit out of luck, because he had no idea what to do to fix that scenario. Hopefully, not a cranial bleed.

Fainting could be a sign of internal bleeding. The good news was that she hadn't puked. Blood or otherwise. Her chest rose and fell with smooth, slow, easy movements. She wasn't short of breath. He ran down as many symptoms as he could think of that would cause her to be unconscious, and, more worrisome, for this length of time.

The other very real possibility for her losing consciousness was some kind of poisonous bite. God only knew his backyard was filled with any number of snakes, spiders, and other venomous denizens of the jungle. Barefoot, and all but naked, she was a walking target.

Sin brushed his thumb across her full lower lip, careful to avoid the abrasions at the corners. If they'd been in a different time and place... But they weren't. No matter who she was, or what her purpose was with Maza, she was his enemy. The ANLF's enemy. Her presence was dangerous to all of them.

She was also a very real danger to his tenuous status quo with Mama.

Of course, if she died, that would no longer be an issue. And if she lived, he had to make the decision of what to do with her. Because Mama didn't give a flying fuck that she was soft, and beautiful, and fascinating. If Mama didn't get the answers she wanted, when she wanted them, she'd kill Riva slowly and painfully just for sport and to fuck with Maza or himself.

"What the hell am I going to do with you, *mi misterio?*" Mystery was an understatement. The fans of her lashes cast shadows on her cheeks, the pulse at her temple and the base of her damp throat throbbed, indicating she was alive.

Shifting his focus from her face to her bare legs, he moved to the other end of the narrow cot. Lifting one slender muddy foot, Sin ran his hands up and down her leg, turning it this way and that, searching for a raised welt, a hot spot, a small hole indicating a puncture wound. Her skin felt warm and silky smooth, but there were no welts. Redness and scratches from her fall through the trees, but no hot spots. Gently returning it to the mattress, he did the same to the other leg and foot. He noted that the long scratch on her thigh was healing well. Mama's poultice had done its job.

Pushing up the too-large T-shirt to expose her bare lower body, Sin kept his focus on what he was looking for, but the smooth skin of her belly, the silky dark hair hiding where he wanted to be, distracted him. He found himself stroking instead of inspecting.

Her abs tightened as he stroked her belly, causing him to lift his eyes to find her watching him, narrow-eyed. Her hand rose to tangle in his hair, riveting his attention to the invitation in her dark gaze.

"You have to stop groping me when I'm unconscious, Diaz." Her voice, low and sultry, shot straight to his groin.

He skimmed his hand up her midriff to the under curve of her breast. Her nipple beaded beneath his light touch as he murmured, barely able to get the words out, "You're not unconscious now." He leaned over the bed, all the while thinking he should be backing away and knowing that he wouldn't.

The sharp sting as she gripped handfuls of his hair in her fists added to the leap in his pulse. Eyes locked on his, Riva pulled him in closer, her lips an open invita—

The hard blow to his chest came out of nowhere, dissipating the sensual haze as Riva rabbit-punched him with both knees straight to his solar plexus. The blow to his chest shocked the shit out of him and he lost his balance, landing on the bed beside her, gasping for breath.

"That's for punching me, asshole."

With unexpected speed, she rolled until she was sitting astride him.

Surprisingly strong, alert, and with murder in her eyes, she pressed down on his elbows with both knees, effectively incapacitating him. For the moment. In her left hand was his Glock, which he'd stuck in the back of his pants.

Fucking hell. She was good, *damn* good.

He now knew one thing for certain: She was absolutely, positively, *not* an aid worker.

"I warned you it was coming," he pointed out.

Her eyes widened, but he only glanced at the surprise that he saw there for a second. Her crotch, inches from his face, smelled enticingly of feminine musk and captured 200 percent of his attention. Sin's dick leapt with excitement. The rest of his body, especially his brain, wasn't so hopeful. Swallowing hard, he lifted his gaze up her body to the cold, calculating intent on her face. "Who the hell *are* you?"

She shot him a bland look. "The woman who just got the drop on you, Mama's boy. And next time you give a warning, make it more than an incoherent mumble. Communication skills definitely need improvement. Where the hell are my clothes, Diaz?"

Sin settled back. With a view of her open pink folds and smooth belly, he had the best seat in the house. Let her rant. He'd had heavier adversaries sitting on him, but none nearly as appealing.

The first faint rays of dawn highlighted her curves and valleys. Sin's gut clenched. She had scars. Faint pink lines, he saw now. Her wrists... Not from Mama's rope. Old scars, faint, telling badges of pain. Christ. He didn't want to feel sympathy for her.

Irritation, yeah. Lust and sympathy? No.

"Whatever you're thinking," she snapped, tilting up his chin with the barrel of his Glock, "forget it. I want my things and then I'll be on my way."

Untidy strands of glossy black hair escaped from the long braid down her back and spilled over her shoulders. Early morning sunlight made the dark strands look as though they were coated in gold. She painted an enticing, exotic picture juxtaposed against the rough, worn gray brick of the walls behind her.

Supremely uncomfortable with her sitting square on his trapped dick, and her hard knees pinning his arms, he was strangely entertained by her. "You'll have to kill me first, and look into my eyes when you do it."

She exerted a little more pressure on his elbows with her knees. "You say that like you think it'll bother me. Trust me. It won't."

If he wasn't looking right at the tempting folds of her vagina, he'd say she had the cojones of a rhinoceros. Riva Rimaldi also had the fearlessness and aggression of a honey badger. Both attributes could have her bleeding out on the floor right now if he wasn't so damned amused and turned on by her.

"If you think you'll be able to walk out of camp undetected, think again," he said easily, shifting his hips just enough to ease a little of his discomfort. Didn't help worth a damn. "My men will shoot you on sight the second you leave this building, and there's no telling what *Mama* will do to you. And if you're lucky enough not to be dead, you'd never find Maza. You won't make it a mile before some animal decides to eat you for lunch."

His gaze darted to her intimate folds and he raised a brow in silent invitation.

"I'd rather take my chances with the animals. Thoughtful of you to be concerned, but it isn't this Maza I want to find."

He almost believed her. "No?"

"I want to go to where the chopper crashed to bury my friends and pay my respects."

That came out of left field, making Sin frown. He shifted his legs to see if he could. He could. Bucking her off would be easy enough. For now he'd see just how far she wanted to take this. He'd draw the line at being shot point blank if he could avoid it. "Crash site's three hours away."

She shrugged. "I'm not on a timetable."

He could smell her heat and was almost salivating to get inside her. "And once that's done? Then what's your plan?"

"Get to Santa de Porres and join my fellow aid workers."

As the sun climbed higher, the camp was wide awake and raring to go. He heard the stomp of booted feet. The sound of weapons being cleaned, low voices. He dragged his attention up to her face. "Lady, you're no aid worker."

"Why? Because I got the jump on you?"

"Yeah, and because nothing I've done to you has scared you. Yet."

"My daddy was a Marine. He taught me how to defend myself on a date."

"If this is how you treated your dates, you were dating the wrong guys."

"I'm going to let you up." She pointed the Glock at the base of his throat. "But I have this trained on you, and believe me, I *will* shoot and not bother with questions later."

She rose on her knees over his body, a move that stole his breath with its possibilities. "Stay still, like a good boy." Keeping the gun trained on him, she eased her way over to the side of the narrow bed, got her feet on the floor, and stood. "Up. Hands behind your head, fingers locked."

Sin got to his feet and obeyed. She took several steps back, out of his reach.

"Now what?" Just by size alone he could overpower her and have her flat on her back, legs spread, in about two seconds flat. It might be worth the risk of getting shot to try it.

"Where are my clothes and boots?"

"And weapons?"

She gave him a dirty look. "Those, too. Family heirlooms."

"Really?" He kept his lips still with effort. "Unusual for an aid worker to carry a SIG-Sauer and a KA-BAR, not to mention that cute little knife you wore as a necklace."

"Let's just say I'm not typical." She gestured with the barrel of her gun. "Clothes?"

"In back." He eyed the barrel, then her face. Yeah, she'd shoot to kill.

"Let's get them." The gun didn't waver. "Move, Diaz."

Fast as a death adder, he wrenched the weapon from her hand, then held it to her temple. "I'm not in the mood for games." Sin gripped her chin hard, forcing her to stare into his molten eyes. "Give me any more shit and I'll willingly hand you over to Mama's charming interrogation techniques just to get rid of you."

He kicked the door shut with a slam without breaking his hold on her, and the gun in his hand didn't waver. "Speak now or forever hold your peace, lady. I'm out of patience. No more bullshit. I'll know if you're lying, and frankly, it would be easier for me to kill you than have you shrieking and giving me a headache."

"Wouldn't taking an aspirin be more expedient than killing me?"

He gave her a cold look. "It wouldn't give me nearly as much satisfaction."

FOURTEEN

She believed him.

Dropping onto the thin mattress, Riva's eyes welled with tears until his rugged face blurred and the room disappeared in a wash of gray and green. A vast improvement.

"You terrify me, you know." She let the tears slide down her cheek, drip off her chin. She sighed for a little more effect. Men hated tears. They hated a woman sighing in despair, too. Playing a victim, as much as it burned her stomach, could go a long way to persuading him of something she wanted him to believe. Maybe.

He was not a pushover, though. This game required finesse and poignancy with a little layer of fear thrown in. She didn't oversell it with a sob. Instead she managed a credible, and subtle, lower-lip tremble. Her ability to cry on cue frequently assisted her in her job. Like her SIG and the KA-BAR, crying was a merely a tool, a means to an end.

She'd stopped crying real tears at nine, because it hadn't helped then. But it had worked outside that Hong Kong bar when she'd been approached by three tangos looking for a T-FLAC operative. She'd persuaded them that she was just a lost girlfriend looking for her soldier boyfriend.

Worth a shot now.

Sin leaned a shoulder against the wall, folded his arms, and gave her a cool, unsympathetic look. Well, damn. Apparently, it wasn't going to work with this hardened man. "You finished yet? If you think that'll make me consider going easier on you, it won't. I don't give a flying fuck if you drown in those crocodile tears. And believe me, they won't deflect the question. Tell me what you're doing for Maza and I'll consider letting you join him."

She gave him a dewy, drenched look filled with girly hope. "S-seriously?"

"How fucking stupid *do* you think I am? Stop the melodrama. I saw the real you when you absorbed my punch like a pro. The real you managed to survive that helicopter crash. Lady, you're a pro. But a professional *what*? Who the hell *are* you?"

Asshole.

Still, maybe she was going about this all wrong. He wasn't a regular guy. He was a live-by-the-sword, die-by-the-sword guerrilla. He was apparently impervious to feminine wiles, and since she wasn't an expert at them anyway, she turned off the waterworks.

She wiped the useless tears off her cheeks, squared her shoulders, and gave him a look that was all Riva Rimaldi, T-FLAC Operative. She gazed at him with unfiltered bravado, hoping he saw exactly who she was: a woman warrior who was tough as nails on the inside and outside and determined to meet her goals. Yeah, she wanted him to know she meant business—*get the fuck out of my way or pay the price.*

He gave her a slightly startled look, then narrowed his eyes, his jaw tight. "Jesus. You are good. Now. Who the hell are you?"

"You're like a damned broken record." She had to give him something since he wasn't buying the aid worker bit, and time was a-wasting. What she gave him, though, had to serve her purposes, not his. "Not *who* I am. But *what* I am."

He raised an inquiring brow. Riva felt a violent urge to punch him. She refrained in an amazing display of self-control as she got to her feet to face him, mirroring his arms folded position. With no room to back up, and since she was a good nine inches shorter, she had to tilt her head to see him. "You hate Maza." Statement of fact. Not a question. Putting them both on the same side would be a good start.

He watched her, unmoved. He could be posing for a *Soldier of Fortune* cover. The flak vest lay open. Hard-cut abs beckoned her hands, her mouth. Her gaze travelled south, following the arrow-like trail of dark hair disappearing beneath the waistband of his pants. Riva dragged her gaze back to his face. Even more distracting.

"Two kings," he bit out. "One mountain. *My* mountain."

Lord, he had a giant ego. "I can resolve that problem." She held his gaze. "I'm here to kill him."

"Kill Escobar Maza?" Eyes amused, mouth unsmiling, he cocked his head. "Are you now?"

Now she had his interest. *What the hell do you want me to do? Knock information into your head with a hammer?* "Yes."

"Why? Did he abandon you and the baby and go back to his wife?"

If she had her KA-BAR, she'd stab him right in the middle of his black, octagonal heart. "He's not married. And no, I've never met the man. I was paid good money to come here, posing as his psychic so I could get close enough to kill him."

"I've heard about Maza's deep belief in psychics." He gave her a considering look, as if assessing her skill level and the validity of her claim. "He's said to be as superstitious as hell, and buys into all that shit. If you have a hope in hell of pulling this off, you'd better be a real psychic, or an even better actress. Are you either?"

Both. And apparently she was going to make Sin Diaz's every sexual fantasy come true pretty damn soon, unless she figured out a way to change that unfortunate future for herself. "Psychic? Of course not." She'd denied it all her life. Most people took her at face value. The ones who heard the truth fled like rats from a sinking ship. Family. Friends. Lovers. *No one* wanted to know what was coming, even if they claimed they did. "But *he* doesn't know that."

"Are you good enough to fake it?"

"I used to be a jury consultant. I was damn good at reading microexpressions and body language. I can play him, and do an Oscar-worthy job. Besides, I don't need to be that good. All I have to do is get close enough to kill him. There won't be time for me to do any predictions of his future."

"The minute he sees you the game will be over, you know that, don't you?"

"Graciela and I are very similar physically. I talk like her, walk like her, and know things only she could know. I'm not worried."

"Maybe he carries a picture of her in his wallet."

"Aw, sweet. You're a romantic. If that's the case I'll be in trouble. I'll worry about it if and when the time comes."

"So you have particular skill sets for the job. Reading microexpressions and all that woowoo stuff."

There was nothing woowoo about her gift. She either saw or she didn't. Frequently she got nothing. And rarely did she have such a strong vision that it was almost in real time. "I'm a woman of many talents."

"Who hired you?"

"No idea." Riva dropped her arms and walked to look out of the window. Jungle. Jungle. Green. And more jungle. Without her weapons, GPS, rations, that package... She wouldn't make it one click. Chance of survival? Not much better than the hostages she'd freed.

Fellow operative Jake Dolan had taught her how to live off the land, and sniper AJ Cooper had taught her how to make her last bullet count. "Maza sent two of his men to accompany me, but I insisted I know his GPS location to assist with my 'prediction.'"

Riva turned and leaned her butt against the wall beneath the cracked window, tugging the oversized T-shirt down her thighs. She would really, really like to have this damn conversation while she was at least wearing underwear.

"Are you telling me you blindly accepted a job from an anonymous employer to go into dense jungle, in a foreign and, may I add, dangerous as hell country, just on blind faith?"

"Blind faith and an obscenely large paycheck. I never know who my clients are."

Dark eyes flickered to her unconfined breasts, then back to her face. His lips twitched. "You're a hitman?"

And turn the hunting knife *slowly*. "If it wasn't for his crappy helicopter, his crappy pilot, and *your* fucking missile, Maza would be dead by now. Help me track him so I can kill him. I'll wire one million into your bank account when I get back home." Hell, she could offer him *fifty* million. But since she had no intention of doing it, she might as well sound sincere as well as realistic.

"Two of Maza's men accompanied you on that helicopter. The pilot was also found in the wreckage. Who were the other two men onboard?"

It never got easier losing a fellow operative. What they did was dangerous, and no matter how good, how experienced an operative was, there were always losses, always the risk of dead in the field. She never thought of her own mortality. And she couldn't allow herself to think about them. Not until she'd done her job and was debriefed. Right now, many more lives hung in the balance. She had to stay focused.

She shrugged as if it was nothing that the two men had given their lives before the op had even started. "They weren't with me. Probably the real deal." He gave her a dark look and a raised brow as she finished. "Aid workers."

"Doubt it. Where's home?"

He'd glommed on to the last word.

"In my line of work I travel too much to bother with one." That part was true. Home was T-FLAC Headquarters in Montana.

He held the Glock steady, no matter where she moved, pointed at her heart. Wasn't his arm tired?

"A million...US?" He quirked a dark brow. A strand of his shoulder-length coffee-brown hair had snagged in the rough stubble on his chin. Seeing it there annoyed her. No. *He* annoyed her. Everything he said and did irritated her. "What percentage of *your* fee would that be?"

Mercenary ass. Both of which he was. "It's a crapload of money for something *you've* failed to do for years. Plus you get the bonus of removing your primary competition. All that infighting with mommy dearest has slowed your reflexes." She gave him an assessing look. "Perhaps you should be paying *me*."

Riva got the impression Sin was a pacer. But the room was too small; even with just the narrow bed and the metal cabinet, there was hardly any floor space. She was across the room from him, and barely ten feet separated them. The very stillness of his large powerful body made her think of a caged panther.

"What makes you think you know what I've been doing?"

Sweat trickled between her breasts. An emerald green lizard scurried across the wall behind him. Riva swiveled her attention back to him. "I make it my business to know everything about my marks."

"Am I also one of your 'marks'?"

"No," Riva said sweetly. "I'd off *you* for free."

Apparently unaffected by her threat, his gaze traveled down the length of her body, lingering hotly at her breasts and making her wonder whether he interpreted "offing him" as an offer of sex.

He pushed away from the wall, his Glock still aimed for a kill shot. "Thanks for your offer to take care of Maza, but I'll deal with him myself."

"Really?" She gave him a mocking glance, then observed two soldiers pass outside the window in her peripheral vision. "He moved in on you. On all your *territories,* didn't he? He's bigger and badder than you. More men. More firepower. A hell of a lot more money. When he's done, the ANLF will be nothing but a footnote in the *Anarchists' Handbook.* You two have been trying to kill each other for months."

"He *tried* to kill me. As you can see, he didn't succeed."

"You've tried to kill him and you haven't succeeded either. You knock off one of his top lieutenants, he knocks off one of yours. Yet somehow you've never managed to kill each other. It's a pathetic game of chess. And you know damn well that five months isn't long in terms of these conflicts. It could go on for decades. Instead of getting ahead, whatever form that takes for you, you'll be struggling to stay in place, and it's looking like that will be a losing battle.

"I can help you. I'm excellent at my job. Let me go so I can get close to Maza's camp, and I'll take care of your biggest problem for you. Cut off the head, and the Sangre Y Puño will be rudderless and scrambling for leadership. Hell, if you want the job, it'll be yours for the taking."

Over T-FLAC's dead body, but Sin Diaz didn't know he'd be just as dead as Maza if he tried to fill the other tango's powerful shoes.

Except Riva didn't have a vision of him dead. Far from it. She saw some kind of metamorphosis, but it wasn't death. She shook her head to dispel the half-baked vision.

"But first I need to retrieve my bag from the crash site." Besides needing the important contents, she wanted her underwear, for God's sake. Being practically naked usually didn't bother her. She was used to being with an all-male team. And while she never flaunted her goods, she wasn't a shy violet either. But she needed more than mere body armor when Sin Diaz was around, because while she thought of him as a ruthless terrorist, she also thought of him as hot and sexy.

The contradictions were getting to her. Evil men normally didn't turn her on, and she'd never before had visions of herself having sex—and so clearly enjoying it—with a man who was her captor.

"You're aware we're in the middle of thousands of square miles of tropical rain forest? Maza and I aren't next door neighbors, *chica*. Think of him as Osama bin Laden, visiting my country. No one knows where his hideout is. He doesn't *have* a camp. Sometimes he hides out up here, sometimes in town, sometimes..." He shrugged broad shoulders. The angle of the sunlight showed his body covered by scars, large and small. Some she'd noticed before, but it was only in this light that she saw more. Car accident? Bar fight? Terrorist activities?

She could match him scar for scar, but most of hers were where they didn't show.

"Always on the move," he finished. "You won't find him."

"Bin Laden was hunted down and killed," Riva pointed out, using her bare foot to scratch an itch on her ankle. A wedge of sunlight illuminated the peeling paint on the headboard. "If you were capable of finding him, he'd be dead. He isn't."

"Like I said, he moves around, a *lot*. It's a shell game. No one can find him, until they find him, and then they're dead. I've searched almost every inch of the city and practically under every leaf in this jungle for months. If he's here, he has some serious wizard powers, and he's disguised as one of the two thousand species of plants. Or any one of several hundred animals."

"If I tell you where he is, will you take me close enough to walk in?"

"If we don't know where he is, how do you?"

"Like I told you, I insisted on having a GPS location for my pre-dictions. I know *exactly* where he is. At least until the nineteenth. Eight days. Then all bets are off."

"Give me the coordinates."

Riva gave him a flat look, then rattled off the GPS coordinates. The intel had come directly from Graciela Estigarribia before she was hauled off to Montana for interrogation. HQ would ascertain exactly what she'd been hired to help Maza decide, and while they had her, they also had questions about a recent Maza bombing in Mexico City, and another in Argentina. Graciela was a busy girl, her sway over Maza absolute. If the psychic said all systems were a go, they were a go. She had many third-world-country dictators, terror-ists, and political martyrs on speed dial.

Graciela had power and she'd wielded it through her tango cli-ents.

Riva now had that power and a clear shot to Maza. Either Sin stepped aside or she'd kill him. Maza's boss was out of the way, now. She didn't need to worry about Stonefish. He was currently enjoy-ing the hospitality in some undisclosed American supermax, await-ing trial.

"Clock's ticking, Diaz." Riva pushed away from the wall. The golden wedge of sunlight had already moved halfway up the narrow bed. A confetti of red dots, her blood and filaments of rope, made an interesting still life on the shadowy end of the bare mattress. "I'm the answer to your prayers. Let me loose, and I'll simplify your life in ways you can't imagine."

Sin walked to the metal locker, pulled open the door, and rum-maged around inside. He came back to sit on the foot of the bed, something in his large hand. Far too damn close. Their knees were practically touching.

"Maza has a jammer blocking our satellite feed. This won't be worth shit until we're on higher ground, if then."

"No GPS?"

"I have an old fashioned compass. It works. I'll input the data, we'll see when it kicks in."

The air was hot and humid as the sun climbed higher, baking the cement block walls. Sweat rolled down her temple and gathered between her breasts as she waited for him to input the coordinates into *her* GPS. It was not encouraging to discover that there was no satellite link.

But seeing the device, Riva's heart leapt. That GPS had been in her pocket. Had it fallen out? Or, he'd found her bag. She'd dreaded hiking to the crash site to look for it. Apparently she hadn't been the only thing Sin had brought back to camp.

"You're sure of this?" He glanced up. Riva simply stared at him. "Of course you are."

If her GPS was close by, so was everything else she needed. Weapons, clothes, insect repellent, her toys. Elated, she could barely stand still. "How long will it take to get me close enough to walk into Maza's compound?"

He shot a glance at the GPS. "Two, three days, give or take. Let's pretend that you really are as good as you say you are. You plan on just strolling into his camp—"

"He's *expecting* me. Or rather, he *was*. Believe me, he'll be extremely happy to see me alive and well. And if it'll take two or three *days* to get to him, I have to go *now*."

Shit. Two or three days could mean the whole mission was FUBAR. Maza had wanted to consult his psychic *before* doing whatever the hell horrible thing he was planning on doing. Riva didn't know if he'd wait if he thought she was dead. Hell. He could just call another psychic. She had to get to him as fast as possible, and have a face-to-face with him.

Maybe she'd get there before he did whatever bad crap he had planned. Maybe she could stop it. She could definitely still kill him, late or not.

"I sweetened the pot by bringing him a little gift." She didn't consider for a moment that Sin hadn't discovered the tightly wrapped package in the bottom of her bag. She had an explanation for that, too, should he bring it up.

"Fake psychic or not, Maza's people won't let you anywhere near him, no matter how you bat those long lashes and flash your pretty tits. Why don't I just shoot you now and save them the trouble?"

SIXTEEN

Without warning, Sin covered her mouth, his hard hand pressing against her lips. He shook his head. His expression told her something unwelcome had surprised him.

With the heavy door open, the space behind his hovel was barely wide enough for the two of them to stand. He'd done an incredible job of camouflaging it, and it really was an ideal place to stash a body. So much for a ceasefire between them. He was back to his macho bullshit. He'd had no intention of letting her just walk away.

Kicking and struggling, she clamped down and bit his finger hard, tasting coppery blood, then drew her arm back for a punch. He blocked her strike with a forearm as hard as tungsten steel.

Yanking his finger from her teeth, eyes on fire, he tightened his large hand across the lower half of her face until she could barely breathe. Oh crap. Was he about to snap her neck after all? She struggled harder, nails digging into the hard hand across her face.

"If you want to live, stop fighting me," he snarled in a voice that was nothing more than a harsh whisper full of gravel and threat. He jerked his chin to the way they had come.

It was only then that Riva smelled smoke.

Oh shit. Mommy Dearest.

Riva had been so focused on Sin and the tantalizing potential of recovering the backpack containing all her fun
toys, that she hadn't caught the stink of cigarette smoke or
the sound of footsteps soon enough.

She wanted that Glock back.

Okay, so he wasn't going to kill her.

He shook his head again, eyes warning her to be still as
he pulled her hard against his hot, hard body. Heat radiated off his skin as if he was on fire. He shifted slightly so
he could shut the heavy metal door. It swung closed with
an expensive, quiet snap as the locks automatically en-
gaged. Ruffling the vines so they tangled over the small
building's entrance, he stepped back, dragging her with
him.

"I can hear your brain working," he said dryly, right in
her ear, his breath hot and humid against her temple. "Shut
it off and listen. When I lift my hand I want you to scream
as if you mean it, understand?"

He waited a second for her to nod, which she did. Something in his hard gaze told her to do as he said when every
rebellious cell in her body wanted to tell him to go to hell.

"Don't stop until I tell you. Make it loud and make it
fucking convincing. *Now.*" His tight expression told her
that to disobey would bring swift retribution. Or an opportunity to screw him and escape.

He removed his hand. Riva screamed as if she were being tortured.

"Keep it up. Move." He used her as a fulcrum and
marched her ahead of him, then strong-armed her around

to the front of his hovel to see his mother accompanied by four heavily armed men standing at the open door.

Here we go again. "Geez, short umbilical cord?" she muttered under her breath between screams.

"You allowed her to escape *again*?" Mommy Dearest snapped, black, soulless eyes on her tall son.

Sin held the Glock so his mother could see it, and used the barrel to indicate he had Riva in a death grip, her skin turning white under his fingers on her upper arm. "She had to pee."

"Why haven't you restrained her? What has she told you?" Angélica Diaz, aka the Angel of freaking Death, stepped forward in a ridiculously aggressive manner, considering they'd left her less than thirty minutes earlier.

Riva controlled her instinctive reach for her weapon. For crapsake, she still didn't have on underwear, let alone a holster and gun. Her weapons had been so near and yet so frigging far.

"Where could she go?" Sin's tone was hard, rough. He was cutting off the circulation in her upper arm, but Riva was riveted by the animosity pulsing between them.

Uh-oh. More trouble in paradise? Awesome.

The more than a foot difference in heights between Angélica and her son should've made her look ridiculous. Instead it was like watching two attack dogs squaring off. One large and menacing physically, the other scary and threatening through sheer intent.

Had the woman seen them slip behind Sin's hut? Did she know about his secret room back there? While Riva continued screaming, and struggling against Sin's punishing grip on her upper arm, she wondered how to use their hostility against both of them. Pit them against each other

harder, and they might just forget she was around. Taking
her screams up a notch, she yanked and pushed to break
his hold.

Sin shook her hard enough that her teeth snapped together. "Shut the fuck up, woman," he warned in biting
English, eyes telegraphing just how serious the situation
was. "Or I'll hit you even harder." The implication was that
he'd hit her hard before. Not that tap in front of his mother.
Nope. He wanted Mommy Dearest to think he'd hit his
prisoner hard and often between then and now.

He raised his voice over hers, and squeezed her arm.
Happy to comply, since she was getting on her own damn
nerves, and breathing hard with exertion from the act, Riva
cut off at mid scream.

"The prisoners escaped," Mama said, her tone angry and
accusatory.

Damn. Riva had hoped they'd have more time before anyone was aware of their disappearance. Attuned to the
thick undercurrents, she noticed the infinitesimal tightening of Sin's steely fingers biting into her bicep.

"Send people to bring them back," he told his mother
coldly. "They can't have gone far."

"You miss the point. They didn't find the key and unlock
the door themselves."

"Then I suggest," he told his mother, frost dripping from
every syllable, "you find out who's responsible, and go
and *find* them. Those prisoners are worth upward of five
million US a piece. Don't waste time bitching. Get them
back. And next time, be more careful with the merchan-
dise."

It was clear to Riva that Angélica had an angry retort on
the tip of her tongue, but instead of spewing it, she seemed

to gather herself, making herself even smaller as she said in a respectful tone. "We can still get the ransom from their families."

The about-face was masterful and unexpected. It was also, Riva was well aware, not in the slightest bit sincere.

"Then *don't* go looking for them," Sin told her, voice even and disinterested. "I don't give a shit. We get the money either way."

Even as she kept her tone modulated, Angélica's evil black eyes darted back to Riva. This had all kinds of potential to slide sideways. Two dogs. One bone. The only problem was that *she* was the bone, and these damn dogs both looked like they were used to winning.

"*Someone,*" Angélica sent a pointed look at Riva, "released them." She leaned in closer, her spittle making wet contact with Riva's cheeks and ear. "Is that why you came here? To take my hostages?"

"The helicopter she was in crashed," Sin answered for her, voice tight; he sounded at the end of his rope. He was just better at controlling his temper than his mother was. "It wasn't fucking premeditated. For Christ sake, listen to yourself, you're paranoid! Do you have nothing more important to do this morning than bother me with household business? If you're bored, I suggest you clean weapons, or go out on patrol."

Riva kept her own expression apprehensive and confused, since she "didn't speak Spanish." She read the woman's angry face. Angélica was livid. Her facial expressions and body language said she wanted to hurt, no, *grievously wound* somebody. Problem was, Riva couldn't tell if it was her, or Sin, or both of them.

Her microexpressions were fascinating. Angélica had prominent canine teeth—a sign of determination to win, a killer instinct. Something Sin had said or done had made her feel threatened. *Vulnerable.* The Angel of Death didn't do vulnerable, apparently. Weakness made this woman lash out like a poisonous snake until her victim was dead. And had suffered beforehand.

A vertical forehead furrow over her right eyebrow indicated stored-up anger related to work. Interesting. Anger about being thwarted at *work.* Not anger stored up over time related to a personal relationship.

Her son meant absolutely nothing to her.

It was the ANLF that was everything to this woman.

"I want to know who she is, and what the fuck she's doing here. *Now.*" She shot Sin a look so filled with loathing and venom that Riva waited for him to fall over stone dead. The switch from malice to benign and back to venomous was so rapid, it was hard to keep track.

Easily agitated, Mama Diaz was volatile and prone to emotional outbursts, including fits of rage. She was a sociopath, and therefore unpredictable.

"She claims to be an assassin, here to kill Maza." Sin said it so deadpan cold that for a moment, Riva doubted Mama would believe him.

Angélica glanced at her with the unblinking stare of a lizard. Her eyes lingered on the swell of Riva's breasts as if weighing them, then slid like a noxious oil slick down her bare legs and back up her face. Riva felt as though something slimy and poisonous had just crawled all over her. Mama's beady black eyes summed her up in a disparaging glance. "You believe her?"

"Why not? What other purpose could she have for being here?" Compared to Mama, hard-ass Sin was a prince.

His mother narrowed her eyes suspiciously. "That makes no sense! Why would Maza fly in his own killer?"

"She hitched a ride, posing as an aid worker."

"And this you believe?"

"Excuse me," Riva inserted, because no one would stand there not responding if people were talking around her. "Could we please have this conversation in English?"

Sin's attention didn't so much as flicker away from the older woman. "My mother doesn't speak English."

Yeah. Just like I don't speak fluent Spanish.

"Notify Maza that we have her. See how much he'll pay. If he doesn't want her, find out where her family is. If they have money, we'll ransom her to them instead." The older woman raked her with another glance. "She's clean. Not ugly. Sell her to Vargas if Maza shows no interest or she has no family. He'll give us two hundred American for her."

Two hundred dollars? Riva was mildly insulted. She could sell her organs for more than that.

Sin snapped out, "No."

"What will you do with her? Keep her here to fuck? *You* want to buy her?"

"I *found* her. I don't need to buy her. I already own her. I'm going to send her to Maza. Let her do what she came to do. If she's telling the truth, it's one less obstacle, removed without us losing any men. If she isn't, Maza's men can waste their bullets shooting her or the jungle will eat her alive. Either way she's eliminated."

From beneath her straight-cut black bangs, *Angel de la Muerte* shot Riva a withering look, then returned her attention to her son. "If Maza sees you again, he *will* kill you," she warned, tone dire. "The man is *está bien loco* and you know it. He left you for dead once. If he sees you alive he will make you *pray* for death and there'll be nothing I can do to help you this time. Between Maza and this one, you'd better sleep with your eyes open."

"I always do," Sin said.

Riva figured she'd killed plenty of men with their eyes wide open. Sin Diaz would just be one more.

"She might choose *you* as her next target."

"You have so little faith that you think I *trust* this woman? I do not."

Ditto, Dick.

Angélica drew deeply on the pungent, unfiltered cigarette she hadn't bothered to remove from her lips, as she tried to figure out how she could gain the upper hand in the situation.

Riva didn't make the mistake of dismissing her as a bitter middle-aged woman. Looking into Angélica's eyes was seeing pure evil.

I rebuke you Satan came instantly to mind.

She had to fight the urge to cross herself. With a Mexican mother and Italian father, no matter how long ago and far away her upbringing was, she wanted all the talismans she could get to ward off evil.

T-FLAC intel, studied in hasty preparation for the mission, gave her plenty of stories on Angélica, some factual, some mythical. One of the many substantiated stories was how the Angel of Death had scooped out the eyes of a hostage as proof of life, *after* the payment had been made, then she sent the girl home, more dead than alive, to her terrified parents. She'd kept hostages for years, using them as toys, breaking their bones and allowing them to heal in un-natural ways. She shipped one man's remains home to his family ten years after his kidnapping. Every bone in his body had been broken while he was alive.

Riva controlled a shudder at the woman's depravity.

Angélica was the most dangerous, but not by much.

Even though the microexpressions of the man who stood before her didn't reveal it, T-FLAC intel told her Sin Diaz was known for his brutal interrogation techniques, too. Torture. Violent coercion. Unspeakable acts too numerous to mention. He was sexy as hell, but she would not for one second forget he was as lethal as a bullet between the eyes. She'd be wise to ensure those marauding lips and hands stayed the hell off her, no matter how much her vision suggested she would enjoy having him on her.

Sin shrugged. "Why do we care? With Maza's top lieutenants now dead, if she succeeds, the SYP will be thrown into chaos, yes?"

Without comment, Angélica took another deep drag of her cigarette.

"Without a leader," Sin continued, "the SYP will be unable to do whatever it is they have planned. Leaving the field open for us. They'll do all the work and we'll reap the rewards."

Keeping up the sham of not understanding what they were saying, Riva kept looking back and forth between mother and son, and as she did, she began to focus on the disparities between the two.

Angélica had the face and body of a squatty peasant while her son had the even features and the physique of a well-honed athlete. They didn't look related. They barely looked like the same species.

Even wearing combat boots, camo pants, and the open flak vest over his bare chested, Sin looked like he came from privilege, as if he'd been born to it. Riva could easily picture him wearing a stark black tux and a pleated white shirt at the opera. Or crisp white shorts playing tennis on a clay court in Cannes. A vision flashed before her, more clearly than her picturing him at the opera or playing tennis. A vision of Sin in a beautifully cut suit at the head of a boardroom table. All superimposed over the ramshackle surroundings of this jungle hut.

Taken out of his native habitat he was vaguely familiar, but Riva couldn't figure out how that could be. She'd never seen him before she opened her eyes after the crash. Not in a picture, or sketch, or live. Could he have really been the son of a famous hostage and looked like his biological father? Was that why he looked so familiar to her?

Who the hell *was* this guy? When and why would he have worn either a tux or white shorts in the jungle? The answer was never, which meant her visions were on the freaking fritz.

Remembering that she was supposed to be struggling against Sin, she resumed fighting to get free of his restraining hand. With a sharp jerk, he pulled her against his side, imprisoning her against the hard length of his body with a vise-like arm, holding her almost immobile.

Riva smelled his hot skin, clean sweat, and fought not to take a deeper breath. Powerful and elemental, his aroma was a siren song to her hormones. At the brush of his heat against her arm, a shudder rippled across her damp skin. Something inside her coiled and tensed with unwelcome need.

She didn't struggle this time. Instead, she mentally made herself disappear, standing silent and dead still. The sultry heat of his body surrounded her like an all-enveloping cloak.

"When will you take her?"

"When I'm ready. Go and find something to keep yourself busy, woman."

Without waiting for a response, Sin jerked Riva completely off her feet and spun her around, pushing her ahead of him into his shack, then kicked the heavy door shut in his mother's face.

SEVENTEEN

The second the door closed, Sin lowered her until her feet hit the floor. He stepped away from her, closing his eyes as he squeezed the bridge of his nose.

Riva gave him an assessing look. Pain pinched his features. "You ordered me to scream like a deranged girl, don't blame me for that headache, Diaz."

He dropped his hand and gave her an amused, if pained look. "Like a *deranged girl?*"

"You know what I mean." With each high-pitched shriek, the muscles beside Sin's eyes had contracted as if he was in severe pain. "You and your mother seem to be having a battle of wills. I hope it doesn't have anything to do with me?"

Something passed behind his eyes, a fleeting telegraph of his next action, which she completely misread. Grasping her upper arm so that her shoulder hunched under her chin, he propelled her backward until her legs hit the side of the mental bed frame. The skin stretched across his cheekbones as his eyes telegraphed pain and intense annoyance. Another shake. "Can't you be quiet for thirty fucking seconds?" Hazel eyes glittered green. "*Enough.*"

Riva opened her mouth to tell him—

He crushed his mouth down on hers in a kiss that wiped the pleasure of causing him a twofer of annoyance and pain right out of her brain.

The kiss was hard enough at first to mash her lips against her teeth. But then, suddenly, he was inside with a sweep of his tongue. The taste of him was startling, metallic, slick, heat and lightning. Pulses long dormant soared to life as he explored her mouth as if he had every right to do so. He used his tongue and teeth, punishing, then more dangerously, passionate and compelling.

Adrenaline, already racing from the confrontation she'd just witnessed, went supernova in her bloodstream. The kiss shot her hormones into the stratosphere, increasing the rate of her blood circulation, making her breathing ragged and preparing her muscles for exertion.

Holy hell.

Sin Diaz *was* a dangerous man.

The thrust of his tongue was unbearably intense, and erotic enough to make Riva shudder. She didn't want the son of a bitch to put his hands on her breasts. No. She didn't want his touch, but she inexplicably ached for it. His kiss was a powerful aphrodisiac, an elixir she couldn't resist. His taste, the rasp of his tongue sliding on hers, made her want one simple thing. More.

Pressing herself tightly against him, she used his hard muscular chest to try to ease the ache of her nipples.

This. Had. To. Stop. *Now*.

Heart tripping unevenly, she hit his chest with both fists as tension burned like a fiery brand in her belly. No. No. No!

In her mind—damn her visions—a future image shimmered into life. How far it was in the future, she had no idea. Five minutes? *Mio Dios,* she hoped not. Two hours? Better. That would give her time to change the course of action that had her spreading her legs for him, drawing her breath in anticipation.

Riva felt a ghost of the powerful surge as he entered her. Heard the phantom sounds as his hips pounded against hers. Experienced a shadow, like a distant thunderclap, of his powerful thrusts as he brought her to a screaming, breathless climax over and over again.

Her visions were never wrong. They always came true. Could the circumstances leading up to them be changed, and would that change negate the outcome? Possibly. Problem was, she didn't have visions for herself. This vision was Sin's future.

It told her that no matter how much she resisted, how much she fought him, they were going to have sex. Not only were they going to connect, she was damn well going to enjoy it. The future image was so powerful she almost reached an orgasm, as her vision of the future merged with what was happening in the now.

Her fists unfurled. Her fingers gripped the soft, damp hair on his hot, naked chest as his fingers dug into the balls of her shoulders. No room to move, no way, other than to stand on her toes to better reach his mouth. Eyes squeezed tight, Riva lived a dual sensation as he kissed her in the now, and her mind showed her their future in sensual technicolor.

The morning sunlight flooding the small hut faded. Cave-like darkness surrounded them, and there was nothing but the feel of him inside her. His mouth sucking hard on her nipple, his fingers gripping the globes of her ass as he thrust into her wet, pulsing—

No, dammit. That was the vision. It didn't have to happen. She, like the prisoners, could zig instead of zag. She'd make different choices. Make damn sure that never happened.

In the now, he was only kissing her. His hands were on her shoulders, holding her in place.

It was *just* a kiss. His attempt at domination. Using sex to control her. Been there. Done that. Didn't need a repeat to learn her lesson.

The hard jut of his penis behind his cargo pants reminded her that her vision could very possibly be about to happen. Sooner rather than later. God knew he was ready enough and so was she.

Bringing her arms up between them, she slammed up on his wrists, breaking his hold and took a giant step backward, out of reach.

"Was that necessary?" she demanded, scrubbing her wrist across her damp mouth as his arms dropped to his sides. He dragged in a breath, a predatory gleam in those hot hazel eyes. He made no move to grab her, force her.

Riva's heart pounded hard enough to feel the beat behind her eyeballs and in every traitorous pulse point in her body. She could still feel the phantom brush of his hands on her breasts, and the very real wetness between her legs.

"It did the job of shutting you up," he told her dispassionately, gaze steady. The quick, pumping tic of pulse at his throat told her he was not nearly as disinterested as he'd like her to believe. "Trust me. I saved you from a fate worse than death out there." He jerked a thumb toward the closed door. "You should be thanking me."

Riva made a rude noise. "Not going to happen."

"Stay put. I'm going around back to get supplies, don't even think of making a run for it," he told her briskly. "You won't make it halfway across the compound. Mama doesn't like you. She's just itching for an excuse to use you as a punching bag. Make no mistake. *She* won't pull her punches like I did."

"Yes, sir," she said, saluting smartly.

He paused, hand on the door handle. "I bet that mouth of yours has gotten you into a shitload of trouble. Stay."

He opened the door, and shut it behind him.

"Sit." Riva plopped her butt down at the foot of the bed. "Clearly all these years of therapy aren't working," she muttered, unwinding her braid, then finger combing the long, thick strands with her fingers. Too damn thick, too long. When she got home she was going to shave it all off, and keep it that way. Nothing wrong with a bald operative. "A few hours with Sin Diaz and I'm reverting back to my mouthy-living-dangerously self."

Getting to her feet, she put both hands behind her head and executed a tight French braid, tucking it underneath securely. "*Stupid,* Rimaldi, *damn* stupid." She started to pace the small room. "You have to get a freaking grip here. He's a Latin male, you *know* Latin males." She had to be silent, and feminine, and not challenge his authority if she had a hope in hell of doing her job.

Surely he wouldn't send her out into the jungle without some sort of weapon? Would he give her the SIG back? The knife? She'd be grateful for either.

The door opened, and she was on her feet. When she saw it was Sin, she breathed a sigh of relief and almost kissed him again, but she refrained. "That was quick."

"Here, hurry and get dressed." Sin tossed her clothing in a heap on the bed, and placed her black backpack on the chair. "We're leaving."

EIGHTEEN

As Riva untangled pants from shirt from boots, Sin got a flash of smooth olive skin and a hint of silky, dark pubic hair before she zipped up.

"*You're* taking me to Maza?"

"I'm your ticket there." He was sorry to see that she'd tamed the wild tumble of her hair into a tight, complicated braid. Not a strand out of place. He liked her a little wilder looking. "*If* he's still at the location you have."

She found a sports bra and managed to pull it on under the cover of his T-shirt without flashing her tits.

Damn.

Sin felt an urgency he didn't understand. But he trusted his gut, and his gut said to take this opportunity to get the hell out of camp. It was a flimsy as hell excuse. His reputation alone would lead anyone to believe he'd have sex with Riva, then toss her into the hovels they called holding cells until a ransom was paid, or he sold her to the highest bidder.

Instead he was going to watch her back until he knew what the fuck he really *was* going to do with her. Or until he handed her off to Maza.

Taking the chopper was out of the question. Maza's men patrolled the jungle. The helicopter was only to be used in emergencies. The second the SYP saw it lifting over the canopy, they'd be shot down. There wasn't a road for hundreds of miles. The river was a possibility. He had a small outboard hidden six miles away. It was nowhere near where Riva claimed Maza was waiting for her, and that was okay; he wasn't getting close to the enemy until he had a better bead on how much he could trust her.

Once he got to the boat he'd decide what to do with her. He was loath to leave her with Andrés, knowing his friend's view of women, and he was sure that Andrés wouldn't think twice about turning her over to Mama, once he was done with her. He also felt strangely conflicted about her going into Maza's camp alone, if it came to that.

Decisions to be made in three days.

In her fatigue pants and his T-shirt, she grabbed up her bag. She saw he'd placed her gun on top and took it out, looking pleased. "I don't suppose this comes with the clips?"

"I'm saving them to give to you for Christmas. Get your ass in gear."

Her sigh was lugubrious as she laid the weapon beside the rest of her clothes. "You should keep things interesting and not be so damn predictable, Diaz."

"I predict I'm leaving without you if you're not dressed in five. Socks in your boots. Move it."

Sin left the door ajar. If she ran now it was her choice as to the outcome. He paused until the two men patrolling passed, told them to tell Andrés to prepare for a weeklong trip, and to bring the rest of his team with him. They'd meet in fifteen minutes at the generator.

Going round to his storage unit, he'd mentally packed a backpack with supplies. After unlocking the heavy door, it took just a matter of minutes to find what he needed and pack everything tightly into two canvas bags. He grabbed a few extra boxes of bullets, and why not? Another submachine gun.

Andrés would bring only their most trusted men, they'd head in the general direction of where she wanted to go, then veer off to the river and go to Abad, to the south. Closer than Santa de Porres, and where his son was located. He didn't remember the woman he'd assaulted or the event. He didn't even have a picture of the kid. But it was high time he met his only child and gave the woman some kind of financial assistance. An apology wouldn't go amiss. What better opportunity than now? Kill several birds with one stone.

He didn't have a long life expectancy.

He cracked the door open, listened for a few moments, then slid out, letting the door close and lock, and slipped back into his hut, where Riva was still dressing.

As she wriggled to pull a tank top under his T-shirt, Sin ran his fingers over the tightly folded square of a glossy magazine page in his back pocket, the one with that tantalizing picture of the two men. He'd finally run a ZAG image search and see what came up.

Perhaps if he found them, they could tell him something about himself that made sense or at least jog his memory. *His* real memory, the kind that came from within his own gray matter. Not the memories of himself that came from the mouths of other people.

He adjusted the pack on his back. "Ready?" God, yes. She now wore a form-fitting black tank top that revealed well-toned muscles and caramel skin. She looked lickable and good enough to eat.

"No, I thought I'd hang around, maybe grab a drink with your terrifying mother so we can bond."

Sleek, bad-ass, and sexy as hell. Too bad she'd confined the natural swell of her breasts. Too bad for his viewing pleasure, but a good decision considering where they were going.

She shook her head as she stuffed the rest of her belongings back into her backpack. "Shit. Sorry. Yes. I'm ready." Slinging the straps over her shoulder, feet spread, she gave him a measured look. "Let's get the hell out of here. I have places to go and people to kill."

The pack was heavy. He didn't offer to help the little lady with her luggage. She wanted her own crap, fine. The pack on her back held emergency supplies and he was glad to have it with them on the hard, long, dangerous trek.

He took a quick look around. Something told him he wouldn't be back.

Indicating that she precede him, Sin closed and locked the door behind him. They walked down the middle of the wide dirt path. The sun was high, but the camouflage netting strung over the small settlement blocked out the brightness and cast a greenish tinge to Riva's skin. It also trapped in the sweltering heat.

"We're meeting up with some of my men." He felt eyes watching their progress. "Safety in numbers," he told her.

She shot him a look under her lashes, clearly aware their every move was being monitored. They met Andrés and the other five men beside the generator, then headed south. The first three or four miles were relatively easy going, as they were well-traveled by the patrols. Later, they'd have to hack their way through the thick vegetation.

If Sin was alone, it would take the better part of a day to reach the river. Riva was strong and athletic, and should be able to keep up with him, but he had to keep in mind that she was still recovering from the crash.

He was sorry to see her dressed; he'd enjoyed her long, toned legs, and the gentle bounce of her unfettered breasts under his T-shirt. Now she wore her own camo cotton pants, which nicely cupped her firm ass as she walked slightly ahead of him.

Concerned about the slice in her leg—cuts could kill in this climate—he'd patched the corresponding rip in the pants with duct tape to keep the bugs out. The black tank top showed off her lightly muscled arms and straight back. She'd shifted her back pack over one shoulder, and her dark, glossy braid, thick as her wrist, hung between her shoulder blades, swaying like a metronome as she walked.

Andrés had brought the five men they trusted most, all heavily armed. If they walked into a Maza trap, they were vigilant and more than ready.

"You don't believe her, do you?" Andrés demanded quietly as the two of them dropped back slightly, allowing Riva to be flanked by the others.

Sin shrugged. "I don't not believe her. If she thinks she can kill Maza, I'll let her try. Why not?"

Andrés shot him an amused glance. "When you're done fucking her, can I have her next?"

The thought of his friend touching Riva roiled something deep inside him, a reaction he was careful to keep off his face. "She won't be around that long. Keep your snake in your pants, *amigo*." Adjusting the strap of his pack more securely, Sin kept her in his sights at all times. Inside his pack was Mama's precious laptop computer. He'd retrieved it before getting their supplies, while his mother was out on patrol. It was never to leave her quarters, and certainly never to leave camp. When she discovered it missing, she'd be hot on Riva's heels.

Mama was sure to think their liberated prisoners had stolen it and he bet, without doubt, she'd blame Riva for the theft as well as their liberation.

Sin needed time and an Internet connection. With any luck, he'd have both in a few days. Either when they reached higher ground, or they got to town.

Ahead, Riva carried both the heavy backpack and her black nylon bag. Sin knew how heavy it was. He'd carried it, and Riva, all the way down the mountain the night before. In it were her weapons, minus the clips he'd held back, three fluffy, battery-operated teddy bears, a Ziploc bag of coiled, colorful hair ties, another of cheap disposable cell phones, a giant jar of petroleum jelly, and a semiautomatic assault rifle.

Plus a no-longer-tightly-wrapped brown paper parcel containing a selection of paraphernalia Sin was more than familiar with. All of which had been locked in a bulletproof black case. The lock was fingerprint secured. Easy enough to press her finger to it as she lay unconscious. He'd removed all the bells and whistles, but let her keep her toys.

All pretty innocuous on the face of it, unless one was adept at bomb making. Which Sin was. The "hair ties" were, in fact, cleverly disguised detonation cords filled with RDX.

Whatever else was necessary for making a bomb or bombs would be relatively available on any site. What did she plan to bomb? An explosion seemed melodramatic when a single bullet to Maza's head would do the trick.

Behind him, Andrés talked quietly into a basic walkie-talkie. All that currently worked because of Maza's jamming of their satellite connections. The walkie-talkie was a step up from two tin fucking cans and a piece of string.

Hopefully his friend was getting information that would help them. Or he was talking to one of his numerous lady friends in Abad or Santa de Porres, which was a no-no.

He turned to give his friend an inquiring look.

Still talking quietly, Andrés gave him a thumbs-up. Which could mean anything. Andrés could have information about what the hell Maza was doing or he'd just made a date with a pretty girl. Although not all of his friend's dates could remotely be called pretty, Sin thought, waiting for Andrés to catch up with him and keeping his eye on the back of Riva's head as she walked ahead of him.

He motioned Hernán Alejos to overtake him, and to keep a close watch on Riva, then dropped back. Hernán, a stocky man in his early forties, carried his AK-47 like a club. His casual grip was deceiving. He could whip that puppy up and be firing it in two seconds flat.

Andrés shoved the walkie-talkie in his vest pocket, gold tooth sparkling in his wide grin. "That was Loza. He didn't want to wait until we reached town to make a deposit in his bank account. I told him to lift the jam, and we'd be happy to. Fucker will charge us double, plus interest, for the delay."

"What he had to tell us better be worth it. What did he give us? Are we headed in the right direction this time?"

Andrés tugged his bandana back over his ear, exposed so he could use the walkie-talkie, as they resumed walking. Riva and the others were now hidden by dense foliage. Sin walked faster, and his friend kept up. This outing would kill several birds. Get him away from camp. Lose Riva. Access a computer.

He was done being defined by other people.

And when he was in Abad, he'd search for the son he'd never met.

"Two pieces of valuable info," Andrés said, keeping his voice low. "Whatever's happening is happening in Santa De Porres, and it's set to happen on the nineteenth."

Eight days to fuck with whatever Maza had planned. So Riva hadn't lied. Not about Maza's timetable, at least. "That's it?"

"That's more than we had five minutes ago," Andrés pointed out.

"True. If it's profitable and/or beneficial to the Sangre Y Puño, it will be profitable and beneficial to us."

"Another thing of interest. The buzz is that Maza's bringing in an expert."

Sin shot him a glance, tired of having to drag every damn little thing out of his friend. It was almost as if Andrés was toying with him. Playing cat and mouse. Sin hated to think his friend and mother were in cahoots, but that was frequently what it felt like. "An expert at *what*?"

Andrés shrugged, then raised his eyebrows, and pointed to the wall of green ahead with a jerk of his chin. Indicating, Sin presumed, Riva.

Sin rubbed the back of his neck. Yeah. She claimed to be here to kill his enemy, but there was a lot more going on behind those beautiful features and big brown eyes than she let on.

"An expert at fucking? You tell me. Is that what she's the expert of?" Andrés laughed.

Sin's hand fisted, and he spoke through clenched teeth. "Push Loza. See if you can get more."

The question now was, was she really here to kill Maza? With a bomb? Or was she here to *build* a bomb for Sin's enemy?

"Whatever's happening in Santa de Porres is some fucking kind of well-kept secret. We haven't heard a breath of any big happenings. What group of any importance is expected? It can't be a coup. *El presidente* is still in Washington, DC, with his family."

Andrés shrugged. "Haven't heard anything."

"Well, listen harder. Eight days isn't a lot of time to counter whatever Maza is planning." Whatever it was, it would affect the ANLF, and himself, adversely. That was a given.

Instead of being there to kill Maza, was Riva bringing the hard-to-find-locally supplies to Sin's enemy? Or some other skillset Maza needed? Like what?

Even without the detour to the river and the hidden boat, it was a long hike through rugged terrain to reach what Riva claimed was Maza's location. And that was if he didn't move before they reached it. Like the ANLF, the SYP was sure to have sentries along the way, just waiting to pick them off.

Was he, in fact, walking into a honeyed trap?

He felt...off kilter. A strange sensation when he was usually completely self-assured. And how the hell did he know if he was usually self-assured, or a complete pussy?

He. Didn't. Fucking. Remember.

Yet being in charge seemed to come naturally to him.

It was as though he'd seen everything in black and white for months. But those facts had all been told to him by

Mama, Andrés, and the others who claimed to be his friends. Now, suddenly, everything was in color, albeit somewhat blurred. Not that he'd give his men even a hint that he wasn't in top form, but it was as annoying as it was puzzling.

If not for Riva Rimaldi, he'd be holed up in one of his secret lairs, working at getting his shit together before either the SYP or his own shot him in the back of the head, execution style.

Perceiving everyone as an enemy was damn disorienting. He had expected the paranoia to dissipate as he weaned himself off of Mama's headache potions. Instead, the distrust became more acute, his doubts more alarming.

Whether the residual effect of the injuries he'd suffered at the hands of Maza was brain-trauma-induced paranoia, or whether he had any legitimate basis for questioning everything he'd been told since he'd awakened, was a fucking mystery. He was damn tired of trying to reason through it. No wonder he couldn't fucking sleep.

NINETEEN

They'd been walking for what seemed like days to Riva. It was hard to gauge the time of day with most of the sky obscured by the tree canopy. But her internal clock said it was late afternoon. They hadn't stopped once, not even to drink water or gnaw on jerky and protein bars. They ate and drank as they walked.

The process of putting one foot in front of the other was mindless. The men had the machetes and they hacked away, producing a long tunnel of trimmed foliage for them to walk through. She kept her eyes out for predators, both human and animal, and watched out for snakes and spiders and thick vines across her path.

A million shades of green were broken up occasionally by a brightly colored spray of acid-yellow colored orchids or a blue and yellow macaw. Now and then a small monkey followed overhead, eyes curious. She saw a couple of five-foot-long green snakes, and bunch of cute black-faced monkeys trailed them for a while.

Riva trudged along beside a guy who looked like a sumo wrestler, called Tomás Saldana. She recognized Saldana from T-FLAC intel, which told her that Saldana had died three years earlier at an ANLF hospital bombing in Argentina. Wrong intel. Beside Saldana was a giant of a man named Nicanor Pando. Her two bodyguards, apparently.

Clearly done talking to her, Sin stayed at the end of the processional. Fine with her. Having him out of her face was a blessing. She wasn't attracted to *Pando's* ass, didn't have visions of having sex with *him*. Let Diaz stay out of sight *and* out of mind.

Concentrate before you get killed, Rimaldi.

Five men, plus Sin Diaz.

Tomás carried one of the compasses and a Russian-made PP-200 submachine gun. The ANLF were in bed with the Russians, no better than the SYP being in bed with Iran. Six of one and half a dozen of the other. She swatted a moth the size of her palm off her cheek, then wiped the dust-like residue off her fingers on her pant leg.

Riva wanted both her GPS and either her SIG or her own Bushmaster 15 semiauto from her gun case, with its full clip, and spare. She presumed her clips were in Sin's back-pack; they certainly weren't in hers. All she needed was an opportunity to help herself.

For barely a nanosecond at the start of this long trek, what seemed like days ago, she'd weighed her chances of taking down six heavily armed men. All together? No. Couldn't happen. Not here. Not right now. Separate them and take them out one at a time? Yeah, *that* she could do. She just had to bide her time.

Problem was, they weren't the only ones she had to deal with. They'd been followed for several clicks. Whoever was tailing them was passably good at remaining far enough away not to alert them. Her heart leapt. Maza's people? So soon? This was going to be easier and quicker than she'd hoped. She'd been anticipating this for hours; it was almost a relief to know they were being less than subtle now. She felt a pang imagining Maza's people killing Sin. And his soldiers. But while her vision included men dying, Sin wasn't one of them.

She wasn't surprised when a heavy hand grabbed her shoulder, almost pulling her off her feet. She'd sensed the guy coming up behind her for several minutes. *"El jefe quiere hablar con usted." The boss wants to talk to you.* Andrés jerked his thumb over his shoulder. Riva glanced back through the cleared green tunnel behind her. Sin.

Not one of the men tracking them. Still. If Sin wanted to talk to her, he could come to her. She gave his messenger a blank I-don't-speak-Spanish look. In response, he grabbed her upper arm, meaty fingers digging into her flesh, and yanked hard as he pulled her back the way she'd come.

She was sweaty, tired, thirsty, and cranky as hell, and being manhandled for the umpteenth freaking time was the last damned straw. With both hands, Riva grabbed Andrés by his shirtfront and flipped him. He gave a very surprised and indignant shout as he spun ass over heels to land on his back in a thicket of dense shrubbery six feet away. "No grabbing, buddy. No damn grabbing."

Sin came alongside. His lips twitched, but he didn't crack a smile. "I think you broke Andrés's back, *chica.*"

Riva didn't bother glancing Andrés's way as he untangled himself from the vegetation. "He looks fine to me."

Sin waved the men forward. After a feral look from Andrés, who was plucking leaves off his clothing as he staggered to his feet, the other men moved ahead without comment. He joined them, every line in his body tight and furious. She'd embarrassed him in front of his boss and coworkers. Riva hid a smile. *Too bad, so sad.*

Now what? She shot Sin an inquiring look. He indicated something off to his left with a quick jerk of his chin.

"Just wanted to check to see how you're holding up," he said easily as he underhanded her SIG to her. By its weight, she knew it held a full clip. So he'd observed their shadows, too. And he was trusting her enough to give her a loaded weapon?

"It's tough going over all these vines and wet vegetation," he said. He gestured at the foliage, conveying a simple message: She was to go right when he went left. "Don't want you to slip and fall." Against his thigh, Sin flashed four fingers.

"Let's catch up to the others. Close the gap." She nodded, but lifted her weapon instead of walking, looking beyond him.

The men came out of the understory so quickly, so silently, that if Riva hadn't known they were being followed, she'd have been taken by surprise. Their very silence made the attack the work of professionals. The susurrus of vegetation being disturbed and the men's breathing was all the notice they were given before being converged on en masse.

Two men headed her way and she was already gripping her SIG two-handed, more for show than intent. The second they ID'd themselves, she'd accompany them back to Escobar Maza. Riva had a twinge of conscience. She didn't want to kill Maza's people—a bad form of introduction—but she didn't want Sin injured either. In no way relaxed, she held her stance, waiting to see how they were going to handle this. She watched the first man's eyes as he approached, the muzzle pointed at his heart so there'd be no mistake that she'd shoot him if she had to.

Out of the corner of her eye she saw three—no, four—more converge on Sin. No shots. They didn't want to alert Sin's men up ahead. But his men must know, otherwise he'd be calling for them. They were probably circling back.

Not that Riva anticipated needing assistance. She had this.

"They've come for me," she shouted at Sin, wincing as a man punched him in the belly and another struck the side of his head with the butt of his submachine gun. What was *that* about? "I'll go." She held her weapon up on the flat of her hand and showed that the other was empty. "Maza sent you, right? I'll g-"

Wait.

She *knew* these guys. Not *knew,* but recognized. What the hell? Hadn't she seen the guy punching Sin walking past his window a couple of times back at the ANLF camp?

Holy shit.

These were *Sin's* men.

Dropping the backpack quickly and struggling to get the heavy pack off her back, Riva spun a quarter turn to go back to help Sin, but more immediate problems distracted her. Two men came at her like rhinos across the plains. Except there was no flat ground and no open spaces as they charged her. She got off a shot, hit Number Two between the eyes. Number One kept coming, beefy arm outstretched to grab her.

Off balance herself, with the backpack half on and half off, Riva used his extended arm as a fulcrum, spinning One around, then twisted his arm, high on his back. Ignoring his struggles, grunts of pain, and inventive swearing, she used his body as a shield against a third man.

Number Three, heavyset, a dirty blue bandana wrapped around his head, came in from the side. Like a gangbanger, he wielded a knife and a sadistic leer. Riva shoved Number One at Number Three, and with shouts of fury the two men tangled together. They fell to the ground, but not before Number Three–Blue Bandana got the tip of his knife on her arm. Her SIG flew out of her hand. A thin slice of icy-heat seared her bicep as Bandana scissored her legs, knocking her onto her back beside him. Everything hard and lumpy in the backpack dug into an organ, knocking the wind out of her. *Ow. Shit.*

He laughed as he dropped his ass on her midsection, pressing down on her diaphragm, restraining her with his superior weight and the knife at her throat. If he put his knees on her arms, as she'd done to Sin earlier, she was screwed. Fortunately he wasn't that forward-thinking.

Burdened by the heavy backpack, for a moment Riva was like a paralyzed turtle on her back. The trees swam sickeningly in her vision, mixing with black and sparks of brilliant white around the edges.

Daylight was fading fast, and the smell of blood would draw animals. Where in the hell was Andrés while their men attacked their leader?

Twisting was futile. He was just too damned heavy for any kind of movement. Kicking out was useless.

Digging her heels hard into the ground, she attempted to arch her hips to buck him off. He was too well-seated and didn't so much as budge. He laughed, telling her to do it again, that it made him hard when she pushed against his balls.

The ground was hard and slimy with rotting vegetation. She tried to claw up wads of whatever the hell she was lying

on to use as a weapon. His punch missed her face by milli-
meters when she deflected the blow with her forearm. Pain
vibrated like a buzzy tuning fork through her bones and
tendons.

Managing to shift the strap of the backpack enough to
free one arm—all the opportunity she needed—she used
the heel of her hand in a swift palm strike to the underside
of his nose, driving the bones into his brain. The crunch
and spurt of blood was satisfying, but she didn't stop to admire her own survival skills. Turning her head just in time,
she avoided the splatter of his blood, then shoved his limp
body off her and lunged to her feet, shaking off the backpack so she'd have both arms free.

Number One, still trying to figure out what the hell had
just happened, grabbed a thick tree trunk as he attempted
to stand. His swarthy face was gray with pain and beaded
with sweat as he used the trunk as ballast. *"¡Me rompiste
el brazo, puta!"*

Yeah, she didn't need him to tell her she'd broken his
arm, judging by its angle. He wouldn't be grabbing anyone
for a while.

"¡No le pegues a una mujer, verguita!" Don't hit a
woman, little dick, she replied.

"Jesus, you're just like my brother!" Sin grabbed her upper arm and hauled her the rest of the way to her feet. All
the while he had his submachine gun trained on Number
One, ten feet away. "You have a death wish, woman."

"You have a brother?" she asked, walking over to divest
the guy of his weapons. She now had a cheap-shit hunting
knife and an AK-47.

"That's the part of that sentence you picked out?" Sin
shook his head, his dark gaze sizing her up from her head

to her toes and lingering for a moment on her upper arm, then turned his attention to the guy clutching the tree trunk. "Who do you work for, Basto?" he demanded in rapid Spanish.

Riva left the two lovebirds to their convo and went to retrieve the bags and her SIG.

Shoving both arms into the straps of the heavy pack, she was careful to avoid the bloody cut on her other arm. Then she repositioned herself in the spot where she'd been standing when she'd lost her grip on the SIG and began walking in the direction it had flown, cursing the vines and leaves that seemed to have swallowed it whole.

Breaking off a branch she used it to push back the greenery until she caught a telltale glint on the ground. Just as well; it was starting to get dark and she would have hated to lose her favorite gun. She picked it up and headed back to Sin. The wound needed to be tended to, she knew, but she didn't have anything clean enough. Not even anything clean enough to mop up the blood. A sweaty tank top or filthy bandana would just exacerbate potential infection.

Ignoring the blood sluggishly dripping down her arm, she wondered what had happened to the other men who'd attacked them. And where the hell were Andrés and Sin's small, trusted dream team? She paused for a second, focusing her thoughts internally. No. Not one damn prediction or premonition. The lack of a vision was inconvenient as hell.

She heard a shot and sped up, SIG in one hand, AK-47 in the other, as birds flew from the trees in a noisy flurry of wings and loud cheeping.

Sin met her halfway, at a dead run. *"Move!"* He shoved her back the way she'd come.

Riva moved. Hard not to when he had her by the wrist and was crashing and thrashing his way to God only knew where and almost breaking her bones. He wasn't using the machete. Just pushing through where he could, or changing course when he couldn't. It would be hard for their pursuers to track them in the gloom without having a tunnel of hacked branches to follow.

Shots sounded behind them. Close, but the shooters weren't visible. Turning, she brought up the SIG. Sin grabbed it by the barrel and shook his head.

"You idiot," Riva whispered furiously. "I almost shot your hand off."

Pushing aside a fern frond twice his height, he shoved her through it, then let it fall like a curtain behind them. "Muzzle flash. Go. Go. *Go.*"

They picked up speed. Not by much. But faster than was safe in this environment. The alternative was worse.

A volley of shots echoed behind them, and voices carried in the semidarkness. A muzzle flash. Then another. The sound set off the animals so that the understory was alive with darting creatures. Her eyes had adjusted to the low level of light, but they weren't going to be able to see anything when it got pitch-dark, and a flashlight, when they had people hard on their tails, was out of the question. "Who?"

"No fucking idea." He held her upright as she tripped over a thick root, or an anaconda for all she knew. They were running. Or rather, walking as fast as possible, considering they were in dense jungle. "Almost there."

She didn't bother to ask *almost where?* Apparently she was about to find out. Sin released her wrist, but she still felt the steel bands of his fingers circling her arm. "Stand right here," he told her quietly. "Don't move."

He melted into the trees.

Straining for any unnatural sounds, Riva didn't move for a good ten minutes, until she thought he'd either been killed or had decided she was a liability.

His footfall was surprisingly light as he returned at a run. Without a word he grabbed her around the waist and ran with her. Straight for a wall of dense vegetation.

She heard them then. Whispered voices, arguing.

Sin had his arm around the backpack on her back, motivating her to move fast. Riva didn't argue.

"This is far enough. Hang tight. As far as I know nobody knows about this place. But be prepared to shoot the first person you see."

"I see you," she whispered, only half joking as she turned the way they'd just come, weapon raised. It was getting dark and everything looked a mottled gray. With her attention fixed ahead, she was peripherally aware of a vast space behind her, the smell of damp earth, animal droppings, and Sin.

There was only one smell—his—that could distract her, and it became even more distracting when he reached across her to lift the strap of her bag from her shoulder and set it down, then moved in front of her, blocking her view.

Nudging his arm with the barrel of the AK-47, she moved to stand beside him. "Chivalrous, but unnecessary," she whispered, inexplicably touched that he'd risk his life for someone he didn't trust.

In response, he slid one arm around her waist. She felt the rock-hard length of him against her back. Felt the steady beat of his heart against her shoulder blade. Felt his arm across her body, his big hand splayed, unnecessarily she thought, across her midriff. She was aware of the weight of each finger, and the promise of his thumb moving a few inches to touch her nipple.

They both held their weapons pointed at the arch of greenery at the end of what appeared to be a rock cave, the entrance obscured by foliage. Sin pulled her more tightly against him as the voices got closer and closer. Braced, she wondered how he could be so completely relaxed and focused when she was as tense as a drawn bowstring.

The beam of bright flashlights cut across the dirt ten feet in front of her boots. It was filtered, diffused by the leafy vines. She held her breath...

TWENTY

Unless one knew where to look, the labyrinth of centuries-old, played-out emerald mines crisscrossing the mountain were obscured from view by downed trees, or—like this one—covered in wrist-thick vines and deadfall.

Three months ago, when he figured out his life was going sideways, Sin had discovered a series of old mine entrances when scouting. He'd marked them, then returned when he was alone. He'd outfitted several bolt-holes to the south toward his hidden boat on the river, one to the south toward Abad, and several more in the direction of Santa de Porres. Four in all. Some with enough supplies to outlast a weeklong siege, others with just bare necessities.

In case of *what,* he hadn't been sure. Now, he knew his instincts were sound, and weren't simply fears based on paranoia.

This particular mineshaft was deeper than it was wide. The decades-old wooden support beams had long since rotted, and the roof had collapsed in places, leaving piles of rocks on the uneven ground. They could stay here for days if necessary. Although he didn't relish being trapped here for any length of time, darkness was already blanketing the jungle. Inside would be safer than out.

Sin realized that if he held Riva any more tightly, she'd be behind him. He loosened his death grip only slightly, enough to feel her chest expand as she drew in a silent shuddering breath. Surrounded by his arms, her back flush against his chest, she remained motionless, her SIG trained on the heavily armed men outside, her arms not wavering.

Sin had believed them to be friends, yet their intent was crystal clear. Kill.

Question was: Him or Riva?

What the *fuck* was going on?

He'd caught glimpses of the faces of the men pursuing them, and recognized their voices. Cesar. Vincente. Geosue. Men he'd worked beside for months, if not the years they assured him he'd known them. Now they appeared determined to *kill* him?

He and Riva had killed Lamora, Deltz, Alejos, and Basto. Four men dead. And no answers.

And how the hell did Andrés fit into this goatfuck? Because his friend hadn't U-turned to come back to assist. Unless Andrés had been killed in the attack? And how the hell would Sin know one way or the other?

The three men stood less than half a dozen feet outside their hiding place, their voices low and indistinct.

He gripped Riva's shoulder and pressed down, firmly, a clear "stay here" order, and crept slowly, silently, to the greenery. He moved one of the inner vines just enough to be able to see the men. Geosue rolled a stick of gum into his mouth. Clearly Sin's admonitions that the smell of mint would tip off an adversary were for naught. Crumpling the paper, he tossed it into the foliage nearby.

Moron.

Sin trained the barrel of the Glock right in the middle of the man's sweating forehead. One move toward the entrance, and he'd be dead.

Go away. What the hell could they be discussing? They'd failed at the task. He and Riva could be miles away by now. Go. Rest up. Hit harder tomorrow. For fucksake, that's what he'd trained them to do. Go fucking *do* it.

It would serve them right if he blew them all away right now. No question he could do it without any of them being able to get a shot off. The catch was that he couldn't be sure if there were more men with them, who'd come running, find the bodies, and start the search again. All things considered, it was better to stay hidden for now.

Riva had a knife slice on her upper arm that needed tending, and he'd taken a hard blow to the temple from the butt of Cesar's submachine gun. Sin blinked back a blur of blood from the corner of his eye.

Riva had fought hard and well. Trained, without a doubt. That could prove to be an asset or a fucking liability if she turned those skills on him.

The inside of the cave, dark and shadowy, smelled of moss and damp. It was a hell of a lot cooler than the temperature outside. The smell of Riva's skin, clean sweat, the coppery tang of blood, and the faint, unmistakable scent of herbal shampoo filled his senses, even as his attention remained on the glimpses of the men gathered right outside their hiding place.

Clearly they'd switched allegiance to Maza. How had he not noticed? When had the betrayal begun? How many of his men were involved? Or had Mama finally snapped and decided she wanted to run the ANLF without his interference?

Jesus. He was fucked. He didn't know who to trust, who to get answers from. Or where he'd be safe until he figured it all out. If he figured anything out before they managed to kill him.

To compound the problem, he had Riva with him.

Protect her or let her go? Would she go straight to Maza if that really was her plan? Could she make it to his nemesis in one piece without him riding shotgun?

Was she an innocent in all this, or was she the precipitating event that had set everything in motion?

His head ached like a bitch as he strained to listen to the muffled convo while he peered through the tiny slit in the thick veil of vines. Eventually the men's voices faded, but Sin stayed where he was.

After several minutes, Riva turned to face him. "They're gone. Now, let's figure out what just hap— Why are you looking at me like Simba looking at a gazelle?"

"Wrong continent." Lifting his hand, he gently brushed a strand of hair off her cheek. He paused for her to stiffen, brace, watched her eyes for fear, refusal, or any number of other get-the-hell-away-from-me signs. Tough to read her in the semidarkness. She didn't jerk back, but she did tuck her SIG in the small of her back.

Progress.

Riva's lips parted as he bracketed her head between his hands, shivering erotically under his touch as he brushed his palms slowly against her ears. He stroked her hair, most of which had come loose from the braid, pulled and tangled by their race through the trees. "Of all the uncertainties," he murmured, lowering his head. "With all the confusion and doubt, one thing I knew for sure. I wanted you the mo-ment I saw you." He cradled the back of her head as she curled one hand around his waist. "But could you please hold off shooting me, stabbing me, or otherwise ruining the moment until I'm done kissing you?"

Riva brought her cupped hand up between their mouths. "Is this a one-sided sport or can we both participate?" she asked, voice husky.

In the midst of trouble and darkness, she amused the hell out of him. It was worth taking the risk she'd kill him while in such proximity. He whispered, voice thick with need, "Move your hand. I'll show you."

Then the barricade of her fingers was gone, and Riva fisted in his hair. "No, Diaz." Her eyes dropped to his mouth. "*I'll* show *you*."

The naked hunger Sin saw in her dark eyes matched his own. His heart hammered against his breastbone as their mouths met. Petal soft, and damp, her lips parted as he swept his tongue inside the hot cavern. She was there to welcome him. When he explored, she reciprocated.

Sliding his hands down her slender back, he gripped the globes of her ass in his palms, pulling her up higher and tighter against the pulsing hardness of his erection. It wasn't enough. Not nearly.

He felt the heavy strum of her heart, the soft brush of her lashes on his cheek as she angled her head. Her hot, salty, female scent was intoxicating.

The sharp stinging nip of her teeth on his lower lip shot directly to Sin's already painfully hard dick. She shifted against him, curling a leg around his like a jungle vine. Mouth avid, slick tongue exploring, she drove him insane as she gripped his hair.

Despite the exertions and hellish heat, the perspiration and humid perfume of vegetation, she smelled-delicious.

No lotions or perfume, just the natural fragrance of her damp skin. Pheromones, he knew. Inhaling her was intoxicating, and his body reacted as though he'd been given a shot of high-octane adrenaline.

Riva's body was sleekly muscled, with graceful curves and slopes. Smooth, hot skin came alive under his hands. He wanted her naked. He made do with rediscovering the shape of her breast, full, small and responsive. The cleft between her legs, behind the barrier of cloth was already damp. She moaned, as he moved urgent hands over her, her breath as rapid as his own.

The kiss was unlike any Sin had ever experienced before, not in his recollection anyway. The taste and feel of her, her avid responses, shot the hot, devouring melting of teeth and tongues, of frantic hands and harsh breathing, to another level.

Dick, taut and hard, his pulse thrummed relentlessly as he pressed his hardness against her moist heat. If they didn't stop, he'd be fucking her right there on the dirt floor of the cave. A tasty meal for any creature using the cave as a refuge.

He placed his hands on her upper arms, and dragged his damp mouth from hers, letting her go with some reluctance. He'd felt the hard nubs of her nipples pressed against his chest, the heat of her body even through the cotton clothing she wore.

"I want you more than my next breath." He didn't recognize the gritty sound of his own voice. "But we have to secure the area. Anyone could've walked in and shot us point blank."

Looking as dazed as he felt, Riva unwound her leg from around his waist and cleared her throat. "God. That was unprofessional." Stepping back, she ran her hand over her hair, which was gloriously untidy. Her lips looked bee-stung, her nipples, sharp points beneath the close-fitting black tank top. She took another step back, putting space between them that was filled with pulsing, pent-up need.

"It won't happen again," she said, looking him straight in the eye. He knew it for the lie it was. It would happen again until they got each other out of their systems.

Sin drank her in, then noticed that the wound on her up-per arm had started bleeding again. "Shit. We have to patch that up."

"Believe me, I didn't feel any pain." She glanced down at the oozing blood. "It'll stop in a minute. I'm good."

Yeah, she was. More than. "We'll get a few hours' sleep, then head toward the river."

Riva grabbed the straps of her backpack, slinging them over her shoulders, then picked up the guns, brushing off a few damp leaves as she did.

"They'll be back with reinforcements." He took his Glock from her and tucked it in the small of his back. "They'll re-convene where they attacked us, spread out from there at first light. I have some supplies stashed behind that rock-fall. Food, water, flashlight."

He indicated the wall of rocks, collapsed from the ceil-ing. All but hidden was a narrow opening, just wide enough for him to squeeze through sideways. Just a week ago, he'd fixed a heavy tarp across the narrow entrance from the other side. Pushing through it, he held it aside for Riva to pass through, then dropped it back.

It was pitch-dark. Sin was going more by memory than by sight. Riva bumped into him as he paused to let his eyes adjust. She stepped away immediately. But not far, as he felt her heat close by. "Hang on to me until I find the flash-light."

She slid her fingers into his waistband, fingers hot against his skin. What he really wanted, needed, was her hands on him everywhere. And being in the dark with her touching bare skin gave him a boner he was grateful she couldn't see, especially since she seemed to have recovered from the kiss just fine.

"Those were your own men." She pitched her voice low. "Do you piss off everyone, Diaz?"

"Apparently." He found the boxes of supplies and fum-bled for the latch, then held on to the lid so it didn't fall back against the rock walls and make a noise. He'd left a flashlight and a loaded H&K MP7A1 submachine gun on top. Just in case.

Fuck. His life was made up of a series of questions, but "Am I in danger?" was not one of them. He was constantly on alert, always looking over his shoulder, ceaselessly aware that he had enemies. *Always* in danger.

He retrieved, and clicked on, the powerful flashlight, filling the cave-like area with light. "Put the weapons down, you'll need both hands, and put the bags down on the rock next to them, not on the ground. This section of the mine is twenty feet wide and sixty feet deep, to the next cave-in." The ceiling of rough-hewn rock fifteen feet overhead.

He waited as Riva put their weapons and the bags on a nearby slab of rock. He handed her the submachine gun. "Loaded," he cautioned. She placed it beside the others with exaggerated care. "Hold the flashlight." He adjusted her aim so he could see what he was removing. "We'll spend the night here, then head out before first light."

Riva shone the light around the walls. "Two cave-ins? Is this place safe?"

"Happened decades ago. We're good. I need that light over here."

She returned the beam to where he was taking things out of the plastic container. "Shouldn't we check to see if anything's lurking back there?"

"Trust me, if anything's sleeping in here, it would've woken up and come to investigate the second we came inside. Doesn't mean animals won't come in later, though. We'll keep our weapons close at hand and I have deterrents so we can sleep safely." He started loading her arms with supplies. The meager light reflected on the loose hair around her face and shoulders so that each strand looked like a silver filament. Dark eyes unreadable, she watched his face.

Reading him? Sin wondered what she saw.

"This isn't a cave, it's a played-out emerald mine. I'm starving, and want to take a look at your arm before we bed down."

"My arm's just fine. I'll slap some Neosporin on it in a minute. Where do you want me to put all this?"

He lit the small camping lantern. It gave off just enough light to see their surroundings. He'd tested to see how far the light could bleed to the outside of the tunnel, waiting for a pitch-black night, and nothing could be seen from outside. "Right where you are, tough girl. If you open that top plastic container, you'll find a sleeping bag and a camp stove. I'll get the tent and the food."

She put down the things he'd handed her, went over and lifted the top plastic box off the short stack of similar containers. "You planned for this?"

"I plan for everything. Don't put that bag on the ground until I have the tent set up."

She removed the stove and a handful of freeze-dried, ready-made meals. A five-gallon plastic container nearby held fresh water. "We're inside a cave. Why do we need a te—"

Sin pointed to a large, hairy, brown Tarantula the size of his fist, scurrying across the mossy ground away from the light.

Riva pulled a face. "Tent it is."

He set it up quickly. With its thick floor and solid, canvas walls, nothing short of a saber-toothed tiger could get in once it was zipped.

They worked in silence for several minutes. By the time he had the tent up, and lined with the unzipped sleeping bag, she had a couple of MREs open. Not that appetizing, but filling, and high in protein. He started the coffee, and her mouth watered in anticipation.

After closing the lid on the supply box, he told her to take a seat. "Let me attend that scratch before it gets infected. Here, hold this." He handed her the open, well-stocked first-aid kit and removed antiseptic and gauze as she sat down. "Hold the light, keep it steady. While we're at it, how's the leg?"

"Leg?"

"You fell out of a helicopter, remember?"

"Oh. That leg. Fine."

He'd check that as well. "Let's clean this up and see what we're dealing with."

After sluicing the four-inch gash on her arm with water, he patted the wound dry with the gauze, then dabbed on antiseptic liberally. She hissed in a breath, but remained stoic.

"You need stitches. All I have are butterfly bandages." Hell, she needed more than stitches, she needed a hospital and antibiotics. Untreated open wounds could kill you in the jungle. Topical antiseptic and a couple of bandages weren't enough. Now the urgency to get her to Santa de Porres was imperative.

"That'll be fine. I'll live."

She had as many scars on her body as he did. He wanted to kiss all her hurt places, the cuts and scrapes, the new bruises and the old scars. But it was the ones on her slender wrists that made his balls clench, and his stomach turn over.

Cupping her hand in his, Sin ran his thumb over the scars on her left wrist. Some had been neatly stitched, and healed well, others were irregular. "What or who caused you this much pain?"

TWENTY-ONE

Riva swallowed the tightness in her throat. "He's dead now."

"Who?"

"Not a story I share—"

"*Who?*"

She'd never told anyone all of it. Probably never would. But here, in the stillness, and darkness, with Sin so close, there was an intimacy she'd never allowed herself to feel before. What harm could it do? In a few days they'd part. "One of my mother's boyfriends physically and verbally abused me from the time he showed up when I was twelve until he died four years later."

"Abused? Physically? That's why you have these?" His eyes in the dim light were keen, intense. He looked...tempered. Contained. Holding it together. It was remarkable to watch him gather himself like that. *That* was control. Incredible inner strength.

He touched the scar hardly anyone ever noticed under her chin.

Bent over the kitchen table, her mother sobbing as she held her screaming child down so her lover could beat some sense into her. Joe standing between her flailing legs, that metal-tipped whip rising and falling on her bare back for hour after hour.

Powerless, no way out, too small, too weak to fight both of them, she'd tried to finish off what Mom and Joe had started. Her first attempt with a razorblade had been a few days after her ninth birthday. *The babysitter had found her that time.*

She had to jerk her gaze away from the leashed anger she saw on his face, wait while her lungs unlocked and she could drag in enough badly needed air to finish. She wished she hadn't started. Showing him her vulnerability was stupid and dangerous as hell. "Most of them," she said on an exhale. The next breath came easier. *Tie it up neatly. Be done with the confessions. Enough, Rimaldi. Just... Enough.* "Some I got on the job, but most were inflicted by Joe.

"A small leather cat o' nine tails whip with metal tips was a favorite. But he was eclectic. A table, a bowling ball. My mother's cigarette. Or when he was drunk, his fists." She ignored the sting of antiseptic as Sin tended her arm.

"My mother started the abuse long before he arrived on the scene. Mostly whatever she could grab. I shared a vision of her banging her best friend's husband—shared it with her and her best friend—when I was two, so it started about then. But Joe upped the fun when he introduced the whip." Did he notice what she'd just admitted?

Riva read his microexpressions. Disgust. Fury. Sympathy. She hadn't even told the full story to the social workers, and her shrink knew better than to let those feelings show. "My mom claimed afterwards that she'd had no clue about his criminal past, but I found out later that she'd met him through a prison pen pal program."

"Jesus." He traced a finger along the row of small puncture wound marks on the side of her neck, where Joe had stabbed her with a fork. Then used eyes and fingers to trace her arms until he found the one in the bend of her elbow, where Joe had snapped her arm in a fit of rage when she'd described his death. In minute detail.

It had been worth it.

The small lantern flickered, sending dancing arcs of light and shadow up on the rock walls. "Three murders, and a string of other felonies," she told him unemotionally as he applied the first butterfly bandage. She'd learned to separate the helpless child from the accomplished, strong woman she'd later become.

"He'd just gotten out of prison when he moved across the country, changed his name, and came to meet my mother... I tried to keep the knowledge of my visions to myself. They already freaked out my mother, and isolated me from my peers. I could never keep my mouth shut. I was always in trouble, at home, at school... When Joe realized that I was predicting his future with pinpoint accuracy, he went ballistic." *And took up where good old Mom left off.*

Sin took up another bandage and applied it gently to the wound, his lashes short and thick and gold-tipped in the lantern light as he tended her.

"You're not asking if I'm psychic or not."

"Whether you are or not, is irrelevant," he said with suppressed anger painted quite clearly in the muscles of his face "These were the very people who should have protected you. They didn't.

The familiar rich scent of strong, boiling coffee filled the small space. Jarringly normal. Riva's throat ached. "Joe freaking terrified me as much as I terrified him, and I retaliated by trying to scare him even more. Then he'd use the whip or his fists, then I'd smart-mouth him and tell him *more,* hoping to scare him enough so that he wouldn't touch me, or better yet-*leave.* It escalated...

"After years of therapy, I now know he was shit-scared I'd see who he really was and turn him in. Of course it didn't help that I relished telling him what he'd be doing in a week or month. But my mother was so in love with him, she would never do anything to jeopardize their relationship, and between his physical abuse and her verbal abuse, I was too scared to do anything."

Riva swallowed down a dry throat. "I swore I'd never be that weak, that vulnerable again. And I haven't been."

"That's why you became an assassin for hire?"

"I searched out a local martial arts dojo. Hell I didn't know what I needed to know, just knew I needed to know...*something.* I was ten. The owner's grandfather taught me everything he knew for a few years. I tried to teach him English. I perfected my craft, loved the strength and power it gave me."*Loved Sensei Kobbayashi.* "That all turned to shit when I told him his daughter was stealing the dojo blind for her drug habit. I moved to Boston after that. Kept moving until I— Never mind." After joining T-FLAC, Riva had honed her skills with a vengeance. Practice made perfect.

She hadn't fared as well with other personal relationship. Hard to do when she was always braced for attack. Verbal or physical. The visions wouldn't stop, so she was isolated by them. She usually went on the attack first which put paid to any hope of a romantic relationships. Romance just wasn't in the cards for her. She lived just fine without it. She was unlovable anyway, so that worked out just fine.

Sin paused, the last bandage in his large hand as he listened. The tiny butterfly bandage crumpled between his fingers and he tossed it aside, unpeeling another.

Riva touched the back of his hand. "I told you I didn't talk about it—"

"Tell me the rest." He carefully stuck the last bandage across her wound, then lifted his gaze to meet hers. His eyes were filled with impotent rage.

It was as though he'd just given her a gift. She curled her fingers into his palm. Their knees touched, the smell of antiseptic hung in the air, and she'd never felt more in sync with another person in her life.

Just because the moment was fleeting and couldn't last was no reason not to allow herself to experience a deep emotion she couldn't name. Whatever it was, she'd enjoy the now of it.

Wanting to get the revealing over with, Riva talked a little faster as she got up and poured a mug of scalding coffee. "I could only find one m—"

He took it from her as she returned to her seat beside him on the box, and took a sip. "We'll share."

"I saw his violent past and made the mistake of telling him his future. He did his best to beat the visions out of me."

"Jesus, Riva. I hope you killed the son of a bitch."

She took the metal mug from him and drank. It was too hot, bitter as hell, it smelled a lot better than it tasted. "He was six foot five, and built like a Mack truck."

Sin waited.

"I shot him with his own firearm." Bloody and messy, that night had haunted her dreams for years. "The police called it self-defense. They had the records from eight different hospitals, a couple of psych holds because of these..." She held up her wrists as though he were about to handcuff her. The pity she read on his face almost undid her, making it hard to breathe. She shrugged. "Case closed."

Not nearly that neat and tidy. She was a child who'd grown up far too quickly. She'd been terrified, alone, and without resources. The many trips to ERs and clinics across the country had saved her from prosecution.

"Where was your *mother* in all this? A priest? A teacher..."

"My mother was the type of woman who needed a man in her life to feel beautiful. There was a succession of 'uncles' before Joe, and we moved a lot. She always took her lover's side, because she was afraid I'd frighten him away with my crazy stories. Joe was no exception. I *wanted* to stop telling people what I saw, I honest to God did. But when the visions came I didn't know how to keep them to myself. Believe me, I've learned how to, because otherwise someone else would've killed me over the years. Most people are freaking terrified when I tell them I just had a vision of their future. Even if it's something favorable, they're afraid."

Beneath the scruff on his jaw, Sin's jaw clenched. "Does your mother know what you do for a living?"

Riva shook her head. "After I killed Joe, she kicked me out. She still wasn't speaking to me when she died of emphysema eight years ago."

Sin lifted her hand and pressed his lips to her inner wrist. The warmth flowed from his mouth to her skin, then was carried by her veins in a dizzying rush through her body. His touch was a healing tonic. Odd, that this man would provide healing. No, not odd at all, because all of his microexpressions indicated a deep kindness. He was a paradox, because T-FLAC intel said something far different about Sin Diaz.

"I'm okay now. Plenty of ongoing therapy," she murmured dryly, sifting her fingers of her other hand through his hair, but having no memory of lifting it to his head.

"It explains why you're so fearless."

Brushing her fingertips over the flexing muscle in his jaw, she saw she'd freaked him out, too. Riva dropped her hand into her lap. So be it. She was what she was. Her psychic abilities had built a damn nice career for her, where people depended on that skill when she did her job.

"I'm sorry."

Oh, God. His words were exactly what she needed to hear. The fact that it was this man saying them was right, and so, so damned wrong. Enough soul baring. "Sin? I might bleed to death here," she kept her tone light, but it was a little thick with pent-up emotion.

He dropped another kiss to the scars, then released her hand. "Let me take a look at your leg."

"You just want to get my pants off."

He smiled. "That, too."

Since she was commando, Riva yanked down her shirt to cover herself. He grinned as he bent his head. Her leg looked fine to her, but he wasn't distracted by her semi-nu-dity. Focused, he applied antiseptic, and called it good.

She angled her head to look at his handiwork. "That looks great," she pulled up her pants. "Now I'll do you. You have a pretty bad cut over that eye."

He allowed her to clean and dress his slashed eyebrow. The cut was small-head wounds bled a lot, but Riva liked touching him. Liked the feel of his prickly jaw against her palm, liked the feel of his humid breath on her wrist as she worked over his eye. "Good as new." Reluctantly, she started putting away the first-aid supplies.

"We'll eat inside the tent, it'll keep insects out of our food."

Fair enough. Dozens of small, assorted bugs flew around the light.

After filling their plates and grabbing his canteen, they crawled inside the tent. Sin reached back for the lantern, doused it, zipped the flap closed, then set the Mag light on the edge of the thick sleeping bag.

Sitting cross-legged, Riva picked up her spork and lifted it to her mouth. "Why are your men trying to kill you?"

The one-man tent wasn't that big. Sin took up most of it. It was a tight fit, with their knees touching. "I have no idea."

"They don't like you?"

"They like Mama even less. Apparently she scares them more than I do. Or they've switched allegiances, and are now working for Maza."

"In which case they would've been trying to separate us to take me to him, not trying to kill me. And they won't kill you. Not in the next few days anyway."

"Is this speculation or a vision?"

"Visions."

"That's comforting at least."

"God, I really am starving. This tastes like ambrosia even though I know it isn't."

Finished with his meal, Sin placed his empty plate near the tent flap and twisted open the lid on the canteen. "Are you really here to kill Maza?" he asked, taking a swig.

She figured he was taking the psychic part of her sorry tale at face value for now. "If I answer you, will you answer a question for me?"

He hooked an arm around his bent knee. "Hell. Why not?"

"I'm going to kill Maza before he does something irreparable. And to answer your earlier question about who commissioned me to do the job? I'm an operative with T-FLAC- Terrorist Force Logistical Assault Command. A privately funded counterterrorist organization."

"Not a hitman?"

"In this case, yeah. I *will* hit him. But that's not my job, usually. No."

"Makes sense. You're neither weak nor vulnerable. You give as good as you get. Plenty of training there. How did you hook up with a counterterrorist group?"

"I was working as a jury consultant. I was good at reading people's microexpressions and body language, plus—" Riva shrugged. T-FLAC had appreciated her skills, wanted them, honed them. "The organization liked my skills and recruited me."

"That's why they sent you in to take Maza's psychic's place. You really *will* be able to tell him his future."

"It's not that easy. I don't always see visions, and I can't do them on command. I have them or I don't, but my training has allowed me to be able to fake it when necessary. Like I said, I'm damn good at reading people. That part of my skill is proven science."

He gave her an assessing look. "Fascinating."

She wasn't sure if he was talking about her job, or *her* personally. "We've been monitoring calls between Escobar Maza and a psychic named Graciela Estigarribia for months. We've also been monitoring chatter world-wide. There's a BRICS Summit in Santa de Porres in eight days—"

"BRICS?"

"It's an acronym for an association of five major emerging national economies."

"Brazil, Russia, India, China, and South Africa. Yeah. I know," he said dryly. "For months I've been trying to expand our sales into those countries."

"We believe Maza plans to either take the principals hostage, kill them, or— Shit. We have theories, but no definitive proof of *what* he has planned."

"And this—*T-FLAC*-sent you in *alone* to protect the BRICS delegation, and take out Escobar Maza? What the fuck's wrong with them?"

"First of all, I'm a trained field operative. This is what I *do*. And I didn't come alone. I came in with two fellow operatives. They were two of the men killed in the chopper crash. Plus, I have a team waiting for me in Santa de Porres and another in Abad. There was no intention of sending me in alone. Although I'm well trained for jungle combat."

"They aren't able to help you here, are they? Don't they know who and what that fucker *is*? A sadistic psychopath. While I hear and compute what you're saying about your people having intel about the BRICS Summit, I have to wonder just what it is that he hopes to achieve. Maza does nothing unless it benefits himself, or the SYP. How will doing *anything* benefit them directly? These people, while powerful in their own rights, are merely appointed by their respective countries to form this alliance. Kill them, more will pop up. It's a renewable resource, right?"

She shrugged. "My people are gathering more intel. They may have even answered the very questions you're asking now. I just need to communicate with them."

"He works for someone. But I guess you know that. Kill him, and his boss will just send in someone else. It's like cutting the head off a Hydra."

"How does a guy raised in a jungle know about a Hydra? That home school nun?"

He shrugged. "Maza's boss—"

"His boss is Stonefish. Yeah, we know. We caught him a year ago. He's in a supermax, so his wings are clipped, if not cut off. No human contact makes playing phone tag impossible. Maza isn't crying about his boss being incarcerated and having the key thrown away. He's aiming for top spot. Why do you think he moved into Cosio? I'll tell you. Because he wants to take *your* job. He's been working diligently to take over all of the ANLF business worldwide, as I'm sure you know. He's taken you in South Africa, he's taken you in Spain, and also in Portugal. Having a hard time ousting you in Great Britain, France, and North Africa, but it's only a matter of time."

"Not news. The son of a bitch has been breathing down my neck for months." He paused to offer her the canteen. Riva shook her head. "Is he working with Mama?"

She shot him a startled look. "Not that we know of, but of course anything's possible. Why?"

"She doesn't like me. Understatement of the year."

"Aw. That's not very maternal of her. But if it makes you feel any better, I doubt she likes anyone."

"Believe me, people feel the same way about her. What do you know about me?"

"What do you mean?"

"What does T-FLAC know about Sin Diaz?"

Dropping her hand from the top of her head, she counted off on her fingers, "Terrorist. Extortionist. Kidnapper. International arms and drug trafficker..." She ran out of fingers and switched hands. "Violent. Ruthless. And those are your good qualities." She flashed him a smile.

"My reputation has preceded me, then. So you recognized me when you saw me?"

"We don't have any images of you, if that's what you mean." She gave him a considering look. "But when I first saw you, you did look vaguely familiar, so I guess I saw a picture of you somewhere. Or you remind me of someone I know."

"Who?"

"No idea. Probably the villain in some movie franchise."

"Shit."

"Shit? Awwwww. You wanted to be the hero?"

"I was hoping you'd be able to tell me what I was doing prior to five months ago."

TWENTY-TWO

She gave him a startled look. "You really don't know what you were doing half a year ago?"

In the iffy light, her tawny skin looked dewy and touchable. He could smell her. Hot, musky woman. She ran her hand around the back of her neck, then lifted the braid on top of her head as if that would cool her neck. All it did was shift her breasts, and make him want to bury his face in the crook of her damp neck. God, she was pretty—no, *exotic* with those patrician features, long-lashed dark eyes, and creamy, pale olive-toned skin. The black tank top showed off her streamlined biceps and the upper swell of her breasts. Fit, healthy, and in her prime. Riva Rimaldi was a siren song.

But it was the intelligence and compassion he saw in her dark eyes, the belief that she *saw* him, that made Sin draw in a breath, then take the plunge. "Apparently I had a run-in with Maza. The injuries I sustained kept me in a coma for months. When I woke, I'd lost my memory."

She cocked her head, causing her long braid to slither over her shoulder and snake against her breast. "You know that only happens to people in soap operas, right?"

"Then this is a particularly bad one. I *think* I remember flashes of things. Maybe I'm having hallucinations. Whatever they are, a recurring one is me thrashing through the jungle. Running like hell. Shots being fired—"

"You just spent the better part of today doing that." She rested her elbows on her knees. "In your line of work, I imagine there's lots of jungle running, and people shooting at each other. You're a terrorist in a friggin' jungle, for God's sake."

"Yeah, that one mostly makes sense and reflects my day-to-day existence. I get it. But a lot of the memories or flashes I see— Shit. I don't know what the hell it is I think I remember. I could be stitching together a bunch of random events and making them into something else entirely. But skydiving? Parasailing? Volcano boarding... Paris? SCUBA diving in Greece? Where do *those* images come from? I don't have that good an imagination."

"Welcome to my world. Are you sure you're not psychic? How about this: Playing tennis? Wearing a tux at the theater—"

He pressed two fingers against the throbbing headache centered on the cut over his eye. "No," he corrected, dropping his hand because pressing didn't fucking help. "I don't have *those* memories at all."

"Maybe not. But those are at least two things you've done. I know, because I 'saw' you."

Sin wasn't sure he bought into this psychic crap. But then he wasn't sure what the hell he believed any more. "Do I look like a tennis player type to you, or a man who goes anywhere necessitating wearing a tuxedo?"

If it looks like a duck, quacks like a duck...

"Why do you believe you *haven't* done those other things? You could've gone to Paris or done any of those extreme sports before you were injured. Gone to the theater, mingled with the jet set..." She gave him a considering look. "Are your people telling you something different? The same people who just tried to kill you?"

"From the moment I woke up, Mama has regaled me with somewhat terrifying stories about my past. Paris and parasailing were *not* included in my list of nefarious past activities. And what she was telling me didn't feel...right. Most of the events were downright horrific. I can't imagine myself doing most of them. And yet, if none of them were true, why the fuck lie to me?" Sin paused, trying to formulate thoughts he'd had for months into something even *he*could believe.

It all sounded surreal. The fact that he was entrusting this woman, whom he barely knew, with his deepest, most terrifying secrets was probably as unwise as hell. "I considered the possibility that the blow to the head had scrambled my brains and that my personality had drastically changed."

Riva didn't say anything, yet her steady focus on him encouraged him to continue.

"At first I went along with what everyone was telling me. It made sense to do so and I didn't have to think about it too much. I couldn't. I had debilitating headaches. Mama gave me medicines to help with it. The meds made me feel...off. I stopped taking that shit, and over the next several weeks my head became clearer, and I started questioning what everyone had been telling me."

"She was drugging you to keep you compliant. The question is—why?"

"Yeah, I figured that out as my brain came back online. *Why* is just one of many questions I have. Who is another." It had to be said. "If I'm *not* Sin Diaz, and the best thing about *that* scenario is that I am not that woman's son, then who the fuck am I? None of this makes sense."

"If we had a computer I could take a picture of you and send it in to my control. He'd ID you in a minute."

"Not if no one has ever seen an image of me. I could be anyone."

"What about your friends? Andrés has known you forever, right?"

"He *says* we were raised together and he has encyclopedic knowledge of everything I've ever done. He's extremely convincing. But if Mama isn't my mother, he's lying, too."

"Where was he when your men attacked us earlier?"

"Dead, maybe."

"Do you really believe that? There's a strong possibility that you're being gaslighted." She chewed on the corner of her lower lip, and gave him a considering look. "That you aren't who they tell you you are. Still, it's pretty far-fetched to think that there is such an enormous and far-reaching conspiracy to make you believe you're someone you aren't. And that you've done things in your past that aren't true. If that is the case, it's a fantastical, complex, and elaborate hoax perpetrated by a *lot* of people. What do they gain from it?"

"When you put it that way, it sounds ludicrous."

"Not if we figure out why a large group of very bad guys are trying to make you believe you're someone you're not. If you weren't *el jefe* of the ANLF, who'd be boss?"

"Angélica. If not, Andrés."

"He's weak, and lazy, right?"

"That pretty much sums him up, yeah." Her assessment was correct and she'd only know Andrés for a handful of hours.

"But if a *woman* were to be the head of the ANLF, how many men would listen to her? How many of these macho Latin men would respect her law? What if Angélica needed a big, strong guy to be *el jefe,* while she ruled in the background? No one's the wiser? Keep you drugged and confused, keep you out of sight here in the jungle..."

"Doesn't make any sense. Where did she conveniently find me? In some bar? And then what? Kidnapped me. Knocked me over the head, which handily induced a coma and fortuitously caused me to have a total memory loss. That makes even less sense.

"We kidnap people to extract large ransoms," he continued. "She would've sold me—probably in small, bloody pieces—back to my family. Besides which, anyone who'd been in the ANLF for longer than five or six months would know damn well that I wasn't her son; how could she keep them all in line?"

Her dark eyes watched him with unwavering intensity. Their faces were so close that he saw each individual eyelash, and the faint trace of blue veins on her lids, and felt the gentle rise and fall of her breasts although they weren't quite touching.

"That woman could scare the devil himself into keeping his mouth shut. And she might be as in the dark about your ID as you are. If she didn't know who you were, didn't know if you had family or where they were, it must've been like manna from Heaven to have a big strong man show up."

Riva was putting into words his very thoughts. "Show up where? And why would she take the risk that eventually my memory would return?"

"She was playing for time; she already got seven or eight months of being in charge, thanks to your coma and having kept you fooled since you woke up. I think she's aware that your memory is back. She just tried to have you killed not two hours ago."

"Good point."

"Everyone at the compound claims to know Sin Diaz?"

"Sure. Most of them grew up with me. Plenty of stories there. She showed me some old newspaper clippings from some of my more salacious deeds. I'm a very, very bad man."

"So you keep telling me and so my intel confirms. Whoever Sin Diaz was or is, he's one hell of a badass. Help me dispose of Maza, and get me to a town with a computer and a phone. Between T-FLAC and ZAG, we'll figure out who you are in minutes. Rest assured." She gave him a bland look, her eyes somber. "If you are Sin Diaz, I'll be executing a kill order on you so fast you won't have more than a few seconds to regret your past actions."

"Then the wisest choice is for you to keep believing that's who I am until I prove differently. Not the kill order, but I certainly wouldn't trust me until further notice."

"Heard and acknowledged. But I've seen you dressed for the opera, so I *know* you aren't who they tell you you are." Her features softened, and her eyes smiled. "I've also read your microexpressions. I knew you weren't Sin Diaz—whoever that might be—the minute you didn't rape me when you first had the opportunity. But I'll keep the possibility under advisement until we have confirmation. And by the way, you look hot in a tux."

He shook his head ruefully, wishing he could just believe her. "I'm unpredictable. Violent. Aggressive. And a killer."

"*Sin Diaz* is those things."

"And if nothing else, I've *been* Sin Diaz for the past five months." His tone was grim, his thoughts more so. He met her eyes. "The safest bet is to get you to your people ASAP."

She shook her head. "My directive is to discover exactly what Maza has planned, and then to kill him. I'm not leaving until I've done my job." She wiggled around until she lay on her side. "How many hours dare we sleep?"

"Three."

She closed her eyes. "Want me to wake you? I'll set my body clock."

Three hours' sleep would be a luxury for him. His insomnia was legendary. Sin shifted so he could lie down, too. They were practically nose to nose. God, he loved the smell of her. Earthy woman, apricots, and a scent uniquely Riva.

Pillowing her head on her arms, she murmured, "Turn off the light."

"In a sec." Sin reached back into his pocket and withdrew the folded magazine page. Wordlessly, he unfolded it, and handed it to her.

"What's this?" She looked at him with a small smile. "A recipe from *Good Housekeeping*?"

No. My talisman. Sin was almost reluctant to give her the one thing he'd been hanging on to for months. The one thing that tethered him to another life. Another man. Chest restricted, heart hammering, he gave her the flashlight. "Do you know who these two guys are? They look— Hell, I don't know. Not familiar, but as if they *should* look familiar."

Her eyes widened. She sat up on her elbow and brought the circle of light closer to the page.

"What is it?"

Her gaze shot from the paper in her hand to his face. "Holy crap. I know *exactly* who you are."

His heart leapt and started to pound. Anticipation, fear. Excitement. "From a picture in a years-old magazine?"

"You're famous."

"Oh, Christ. Don't tell me. I'm an *actor*."

"You're *Gideon Stark*. This is you"—she pointed with the hand holding the flashlight—"and your brother. Hell, what's his name? Hang on." She closed her eyes for a second. "Let me think. ZAG... Z...and G. Z? Z? *Zakary!* You and your brother founded the ZAG search engine. Damn. Something happened to the two of you. I think. I'm trying to remember. It was all over the news..."

He waited impatiently in silence as she tapped her fingers on the folded magazine picture, hoping she held the memories he did not of what happened to him. "Sin... Gideon." She looked at him. "I think the two of you were kidnapped—"

"They killed him?" Shit, he was suddenly mourning a brother he hadn't known existed until ten seconds ago. A brother he didn't remember except for a vague sense of familiarity from a photo in an old, folded magazine page.

"No. He's still around. Alive. Seattle, I think."

Seattle was a long goddamned way from the jungles of Cosio. "So he abandoned me to my fate. Nice fucking guy."

"Assumptions. You better than anyone else know that's a huge mistake. Maybe he thought you were dead."

He needed to pace. To *move*. Walk. *Think*. Those were not options at the moment. "Which one do you think I am?"

"*Gideon*. Gideon Stark. Hot damn! I'm sure of it."

"Maybe." And maybe this famous brother of his had escaped their kidnappers and saved his own ass, resuming his successful life of fame and fortune and leaving Sin—Gideon—behind. "Where did the kidnapping happen? Cosio? That would make sense."

He didn't wait for her to answer. He didn't need to. He knew the answer. "Angélica kidnapped us. Crap. He had to have escaped, or was let go to drum up ransom. For whatever reason, he didn't return to get me. She kept me. It explains how she got her hands on me. How long ago?"

She shrugged. "Honestly, I'm not sure. The whole thing was all over the news for several months. I got a glimpse of the headlines about a year ago when I was on an op in Samara. But who knows how old it was by the time it made its way to where I was in Russia."

"A year? Maybe longer? And I've been out of my coma for five months. Where was I before that?" He took the magazine page from Riva and studied the two men with fresh eyes. *Was* this him? "To be honest, I don't feel like this Stark guy either. I don't remember wearing a suit. This guy looks like a fucking urbanite. If this is me, how in the hell don't I recognize myself? "

Riva touched his chin. "Maybe the scruff is new. You probably didn't have this scar." She lightly touched his eyebrow, then his jaw. "Or this one either. I'd hazard a guess that you don't stare at yourself in a mirror very often. If and when you shave, you're more likely to do it by feel than by sight. Am I right? You're more a Stark than a Diaz, I assure you."

She was right. He actually didn't recall the last time he'd glanced in a mirror. Still, he didn't feel like either man. "If *I'm* not Sin Diaz, then where is he? Dead?"

"Or made up. A terrifying, threatening, ominous urban legend. There are no pictures of him. He's never been identified. But T-FLAC has been well aware of his existence for at least a decade. Together, father and son were hell on wheels, terrorizing the emerald miners, kidnapping, selling drugs, et cetera. But Sin became even more powerful, and considerably stronger, after Carlos Diaz's death about seven years ago."

Sounded right. Mama had multiple stories about his accomplishments after his father's—*Sin's* father—death "He came into his own."

Riva spread her fingers on his chest over his heart. "Or someone wanted the world to *think* so."

"Angélica."

"Oh yeah."

A piercing headache made him grit his teeth. "She took away my life, planted false memories, and removed any opportunity for me to reunite with my family. She has a lot to fucking answer for." And he'd get those answers, one way or another. He folded the slick page more carefully, now that it gave him an anchor to his past. "She told me I have a son."

Dropping her exploring hand, she blinked. "That came out of left field."

Sin turned off the flashlight, plunging them into semidarkness. He'd loved the feel of her cool fingers learning the contours of his face, now his heart leapt with anticipation as she stroked his chest. "He's five and a half." His voice sounded foreign to him, thick with regret, guilt, and love for a child he'd never met, never seen, knew nothing about. Surely, if he wasn't Sin Diaz he wouldn't care so deeply about this boy?

"I was told I raped his mother, beat her half to death when I found out she was pregnant, and abandoned her." And now, he felt guilty about an offense he had callously committed, wondering whether, at the time, he'd felt remorse about the evil act. He could not, for one second, reconcile the act of rape with the feelings that he now had. Committing such a heinous act seemed so foreign to him that the thought that he did it made him sick to his stomach.

"If today is any indication of your true nature, you're most definitely not a rapist. You could've assaulted me any number of times while I was unconscious or restrained. You didn't."

"I just asserted my amazing self-control," he said wryly.

"That's my point. You *have* control."

He felt the heat of Riva's body down the length of his, tasted her breath on his tongue as she asked softly, "Are you saying *Sin Diaz* has a five-and-a-half-year-old son?"

He picked up the tail end of her braid, pooled on the sleeping bag between them. "So I've been told." Running the silken twists of dark hair across his palm, he played with it like a string of smooth worry beads. "Never met him."

"It's unlikely you have a son that age, Gideon; *you* were living in America when he was conceived and born. You're clearly highly intelligent, well educated, a seasoned traveler. I know nothing about you, but I can pretty much guarantee that you wouldn't use violence on a woman."

Gideon. "I might've done that when I was here on a visit." Was he trying to convince himself that he really *was* Sin Diaz? He knew in his gut that Riva was right. But he had to be 1,000 percent *sure.*

"And it might be another bullshit story that Mama told you to keep you in line."

TWENTY-THREE

We'll get to the bottom of it, I promise." She meant it. She wanted to help. "But one thing I'm sure of: You *are* Gideon Stark." She liked the feel of his fingers gently playing with her hair. Even the lightest touch seemed to make each follicle feel alive, as though individual nerve endings connected directly to her nipples. The sensation also inspired a throbbing ache between her legs.

"You know this only from that photo." He blew out a breath. "I've been lied to for months, living a life that I never felt connected to. Now, you tell me I'm a different man, someone I don't feel a connection to either." He sounded at once doubtful and hopeful.

Riva gave a small, one-shouldered shrug, which he wouldn't be able to see in the dark. "I'm not lying to you. I have nothing to gain from it. I know you're Gideon from that magazine picture and from my intuition, which is never wrong. Plus the fact that despite being convinced of all your nefarious deeds, you remain conflicted and repulsed by who they claimed you were. I have something else to offer you. Earlier today you told me I had a death wish.*Just like your brother."*

"God—"

She reached out to him in the darkness and touched his face. His jaw was heavily stubbled, but the hair was soft to the touch. Enjoying the tickle of it beneath her palm, she stroked his cheek, wondering if her touch affected him the same way his affected her. "Help me find Maza, and put a stop to what he has planned. Then we can figure out what happened between the time you last saw your brother and now."

"Maza's a sick fuck, you know that. I can't dissuade you from looking for him?"

"I came here to do a job." Riva stroked her thumb across his lower lip. Parting his lips, he nibbled on the pad. The sensation shot directly between her legs and remained there, damp and heavy.

Having him swirling his tongue against her finger was too damn distracting. "Look, honestly? I can't ask a civilian to go into a dangerous situation like this, especially since there's a damn good chance that you might be killed. Or worse, knowing how Escobar Maza operates. But we both know I'll be better off *with* you than going in alone. Don't get me wrong, I'm good at my job, damn good. And I could probably take him alone. But I'm used to working with a team." She thought of Sanchez and Castro with a pang. She'd barely known them, but their deaths gave her a heavy heart. Death was a daily part of a T-FLAC operative's life, but she didn't have to be immune to the sadness that came with it, and she didn't have to like it.

"My fellow operatives were killed in the chopper crash, remember? Until I reestablish contact with my control, I have no backup. And honestly? It's just not smart to try and go it alone."

"There was zero possibility of that ever happening, I assure you," Gideon told her, then turned his face into her palm, kissing it. "Since I can't persuade you to come with me to Santa de Porres, I'll be fully locked and loaded beside you."

Relief flooded her. He knew the jungle better than the newly arrived Maza did. Certainly a damn sight better than she did. Knew Maza's methodology, and even better still, had resources here that she didn't have access to. She needed him. Yeah, she could probably pull off killing Maza if she was smart about it. But alone, there'd be zip possibility of leaving his camp alive.

But it was damn hard to follow a conversation when the prospect of being eaten by this man was becoming a reality. "Okay. Good. Fine. Thanks."

Gideon chuckled, and since he was proceeding to nibble her thumb, the sound shot through her in a delicious wave of anticipation, ricocheting off all her pleasure points like liquid fire. Unfortunately, he was apparently done sucking her fingers, because he gently took her wrist, removing her hand from the vicinity of his mouth. "Turn over and go to sleep. Tomorrow promises to be an exciting, fun-filled day, and we both have to be sharp and on our toes."

Riva realized how strong he was as he lifted her with one hand, and managed to flip her over. Slinging a heavy arm over her waist, he pulled her tightly against him, then cupped her breast in his palm as if he had every right to do so. "Sleep," he ordered.

"Easy for you to say," she mumbled, pillowing her head on her bent elbow, and snuggling her butt against his impressive erection.

"Do you always have to have the last word, Rimaldi?"

"Yes."

His warm breath fanned her nape as he chuckled, then his breath became heavier.

Damn it.

The man was asleep. He had a will of steel. She could feel his erection pulsing. She knew he wanted her, but he was a jungle survivor and knew sleep was a means of self-preservation, while sex was recreation. After the day they'd had, and the day that was in store for them tomorrow, he had decided which was most important. Training told her she should be agreeing with him, but desire had her thinking that the two activities weren't mutually exclusive. After all, they had a few hours. She sighed in resignation when his breaths became even deeper. She covered his hand cupping her breast, nestled into his warm, hard body, and fell off the precipice into sleep.

TWENTY-FOUR

Always a light sleeper—it had saved her bacon more than once—Riva woke to darkness. Instantly alert for sounds or movement outside the small tent, she heard nothing but the distant call of a bird.

Hmm. She was sprawled on top of Gideon Stark as though he was a Heavenly Comfort bed. Comfortable he wasn't. He was as hard and unyielding as the ground had been when she'd fallen asleep. How or when she'd climbed on top of him was a mystery. When she slept she usually didn't move for the duration.

Eyes closed, she was wide awake now, nose buried in the curve of his neck. The smell of his skin, musky, something uniquely Gideon, made all her molecules hop, skip, and jump inside her body. What was it about the smell of him that supercharged her? Sex was okay. Sex had its place. But this... She wasn't sure *what* the hell *this* was. Riva felt like an adolescent girl noticing a boy for the first time.

Her knees cradled his hips, her center directly on top of his enormous erection. A full body shudder racked her, and her heart started thumping harder and faster. *His* breathing was deep and even, and he'd loosely draped an impersonal arm over the small of her back.

Somehow her hair had come loose from its customary braid, and hung around her shoulders and over half her face. Not that she could see anything in the pitch-darkness anyway. She really should go back to sleep. They had maybe an hour left before they had to move out. Yeah. Sleep. She needed that hour to reenergize and prep for the day. His penis shifted, through several layers of cloth, as if trying to escape the confines of his pants and get into hers.

I'm so with you there, buddy. Come out and play.

Slowly, Riva slid her hand down his side. Heat radiated through his T-shirt as she lightly explored the part of his abs she could reach without moving off him. And she wasn't going to do that. She liked being exactly as she was. She'd like it a hell of a lot more if they were both naked, and he was awake to participate.

Gliding her fingers under the soft cotton, she was rewarded with hot, satin-smooth skin, and the tantalizing dip between torso and thigh.

Dare she? Would he wake up? She had no idea how hard he slept. Would it be so bad if she availed herself of a perfectly good hard-on?

"If you think for a minute I'd sleep through this, you're out of your mind." Sliding his fingers beneath the cape of her hair, he cradled her nape. His hand rested cool against her hot skin, the abrasion of rough callouses at the edge of his palm like a cat's tongue against her sensitized nerve endings.

Her answer was to lower her lips to his. He plundered her mouth in a rough kiss that made Riva's toes curl and heat blossom on her skin. As he devoured her mouth, he took her marauding hand, pressing her fingers over the rigid length of his penis. With a sharp hiss, he went rigid as she cupped his balls.

His penis, hot and silken, jumped and twitched in her hand, pulsing so Riva felt his throbbing heartbeat in her palm. She kissed him back hungrily, wrapping her fingers around as much of him as possible. Desire leapt and danced inside her, making her fingers tighten around him.

Heat coursed through her, flushing her skin, making her blood surge through her body. It raced through her veins and tingled in her fingers and toes.

He turned his mouth from hers enough to suck in another breath, then plundered her mouth again as he tugged at the waistband of her pants.

Riva lifted her hips to help him, their hands tangling as they both fought with zippers and fabric, need and a driving urgency, all of which made her breathing harsh and her heart pound erratically. *Less haste, more speed.*

She wanted to see him, wanted to watch his eyes as he came into her, but that was for another time. If there ever *was* another time. Now they were both on fire, both fighting for the same seemingly impossible goal. The setting was confined, the darkness complete, the urgency maddening.

Riva whimpered. "Can't—"

"*Must,*" he insisted, freeing himself with one hand, then pushing hers out of the way. The brush of silken flesh, hard and searching against her belly, caused Riva to shudder. "Oh, God, Gideon! *Hurry.*"

"Push th—" He fumbled with his clothing, hers, cursing, frantic. "No. Here. Let me. Lift."

He managed to yank her pants half off. Gripping her thigh, he grunted. "Knees on either—" Her breath hitched as Riva bracketed her knees on either side of his hips. His

skin was beyond sensitized, and he shuddered as she strad-
dled him. There was barely any room to move, she couldn't
sit upright, her head brushed the roof of the tent. Leaning
over him, she dug her nails into his shoulders. Her thighs
trembled as she held her open, pulsing heat directly over
the spar of his penis.

She was wide open, exposed. Her heart trip-hammered,
and she hesitated, feeling naked, vulnerable, and suddenly
afraid. Not of Gideon Stark, but of herself. Too much feeling. Too much passion. Just too damned much. Riva
started to pull away, but he grabbed her waist and held her
in place. The time for hesitating was past. Long past.

"Killing me here." Impatiently he shoved up the sports
bra with her tank top, allowing her to drag in a shuddering
breath. "Arms up!" She lifted her arms so he could pull both
over her head. The moment she was liberated from her
clothing, her hands were back on his chest.

He positioned the blunt tip of his penis at her entrance.
She was tight. He thrust up, opening her wet heat with hard
strokes that stole her breath. It had been years...

She made a choked sound of need as he drove into her.
Calloused hands gripped her ass cheeks. His mouth closed
over her nipple as Riva guided him, then seated herself to
take every throbbing inch of him deep inside her. He felt
huge, stretching her around the spar of his penis. Breath
jerky and shallow, she scored his shoulders with her nails
as he thrust up his hips to meet her.

"Yeah... Wet. Perfect... Christ. Yeah, just like—*That.*"

The sensation was so sharp, so intense for several moments, that she just squeezed her eyes shut and bit her lip
to prevent crying out and alerting two- and four-legged

predators to their location. She dared not move, but her internal muscles pulsed, until Gideon gripped her hips with hard fingers and plunged impossibly deeper, setting her to a manic rhythm.

Lust clawed at her. Riva's fingers dug into his muscular shoulders for balance as their hips moved fast in counterpoint. The slap of flesh and their heavy breathing filled the small space. Her hair whipped across her back and shoulders as she rose and fell. Faster and faster. Teeth clenched, caught in a storm of sexual frenzy, she blinked sweat from her eyes and hung on, giving as good as she got. And God, she got a lot.

The tight, slick heat of her gripped the length of him as he plunged in again and again. And again. Locked into her own world of intense pleasure, Riva rose and fell against him like a savage tide beating against the rocks of lust and desire. Her breathless, barely muffled cries came at her from a distance, mingled with his rough sounds of pleasure. Riva's first, relentless orgasm bore down on her like a Japanese *shinkansen,* a hurtling, unstoppable bullet train, wrenching an explosive climax through her with brutal force.

Shaken, sobbing, her wet face pressed in the crook of Gideon's neck, she felt his entire body shudder and quake in the aftermath.

Gideon kissed her temple as she collapsed on top of him. "Incredible. I think you broke me in half."

"No stamina," Riva said weakly, patting his hip because it just happened to be under her hand. She could barely move.

Gideon stroked his palm down her thigh. "Straighten."

She straightened her legs on either side of him, hooking her toes over his calves. He still wasn't the most comfortable bed, but she was bonelessly relaxed, and quite content to use him as such. Caressing his hand down her bare back, he stroked her ass. Not in a sexual way, but rather to just touch her. Connect. His hot breath fanned her throat, and the only sound for several minutes was their ragged breathing.

The duel syncopation of their heartbeats slowed into a steady rhythm, as if it was one heart beating. *Odd,* Riva thought, yawning. *Odd but interesting.*

Finally, Gideon said softly, "Sleep. We only have another hour."

There was absolutely no way she'd sleep after that. But it was warm, hot really, and dark, and her muscles were already relaxed. Melting into him she closed her eyes.

"You're hard all over," she whispered sleepily. She didn't hear his reply.

A gentle hand shook her awake. So much for her internal alarm. She'd slept like the dead for what felt like thirty seconds. This time, he was leaning over her. Lifting a heavy arm, Riva stroked Gideon's soft stubble. He brushed a brief kiss to her mouth. "Hmm."

Pulling away from her urging hands, he clamped tight fingers around her wrist to hold her at bay. "I'm going outside to take a leak and reconnoiter." His voice was barely above a whisper. "There's hot water so you can wash up. Change your clothes. Eat a protein bar, drink some water. All your weapons are loaded, and there are several new boxes of ammo in your pack, plus water and more protein bars. The compass is on top of the supply box. If I'm not back in thirty minutes, head southwest toward—"

"I'm a trained operative, Gideon." Riva kept her voice as low as he'd done as she sat up. Still bare-breasted, her pants were around her knees and her hair was a wild tangle down her back. Good thing he couldn't see her; she must look like the Wild Woman of Borneo. "Maza is still my directive."

Unerringly he grabbed her by the chin, tilting her face up, his fingers rough on her skin. He'd brushed his teeth, and his minty breath fanned her face. "Fuck your directive. Listen to me, Riva. I know Maza better than your intel does." It was too damned dark to read any expression, but she didn't need to see him to know what it was. Focused, intent. Deadly serious.

"If I'm not back in thirty, head directly to Santa de Porres. Follow the river down. One, maybe two days barring complications.

"Minimum supplies, maximum weaponry. Don't collect two hundred, don't fucking get caught. We have two factions on our asses. On *your* ass. Death will be the least of your problems should either capture you. You hear me? Meet up with your people. Come back for him, if you must. But not alone."

"Where will y—"

"I'll be back in thirty. If not, I'm dead." He silenced her with a hard, deep kiss, then soundlessly melted away.

Riva wrapped her arms around her legs, resting her chin on her knee. "Neat trick, Gideon Stark."

Even though he wasn't Sin Diaz, he had the smarts and the skills to be useful out there. She spared a moment to wonder where and why he'd acquired those skills; they didn't go along with the millionaire playboy lifestyle. But the thought of him dying made her hesitant to involve him in the op. If it weren't for the other visions she'd had of him, which told her he wasn't going to die any time soon, she'd seriously thought of leaving him out of the op altogether.

Riva considered his order for a few moments. She now had seven days, maybe less. Get to Santa de Porres, connect with her team, and bring them back to find Maza.

Considered and rejected. The to-ing and fro-ing would eat up too much time.

The operatives already in Santa de Porres were well into their portion of the operation. They had contingency plans in place should the team in the jungle fail to make their rendezvous with Escobar Maza. Let them do their thing. She'd do hers.

Crawling out of the small tent, she used his thoughtfully provided hot water, chewed a protein bar as she dressed in clean, dry clothes, checked her weapons, broke down the camp, and departed the cavern in less than nine minutes.

"Now," she whispered, adjusting her NVGs over her eyes, and stepping from the shelter of the mine entrance. "Let's see what you've discovered, Mr. Stark."

He hadn't left much of a trail for her to follow. A bent leaf here, a flattened fern there. The man knew what he was doing, and had practically vanished into the jungle. She turned north, eyes scanning the underbrush. Riva had been trained by Jake Dolan, a fellow operative and a tracking expert. She added her own special psychic skill to the mix, something she couldn't share or explain.

A feeling, an innate sense of where someone had passed, like an invisible trail. She was able to track almost anyone, whether it was through a castle ballroom or the deep jungles of Cosio. If there were any clues, she'd follow right on his heels. Watch Gideon's back. From now on, where he went she'd be right beside him. No telling the little lady to stay home and darn his socks while he went off to fight the Bridge Trolls.

She was quite capable of handling Bridge Trolls on her own, but having him at *her* back would make things easier when it came to killing Maza.

TWENTY-FIVE

No moon, and even if there had been, the night sky was blocked by dense tree canopy. It was blacker than Angélica Diaz's heart, but Gideon wore a pair of bulky NVGs, which picked up the unblinking glowing eyes of small animals observing his passage. Not optimal conditions for indulging in deep thinking. Especially since he had to watch not only his back, but his front as well.

He pushed on, a small machete in his left hand, and a larger one slung over his shoulder with his AK-47. He hadn't used the machete as he made a narrow path through the undergrowth and headed back in the direction of the ANLF camp.

No cutting a trail for anyone to follow. He was making as small a path for himself as possible.

The fog dampened his exposed skin and wet his clothing. In a few hours, it would turn to rain, obliterating his tracks and making it even harder for anyone to follow him. It would also make it harder for him to track anyone himself.

There was no damned way she'd wait for him for the full thirty minutes; he bet himself that the second he'd left her, she'd left the mine and was forging her way to the SYP camp alone, fool woman. He shook his head. He had to concentrate on what he was doing, not be distracted by thoughts of Riva. He tried to guesstimate who might have remained patrolling the area, and how many had returned to camp.

Shoving up the NVGs, he pressed a button on his watch to illuminate it, cupping the dial to block the light, and noted the time. The men who'd followed them had had time to return to camp by now. It would take them another half hour to get the men up, weapons assigned... He knew the drill.

He figured the men would be on his ass approximately four hours from—*Now.* Setting the timer on the watch, he turned off the illumination and paused for his eyes to readjust to the stygian darkness before drawing the NVGs down.

As soon as he verified that no one was in the general vicinity and could follow them to or from the mine, he'd return for Riva. Traveling down the river would be their best bet. They'd retrieve the small boat he had hidden, get downriver unseen by either faction, get her safely to her people in Santa de Porres.

Then he'd return to take out Maza while she and her people protected the members of the summit from harm. And when he was done with Maza, he'd deal with Angélica Diaz. Personally.

Neither side knew his real identity, of that he was sure. Maza had no reason to know. Angélica Diaz knew he wasn't Sin Diaz, and his coming to the same realization was probably what had set her off. As it was, he figured she'd been trying to find out who he was, just in case he was worth good money. If she had known he was *Gideon Stark,* if indeed he *was* this Gideon Stark, he sure as hell wouldn't be roaming free.

He'd be sitting in a holding cell behind the barracks right now, waiting for a ransom to be paid. And since he knew Mama, he'd be praying for death. He was damn sure her torture techniques would reach a new high in creativity with him. Both the ANLF and the SYP would like to get their hands on a prize like Gideon Stark. And while he didn't know any more about the man Riva claimed him to be, if he was as well-connected and as wealthy as she'd implied, he was worth a shitload of money in ransom alone. Not to mention access to passwords and worldwide Internet access, if only he could remember. It was only a matter of time before everyone figured out who he really was.

He'd like to fucking know *first*.

Of course, that assumed there was anyone back in Wherever, USA, who *gave* a flying fuck if he was dead or alive to pay a ransom. *That* was the question. His brother had better have a damn good reason for leaving him in this godforsaken place.

Fuck.

Gideon stopped dead in his tracks.

For all he knew, the same brother who had left him there had refused to pay ransom. Seeing Gideon's absence and death as a means to keep the wealth they'd acquired to himself. Even as he thought it, his gut told him he was wrong.

Maybe he *was* wrong, but he knew two things for certain: He'd never have left his brother in this godforsaken jungle, and so far, no one named Stark had come looking for him.

He reined in his suspicion about his brother. Best to fight the closest enemies first, and if he really was this Stark, and he did have a brother, that asshole was nowhere near.

All this damn speculation was useless. One thing at a time.

Right now, staying alive and undetected as they got the hell downriver was priority one.

Riva. He hadn't wanted to leave her, and not only because the sex had been mind-blowing, and he'd like to repeat it again and again, in a more relaxed setting. That was a given. He hated leaving her because she was a woman. That seemed wrong, he knew, because she was a well-trained field operative for this T-FLAC. But he knew that even a woman with deadly skills, one who had family support in these parts, was fair game. She did not. She was alone. Another reason to keep her around was that she claimed to know who he was. He wanted to see if he could mine her for more information.

Her goal was to kill Maza. An admirable goal and one he concurred with. That part was of interest, but what interested him more was something Riva Rimaldi also wanted to know. What the hell did Escobar Maza plan for the summit? Killing one or more members of the group meeting there? Killing them all? To what purpose?

Other delegates would be brought in. There were always other people. Or did he plan a mass kidnapping, with the intent of getting millions from their governments in ransom? He thought more about that and rejected it; the logistics of getting them, hiding them, and dealing with multiple payments made it a poor choice. Death and destruction was so much easier.

And what was the plan?

Sniper? Bomb? Neither were out of the question.

For now, he planned to make a two-click circle around the mine, checking to make sure that no one had followed them, that men weren't waiting to ambush them when they left the mine.

Half a mile from where the earlier skirmish had taken place, he smelled spearmint. Geosue and his ubiquitous chewing gum. *Asshole.* He'd warned him countless times that the telltale smell would get him killed one day.

Today was that day.

Adjusting his weapons, Gideon carefully set each step as he closed in, getting near enough to hear the soft susurrus of the men's voices. Now the question was whether they were ANLF or Maza's men.

Three members of the ANLF. Cesar, Vincente, and Geosue stood in a small clearing. The three men were usually together, causing more trouble together than separately. While not the brightest ANLF bulbs, they took direction well. All three of them were like pointing an Uzi at a target and opening fire. Their MO was mass carnage. Case in point, the slaughter of that small group of SYP soldiers who were merely boozing it up with a few local *putas.*

He knew Andrés's role in that.

Using the NVGs, he scanned the area for another heat signature. Just these three.

Vincente said something about a new whorehouse outside the Santa de Porres place. His voice, low and excited, covered the rustle of leaves as Gideon moved in. Geosue, standing a little apart from the others, glanced up. The sudden stiffening of his body indicated he'd made out Gideon half-hidden in the trees, close enough to touch. Opening his mouth to warn the others, he started to bring up the muzzle of his AK.

Clamping a hard hand across Geosue's mouth, Gideon pulled him into the shrubbery, brought up the sharp knife, and efficiently slashed his throat. Jerking the limp and heavy body backward, he allowed it to drop as the other two abruptly stopped talking.

After a moment, Cesar whispered, *"¿Geosue? ¿Adonde fuiste?"*

He's gone to hell, asshole. He remained still.

The two men weren't complete idiots, and Gideon heard the snick of their weapons being drawn as they looked around nervously. Shots would bring reinforcements. An added complication he didn't need.

"Hey Vincente, Cesar," he called out, and stepped into the small clearing. "Geosue's taking a leak," he told them easily.

Like himself, the men wore bulky NVGs. They looked like space aliens.

"Sin," Vincente said nervously. "What are you doing here? We've been looking for you. Mama—"

Gideon held the blood-edged, razor-sharp knife loosely at his side, watching the man's body language for any sign of attack. "What's happening in Santa de Porres?" he asked easily, not bothering to answer the other man's question. Cesar looked to Vincente for guidance.

"We have Maza pinned there," Vincente told him, not relaxing his stance. If anything, he looked more uncomfortable and ill at ease. He glanced over his shoulder briefly before looking back at Gideon. "He and his men are visiting the new *burdel.*"

Handy. *If* it was true and they were really at the whorehouse. It was a hell of a lot closer than the GPS coordinates Riva had been given for his nemesis's location. Hell, he was already more than halfway there. He'd give Riva an early Christmas present, kill Maza for her, and catch up with her *en route* to the river. "Then what the fuck are you doing *here,* wasting time?" They might've been given the order to kill him, but he was still *el jefe* as far as they were concerned, and his tone and aggressive stance clearly reminded the two men of who and what he was.

Dangerous as hell.

Cesar took a step back, lowering the barrel of his weapon. Vincente ducked his head and shuffled his feet nervously. He didn't drop his hand and lower his weapon completely, but the barrel dipped toward the ground instead of Gideon's chest. "Mama said—"

To eliminate him; yeah, he knew. "*She's* deranged," Gideon stated flatly, keeping his voice low and his body coiled for immediate action. Because of the NVGs strapped to their heads, he couldn't watch their eyes, but he read their body language. "You know this."

They were afraid. His knife hand twitched. Scared men behaved irrationally. "Our enemy is Escobar Maza," he reminded them, to distract them from the dilemma of killing him or obeying his leadership. "I presume we have a plan of attack? Who's in charge? Andrés?"

"*Sí,*" Vincente mumbled reluctantly. The man was more brawn than brain, and he was confused as hell. Used to obeying Sin without question, he'd now been given orders to kill him, presumably by Mama, a woman he'd known and obeyed for a hell of a lot longer. Where Mama was concerned anything was possible. And it was also entirely possible that the order had come from Andrés, whose "friendship" was clearly as false as Mama's claim to motherhood.

A faint brush of leaves to his right alerted him to another human presence. Like an animal scenting his mate, he knew Riva was near. Damn it to hell, he'd given her explicit instructions to go in the other direction. Stubborn. Focused.

Reminded him of someone else...

"Then we must join our men there," he told the two men, covering the snap of a twig underfoot and ignoring the shooting pain in his temple. *"Vámonos. Ahora."* Once the men walked ahead, he'd figure out what to do with them. Kill them as he'd done with their buddy? Or put the fear of God into them and send them back to Mama?

That decision was taken out of his hands when Riva tripped over Geosue's body. With a bitten-off curse, she came flying out of the vegetation as if catapulted. She didn't scream in surprise, but she made a shitstorm of noise nevertheless. Arms extended to break her fall, she crashed into Cesar's back.

TWENTY-SIX

Honest to God, they must've heard her back in the States as branches snapped and leaves rustled like castanets when Riva stumbled over what could only be a body hidden in the undergrowth. She'd seen it a nanosecond too late. *Shit.*

Gideon stood a few feet to the left of the guy she'd stumbled into. The other man started lifting his AK. It all happened fast.

Riva brought the butt of her SIG up, slamming it into the side of the guy's head as he stumbled forward with her weight slamming into his back. He half turned and she hit him again. This time the blow shattered his cheekbone with a satisfying crunch of bone and cartilage and the hot spurt of blood. His weapon went flying.

He cried out in pain and outrage and turned fully to confront her, blood pouring from his nose. Using their forward momentum, she knocked him to the ground, then slapped her palm across his mouth as he started to scream.

His surprise was to her advantage as she scrabbled on top of him, drawing the KA-BAR from the sheath on her leg as he bucked and heaved to get her weight off his chest. With a quick swipe of the sharp blade, she silenced his muffled shouts for help. He went limp beneath her. Riva rose fluidly in time to see Gideon picking up both dropped AK-

47s from the shrubbery. At his feet, the body of the third man lay sprawled on his back, arms and legs out-flung.

He shoved up his NVGs. "I told you to head toward the river," he snapped, his voice low and pissed as he handed her one of the guns.

Holding it loosely in one hand, Riva picked up the SIG and tucked it into the small of her back. "I got lost," she told him dryly. There was no point reminding him that he wasn't the boss of her, and that she had no intention of going in the opposite direction to Maza.

Bending, she wiped the blade of her knife on the dead guy's shirt, then shoved it back into the leg holster. "I thought you might need help."

"I didn't until you crashed the party."

Riva shoved her NVGs on top of her head. "Then you shouldn't have left your trash for me to fall over. Do you think these guys brought friends to their party?"

"Probably not. But let's not wait to find out. Fortunately, no one got off a shot. Come on."

Riva didn't move. "I'm not going to Santa de Porres. Not until after I find and kill Maza." She had suddenly remembered, after he left, that Maza was supposed to be responsible for Gideon's lack of memory. Damn. He *couldn't* come with her after all, not and risk Escobar Maza recognizing him, which would blow her mission. "As much as I'd like the company, you can't come with me. Maza knows you—"

"Or not. That might very well be another bullshit story told to me by Angélica to explain the bump on my head and the lacerations. Who knows how she came to get her hands on me? I suspect Maza had nothing to do with it. But rest assured, I *will* find out."

"Maybe. But what if it's not?"

"I'll risk it." He didn't sigh with exasperation, but Riva sensed him holding in his annoyance. Too damn bad. "I'm not letting you anywhere near that lunatic alone."

"That's heroic, but incredibly damned stupid," Riva informed him tartly. "*I* can't take the chance that he takes one look and recognizes *you*. If he does, my cover will be blown, the whole mission compromised." Without the NVGs on she couldn't see his face. She could barely make out the height and width of him, a denser black against the mottled blackness of the vegetation.

"Then you tell him you captured me and brought me to him as a fucking gift. Tell him whatever the hell you like. We're not separating until you hook up with your people."

Holy crap he was stubborn. "*I'm* trained for this."

"Christ, you're stubborn," he said with irritation, repeating exactly what she'd just thought. "You going in alone is *not* an option, Riva. If Maza and I *have* met, I'll deal with that when the time comes."

Gideon was the first male to insist on taking care of her. Her fellow operatives always had her back, but this was...different. Short-lived, sure. But what relationship wasn't?

A soft, warm emotion unfurled cautiously inside her. It didn't mean anything to him, and it wasn't personal, Riva knew that. Machismo was his middle name, and to him women needed protection. He couldn't know that years of abuse, then many years on her own coming to terms with that abuse, had honed her to a fine, self-sufficient point.

T-FLAC training and experience had added another several layers of hard-ass to her so that she'd reached this stage in her life where she didn't need anyone. Still, the fact that he'd thought to offer his help, his support, warmed her to the core.

She tried one more argument, even while she knew it was futile. "I can't allow you to compromise my mission."

"I know this jungle, and how to cut straight through it to get where you need to go. You don't."

Riva drew her NVGs back over her eyes, as Gideon did the same. "Lead on, MacDuff."

The dark jungle paid attention as they moved through it. Animals generally gave humans a wide berth, but a few curious monkeys trailed them as they walked, swinging from branch to branch overhead.

Riva had been afraid that the kerfuffle with Gideon's men might alert anyone close by, but so far so good. No one was following them, and if they were, they were damn good, because she didn't hear anything to alarm her, and neither did the other jungle denizens.

Without warning, the soft, cool mist suddenly turned into a torrential downpour. Gideon forged ahead, not missing a step as hard drops bounced off his bare head and shoulders.

"Hold this." Handing him her backpack, she took a thin jacket from the bag. After shrugging it on, she crammed a ball cap onto her already saturated hair. Before taking back the pack, she readjusted the NVGs. Slipping her arms into the straps, Riva readjusted the weight on her back. "What's our ETA?"

"It's not that far as the crow flies, but we have a river, a large chunk of mountain, and dense jungle between here and there. Barring complications, as I said, two days. How do you want to play this?" Gideon asked quietly, dropping back to walk beside her.

"I'm going in as Graciela. Let's assume he doesn't recognize you, that *your* people aren't there partaking of the party favors, and that we make it there in one piece. You'll go in as my bodyguard. That'll keep us together for the duration."

"Hell, I'm willing to risk anything at this point."

"Okay, tails it is. Bodyguard."

"What was heads?"

"My...brother." She'd been about to say "sex slave," but decided that was too inflammatory, and far too close to what she'd like the truth to be.

He made a rude sound. "Brother?"

Riva shrugged. Rain pounded the top of her ball cap, spraying off the visor. It beaded on the NVGs, making it impossible to see where she was going. Gideon must have radar, because he didn't hesitate as they moved through the lush, drenched foliage.

Everything but her feet in her waterproof combat boots was soaking wet. Rain sluiced down between her collar and neck, soaked into her T-shirt, wicked by her braid. Not that it was imminent, but she almost felt the heat and smelled the sweet steam of a scalding hot shower. More wishful thinking than psychic ability. Cold water gathered beneath the under-rim of the NVGs, trembled on her cheekbones for a few seconds, then spilled over her cheeks to wash her face.

"Okay?" Gideon leaned in to speak in a normal volume. Or rather she figured that was what he asked, since the thrashing of vegetation, and the spatter and spray of the rain whipping the leaves around them lashed away his words.

Riva gave him a thumbs-up. It was just rain, she wouldn't melt. Catching the edge of his smile, she smiled back as he continued walking. No use complaining about being cold and wet. He was just as wet. Eventually they'd reach civilization. Of course, that didn't mean a respite from the weather or their wet clothing. But a girl could dream.

She'd had it worse. Worse ops. Worse terrain. Worse weather. Worse companions.

As it was impossible to converse, each kept to their own thoughts. Riva's became more and more erotic, and while she was pretty sure she was just using her imagination and it wasn't a vision, the images kept her toasty warm and ridiculously aroused, under the circumstances. Rain ran down her neck, wet fabric clung to her skin from her throat to her ankles, and none of it mitigated the heat generated by her thoughts. She shook her head at the absurdity of the situation, grateful that Gideon couldn't see the images playing in her mind.

Placing one foot firmly in front of the next, she kept her wits about her as best she could and focused on what was ahead, maintaining clear peripheral vision and her weapons quick to hand.

They walked for another thirty minutes. Riva tried to switch from conjuring images of hot, wild, monkey sex to fantasizing about being chin deep in hot bathwater, sipping a cup of strong coffee. Her stomach rumbled as she imagined the spicy smell of hot chili cooking when, without warning, Gideon barred her way with a hard arm across her chest. Riva immediately stopped dead in her tracks, ears and eyes alert.

Adrenaline raced through her veins as she strained to hear any sounds not associated with the deluge. Nothing but pounding rain and the timpani of her own heartbeat, loud in her ears.

Taking her by the shoulders, Gideon turned her to face him, then unhooked his machete and AK from his own shoulder, hanging them on a nearby branch before reaching for hers.

Riva's fingers tightened around the stock of her weapon. What the hell? He gave a sharp tug, dislodging her wet fingers.

Eyes narrowed, she tried to look around his bulk to see if someone stood behind him with a weapon trained on his back. As far as she could tell, they were still alone. Jungle. Rain. Miles and miles of trees bowed with moisture.

Tilting her face up to ask him what the hell, Riva sucked in a wet breath as he reached over to lift her NVGs, shoving them to the top of her head. Her dislodged ball cap plopped soundlessly to the muddy ground near her boot. Rain pounded her bare head as he raised his own much bulkier glasses so they pointed sightlessly up at the black sky.

Blinking up at him, Riva frowned. "Wha—"

Large hands cupped the balls of her shoulders, lifting her to her toes as he lowered his head to plunder her mouth. The shocking heat of his mouth crushing hers spiked her adrenaline in waves of intense pleasure. She was pretty sure steam rose wherever they touched.

Avid lips. Soft breasts to hard chest. His muscular thighs cradled her hips, and the brace of his calf stabilized her wobbly legs. She shivered at the burning caress of his mouth, followed by the light pressure of his teeth scoring her lower lip.

They were going to be ambushed and killed if they kept this up. She had to push him away. Be the trained operative that she was. And she would be. In a minute.

Long strands of his hair brushed her cheek, and she inhaled the unique fragrance of him as he slid his hot palm around the back of her icy neck, warming it in seconds. His slick tongue danced across her teeth, then tangled with hers in an erotic dance. His fingers tightened, his hand so large it almost circled her throat. Riva had a moment when she remembered just how strong he was. It would be nothing to him to snap her neck in the middle of curling her toes with the passion of his kiss.

Right then she didn't give a damn, as long as he didn't stop.

Holy crap, the man was potent.

Twisting her fingers tightly into his saturated T-shirt, she felt the radiated heat of his body through the wet fabric. She inhaled a brief, shuddering breath as his lips skimmed hers before his tongue reclaimed the cavern of her mouth.

She wanted him inside her. Despite the danger, regardless of the rain and lack of a horizontal surface. Riva wanted. Him. Inside. Her. She craved the driving force of his strokes, the fullness of his penis deep inside her, the hard slap of his hips against hers...

She whimpered when he bit her lower lip, then sucked it into his mouth, his tongue tender as he stroked the small wound. She wasn't aware he'd let go of her shoulders, until he skimmed his warm hands down her ribcage. One hand continued over her hip and around to grip the globe of her ass, pulling her up and in, pressing her firmly against the steely jut of his penis.

"This is insane."

He grunted, "Uh-huh," as his other hand skimmed between them to close over her breast. Goose bumps bloomed on her skin as he brushed his thumb over the puckered peak of her nipple. Riva arched her back, pressing his hand hard between their bodies. Not enough. Not nearly enough.

The heat of his breath caressed her chin as he moved his prickly face down her throat. She arched her neck to give him access. To her jugular...

Nerve endings. Lots of them.

The rasp of his stubble on the sensitive spot between her shoulder and neck made Riva shiver. Tightening her fingers against his pecs, she shuddered and closed her eyes. He kissed and licked up her throat, until the heat and wetness of his teeth and tongue were everything, and her body shivered and shook, not with cold, but with passion.

His mouth skimmed up to her ear where he traced the swirls with the tip of his tongue before murmuring, "Unfasten your pants."

"You're *insa—*" Heat and light exploded through her as he bit her lobe.

"Do it, Riva. *Now.*"

Dragging her hand down between their bodies, she paused to wrap her fingers around the hard spar of his penis tenting his cotton pants.

His chest vibrated with a growl. "Uh-uh." Not waiting for a verbal response, he went back to devouring her mouth until Riva's head spun and her heart raced.

With clumsy fingers, she fumbled with the button at her waist, slipping it from the hole as Gideon raked his teeth over her upper lip, then sucked it into his mouth. She forgot what she was doing, and dug her nails into his chest, too aroused to move. Pinching her nipple through several-frustrating-layers of fabric, he parted their lips by a heated breath to rasp, *"Zipper."*

The fabric was uncooperatively wet, the zipper recalcitrant, her hands clumsy, but Riva finally managed to jerk the small tab down as far as it would go. Chilly, damp air hit the relatively warm skin of her belly.

Still kissing her, Gideon slid his hand, cupping her ass over the bare skin of her hip, and into the open V of her cargo pants. She'd gone commando, and the shock of his hand on the naked skin of her belly caused her to suck in a shuddering breath.

Heated liquid lightning shot through her veins, and her breathing came fast and ragged as his finger combed through her pubic hair to find the damp, swollen folds of her labia. Arching her back, she pushed her mound against his palm.

Riva moaned, thighs unlocking with a shudder of surrender. *Moremoremore.*

When he opened her slickness with two fingers, she was unable to drag in a breath, aroused beyond caring of who or what might be watching or listening. She shuddered as he pushed two fingers slowly inside until she moved urgently against his hand, desperate for more.

Curling his fingers, he pressed the hook to the precise bundle of nerve endings, making her entire body clench. Internal muscles clamped down harder as his clever fingers circled and pushed deeper. He added a third finger, stretching her wider.

She wrenched her mouth from his to bury her hot face against his chest, gasping for air as her internal muscles contracted around his hand. When his thumb found the hard bud of her clitoris, the sensation was too powerful.

She had to muffle her cry by biting his chest right over his heart, as her internal muscles clenched tighter and tighter, torqueing until she was panting, and moving against him. His hand was everything.

She climaxed, an endless shimmering cascade of pleasure shooting her from one peak to the next and the next as the rain sluiced over them.

TWENTY-SEVEN

He'd fucking lost his mind. Worse, he didn't give a shit.

"All right?" Gideon murmured, lips pressed to the manic pulse at her throat. In response Riva's internal muscles, clamped, juicy and fever-hot around his fingers still plunged deep inside her. She surged forward, a clutching glide around his fingers that made his dick leap and try to lunge, independent of his will.

His thundering, erratic heartbeat thudded in his groin as her hips bucked. Cool rain dripped from his hair, down his neck. He shuddered, not from the drop in temperature, but from the hard clamp of her small hand now gripped around the bulge in his pants. Painfully hard, relief inches away, he let the hot wetness of her encompass his fingers and imagined his dick plunged deep inside her pulsing heat instead of his fingers.

Head tilted to grant him easier access to her throat, she whispered hoarsely, "Don't..." as he started to withdraw his hand from her clutching internal muscles.

The wet suck and pull made him reckless. And reckless in the jungle was foolhardy. Here one either ate or got eaten, and the diners were out there somewhere, hot on their asses. Foolish? He didn't give a fuck.

Her next climax almost dislodged his hand, but she rode it to the end, shuddering and coming apart in his arms. He held her tightly against his chest as ripples worked through her body. He savored every jolt, every quiver of release as she pressed her face to his chest. Gideon sucked in her scent as his body braced hers as she came.

Minutes later, she lifted her head. Cheeks hot, skin dewy with sweat and rain, breath ragged, she managed to whisper, "Dear God, have we gone completely insane?"

"I'm guessing that's rhetorical." He eased his hard-on as best he could behind the now uncomfortable tightness of his pants. Her internal muscles still milked his fingers, making him hard as a pike, and just as fucking unfulfilled.

"As much as I'd like to keep going, preferably when we're horizontal and dry, we have to keep moving." The pounding rain had morphed back into a light drizzling mist, doing nothing to cool his heated skin. His heart beat uncomfortably fast in anticipation of a good hard fuck. Wasn't gonna happen. Not now.

Riva pulled his head down, then kissed him deeply, her tongue avid and aggressive. Her pussy clenched around his hand. Her response shot his heartbeat even higher. He craved bare skin, needed to taste her all over. His fingers pushed deeper, and she moaned into his mouth, body arching into his hand.

Finally she tore her mouth free, took a step back and zipped up her pants, the sound harsh in the close confines of the trees. "Next time, finish it," she said. "But let's not do it with men who want to kill us hot on our trail."

Christ she recovered fast. He was a stroke away from coming right there, and she was as nonchalant as if they were strangers introduced at a cocktail party. "It's a date."

They both knew it for the lie it was.

There'd be no opportunity in the foreseeable future for that to happen, and later... She'd go back to what she did, and he'd... He'd resume the search for his past.

Standing a yard away, Riva adjusted her glasses over her eyes. Unlike the bulk of his, her NVGs were sleek, high-tech. Gideon pulled his into position as well. After retrieving their weapons and packs from where they'd been irresponsibly tossed in a fit of insanity, they resumed walking. The rain mimicked them, suddenly going from the powerful downpour to almost nothing at all.

He waited in vain for her to say something about being unexpectedly fingered. But she didn't seem fazed by it at all. Riva Rimaldi was a cool customer. The fact that she could go from hot to cold in an instant shouldn't piss him off. So why the hell did it?

He adjusted his NVGs and was hit by the musky scent of her juices on his hand. Gideon wasn't sure he appreciated a woman who treated sex as a man did. Which was ridiculous. Why *shouldn't* a woman have the same on/off switch as a man did? Especially this woman, considering her line of work. She was complex, and he wanted to know her. All of her. Wanted to know what made her tick. What she was thinking when her beautiful face went blank. Next time they made love, he wanted to see her eyes, the windows to her soul.

For a few minutes as they walked, he fantasized about making love with her in full daylight, the sun gilding her skin and tangling in her loose hair. Yeah, he'd definitely make love to her in the daylight next time.

If there ever *was* a next time. Gideon knew the fantasy of making love to her somewhere clean, safe, and deadline-free was just that—a fantasy, a luxury he'd never attain. The clock in his head clicked away the seconds. In a few days, if they lived through this dangerous mission of hers, they'd go their separate ways. He doubted Riva would give him a second thought when they parted.

He shoved aside a branch, heavy with moisture, then used his upper arm to wipe the droplets off his face, almost dislodging the NVGs. He shoved them on top of his head, able to see shapes and tones of color now. He took a moment for his eyes to adjust, then twisted his backpack around so he could unzip it and toss the NVGs inside. While his pack was open, he withdrew his canteen and drank deeply.

Daylight came slowly to the jungle. Pale yellow filtered almost imperceptibly between the thick dark leaves and branches overhead to spotlight, with delicate, dusty spears of white gold light, lower branches and small, scurrying animals.

"Water?" He offered the canteen to Riva as they resumed walking.

"I have my ow— Sure." She took it and drank, then capped the flask and handed it back to him. For a half a heartbeat, a pinpoint beam of sunlight caught the tips of her eyelashes like gold dust, entrancing Gideon before she moved through it. His heart skipped several beats as he took a mental snapshot. Mental snapshots? Heart skipping beats? Jesus. He was going fucking insane.

Going? For all he knew he'd *always* been insane. How did he know how he was with women in general? Perhaps he was the love them and leave them type. Shit. Maybe he had a wife and kids in America who thought him dead all this time. Maybe...

Useless to speculate until he had solid facts.

One thing he knew for sure—he wasn't going to dick around with Riva. Tough as she was, she had a soft, fragile inner core that she protected at all costs. He wasn't going to be the man to shatter that.

"It would be a hell of a lot quicker if we started hacking at this," she pointed out, oblivious to his observation. "Your little friends are miles behind us, and apparently in no hurry."

His *little friends*? A group of violent killers and drug dealers? "How do you know?"

"I'm psychic, remember? Seven of them. Andrés is with them. They went to some whorehouse last night and they're sleeping off hangovers."

"Christ. I'm gone one damned day and they can't keep their dicks in their pants. The good news is, if that's the case, they can't want to find us too badly."

"They will in about five hours." Riva shot him a sidelong glance as she pulled the saturated weight of her braid over her shoulder and used one hand to squeeze out the water. Much the same way she'd pumped his dick earlier. "You're complaining because they're undisciplined? It's a good thing they are, today, isn't it?"

"Yeah." He had a cockstand again just watching the rhythmic movement of her fingers. "Of course. But I thought I'd whipped them into better shape than this. Getting drunk before a sortie will get them killed."

"Good for us, then," Riva said unsympathetically.

Gideon swept his hair out of his face. He didn't have a tie, and it hung wet to his shoulders. He suddenly wanted to be shaved and clean, appropriately dressed— What the hell? Who was the suave, urbane man he'd just imaged?

And whoever he was, was he the kind of man Riva dated? He doubted it.

"What kind of men do you date?"

She almost face-planted into a tree trunk, her head whipped around so fast. "Who has time to date between flying off to Cosio or doing a halo drop into Uzbekistan?" She frowned. "Why? Want to go steady?"

"I'm not ready to go steady yet, Rimaldi," he teased. "But we could see how the prom goes and take it from there."

"The chances of making it out of the prom alive are becoming slimmer and slimmer." She hesitated, then said, without a glimmer of humor in her voice, "In the interest of full disclosure... I'm not particularly lovable, so I wouldn't hold my breath on any hope of future...romance."

Not particularly lovable? What a fucked up thing to say. "Who fed you *that* bullshit?"

"Sometimes it's best to take a declaration at face value, Stark. This is one of those timα" Her face lost all expression as she stopped mid-step. Eyes glazed, she stared off into the middle distance.

The hair on Gideon's arms rose as if touched by an electrical current. He put a hand on her upper arm, then dropped it when she remained stiff in his hold. The same woman who'd melted over him earlier?

It was over in a matter of seconds, then she resumed walking as if nothing had happened. An intense scrutiny of her profile told him that whatever that was, was now gone. "What did you just see?" The need to touch her was astronomical. He reached out again, this time to tuck a loose strand of hair behind her ear. His fingers lingered on her cheek. Her skin felt soft and supple and seemed to warm to his touch. She didn't pull away, but he sensed that she wanted to.

"Are things going even *more* sideways? More important, is something going to happen to *you*?"

"I rarely predict my own future and if I do get a glimpse, it's usually only pertaining to the people around me. Not necessarily a prediction about myself."

They stood close enough for Gideon to see a glint of something he couldn't name in her dark eyes before she blinked it away. Now her gaze was cool and steady. Unemotional. Had the brief look been fear? Longing? He had no idea. She was the one trained to read microexpressions. He suspected she was trained to hide her own from everyone else, too.

He wanted to explore her depths. Peel her carefully and deftly apart, layer by layer, until he uncovered what was really at her core. And while his thoughts were certainly carnal, in this instance he was more interested in knowing more about *her*. The thought of unraveling the mystery of who Riva Rimaldi was under her prickly, über-efficient persona fascinated him.

Gideon resented whatever the fuck fates had brought him to Cosio. *What*ever, *whom*ever, had derailed his life—whatever the fuck that had been—that brought him to *this*. Standing in the middle of a danger-filled jungle with a beautiful woman he'd never come to know, taking away any chance of ever knowing.

Fate had handed him a fucked-up buffet filled with people like Mama and Maza, when his gut now told him they—and the goddamn jungle they frequented—were a side-trip on the road to his real destiny. The how, the why, and the when were open questions at this point, but he was going to change his fate. That much was certain.

Riva? At the very least, she was a passing breath of fresh air. Maybe she was more. He didn't need one of her visions for the answer. His gut told him he'd find out. Soon.

"Do you have something for that headache?" she asked quietly.

Yeah, she was terrific at reading *his* expressions. His book wasn't closed because he didn't want her to read him, it was closed because he had no goddamned idea what any of this was about. Big fucking difference. "My head's fine. Tell me what you predict for us the next few days."

"I see changes. Big changes. That could mean death, or the end of something, and the beginning of something else." Taking his wrist, she removed his hand from her face and resumed walking, shoving branches and vines out of her way with thinly-veiled impatience. She kicked at a coiled snake sleeping in her path, as big around as her arm. The fat ribbon of black went airborne for several seconds before it fell over a nearby branch and slithered away.

"Even people who claim to want to know their future don't want to hear the truth. I don't sugarcoat."

No, no she didn't. He found that trait both annoying and endearing. He watched her for a moment. Mission notwithstanding, he could at least enjoy the sway of her tight ass as she forged ahead of him. "How long before Andrés and the others reach us?"

"About five hours."

"So a little skirmish to whet our appetites. We should near the location Maza told you he'd be just before dawn."

"If Angélica doesn't join them," Riva said, as if he hadn't spoken. "If that happens, they're going to be on our asses as if jet-propelled. She hates you like the fiery jaws of hell. She won't stop until she kills you. Or you kill her." Riva paused to look back at him. "This doesn't come as a surprise to you, right? She'll kill anyone who gets between the two of you, just so she can have the satisfaction of doing the job herself."

He shot her a cocky grin. "Comforting to know my impression of Mama was dead on target. She's a sadistic, vile bitch."

"Don't smile, it's not funny."

"Knowing I'm *not* related to that woman is funny as hell, I assure you. I'm willing to bet this is one of the biggest reliefs I've ever experienced in my life. Past and present."

"Let's get the lead out. Hand me that machete." She held out her hand. Gideon slid the large, razor-sharp knife from the leg holster and handed it over, hilt first. It looked ridiculously oversized in her slender hand. For a moment he considered offering to exchange it for the smaller blade he carried, then imagined her response to that, and kept his mouth shut.

"They'll." *Slash. Slash. Slash.* "Find us whatever we do." *Slash. Chop. Slash.* "Might as well get ahead faster."

Soon, Riva built up a rhythm, while he admired the flex and twist of her biceps. He knew how heavy the blade would become, and he was used to it. Without saying a word, he took out the smaller machete and went to work beside her.

They walked for twenty minutes, slashing and hacking their way through thick ferns, air roots, and dense vines until he saw the quiver of her arm. She wasn't used to the weight and the resistance when the blade hit a tree limb.

"Let me know when you want me to take a break," he offered, just to see what she'd say. They'd had this conversation a dozen times along the way. Both determined to take the lead.

"Sure."

He laughed. "And hell will freeze over before you ask for my help."

She stopped in her tracks, and he almost walked into her back. "Nope." She handed over the machete, which he slid back into its sheath, then shook out her hands and arms. "Hack away. I'll conserve my strength for later." She stepped into a nearby shrub to allow him to take the lead.

As he came abreast of her, Gideon reached over to cup her chin. "Jesus, you're a piece of work." Holding on to her chin, he lowered his head and kissed her, hard, until they were both panting. Lifting his head, Gideon, wiped moisture off her lower lip with the edge of his thumb. He loved the slightly dazed look in her eyes.

Voice husky, he murmured, "Later..."

TWENTY-EIGHT

He took a few steps past her to take the lead, swinging the machete as if it weighed as little as a steak knife. A swoop of red and blue flew directly over her head as a parrot flew low. It landed on a branch, tilted, and gobbled up a skinny jade-green lizard that had been sunning itself on a spindly branch.

Lizard-tail hanging out of its mouth, the parrot opened its wings, looking like the flick of a can-can dancer's skirts, and took off. Talk about fast food.

Her stomach growled. The scant meal of protein bars in the dark hours seemed a long time ago. "Any more protein bars?" Riva knew she sounded surly, and didn't give a damn.

"Help yourself." He pointed over his shoulder.

Unzipping his backpack, Riva pulled out a bar and broke it in two. Handing him half, she rezipped the pack.

Riva unwrapped the dense bar, stuffed the paper in her front pocket, then took a big, dry, bite. Who the hell did he think he was, flirting with her, and making promises they both knew he wouldn't keep?

She chewed the mass that seemed to grow larger in her mouth with every chew. Unhooking her canteen, she drank the last few inches of water before reclipping it.

She'd already shown she was available for sex whenever the hell he felt like putting his hands—and anything else—on her. He didn't need to waste time romancing her. It wasn't as if flirting with her, sweet-talking her, was an investment in their future.

Hell. She was so freaking irritated she just had to say it. "You know, there won't be a *later*."

He glanced at her, studying her eyes, then looked away with a shrug. "You don't know that."

"How do you know I'm not seeing it?"

"Because when you have a vision you sound...certain and cool. Now you're just pissed."

"Not pissed at all, Stark. This is it. All we have is between now and Escobar Maza. *That* is the duration of *us*. After, there will be no more. Making it seem like there's some kind of future just annoys the living crap out of me."

"Why?"

"Because people like me don't have happy endings. Violent endings, yes. Happy? Never."

"Here's a vision. You in heels and a beautiful dress. Red. Short. You do have spectacular legs. Might as well show them off."

"You've seen them. Seen everything there is to see, as a matter of fact." Of course he'd like to see her dressed as a woman. He was a macho guy, wasn't he? He'd want perfumed skin, fluffy hair, and a skimpy dress. And a damned thong, or hell, he'd probably want her commando, even in a dress and heels. *Especially* in a dress and heels.

Wrong time. Wrong place. Definitely the wrong woman.

"I'm a counterterrorist operative. I don't own either."

He shrugged broad shoulders. His easy expression and body language said I'm teasing you, but his eyes read deadly serious. It was the eyes that told his deepest thoughts. "Easy to remedy."

The conflicting microexpressions confused the hell out of her. She didn't like being off balance. "I don't do red dresses and I don't date."

"Ever?"

"Ever."

"Since when?"

"Since none of your damned business, Stark. Why the twenty questions?"

He glanced back at her as he slashed a clean stroke through the vegetation blocking their path. "Ask me anything you like."

Riva worked predominantly with men. She was used to testosterone-fueled alpha males. But she didn't understand what kind of weird pull *this* alpha male had on her. He was no more handsome than Hunt St. John, no smarter than Kyle Wright, his body wasn't that much more buff than Rafe Navarro.

She didn't just feel an incredible sexual attraction for Gideon. It was as though their very DNA spoke the same language. If she believed in such nonsense, and she hastened to assure herself that she damn well didn't, it was as if they were soulmates.

Riva didn't want to go there, nor did she want to dig deep into her psyche for answers. "That's hardly fair," she told his back. "You don't have any answers."

"Then I can ask you twice as many as you don't ask me."

Riva gave an inelegant snort. "You were known as a playboy. I can see why."

"I was?" His shoulders tensed for a moment. "Hmm. You'd think if that was the case I'd be better at this."

"You're not terrible at it."

"Ah. Damned by faint praise. Want to wield this for a while?"

Not really; she'd been admiring the play of his muscles as he swung. "Thought you'd never ask."

He was ridiculously piratical-looking. Swarthy beard, long hair, a big frigging knife that could be a cutlass in his hand. All he needed was a gold hoop earring in his ear, and a half-clad, skimpily dressed woman draped over one arm, or that parrot she'd seen earlier perched on his shoulder.

"There's a forfeit," he informed her solemnly, handing over the machete.

Riva's heartbeat kicked up as she curled her fingers around the thick handle, dropping her hand to hold the giant knife at her side. A heavy weight seemed to be pressing on her chest, and her skin felt hot and tight. "I don't play games. If you want quick sex, sure. But don't flirt with me. I'm not equipped to deal with it. When I'm out of my depth, I tend to get cranky and argumentative."

He slid his hand under her braid to cup her nape, pulling her inextricably closer. "I don't think you're ever out of your depth, Riva Rimaldi."

"Cranky, argumentative, and *homicidal,*" she assured him. Why was there a damned lump in her throat? He was about to kiss her again. Apparently he felt entitled to do that whenever the hell he felt like it. She really should discourage him, but damn it to hell, she *liked* it when he kissed her. Which made her conflict even worse and soured her mood further. She didn't like entanglements. Direct. To the point. That was her style. That way you didn't get hurt. That way you didn't care when things didn't work out. "Hurry up and kiss me so we can keep moving. I don't want to be in a sensual haze when your little friends get here."

"Sensual haze?"

"I'm armed and extremely dangerous, Stark. Kiss me. Or don't."

His hazel eyes looked as impenetrably green as the surrounding foliage as he gave her a considering look. Every flick of his eyes felt like a physical touch. He took in her narrowed eyes, the slope of her nose, then his gaze dropped to her mouth.

Riva's mouth tingled. She didn't do it voluntarily, but her lips parted in anticipation.

He lifted his head. "I'll take a rain check. We really should push on. After you, ma'am." He stood aside for her.

Riva wondered how much strength it would take to use the machete to slice him off at the knees.

It was arduous, sweaty work. After several hours of pushing, ducking, and circumventing, they were both breathing hard, sweat dripping off their bodies.

Even though the sun was high overhead, it wasn't visible. But Gideon felt its sweltering rays filtering through the tree canopy. The wet earth gave up its moisture, surrounding them like a sauna.

"I've *been* in a sauna," Gideon said quietly, more to himself than to Riva. "After Zak and I did a winged-suit BASE jump in Voss. Middle of Norway's most spectacular fjord landscape. Then we went to this incredible sauna..." The realization stopped his forward movement for a moment. "My God. That's a real memory as Gideon."

Flushed cheeks made her eyes look deep and mysterious. "That's good news." Her breathing was more labored now as they climbed to a higher elevation on the slope of the mountain. "Maybe it'll all come back to you." She wiped her sweaty face with a bandana, then shoved it into her back pocket. With her T-shirt clinging to her breasts and midriff as if painted there, she looked heated, disheveled, focused. And so sexy. Gideon added permanent erection to his list of discomforts.

Their clothing, which had dried briefly after the rain, was soaked again by mid-afternoon, between sweat and the moisture dripping off the vegetation. They'd been walking since well before dawn, eating and drinking as they went. She'd taken back the machete a while ago, gamely hacking away at the endless greenery. While Riva had yet to complain, he could tell that she was tiring. Determined to find Maza she refused to take a break.

"How does anybody find their way around the jungle without GPS?" The way she said it indicated it was more casual observation of the obvious than conversation. At least she was too tired to sustain her pissy attitude for very long.

Adjusting course, Gideon slashed a path through a mass of frilly wild orchids the rich, deep color of a good Burgundy. "There are landmarks if you look hard enough. Or go high enough to see them. Anybody out here without at least a compass could wander around lost for years. Can't see any landmarks from the jungle floor even though we're halfway up Qhapaq. About ten thousand feet above sea level now."

He pointed left. "Mountain peak is that way. And a deep valley will be coming up on our right in a little over an hour. You can't see either for the trees. You'll hear the falls long before we reach them. Rest your arm, we can push through here."

Riva dropped her arm, her fingers gripping the machete at her side. Since his arm felt as if it weighed a hundred pounds, he could only imagine the strain on her slender arms. She hadn't flagged once. His admiration for her went up another notch.

"The falls are about half an hour from here." He heard them over the susurrus of the leaves, and the chirp and whir of insects. "We can rest up there for a couple of hours."

"A couple of *hours*? Are you insane? I don't need to rest. Let's just push on. Angélica just found Andrés and the others. She's on a rampage and has death and dismemberment on her mind. She'll intercept us before we make it to Maza's camp. Gideon, we *have* to keep moving."

Hearing that Angélica was on the move tempted Gideon to encourage Riva to go ahead while he circled back and took them all out. He was damned if he did, and damned if he didn't, but he couldn't second-guess his decision to stay with Riva to the end. Stay the course.

"We've been walking for over fourteen hours. I'm tired even if you're not." Not true. His adrenaline was charged, and he was ready for that fight. He was also used to this environment. But trekking through the dense vegetation at this elevation was taxing for anyone, especially someone not used to the higher altitude.

They were in for high-octane, danger caught as they were between Angélica Diaz and Maza. He didn't know what Riva's limitations were; probably none, he acknowledged ruefully, but discovering them in the middle of a shitstorm would prove fatal. Her disbelief was evident in her tone as she swung around to look at him. "You're *tired*? There's no damn way I'm going to stop to take a tea break when Maza is waiting for me and Mama is on our asses. You need to pop some vitamins and eat your Wheaties, Stark."

He suppressed a laugh, then sobered. "How long 'til the ANLF reaches us if we don't go any farther?"

"We *are* going—" She threw up one hand. "*Fine*. Possibly three hours. A little more."

"Anyone from the SYP patrolling in that length of time?"

She closed her eyes and sighed. "Not that I can see. But that doesn't mean things can't change on a dime. There are hundreds of variables. My predictions aren't always foolproof, and full disclosure: I don't always see everything that might go into an outcome. There could be elements I'm not aware of, factors that I don't see until it's too late."

"Got it." He waited until she opened her eyes again, her gaze connecting with his. "We'll stop. Eat. Drink. Rest. They can run around looking for us. Hopefully the two groups will find each other, and we won't have to do any work at all."

"I'd prefer not to leave that to chance. I'll kill them myself while you put your feet up and sip your Earl Grey."

Gideon grinned. God, she was perfect. Where had she been all his life? " We'll stop at the falls long enough to grab a hot meal and change our socks. Fair?"

"If you insist."

If he knew Riva, and he was starting to, it would be quick. Quick, but he'd get more liquid and some protein into her. Let her body adjust to the climb. They'd check their weapons and be ready. He might not be psychically inclined like Riva, but it didn't take a psychic to know they were in for a bloodbath once they reached Maza.

And that would be after the battle that would doubtless be joined when Mama reached them.

TWENTY-NINE

It was slow going, but they kept moving. Six hours in the jungle felt like twelve hours anyfreakingwhere else. The stifling wet heat made it feel even longer. Just standing still made Riva sweat.

She felt an urgency, as physical as a timer in her head, counting down the minutes to whatever hellacious act Maza planned. Speculation on why there was the insistent tick, tick, tick in her head kept her mind occupied as they mindlessly cut down any obstacle in their path.

Since they were gradually climbing, she attached her headset, hoping the higher elevation and fewer mountains to block signals would help with making contact with control or her team. So far there hadn't even been a faint crackle to indicate a live feed. And if there was a drone overhead, she was unable to see it for the canopy.

But what was Gideon's deal? What motivation did he have for staying with her? She had no freaking idea. Now that he knew he was Gideon Stark, and no longer Sin Diaz, he no longer had a dog in this fight. "You should head to Seattle and find your family."

Turning his head, he gave her a puzzled look. "That's random. What brought that on?"

"There's no reason to put your life in danger." Riva's heart galloped, creating uncomfortable hard knocks against her breastbone. The pressure in her chest hurt, making her eyes sting.

She didn't *do* emotion. Didn't *do*—God forbid—crying. Why the hell now? With *him* right beside her? "You don't need to be here. Go home, Find your brother. Have a nice life."

He stopped her by curling hard fingers around her upper arm, and drawing her to a standstill. "And leave you alone to find your way to Maza's camp? With the ANLF on your ass, and us not sure if Maza hasn't found another psychic, rendering *you* superfluous? Yeah, right." He gave her a hard look, his lips thin with anger. "I should go find a Starbucks and grab a latte."

It would be childish to peel his fingers off her arm, so instead, she gave his hand a pointed look before forcing herself to meet those damned X-ray eyes of his. "Any of those things with Maza is a possibility. But I'm not your problem, Stark."

"True, you're not. And you're right. I don't give a damn if the ANLF and the SYP murder each other in their sleep. Since you seem to have given this some thought, let's see where it takes us. I'd—"

Not wanting him to continue, even though she'd opened this can of freaking worms, Riva put a hand on his chest. Beneath the thin damp fabric of his T-shirt, his body felt hot, his muscles rock-hard. She dropped her hand. Big mistake touching him. Constantly on the razor's edge of lust, she was better off not having physical contact.

"No," she told him firmly. "Let's *not*."

She knew what she was asking, but it wasn't fair that he, of course, did not. Inexplicably, *not* acknowledging that they had no emotional attachment was less painful than knowing for a fact that they were two ships passing at full speed in the night. In this case, ignorance was bliss.

Riva told herself firmly that Gideon Stark was not breaking her heart *right now*. Poking at a wound, visibly bleeding or not, was unproductive. "You're determined to play Galahad and escort me all the way," she said, keeping her tone light with effort. To prove to herself that she could, she walked away from him a few feet. He let her go with ease.

"Thank you." Her smile might be forced, but it said no big deal. "I appreciate it. Please don't get killed on my behalf," she added lightly as she turned in the right direction and forged ahead, only to be halted again with his heavy hand on her shoulder.

"What's going on, Riva?"

Throat tight, she shrugged. His fingers tightened. "It doesn't make sense for you to put your life on the line for a stranger, that's all. But since you can't be dis—"

His mouth came down, quick, decisive, and hard on hers, effectively cutting off her comment and setting her on fire at the same time. His tongue slid and wrapped around hers, as his teeth scraping her bottom lip. Every cell in her body focused on their intimate connection. It wasn't just a kiss. Sin...Gideon—it no longer mattered—branded himself upon her synapses.

When he pulled back, giving her a second to catch her breath, his gaze bored into hers. "You sure you still feel like a stranger?"

Riva pressed her lips tightly together. Way easier to hold back the instant reply from escaping her lips than to keep it from reverberating in her whole body. They were far too intimately connected to be mere strangers now. Death, danger, sex, and emotions she'd not yet had time to fully contemplate while they were running for their lives, all churned within her.

"You have another life you don't even know about yet. Don't throw it away before you find out." Riva turned away from him and pushed forward into the trees.

Hours went by without a word. Sometimes they were slashing at dense vegetation, and occasionally they were able to make good time because the understory was thin and easy to traverse. No humans to deal with, which was good news. And there were surprisingly few animals to be seen, but she knew they were around. Various birds' calls, insects' clicks, and monkeys' chatter came in surround sound.

Over three hundred tree species, shaded by enormous Kapok, Palm, and Brazil nut trees, some towering hundreds of feet over the jungle floor showed the vast diversity of flora in the tropical rain forest of Cosio. Intertwining branches and aerial roots kept them upright in the thin soil.

The tree canopy was choked with woody climbers, bromeliads, orchids, and ferns, all fighting for a sliver of sunlight. Amidst the dense trees and undergrowth it was hard to judge elevation. Hell, most of the time it was difficult to see a patch of blue sky. But Riva could feel the elevation change in the burning of her quads and the need for her lungs to suck in more air with the effort of each step.

As they moved through the dim world, surrounded by dappled sunlight and a green mass of rippling leaves, Riva felt as though she walked underwater. Underfoot, the soggy, muddy ground was covered with leaf litter and a lattice of exposed roots. When—no, *if,* Riva amended silently to herself—she got out of here, she was going to spend a long week on a beach somewhere with endless blue sky.

A howler monkey, following them for a mile, perched on a branch ahead of where Gideon slashed through the branches. The monkey screamed like a woman in pain, making the hair on Riva's nape stand up as it had done for the last hour. "That damn monkey does that on purpose to get on my nerves. Look at it. It's daring me to shoot it."

"Tasty when cooked just right," Gideon told her, not turning around. "But resist."

"No problem." Riva had tasted worse, and she knew a gunshot would bring everyone to the party at a run. She gave the monkey a threatening glare. The animal seemed to meet her eyes head-on, then lunged, screaming, for a higher branch, then a higher one, until it disappeared, screeching all the way.

It wasn't the two humans who'd scared off the nosy monkey though. With a frustrated howl of its own, a sleek, spotted ocelot streaked past Riva's boots, ran between Gideon's feet, and hurled its sleek body up the trunk of the tree after the monkey.

"There. I sent my representative to take care of that little—" She cringed as the monkey did its howler thing, making her hair stand on end again. "It's a dog-eat-dog world out here, isn't it?"

Gideon glanced back. "Don't touch that frog," he pointed. "It's poisonous."

"Pretty, though." Riva gave a tiny blue, leaf-sitting frog a wide berth. Jesus, there wasn't a square inch of jungle that didn't contain some kind of thing that was innately dangerous or actively trying to kill them.

For the last several hours their breathing had become increasingly more labored, as they climbed. To reach both low-lying Abad or Santa de Porres, they had to go over hill and dale. The summit of Qhapaq was twenty-five thousand feet. Clearly Maza wasn't going to position his camp at the top, so they'd find him somewhere between the ANLF's camp, Santa de Porres, and the summit. According to the coordinates she'd been given, the SYP was approximately thirteen miles away as the parrot flew.

Here the understory opened up enough that they didn't need to hack and slash. Her shoulders were grateful for the break. "Are you sure we'll make it to the SYP compound by tomorrow?"

"Yeah. If it's where I think it is, there's a mining road a few clicks away from there. We'll hit that, then walk in. It's a smart place to house his people, well hidden, high vantage points, and a road directly into Santa de Porres."

Riva caught up to walk beside him. Sweat ran down the muscular column of his tanned throat in shining rivulets. She had an overwhelming desire to lean in and lick it off him. Instead, she stepped a little more to her left so they weren't walking quite as close. Still, the image of licking Gideon, of tasting his hot, salty skin, of gliding her hands down his chest, of feeling the weight of his sex in her hands... She used her bandana to wipe the sweat off her own face and neck.

The heat was making her lose all common sense and that damn ticking in her head and feeling of urgency was making her crazy. They had to pick up the pace. Had to move faster.

Just because she was slightly—*slightly*—distracted by her walking companion, didn't mean she could allow herself to get reckless.

"You know what's weird. We haven't seen anyone. I don't mean your little friends, or the SYP. *Indigenous* people. Where are they?"

"My fath— No." Gideon shook his head as if to readjust his thinking. "*Carlos,* Angélica's late husband, got rid of them," Gideon said, clearly oblivious to the sexual time bomb walking beside him. "Killed, sold, scared the shit out of them. Most, I imagine, lived simple lives, way the hell and gone from civilization. He came through and wiped them out. They wouldn't fight for him, wouldn't cooperate when he squeezed the emerald miners and charged massive protection money that put most of them out of business. Eventually they either died off or relocated to less hostile environments."

"He sounds almost as charming as the *Angel de la Muerte.*"

"Worse. He was a sick fuck. She tried to make out that I was a chip off the old block. The best—or in their case, the *worst*—of both of them." He ran his hand over his mouth, disgust in every line of his body. She observed the tightening of his features one by one. Riva read intense regret there.

Gideon's face showed him suppressing the depth of what he felt. His brows were lowered and drawn together, nostrils dilated, lower jaw jutted forward showing his anger.

Puzzlement. Betrayal. All passed so swiftly over his features that they'd be impossible to see by someone not trained to do so. Riva's heart ached in empathy.

"I wish to hell I could forget what I've done for the last five months, as easily as I forgot who I was before." His tight voice didn't betray the intensity of his feelings as much as his unconscious facial expressions did. But it was there all the same. "But that's going to take some fucking doing."

Riva didn't ask. She knew Sin Diaz's reputation. Knew what he'd done, knew what he was capable of doing. He might be Gideon Stark, but for five months he'd been the Ghost, Sin Diaz, and what he'd done even in that short time period was horrific.

"You'll figure out how to live with that knowledge." Her fingers brushed his and without looking at her, he turned his hand so they were palm to palm. A shiver of longing cooled her skin as he slid his fingers between hers. "You'll have to," she told him softly. "Otherwise it'll tear you apart."

Riva realized she'd never held hands with a man in her life. It was the weirdest, sweetest sensation to be tethered to Gideon this way. It couldn't last, but she enjoyed the moment while it did. "I know an excellent shrink if you're interested."

Gideon lifted their joined hands to kiss her knuckles. The brush of his mouth on her skin felt as though she'd just walked through pure sunshine. Odd. Disconcerting. Annoying that her heart skipped an ecstatic beat for no real reason.

She pulled her hand free to unhook her canteen from her belt. He shook his head when she offered it to him first.

"I might take you up on that offer."

Unlikely. Her shrink was in Montana.

She'd forgotten her canteen was empty and she hooked it back to her belt. The distant sound of pounding water intensified her thirst.

Gideon used his machete to point out an enormous red and black banded tree snake coiled beneath a dense fern. Sidestepping it, they kept moving.

Riva was breathing as erratically as if she was nearing the finish line of a 30K marathon. She tried to tell herself that her inability to calm herself had nothing to do with her reaction to Gideon and everything to do with the extreme physical exertion it took to move forward and up the slippery trail.

It was a good thing she was trained for inhospitable terrains, high altitudes, and the unrelenting pressure of being in danger 24/7. She'd studied what she could about the SYP on the flight from Montana to Bogotá, but she hadn't done the necessary cross-training, strenuous exercises to acclimatize herself for scaling the mountain.

So be it.

The good news was that higher elevations meant that there was an excellent chance that the homing beacon in her molar would get through the signal jammers, and activate. T-FLAC would pinpoint her location and know that she was not only alive, but either close to, or with, Maza.

When she and Gideon took that short break, she'd try her comm system, see if she could contact control directly. "The ANLF would be very surprised to discover where we're heading."

"No shit. We patrolled for months trying to find the SYP's main camp outside town. Never did. I doubt the ANLF will follow us all the way in to Maza's camp. But then Angélica's batshit crazy, so perhaps she would."

The sound of a million bees vibrated the air, transferring to the ground beneath Riva's boots and then through her body like a tuning fork.

"That's the falls," Gideon told her unnecessarily. "We'll have to take a bit of a detour to get there, but not far. It's about a quarter mile west."

Another delay. "I'd rather skip—"

Gideon gave her a hard look. "So you've said. We're going. Admit it, you're flagging. What the hell would you do right now if we were attacked by twenty of either side?"

"I'm armed."

"And exhausted. Don't fight me on this. I don't have the energy to argue with you." She saw now that like her, he'd had little sleep, and subsisted all day on a few protein bars and adrenaline. "You know damn well that neither of us has the physical reserves to take on anyone until we refuel and get at least an hour sack time."

He was right, damn him. "A fifteen-minute power nap," Riva agreed with great reluctance. "If we don't get the lead out we'll end up being the filling in a tango empanada."

"There's a cave directly behind the falls. Not much in it. I haven't had time to stock it properly, but enough to get us a filling meal, and there's a sleeping bag—"

"We're not staying long enough to get cozy," Riva insisted, although the prospect of not putting one boot in front of the other, and not swinging the machete for a little while was seductive. In the past forty-eight hours, she'd not only fallen from a helicopter, she'd been on the run. That too-short nap twelve hours ago wasn't going to cut it for much longer. She was trained for high exertion, high adrenaline ops and no sleep, but he was right. She was exhausted. A power nap and some protein would go a long way in helping her to keep going. "Fifteen to twenty minutes and we want to be on our way. Seriously, Stark. Twenty minutes max."

"Hearing you call me that is surreal. It doesn't quite fit, but then neither does Diaz," he said almost under his breath. "Whatever you want." He switched gears.

Whether that gear-switch was about his identity, or the fact that she refused to budge on a lengthy sleepover wasn't clear.

"This dual personality crap is going to drive me crazy until I sort it out," he muttered, proving that no matter what he said and did, that thought never left him. She couldn't begin to imagine how Gideon must feel, with so many questions and no one to supply the answers.

"And that's not gonna happen soon." Using his fingers, he raked his hair off his face. "This way." He headed off, not glancing back to see if she followed.

Riva knew she'd follow this man anywhere.

Damn. She was in deep, deep shit.

THIRTY

The closer they got, the louder the roar of pounding water became. Gideon paused as they cleared the trees to give Riva a moment to take it in. "Spectacular, right?"

"Beautiful," she agreed as she scanned the area, not particularly admiring the falls, but more alert in the open. He supposed in her line of work she was always ready for attack. They had that in common.

A narrow strip of lush grass grew right up to the rocks and boulders lining the edges of the falls. Torrents of white water poured like a silky bridal veil from a hundred-foot drop, then crashed to stair-step off shiny boulders, as big as houses, below. From there it boiled and tumbled another fifty feet in a lacy froth over smaller boulders, then surged between heavily wooded banks in its race to join the river as it curved out of sight.

The cascade—a force of nature as beautiful as it was deadly—sprayed them where they stood, two hundred feet away. Dropping her backpack, Riva lifted her face to the cooling mist. Gideon was more interested in the sublime, peaceful look on her upturned face than he was in the majesty of the falls.

His chest felt heavy, looking at her. How could she claim she was unlovable? And who was the dick who'd convinced her it was true? She might be prickly and hyper-focused, but she was also— *Stop right there,* he warned himself. *Just fucking stop.* This wasn't a trip to Disneyland. This situation had nothing to do with them personally. Both had agendas and while they weren't mutually exclusive, after it was over, *they'd* be over. He had no business feeling anything other than admiration for her mad skills. Not until he ascertained what waited for him in that other world. The world he'd left behind.

She spread her arms and did an uncharacteristic twirl. Gideon knew he'd ventured into unknown, dangerous territory when his heart swelled with emotion. *Fuckit.*

Within minutes they were soaked to the skin. It was refreshing after their long sweaty, clammy walk, but not exactly relaxing for him. Her nipples, responding to the sudden cold and wet, peaked beneath her T-shirt, and with her wet hair slicked back from her face she looked like a flesh and blood statue come to life.

Riva was so beautiful she stole his breath. Gideon choked back a half laugh at his sudden romanticism. It would be nice if he remembered how he'd been with women beyond five months ago, because this poetic mental masturbation felt new. But what the hell did he know? Ascencion's whorehouse was his yardstick.

If he could convince Riva they could spare an hour to rest, that would give them time to indulge in a few of his fantasies before the things went sideways when they finally reached Maza's camp.

He might've guessed Riva wouldn't waste time admiring nature for long. She touched his forearm and motioned eating. Then twirled a finger to indicate*hurry the hell up.*

He grinned, admiring her ass as she bent to retrieve her pack from the long grass. Stretching out his hand to cup her butt, he jolted upright as the crack of a gunshot pierced the din of the falls. They both reached for the weapons at the same time.

A dense group of men, dressed in camo, weighed down with weapons, bandoliers of ammo, and bulky with flak vests, fanned out from the trees a hundred yards from their location. Blood in their eyes, clearly given the directive to kill, they'd made good time from their little party earlier and caught up.

Hurtado. Fernando. Javier. Emilio. Juan. Damián. The rest—a couple of dozen or more ANLF soldiers—were immaterial. Gideon knew all the men, had patrolled side-by-side with them for months, laughed with them, drank with them.

Now he was going to kill them before they killed himself and Riva.

Andrés, beside the squat form of Angélica, both dressed head to toe in Kevlar, took the lead.

"Well, hell. The party just started." Glock in one hand, he pulled the MP7A1 submachine gun from the leg holster, and returned a barrage of shots.

Instinctively he slammed his forearm hard into Riva to push her back. Instead of being knocked on her ass, and the fuck out of the way, she staggered backward, caught herself, and came up on one knee, firing her SIG at the group emerging from the tree line.

Gideon indicated they do a quick tactical retreat to find cover. Riva grabbed him by his backpack, yanking him back, urging him to run in a crouch with her toward the boulders beside the falls. "Keep shooting, I've got you. There's better cover behind us."

Gideon continued firing, allowing her to back him up. She maneuvered them into a decent position behind a large wet boulder, then released her hold to crouch low. Six feet of muddy scrub grass separated them from a five-story drop to the base of the falls. Heavy spray made visibility a bitch, as water obscured the scene and ran into his eyes. Sliding on their bellies in the tall grass, they took up positions. Then, with just their eyes above the grass, continued to fire.

DM11 rounds were capable of penetrating twenty layers of Kevlar with 1.6 mm titanium backing. Handy, since the ANLF were all fucking wearing the vests. He and Riva were not. They had T-shirts and skin to protect *their* vital organs.

The 4.6x30mm 2-part controlled fragmenting projectile increased the chance of a permanent wound cavity and doubled the chance to hit a vital organ. The muzzle energy was comparable to 9x19mm Para-bellum rounds that the *other* half of the ANLF were firing.

It was a clusterfuck of gigantic proportions.

The air smelled more of humid vegetation than the visual of blood and gore. Wiping water out of his eye, he checked out the men still shooting at them. They'd taken a stance about seven hundred feet in front of the tree line.

He fired a spray into the crowd. Other men fell as they squeezed off answering shots. His weapon, one that half the men who shot at them also fucking had, had a muzzle velocity of 720 over two thousand feet. That went both damned ways. So, not only were they outnumbered, they were out-fucking-gunned.

Two men he'd trained and another, a sort of buddy of his, Emilio, went down hard. "Nothing personal, *amigo*," Gideon muttered under his breath. "Three more down."

Riva shot off the top of Damián's head in an amazing piece of marksmanship. Damián's skull exploded like a piece of ripe fruit and he crumbled where he was. Followed by the man behind him, whom she shot in the neck. "Nine down."

Dense spray blanketed the entire scene, soaking clothing and weapons. Water. Blood. Organic matter. The grass and low-lying vegetation was slick, slippery underfoot. Flat on their bellies behind the rocks, he observed the men inch forward. Wet, of course, but he and Riva weren't slithering, and sliding, and falling on their asses like the men shooting at them.

"Who do you want?" Gideon shouted to Riva over the roar of water and the fusillade of gunshots pinging off the rocks nearby. Shards of stone flew in the air to mingle with the heavy droplets of mist.

Brandishing an AK-47A, Iker, a man Gideon had shared an evening meal with four days ago, yelled a war cry as he raced toward them, semiauto firing a steady stream of bursts of light. Riva's bullet felled him mid leap. He dropped into the tall grass and lay still.

"Six," she shouted, without pausing, then answered his question. "From Andrés's left."

A fair division of labor. And one he'd congratulate Riva on. If they made it out of here alive. The odds weren't in their favor.

She returned a barrage of shots as she ducked behind a small boulder. Too damned small. No time to pause to look for better cover. The falls and rocks, with a fifty-foot drop, were directly behind them. The ANLF advanced, firing.

"You're bleeding!" Riva shouted. Her eyes must've been on him for a split second because the observation came as she was reloading and focused on their adversaries.

Yeah, he'd felt the icy-hot slice of a bullet across the top of his shoulder and the chips of rock nicking his skin. But right now he was filled with adrenaline. Blood, no pain. Riva, on the other hand, had a gash on her left cheek that bled profusely, either from a bullet or a sliver of rock. Blood dripped off her chin, and he doubted she even realized she was bleeding. She got off three shots in quick succession, so close Gideon felt the heat of the bullets against his upper arm.

She'd already balanced speed within the context of how many shooters, how far away they were, and how quickly they were advancing. Clearly she wasn't trying for a bull's-eye. She was aiming for their chests. He had the same rule: Shoot as fast, and as many, as he could. Kill, maim, or in-capacitate.

Two men to the left of her quarry dropped, bullet to the chest for one, through the eye of the other. She was a good marksman. Good to know, but he couldn't hang around ad-miring Riva's skill. He had his own people to kill. His rule of thumb was to hit each of them at least once. They couldn't be allowed to run away. This was the last stand at the OK Corral.

"Good one!" Riva yelled as he got a two-fer by shooting through and through and getting two men with one round.

Gideon processed, at ultrahigh speed, the rapidly un-folding events. The men's fast advance. Angélica cradling the Uzi like a beloved child, hatred and grim determination painted like a neon sign on her butt-ugly face. Gideon squeezed off a measured shot just as she shifted. Instead of striking her, the shot hit the man on her flank. *Fuck.* She kept running, nimbly jumping over his body as he fell.

While Gideon's focus was on Angélica, he couldn't exclude secondary, lateral, targets. Tunnel vision wasn't an option.

Angélica was his primary target, but her men also shot at them and those men were starting to fan out.

Late afternoon painted the robin's egg blue sky with crimson and black streaks, magnifying the droplets so they looked like tiny glass marbles with swirling colors as they dropped. The whole damn scene looked like Dante's inferno.

The cacophony of sounds—the thunder of the falls, the incessant whiz of bullets, the cries of the men hit, the screams of the men fallen—was joined by the screeches of several large, carnivorous birds circling overhead.

Bullets ricocheted off tree trunks, scattering bark and leaves. Jagged chunks of their sheltering rock flew as someone got off a good shot at them.

Gideon looked right. Seven men flanked Angélica.

Missed her, but got three in rapid succession.

Bam. Bam. Bam.

He looked left, including Riva in his scan in passing. She remained firing and focused. He looked right again. Squeezed off another shot. No one went down. Someone screamed from the left, his voice high-pitched and faint over the sound of the water and the cries of swooping birds.

Gideon looked for the men with Angélica, then realized she was no longer where she'd been moments before. He frowned. Andrés, too, was MIA. With any luck, he hoped, dead. "See Angélica or Andrés?" he yelled as the unmistakable burn of a bullet creased his upper arm.

"Fucking hell." The Glock dropped from his hand in reaction. His left hand worked just fine, and he continued squeezing the trigger of the MP7A1, spraying the remaining men as they zigged and zagged to reach them.

One by one, he and Riva took the remaining men down. It had been one hell of a fucking battle, but there was no joy in looking over the bodies on the killing field. The men had fought liked trained warriors, full of lethal intent, yet they'd been ineffective. Relief that gunfire was no longer whizzing at them was fleeting, because Mama and Andrés weren't lying among the dead. Riva put a hand on his forearm. "They split."

"Fuckit."

"Let's get going," she responded. "Before the bitch from hell returns. I couldn't sleep now anyway."

He grabbed her by the hand. "Come on." He took three steps in the opposite direction of where they were supposed to head.

She shook her head, taking one step with him but otherwise standing her ground, trying to free her hand from his grasp. "We're going the other way."

"Detour."

"No time."

"Yes. Time. No one will find us there. We'll be there in ten minutes. Cool bath in clear water. Supplies. Bandages. Let's go. Now. And goddammit Riva, we're staying there for two hours. We need to regroup and your head needs a bandage," he said, his words urgent, but his tone calm.

Gideon realized that for the first time in months, he felt right. He was acting true to himself, and that feeling gave him the power to look in her beautiful, dark eyes and know he was making the right move. "Because right now, I don't give a damn about the ANLF, or the SYP, or Mama, or Maza, or whether I'm Gideon Stark or Sin Diaz. All I care about is Riva Rimaldi and the world can goddamn stop turning, but I'm going to damn well focus on you."

And he knew, even as he spoke calmly and rationally, somewhere out there, Angélica Diaz and his ex-best fucking friend Andrés, were planning something much, much worse than a surprise attack with a hoard of their men.

THIRTY-ONE

The evening sun painted the falls a shimmering, ever-moving metallic copper. Thundering water competed with the raucous cries of scavengers who'd come to feast on the dozens of bodies.

She and Gideon had separated an hour earlier, although he'd tried to talk her into them going together. They'd agreed on a half-mile round-trip, then each went in a different direction, forging into the trees to see if they'd run across either Angélica or Andrés. She hadn't. But unless Gideon had killed them in the last hour, they were out there, waiting. Probably for full dark.

Even softly-filtered through the misty spray of the falls, the visual that greeted her return to the scene of battle was the stuff of nightmares. Riva had never before witnessed such a surreal picture of chaos and carnage. Death, yes. But this didn't compare to the dead people she'd seen in her job. And she'd seen plenty of dead people. As justified as those deaths had been, sometimes she still had nightmares about the bloodshed she'd been part of. What worried her was that each time it seemed to get a little easier to stomach. She doubted this would fall into the *get a little easier to stomach* category.

She'd never observed animals in their native habitat doing what wild animals did. It was as fascinating to watch as it was repulsive.

Keeping an uneasy eye on the more than a dozen yellow-headed vultures circling overhead, she saw a dozen more that had already staked their claim on the corpses, plucking out eyeballs and tearing off chunks of flesh. None seemed to notice or care that a couple of living humans walked among them. She wanted to keep it that way.

Two black and white king vultures, with their showy, multicolored heads, ripped open bodies with their strong beaks so their yellow-head brothers could feast. The watchful eyes of the jungle denizens gave her an itch in the middle of her back, as if she had a target drawn on it, and one that would attract more than one kind of predator.

Getting the hell away from here, and killing Angélica and Andrés, would alleviate that problem.

Determined to kill Gideon, they wouldn't stop hunting him until they accomplished their goal. She'd be collateral damage. They might've made a tactical retreat, but Riva knew with utmost certainty they were just biding their time. She also knew with the same determination and certainty that they had to be eliminated before they negatively impacted her mission.

Gideon emerged from the trees up ahead, and Riva went to join him, ignoring the carnage around her, weaving and dodging as she went. Running right now would be a big freaking mistake, but her heart raced as if that was what she was doing. Annoyed by the profound relief she felt at seeing him, she intersected him on the flat, grassy stretch between the tree line and the rocks at the edge of the falls.

"Nothing?" She gave him an inquiring look, one eye on the predators spread out over the grassy area a couple of hundred feet away. Not nearly far enough, as far as she was concerned. Animals were as untrustworthy and unpredictable as humans.

Gideon shook his head, grabbing her arm to guide her around a determined column of army ants, a formidable force on the jungle floor, and even more so now as they swarmed over the bodies like a living blanket.

Damn. So he hadn't seen the duo either. Since it was a waste of time attempting to be heard, he pointed to the falls, and they headed in that direction together.

The stink of the bodies, simmering like stew in the heat and moisture, was already strong enough to make her eyes water and gorge rise. The animals and insects, however, liked it as they feasted on the all-they-could-eat buffet.

Growling and hissing, two pumas fought over a bloody arm, even though there were plenty to go around. The ground shifted, undulating like a living creature as the insect population made their own claims.

A jaguar, sleek and beautifully spotted, flattened its ears, growling low in its throat, yellow eyes watchful as they gave him a wide berth. He wasn't afraid, and he sure as hell wasn't leaving his meal. Mouth and chest wetly red, he remained poised to attack anyone or anything that came near.

Five curious red-and-green-winged macaws flew in close, as if on a reconnaissance flight, then swooped upward. Seed-eaters, they had no interest in carrion, and were not willing to challenge the feeding predators. They were dispatched with speed by an arriving harpy eagle, gray wings spread in aggression.

"There's a small cave just behind the water," Gideon yelled, indicating a midpoint with the barrel of the MP7A1 in his right hand. In his left he still carried his Glock. Riva held both her SIG and KA-BAR knife, the AK slung over her shoulder where she could easily reach it. There'd be no letting down her guard until they were safely in Santa de Porres.

She lip-read the words she missed, and nodded before he stalked off, long legs eating up the ground, putting as much space between them and what was behind them as possible. Taking a moment, she removed her headset. There hadn't been a crackle so far. Disappointed that even at this elevation she couldn't make contact with control or her team, she twisted around to shove the comm into an outside zipper compartment on her bag as she caught up with Gideon.

The thin, wet cotton of his tank top clung to his hard body and his damp pants hugged his muscular legs and prime ass. Water gleamed on his bronze skin, defining his shoulders and highlighting the curve of his well-defined biceps. All ruined by streaks of dried and wet blood. His face, his shoulder, both arms...

"You okay?" He shot her a puzzled glance.

Good thing she wasn't a woman who blushed. It would be unfortunate if she killed herself falling down the waterfall because she was staring at his ass. *Get a freaking grip, Rimaldi!* "Where?" she mouthed. She didn't see any cave opening as she searched the surrounding area.

He pointed about twenty feet straight ahead, into the middle of the falls. "Not huge, but big enough for our needs right now." Oblivious as to where *those* words just took her, he stopped at the edge of the grassy bank. The thirty-foot-wide cataract of opaque water plummeted in a straight, flat sheet from a plateau a hundred feet above her. The water at the first base spumed over an almost level talus of large boulders, and from there cascaded over the rock shelf another five stories, in a churning froth, down to the base.

"Here." He held out his hand as he stepped onto a wet boulder as tall as he was. "Take my hand. It's slippery as hell right here, and I'm too tired to climb down there to get your broken and battered body if you fall."

Riva put her hand in his. His fingers closed around hers. Ridiculously, holding his hand made her feel invincible, and at the same time hellishly weak. Which in turn made her want to pull away from him. Her balance had always been exceptional and training had honed it. Still, she stepped where he stepped on the slick rocks, and didn't look down.

"Why would I fall if you won't, Stark?" she shouted, clutching his hand because, damn it, it felt good to do so. "Are you going to keep going macho on me until I take you down? I *am* a soldier, remember?"

"Yeah, and a damn good one. Maybe I just need to hold on to you so *I* don't plummet to my death, did you think of that?"

"I think you're full of crap." Since most of their dialogue was swept away in the roar of water, the exchange had no heat.

He pulled her up beside him onto a flat-topped rock a couple of feet in front of the sheet of water. "There's a deep hole three feet to your left the minute you get inside. Stay right behind me and keep right to circumvent it. Ready? Hold your breath, going through."

Riva barely had time to suck in a breath before he yanked her from one flat surface to the next, pulling her through the curtain of water. It felt like walking into a brief, hard, cold shower.

The temperature dropped a pleasant ten degrees inside the cave. The moving shadows of the water closed them off from the drama outside. Riva glanced around as she squeezed water out of her braid. The cave, approximately fifteen feet wide and ten feet deep, rose to about a foot over Gideon's head. The front section was wet, the back, moderately dry.

The changing coppery shimmer of the water made it appear that she was inside a translucent stained-glass window. The movement painted shifting lines of bronze on Gideon's face and arms.

Maintaining eye contact, a predatory gleam in his eyes, he shrugged off and dropped his backpack. "Drop the bag."

Riva shivered. She was soaking wet. Cold. The pack was heavy, and she was so damn spent she could barely blink. "Give me a sec—"

"Time's up." Ripping the straps of the heavy bag off her shoulders, and down her arms, he let it thud to the ground, then pushed her backward against the rock wall. "What the fuck do you expect from me when you look at me like that, Rimaldi?"

The naked hunger on his face stole Riva's breath. Inappropriately, her stomach growled. "I'm starving," she said thickly, struggling to toe off one boot. No easy task. It was wet and still had the laces tied. She almost gave herself a hernia forcing it off her foot.

"So am I." Rough and urgent, Gideon closed his hands around her face, curving them to shape her skull. His more green than hazel eyes sparked hungry and slumberous with desire. Heat emanated from his body, and his musky, emphatically male odors of sweat, rain, wet cotton and his own essential, indefinable *him* sent Riva's senses swimming. "God, so am I."

His mouth softened, sensuous and unsmiling. "Keep wiggling against me like this, I'm going to go off like a rocket."

Riva tried to toe off her other boot, but she was distracted by his mouth, and the way his hands molded her body. And, if those things weren't enough, she was totally taken off her game by the tantalizing, and out of reach, press of the hard bar of his penis.

"That's it," he growled, plundering her mouth with no more preliminary forays.

Heat prickled her skin as if she had severe sunburn. The warm slickness of his tongue clashed with hers. He tightened his fingers, pulling her hair in the process, and the small sting shot her arousal up several notches.

He bit her lower lip, then lifted his mouth from hers a fraction of an inch. "Take down your hair," he ordered in a harsh, gravelly voice as he dropped his hands to grip her hips, and slid his knee between hers to press at the juncture of her thighs right where she needed it.

Squeezing her eyes shut, Riva shuddered, the sensation so piercing, so *necessary,* she couldn't move. Seconds later, she pulled her braid over her shoulder. Gideon's dark eyes held hers as she slid the elastic off her braid. Her wet hair brushed cold against her throat as she picked it loose with trembling fingers.

He ran a line of hot kisses up the underside of her raised arm as she unwound the strands. Goose bumps sprang up when he stroked his tongue up the sensitive skin of her inner arm. Something sweetly painful unfurled in her chest as he kissed his way from her inner elbow, to her forearm, to her hand, to her temple.

Combing his fingers through the bumpy wet strands, he smiled a predator's smile, spreading her hair around her shoulders like a cape. "Spectacular...better than I ever im-agined."

Her hair, too dark, and far too thick to cut practically short, had always been the bane of her existence. As a teenager, Riva had wanted silky, blonde hair. Now she was glad for the long black weight of it as it fell between Gideon's fingers.

With a shiver, she arched her throat for his mouth as he gathered her hair in both hands and resumed kissing her. He surrounded her. The blazing heat of his body scorched her from breast to knees, setting her internal thermostat to a roiling boil. Squeezing her thighs around the muscular pressure of his knee, Riva wrapped her arms around his waist, then curved her hands down to grip the flexing muscles of his butt.

Fully aroused, the hard length of his penis pressed against her thigh. Riva stroked a hand over his hip and ran a finger along the edge of his arousal. "This. Now," she instructed, shifting to grant him better access.

His expression tense, she read his searing, primitive intensity on the taut muscles of his face. A look that heated Riva to her very core.

His chest vibrated, but he reached between them with one hand to undo the top button of her pants. Straightening his legs, he stood between her spread feet.

Struggling, she couldn't get the second damned boot off. She whispered, kissing the tense cords of his neck as she worked at it with her bare toes, "You know, this always sounds better in theory than in application." Hard fast sex was good. Hard fast sex on a horizontal surface was better.

"Wrong."

He was a magician. With sleight of hand, he made her pants slide down her legs to her feet. Her *booted* feet. "It's not..." Possible.

Hmm. Apparently, it was.

Still kissing her, he slid a large, warm hand down her thigh, then hooked his palm under her knee. Ahh. *That.*

Riva stood on tiptoe and slid her unshod foot through the pants leg, freeing her up to wrap her leg around his waist, opening herself. Taking him in her hand, she stroked along the smooth length of his jutting penis, then cupped the weight of his balls.

Gideon flung back his head with a groan, then brought his hand down to cover hers, squeezing his fingers hard over hers. "As amazing as that feels, I want *in*." Gripping her hips in both hands, he lifted her up, then brought her down, hard, so he entered her.

"Now. You. God. Don't care if I never." He thrust deeper. "Remember. Anything. But. This."

Nice words.

She'd learned not to listen to nice words men said while having sex.

Instead, she focused on the feeling, the sudden fullness that was a perfect fit and managed to steal her breath. What was even more amazing was how powerfully, yet tenderly, he manipulated her body with his arms and legs as he pistoned into her. He held most of her weight with his hands, while the dank wall of the cave gave her stability. All she had to do was lift her legs, hold onto his shoulders, and cross her ankles around his lower back. He did the work, plunging into her again and again, until her moans joined his, until he slowed, until all they were doing was leaning against each other, breathing harshly.

When she could stand on steady feet, she moved away first, inching along the wall to the side of him. Riva put her foot through the empty pants leg, pulled them up, dropped down to remove her other boot, and started to laugh. "I can't for the life of me undo these wet laces, and yet—" She indicated the other boot, which had landed six feet away.

Gideon crouched beside her and deftly undid the laces. While his head was bowed to do the job, her fingers hovered over the crown of his head. In a wild-hair burst of temptation, she wanted to comb her fingers through the chocolaty strands. Uncharacteristic, and not in her wheelhouse to be sentimental or tender. Sex was merely scratching an itch and dear God, he knew how to scratch with precision.

They both knew the score.

It was just sex, Rimaldi. Just sex. No cuddling, no romance to follow. Just the way you prefer it. Try to remember that.

A vision came. Clear and sharp. A hotel room. Sunlight streaming over a wide bed. Air conditioning on high. Sweaty skin, avid mouths. Pulses pounding. The vision of them making love. Lingering. Tasting. Touching. Breathing him in. Riva's heart raced with the start of what felt like her first panic attack. *Dios...*

"Thanks," she said easily and dropped her hand before he noticed she was about to pet him. *Foolish, foolish woman. Get a damn grip.*

Tossing the boot in the general direction of the other one, he pulled off her sock. "These are wet. Have another pair?"

"I d—" Hand warm and strong, he cupped her foot in his palm. She cleared her throat. "I do. Yeah."

Stroking his thumb in a sensuous path along the side of her instep, he met her eyes. Hot hazel. Short, black spiky lashes. Hot intent. "That was just an appetizer," he murmured, in an intimate, smoky voice.

Carefully, Riva pulled her foot from the cage of his fingers. She wasn't touchy-feely. Never had been, but the urge to fling herself into his arms, to feel...safe and cared for was overwhelming. Holy crap. What the hell kind of thought was that? Her insides knotted, and her chest ached. All of which pissed her off.

Getting to her feet, she curled her toes on the cold, damp rock floor. "Good to know you have some stamina, Stark. I'm absolutely starving. We need to get cracking. Food. Rest. Go."

For a few moments he looked up at her, his forearm braced across his knee. "I needed that," he murmured, not addressing her statement, but on a tangent of his own. Rising, he looked as though he wanted to reach for her. Riva stiffened, but he merely combed back his hair with both hands. "If I'd waited another five minutes it would've been too late."

"Fortunately, I felt the same way." *Dios,* she did *not* want to analyze what had just happened. Didn't want to talk about getting and giving, needs met, expectations unmet. "Do you always Monday morning quarterback after sex?" Riva waved the words away with a quick flourish of her hand. "Never mind. Don't answer that. None of my business." Rubbing her hands, she went to her pack and unzipped it. "I could drop nose first onto this hard ground. I need real food, what do we have?"

"MREs." Gideon went to the small pack he'd secreted in the cave a couple of weeks earlier, watching as she unpacked, not dry clothing or food. No. Her weapons and cleaning cloths for her guns.

He hid a smile. "Camp stove. Coffee. Chocolate bar." In the last light of the dying sun, she looked like a pagan goddess sitting there, glossy black hair, a shiny, patent leather rippling waterfall down her back, skin creamy and luminous, cheeks flushed, pale bare feet looking sweetly innocent. Something roused in his chest, a sensation sharply sweet and unfamiliar.

Gideon didn't know what drew him to her so viscerally. It wasn't the sex, good as that was, or her appearance, sexy, strong and badass as she wanted to appear. There was something in her eyes when she watched him. An aching loneliness. A look that said, I'll hurt your ass before you hurt me. He tried to imagine Riva without her shields up, and couldn't. But damn, he wanted to *see* her—*really* see her.

For a brief moment, when her eyes had fluttered open, when she was disheveled and vulnerable, he'd seen the naked look there. No wall. No smart come-back. Just honest emotion.

She'd lowered her gaze and when she looked at him again, it was the same hard-ass Riva staring back at him.

He started foraging for the coffee and food. When he looked back, she was sitting cross-legged on the floor.

Spreading out a cloth, Riva laid out a neat row of weapons. Her SIG Sauer P230SL, KA-BAR, .40 S&W Action semiauto sniper rifle, a mini boot knife, and a tactical boot knife. Several boxes of ammo, cloths, and oil.

Soaking wet, exhausted, she took care of her weapons before she took care of herself. She picked up the SIG first and removed the magazine. Glancing up again, she shook her head. "Coffee? You buried the lead there, Stark." She removed the tube of lubricant, squeezed some onto a cloth, and started meticulously lubing all the parts. "Let's have it. I'm so desperate for it I might just eat the grounds dry."

Without looking down, she rebuilt the magazine, then reassembled the rest of the SIG. Laying it aside, she reached for the KA-BAR knife. "Want me to do yours for you?"

Yes, he did want her to do his. Not his weapons. Him. Why the hell was she so prickly? She had no problem enjoying sex, but anything beyond the actual act seemed to make her uncomfortable. Anything remotely playful or a show of affection made her uncomfortable. In fact, once sex was over, she damn well acted like it hadn't even happened. "I'll take care of mine."

The fact that Riva approached sex as a man did, didn't sit as well as it should. Less so each time they were intimate. Hell, wasn't that what he'd thought would be the ideal situation with a woman? *The perfect relationship.*

So what the fuck was his problem? Gideon wasn't a guy who liked to cuddle post sex, he didn't think. But Jesus, not even a wow? Or a *thank you*? Or peck on the cheek? She'd barely caught her breath before her clean dismount.

Wham, bam, thank you, man?

Good thing he had a healthy fucking ego, because that kind of response was a ballbuster. Another man might think he hadn't satisfied his lady, but he knew better. He'd seen it in her damn half-unguarded sultry smile when her body was racing to that fucking perfect moment. The corners of her luscious lips eased up ever so slightly right before she came.

Twice.

The interior of the cave now glowed a deep maroon as the dying light pierced the veil of water at the entrance. "How about a bath before it gets dark?" He figured they had about half an hour before night fell.

Yeah, dick, seeing her naked will help your ego no end. Go for it.

The quick look she shot him was filled with surprise and pleasure. His sulking dick stirred.

"You have hot and cold running water in here?" Sarcastic shot fired, she returned to what she was doing. After placing the knife on the cloth, she picked up the small boot knife, inspected it, gave it a wipe, and replaced it. Quick and methodical. Clearly she could fieldstrip and clean her weapons quickly and in the dark if necessary.

"I have a perfectly shaped, smooth as a baby's butt, bath filled with cool water right there." He pointed at what looked like a shimmering sheet of gleaming copper just inside the fall of water. The one he'd warned her about when they'd arrived.

"Four feet deep. Here—" He tossed her a small bar of soap. She caught it overhand. "Soap."

Riva uncurled her long legs to get to her feet, and standing on tiptoe, she gave him a quick, sisterly kiss on the cheek. "You're a freaking prince, Gideon Stark."

When she started to step away, he wrapped an arm around her waist to hold her against him. "We won't always have to make love on the fly, you know. There's a wide bed with clean sheets on it in our future."

She didn't pull away, and while she looked right at him, Gideon knew she was hiding behind those dark, long-lashed eyes. "You must be having different psychic visions than I do." Reaching back, she unpeeled his fingers from her hip. "I don't see that at all, Mr. Stark."

He smiled. "God, you're a hard nut. Yeah, you see *exactly* that, Miss Counterterrorist Operative. I saw it in your face over there."

"The only vision I see is me not getting that hot cup of coffee you promised me in the next ten minutes." Bending, she gathered her weapons and put them away, the cloth folded and neatly tucked beside them.

Gideon pulled out the sleeping bag and supplies from the waterproof backpack he'd left there weeks earlier, while she went to the back of the cave to retrieve her boots.

Returning to her pack, she removed the dry clothes she'd need. She moved with the grace and speed of a dancer, and he couldn't tear his eyes off of her. Economical, no movement wasted. "Coffee brewing, food out—what a good little camper you are. Let's lay out clean clothes and the sleeping bag, and save water."

"You're that disciplined? I'm impressed."

"It'll take a few minutes. I don't know about you, but right now that water looks inviting as hell, I'm starving, and I'm exhausted. Let's get our priorities in order, because if not, we'll both still be hungry and dirty two hours from now when we wake up half naked on the dirt floor."

"We don't want any light in here once it gets dark, right? It'll show through the water and let everyone know exactly where we are."

"Good thinking."

Gideon turned the small stove down so the flame barely showed, just enough to keep the coffee and food warm. Stripping he sat on the edge of the pool. She was a spectator sport as she wound her hair up on top of her head, then stuck a pen she pulled from her pack through the heavy mass to secure it. It left her long neck and the elegant slope of her shoulders for him to admire. "Planning on bathing fully dressed?"

Holding his gaze in the semidarkness, Riva pulled her T-shirt and bra over her head. Wearing nothing but her khaki pants, *unbuttoned*, she placed her hands on her hips. A nerve throbbed at the base of her throat as she tilted her chin. "Happy?"

Hell yes. Her breasts were firm and round, beaded with droplets of spray. The tips hard little points. Holding his gaze, she shimmied out of the pants.

"Happier." He held up his hand to assist her in. After a moment she placed her hand in his and sat on the edge to swing her legs over into the water. "One of these days," he said as she eased into the chilly water. "I'm going to strip you slowly, and look at every inch of your body."

"You can see every inch right now." Standing, the water hit her mid chest. "Yow!"

"You'll get used to it. Want me to wash your back?"

"I can do it."

"I know you can, but I'd enjoy doing it. Hand me the soap, and turn around."

"I-" Clearly thinking better of arguing, she handed him the soap, then turned around and looked at the falling water beyond.

"Holy Mother of God." Her slender back was criss-crossed with long thin scars, white and shiny against her pale olive skin. Fucking hell. How had he not seen them before now?

Because she'd been naked, but tied to his fucking bed. Because they'd made love in the dark. Because he'd been blind?

Gideon had witnessed beatings, he'd seen the result of abuse. But this was more than whippings. This had been premediated *torture*. Fuck. Fuck.

The silver scars, unevenly spaced, ten-to- twelve-inch length, and razor-thin, spread from her shoulders to below her waist. Gideon had to gather saliva in his mouth before he was able to push out the words. "This the work of that fucked-up, low-life step-father?"

"I have no idea if they ever married or not. But he took his paternal duty seriously." She shrugged. "Took up where my mother left off. Stronger wrist. More upper body strength. Excellent stamina. He could go on tirelessly for hours."

She glanced over her shoulder. "Are you going to wash my back, Stark, or do I have to—"

"What the fuck were they trying to do? Beat the visions out of you?" She'd told him as much, but seeing the marks— *Fucking hell.*

"Didn't work." She frowned. "Give me the damn soap."

Jesus. Cupping her slender shoulders, Gideon turned her around to face him. Aw, shit. He wished the bastard was still alive. He wanted to eviscerate him. Empathy knotted thickly in his throat. He wanted to soothe and comfort, but seeing the gleam of the dying rays of the sun on her wet body made keeping his hands off her sexually damn near impossible. He resisted making an overture with every damn thing in him.

"One day," he said tightly, cupping her cheek because he was afraid to touch her anywhere else. His thumb skimmed the plump curve of her bottom lip. He wanted to cover her face in tender kisses until she was convinced of how special, good, and lovable she really was. Hell, what he wanted was the impossible: to change her past.

"We'll lie in the sunlight and you'll tell me everything this fucking prick did to you. Then I want to hear, in detail, everything you did to kill the bastard. I only wish you hadn't already done it, because it would give me great pleasure to rip him apart slowly, and over a very, very, *very* long time."

"I don't think about them." She swayed toward him, tight nipples brushing the hair on his chest. Wrapping her arms around his waist, she dropped her forehead to his chest. "The scars are just a part of me."

Fuck yeah, they certainly were. The scars were the pain he saw in her eyes when she couldn't hide it fast enough.

They were her refusal to get close. The people who were supposed to love and accept her unconditionally were the ones who had betrayed her with hatred and violence. Damn it. It was no wonder she had closed down emotionally.

Was that what she'd learned to do from her shit-for-brains mother and dickhead stepfather, as a result of them taking a whip to her back? Had they beat her into believing that crap she said about being unlovable? Because that was the goddamn expression he saw in her eyes. That's what she thought of herself.

Unlovable. *Fuck that.*

"Scars only show us where we've been." Her voice was muffled, her breath warm against his skin. "Not where we're going. Unless, of course, you focus on them. They've got nothing to do with the woman I've become."

Gideon called bullshit.

THIRTY-TWO

T he smell of stale sweat permeated the air, mixing unpleasantly with the still lingering fragrance of coffee and piney soap. Fuck. He knew that smell.*Andrés.*

"Where's the bitch?"

Good question. Where the hell *was* Riva in the dead of night, in the pitch-darkness? What stunned Gideon was that he hadn't stirred when she left. How long ago? Christ, was she so determined to reach Maza that she'd attempt to go to him alone at night, through unknown territory? Without her go-bag, which they'd used as a pillow and which was still under his head?

Ah, shit. Had revealing herself to him willingly scared her enough to make her run? The thought made him ache for her. But right now he had a more immediate problem. Sliding his hand along the outside edge of the sleeping bag, he closed his fingers around the grip of his Glock. Beside it was the MP7A1. Both loaded before they'd fallen asleep.

"Come to finish me off *mano a mano, amigo*?" he yelled over the sound of the falls. A dime-sized, blurred circle of white indicated a moon, but the light didn't penetrate inside. It was so dark he couldn't see a damned thing, except Andrés, barely backlit by the water-filtered moonlight. Which meant that unless he wore NVGs, Andrés couldn't see him either. From the direction of the other man's voice, he stood just inside the wall of water and about ten feet away.

"Can I at least have a minute to put on my pants so I can die with some dignity?" He was fully dressed and shifted on the bag as if searching for his clothes.

Andrés shifted, boots scraping across the rocky floor. "I told her it wouldn't work."

Since the other man made no comment about his state of dress or undress, Gideon figured he wasn't wearing NVGs. Good. And the switch of subject gave tacit agreement for more time. "Yeah? Why was that?" he responded.

The more Andrés talked, the better. Gideon rose to a crouch, Glock in one hand. He slowly reached over to feel for Riva's KA-BAR. It was right where she'd left it. The tactical knife's handle fit comfortably in his hand, perfectly weighted. Its large finger guard allowed him to wield it comfortably. He adjusted his grip as he started to slowly rise to his feet, then thought better of it. In the same way he could tell that Andrés stood instead of sat, the other man would be able to know where he was situated, too.

On his haunches, Gideon moved another foot to his left.

"I knew you wouldn't believe you were Sin." Andrés's voice held a note of righteousness. "I warned Mama that your memory would come back, and that you'd do everything in your power to extract retribution from her. Just so you know, *amigo,* we *all* lied to you."

"No shit," Gideon said grimly, lowering his voice so that he could barely be heard as he edged another six inches to his left. The knife would work better in the close confines of the cave. Bullets had a nasty tendency to ricochet in confined spaces. His fingers tightened reflexively around the hilt of the KA-BAR.

"When did you figure out who you were?"

"What difference does it make? Surely you two made contingency plans for the day my memory returned."

Fuckit, he did not goddamn want to crouch here in the dark chitchatting with a man whose head he'd like to place on a pike. He wanted Andrés dead, but the bastard might have some answers that would help him put the puzzle pieces together. Still, this was a dangerous game. Only one of them would leave alive, and right now he had the upper hand. A few minutes could topple that advantage the other way.

"Find your family and demand ransom." Andrés automatically raised his voice because he was finding it hard to hear Gideon, which was exactly what Gideon intended. "Kill you."

"So, like the coward you are, you're here to murder me in the dark? Where you can't see my eyes as the life blood flows from me?"

"Do you think I care if I can see you or not?" Andrés said angrily. "You'll be dead, and I can carry on as I did before she came up with this *loco* idea."

"Since you're going to kill me anyway, where did she find me?"

"Venezuela, near Angel Falls."

"Jesus." His fingers flexed on the hilt of the knife. "That's a thousand miles away. What was I doing there?"

"How the fuck should I know? A group there sold you to Mama for a shitload of money. Claimed you were from a very wealthy family. Said they pay any amount of money to get you back."

Gideon lowered his voice a little more. "And?" It like was taking candy from a baby. Andrés's ego, coupled with his competitive streak, layered over his need to please Mama, would net Gideon all the answers he needed.

"But they didn't know who your family was. Until we knew, we had to keep you alive. You were unconscious for months. It was damned inconvenient to take care of you, but always with the promise of our biggest ransom score ever."

"Sorry to disappoint you."

"Then you woke up and we realized that you didn't fucking know who you were. If we couldn't make money from your family, Mama thought you would be perfect to fill the shoes of Sin."

"Where *is* Sin?"

"He died years ago. Mama has been making out that her son is still alive all this time. A few of our men knew you weren't Sin, the others believed us when we told them you'd returned to us."

"From the dead?"

"From Europe, where you were negotiating contracts for our *El aliento de demonio* distribution."

"Ahh."

The sound of Andrés's boots scraping on the wet rock indicated he'd stepped backward where the ground was wet from the spray and was also turning, slowly. Trying to get a fix on Gideon's location. "She told stories about you. Your bravery. Your machismo. She planted fear and dread in the hearts of those that may one day be unfortunate enough to meet you. The stories spread, got bigger, more graphic. Sin Diaz became larger than life. The boogeyman for grown men to fear. You were *El Coco*. *Everyone* feared the Ghost, Sin Diaz."

Andrés agitated movements dislodged a pebble and it splashed into the small pool beside him. He sucked in a sharp breath as he caught his balance.

"I'm no doctor, but *soy inteligente*. Smart enough to have known all along that your memory would come back. I knew for *sure* when you stopped taking Mama's drink. It kept you docile, kept you from remembering. When you stopped— We knew you'd betray us."

Gideon rose to his full height, right behind the slightly shorter man. "Betray...*you*?" Like a cobra strike, he wrapped his forearm across Andrés's throat, gripping him in a tight bear hold. With arms around him, he limited the other man's movement as he edged him, more from memory than anything else, right to the precipice of the small pool. Andrés teetered on the brink. "Seriously?"

He wrenched his "old friend" off center, holding the knife right under his chin. "You took away my past, douchebag, and tried to fucking control my future." He nicked the underside of the other man's chin, felt the terrified sweat pour off Andrés's skin. "You both lied, cheated, fucking hell—*drugged* me—and now you think you can just stroll up to me and kill my ass, and I'll bare my neck? *Inteligente* my ass."

He took another light slice at Andrés's throat with the seven-inch, partially serrated blade. "Feel how close I am to your carotid? I wouldn't move if I was you." Andrés gagged, but quit struggling. "Finish the story."

"If I finish you'll kill me."

"It's not a case of *if*, douchebag, it's *when*." Gideon tilted him a little farther. One move and he'd slice his throat and throw him headfirst into the pool, or better yet, do what he'd do with any other snake: Jettison him through the falls and onto the rocks below. "More importantly, it's a case of *how*. We can do this slowly, or we can do this fast. I can stand here for the rest of the night." He could feel Andrés's Adam's apple move convulsively as he swallowed, gasping for air.

"The timing was perfect. We had you, and Maza showed up in Cosio showing muscle and power. We had to have a show of strength. A woman wasn't enough of a leader—not a strong enough leader. We needed someone *muy fuerte*. Sin was that man."

"Why weren't *you* that man, Andrés?" Gideon mocked against his ear. "Why didn't *you* take over? Was it because she knows you're too weak to take control of such a big enterprise? That you're whoring, boozing, and use of our products makes you unstable? Yeah, that's what I think. And you knew what she thought of you, didn't you? All this time when she made you think you had some control of your own life, she was manipulating you like a *marioneta,*pulling the strings."

"She depends on me." His voice was a mix of indignation and scorn, with a hint of doubt. "Trusts me to get the job done. *You* trusted me, confided in me. Told me about your doubts. I reported back to her. Nothing you did was unknown to Mama."

Gideon separated the sound of a scrape of a boot heel on rock behind him from the other familiar noises and braced for a rear attack. "Where is she?"

"Mama? I don't know. She went back to camp."

"Which is it?"

"I don't know."

"Do you have anything else pertinent to add?"

"I came to warn you," Andrés said desperately. "To help you—"

Gideon slashed his throat, then shoved him through the water and over the edge of the falls. "No, dickwad, you didn't." At a round of applause, he spun around, knife at the ready. "Enjoy the show?"

"It was more radio play than Broadway," Riva told him cheerfully, producing a narrow beam of filtered light between her fingers. "But it was mildly entertaining." She slung her backpack over her shoulders and made an "oomph" as she picked up his. She shoved it into his chest. "Let's hit the road, Stark."

Christ. Why did this woman amuse him as much as she made his chest and balls ache? Albeit for completely different reasons. "Just like that?"

"Why?" She looked over at him. "Were you thinking of moving in and putting up drapes? Angélica is out there somewhere, and if that dickhead found us, she can't be that far behind. Was that my favorite knife you used?"

With a grin, Gideon crouched beside the pool and swished the blade in the water. Straightening, he wiped it dry on his pant leg. "There." He handed it to her hilt first. "Good as new. Let's go find ourselves another bad guy. I'm in a fighting mood. Where'd you disappear to?"

"My comm beeped," she told him, sliding the KA-BAR into the thigh holster. Very sexy and Lara-Croft-ish. Same long dark braid, same steely look in her eye. But she wasn't an actress, and bullets, and knives, and assorted other lethal weapons *would* make her bleed. Or worse.

"I climbed a bit to try for better reception."

Gideon's heart thumped hard. The climb up the side of the falls was practically vertical. The rocks were wet and some were slippery with algae. There would've been nowhere to hide if anyone saw her. Fully exposed on the mountainside, with a moon, as small as it was, no help. It was suicide. But he merely said, "Did you connect?"

"One of our drones spotted us this afternoon. They ID'd me. Asked about you."

"And?"

"I told them you were Gideon Stark, international playboy, inventor, and head of the ANLF."

"What?"

"Okay. Not the last part. There wasn't time, and the connection sucked. My team is assembled in Santa de Porres. I'm to complete my op. Meet them there when I'm done. They believe whatever is happening is going down tomorrow instead of in a few days."

"What *is* happening? Something to do with the delegates of the BRICS summit? An SYP takeover of the ANLF? Word War Three or Four? A coup while *el presidente* is meeting with the US president?" He bit the words out, annoyed. "Seems to me we have multiple questions and no fucking answers. You should probably have some fucking clue before you stroll, whistling a happy tune, into Escobar Maza's stronghold, don't you think?"

"You sound cranky." She tilted her head to look him up and down. "*Are* you cranky? If so, why?"

"They know you're alone, right?" He'd asked the same fucking rhetorical question before. It bore repeating. He didn't give a shit that Riva was a well-trained operative. Call him a chauvinist. She might be able to outshoot and outsmart most of the predators in the jungle, but she was still female, and vulnerable. She was still about to walk up to one of the most dangerous, most unpredictable, sadistic terrorists in the world.

She readjusted her pack on her back. "Each of us has our own section of this operation to complete, Gideon. Just because the two men who were supposed to go in with me are dead, doesn't mean I run to the others crying. My directive hasn't changed." She hooked the second strap over her shoulder. "Coming?"

Unfortunately not. "Yeah. After you." And he'd stick to her as if they were goddamned Siamese twins until this was over. He might not be a trained T-FLAC operative, but he brought similar skills to the table. From the fragmented memories of his past, he was discovering that he was a daredevil and unafraid of the biggest, most terrifying challenges. If he trusted his disjointed memories, he'd BASE jumped the tallest buildings in the world. He'd forded rivers that few people had even seen, let alone white-water rafted. He'd hiked deserts, dived with sharks, and was a marksman if the trophies in his memories were real.

From his most recent past, he was intimately familiar with the jungle, guerrilla warfare, and the inner workings of the ANLF and, to a certain extent, the SYP. He knew his way around guns, knives, bombs, and booby traps.

And like it or fucking not—and he knew *not*—he was Riva's bodyguard.

"There's some good news," Riva told him, shining the narrow beam of light around the cave as if committing the space to memory.

Since she had to be the least sentimental woman he'd ever met, Gideon presumed she was checking to make sure she wasn't leaving anything behind. He was ditching what-ever had been there when they arrived. He'd never be back here, he knew for damn sure. "Your people are sending in a chopper to evac us when we get to the base?"

"Better. They'll have a truck waiting for us on the road up to Maza's camp. I have the coordinates. It'll cut six hours or so off our walk. We should be there just in time for breakfast."

Gideon finished packing his stuff, slung the backpack over his shoulders, grabbed Riva's hand, and together they walked through the falls. He couldn't fucking wait.

A waning crescent moon did little more than limn the edges of the leaves as they headed to the location where a truck would be waiting. From there, it was, apparently, a twenty-five mile drive up a series of dirt roads to Maza's stronghold higher in the mountains

"Angélica isn't lying in wait for us," Riva told Gideon, large and moody beside her. "She's in some sort of bar. Not drunk and not socializing." Riva had seen her surrounded by men, drunk, and raucous.

As they'd left the carnage several miles back, the air smelled pleasantly of wet dirt and vegetation. She held back a leafy branch as it curved at her head, then released it when she was clear. Her breathing, now that she was more acclimatized to the elevation, was no longer labored, even though they were still climbing. It was too dark to read Gideon's microexpressions, but she could certainly read his body language and feel the heat of him every time he got close. He'd been quiet and introspective for the past hour.

"Good to know she's boozing it up, and not hot on our trail," he said in a low voice, not bothering to hide his sarcasm. Every line of his body showed he was hyperalert. Coiled, tense, ready to spring into action. He didn't believe her. Hell, in his situation, she wouldn't believe her either.

"I feel compelled to point out that we have— *She* has three hundred soldiers back at camp to do her bidding. Several thousand more in both Santa de Porres and Abad. She's sitting at a bar somewhere waiting for the report to come in of who gets the kill fee. Maybe she's waiting for Andrés to return."

What Riva saw was a black mist surrounding the woman who'd lied to Gideon for months. Riva saw death. But whose? It was moot to tell Gideon that. She didn't know who was going to die, nor did she know whe—

Another vision slammed into her as they navigated an enormous section of densely growing ferns taller than Gideon. She sucked in a shuddering breath. Placing one foot in front of the other, she didn't have the sensation of walking on solid ground. The world around her became ephemeral and insubstantial.

Dios. Not Angélica. This time, the intensity of the emotions filled her with sheer terror like a body blow. Piercing pain pulsing around her in flashes of red and deep bloodred almost brought her to her knees. Swaying, she stopped in her tracks.

A stride in front of her, Gideon half-turned. "Okay?"

His words came through a thick fog of deafening, gutwrenching fear. "Charlie horse." Bile rose up the back of her throat. Prickles of hot and cold roughened her skin. Dizzy, disoriented, it was impossible to focus her eyes, and Riva stood there, the trees pressing around her, unable to move or breathe. "Second."

This was unlike anything she'd ever seen before. The vision consisted merely of violent, swirling colors, and a feeling of the most intense, profound sorrow she'd ever felt in her life.

Despair. Death. Unimaginable pain.

It felt like years, but as suddenly as the vision came it was gone, leaving only moon-tipped leaves in her vision.

"Riva?" He said her name as though he'd said it several times before. Instead of having the weight of her pack on her back, Gideon's arms were wrapped tightly around her.

Not wanting to appear weak, she knew she should pull away, laugh it off. Instead, she dropped her clammy forehead to his chest, and wrapped her shaking arms around his waist.

"*Cariño,* talk to me."

"I don't know what that was. I saw." Her arms tightened around him. "Whatever it was, it scared the crap out of me." Understatement of the century.

"Tell me." He ran his hands over her back in comforting, even strokes. His large hand warmed her icy skin, the steady beat of his heart flub-dub-flub-dubbed under her ear. "Jesus, Riva. You're shivering."

"I feel as though I just walked through an ice storm. That's never happened before. Give me a second to get my equilibrium back."

Gideon slid a hand beneath the length of her braid, his fingers warm on her pebbled skin as he cupped her nape. "Take as long as you need."

Breathe in. Breathe out. In. Out.

Calmer, she spoke quietly. "Usually the visions play out in front of me. I saw Angélica a few minutes ago, in that smoky bar. Sitting in a dark corner like a black widow spider, nursing a drink in a fingerprint-smudged glass, staring at the door. Waiting. For something? For someone? Crystal clear, no ambiguity. In microscopic detail. This—" She shuddered. "*This* was different."

"Can you tell me how it was different? What did you see?"

Riva shifted to get out of his hold. His arms tightened around her for a second before he released her. She stepped away a few feet and straightened her T-shirt, pulling it down, and adjusting the KA-BAR on her thigh. "I need time to try and process what it was."

"And then you'll tell me?"

Bending, she hefted up her pack by the strap, then swung it over one arm, indicating with the barrel of her SIG to keep moving. "Sure."

A stray glint of white moonlight gleamed in his eyes, and *she* saw in them that *he* knew that they'd never have that conversation.

THIRTY-THREE

Unseen monkeys chatted, birds chirped, and a jaguar roared. Time for the animals to rise and shine with the sun and forage for breakfast. Gideon's stomach rumbled even though he and Riva had had their protein bar breakfast several hours earlier when they left the falls. They'd seen no sign of humans, but Gideon knew that would change by day's end, if not sooner. In about four hours, they'd reach the location where the truck would be hidden beside the road.

Mama was out there lying in wait. But if Riva's vision held true, the bitch was holed up in a bar somewhere. And Riva's word was good enough for him.

The sky lightened enough for them to remove their NVGs, and the ground was more flat than sloped, making walking easier. They were making good progress.

"Okay, *that's* gross." Riva grimaced. The strong stink of putrefying flesh, similar to the stench they'd left several hours earlier back at the falls, made them breathe through their mouths.

"Could be a carrion flower, or a dead animal."

"No flower smells like *that*. That's something large and dead."

"My vote is something dead, but the plant is a strong contender. A lot of the plants here have developed methods to prevent their leaves from being eaten by animals and insects." Gideon smiled as she sent him a disbelieving look. "Tough, poisonous, waxy, or strong-smelling leaves enable them to resist predators. Admit it, even if you were starving, you wouldn't take a bite of something that smelled this bad."

They'd barely spoken in the past four hours and his weird rush of memory had been the catalyst to her actually engaging with him again instead of just responding by rote.

She'd tamed and controlled her thick braid down her back as they walked, and despite little sleep, and the stress of that last vision, she looked determined and eager to get where they were going.

Eager, Gideon knew, to do her job, and move on.

To what? To whom? None of his damned business. God only knew he had his own issues to deal with. He didn't know the what or whom of his situation either.

While the trees provided overhead cover, they were sparser here, allowing washes of weak, early morning sunlight to bathe the ground. The scant understory made walking side by side possible and they sped up. They were careful where they stepped, though. The uneven ground, bumpy with thick veining of roots, was also a good place for reptiles to coil up in the sun. They'd passed two snoozing anacondas in the space of a hundred yards.

Something struck Gideon on the forehead. He glanced up and smiled. "We have company." He pointed at several dozen playful spider monkeys racing around the branches of a Brazilian nut tree. "Watch out, they're using us for target practice."

"Beats bullets." Unsmiling, Riva put up a hand to deflect a missile aimed at her face, and frowned. "I think you should reconsider. Head into Santa de Porres when we reach the vehicle. We can meet up there in a couple of days."

If they separated as she suggested, that would be the last he saw of her.

He knew it, and he knew she knew it. They were inevitably going to say good-bye, but not when they reached the vehicle. He wasn't letting her go after Maza alone. End of story. Besides, he didn't want to admit it, but he wasn't ready to say good-bye yet. "Have you received a blow to the head recently from something bigger than these stupid nuts, that I don't know about?"

She turned to give him a narrow-eyed look. "What? No. Why?"

"Because we've had this convo *ad nauseam*. The answer remains the same."

"You're being obstinate."

"You're being pigheaded."

She shot him a fulminating glance, then faced forward, speeding up her steps. "Fine."

"Fine." Gideon lengthened his stride to catch up.

Two minutes later, she tried again. "I still wis—"

"Shut the fuck up, Riva," he told her without heat. Had her vision shown one of them dying? Both of them dying? That gave him pause. It made sense with how shook up she'd been and why she'd not wanted to tell him about it. If he went with her, would that change her fate? Would his presence, instead of protecting her, get her killed? He thought about asking. Hell, she had a power they should capitalize on. Instead, he clamped his mouth shut. If he asked, she sure as shit wouldn't tell him.

But instinctively he knew, if *he* was the one in mortal danger, Riva *would* tell him. She'd warn him away without mincing words.

So she was the one at potential risk. Unfuckingacceptable. And if he had any power to stop her, he would. "How close are we to danger?"

Using the elevated highway of vines to chase them as they walked below, the monkeys became more proficient in their target practice. Riva shot out her hand and deflected a flying nut headed for his face. "I'll protect you, don't worry."

That wasn't what concerned him. He needed facts before he calculated the risks. He had no intention of letting her see Maza alone. That was set in stone. "I'm sure you will, but it's not me I'm worried about."

"I'll be fine."

"Good to know. So back to my question. Are you seeing any imminent threat?" he asked as they stepped into a pool of sunlight.

Riva's glossy hair shone blue/black. The curve of her smooth cheek begged to be touched. She was 100 percent focused. Walking fast. Her gaze strafed their immediate terrain for danger. Her SIG was in her hand at all times. "Not that I see."

"Any new visions?"

"Thank God, no. Not yet."

"Good." He reached for her arm above her elbow and drew her to a stop. He ran his thumb in small circles on the inside of the soft flesh of bicep, then slid his hands up, letting his knuckles brush the sides of her breasts. "How about now?"

She cocked her head.

"I really want to kiss you."

Her brown eyes darkened. Golden light gleamed on her creamy olive skin, and sheened the moisture on her lips. "This isn't the time or place," she told him crossly, not moving, but not shaking off his restraining hand.

"Yes." Gideon turned her, then cupped her jaw. "It is. Later will be...later. Now is perfect." He stroked his thumb over her lower lip. "Scared?"

"Shaking in my boots," she snapped. "Hurry up, will you?"

Impatient. Focused. Sexy as hell. Gideon's heartbeat did calisthenics as he looked down at her upturned face. She was beautiful. Exotic. Annoyed. And he wanted her so badly, he could barely control himself from grabbing her, yanking off her clothes, and fucking her right there in the sunlight.

Running his knuckles gently down her cheek, he murmured, "Honey."

"I don't do endearments, Stark."

"The color of your skin. Honey washed in sunlight. Delicious."

She rolled her eyes. "Are you going to eat me or kiss me?"

His dick leapt at the suggestions. "Depends. Maybe both. Anyone going to shoot me in the back of the head in the next five minutes?"

Giving him a pointed look, she held up the SIG.

Laughing, Gideon brought his mouth down on hers. *Now* he felt her answering smile. His heart swelled as she opened to receive his tongue. The hard press of her gun bumped into the small of his back. *That's my girl.*

With a tenderness that surprised him, he pulled her against his chest and kissed her softly. Her eyes fluttered closed and he brushed his lips across the fan of her eyelashes, then trailed kisses down her nose, back to her damp mouth. Kissing her slow and deep, he relished her low moan of surrender. Her fingers tightened on his belt, tantalizingly inches above his rock-hard dick. The SIG dug into the small of his back.

Sunlight poured over them, and even with his eyes closed he felt the warmth penetrate him to the core. It was he who broke the kiss. He loved the soft, dazed look in her eyes as he stepped away.

"Hey," she whispered thickly, tightening her fingers around his belt and giving a hard tug. "Come back here."

He shook his head, though his body wanted to comply. "People to kill, terrorist plots to foil," he told her, keeping it light. Above them spider monkeys chattered from their ringside seats.

Riva laughed. She released his belt and moved back. "I'd give a dollar to see you in your native habitat. You must be a wonder at the...board table."

"Yeah. Probably. I'd rather think about what I would do with you on top of that board table," he said, fascinated when a blush pinked her cheeks.

She raised a dark brow. "Don't get ahead of yourself, Stark; rumors of your prowess out of the boardroom might be highly exaggerated."

"You have firsthand experience, Rimaldi, what do you think?"

"I think a quarter turn to your left and you'll face-plant into that spiderweb."

He was not fond of spiders, and moved forward more slowly. The jungle was filled with hundreds of species of spiders, most of them poisonous. Jorge had been bitten a month ago, and there'd been talk of having to amputate his arm. He'd been in agony for weeks.

The spiderweb wasn't that big, just the size of a dinner plate. No spider in sight. Yet the web was a reminder that danger lurked, even from the smallest denizen of the rain forest.

"Are you scared of spiders?"

"Everyone's afraid of something. I have a healthy respect for anything that has the potential to kill me, especially tiny things that can sneak up on me before I have a chance to kill them."

"You live in a jungle. Everything, including the nut job you lived with, could've killed you at any given time. Hell, given the opportunity, I was planning to kill you."

"I was aware." His voice was dry. "Angélica's afraid of *something*. I'll find out what that is, and deliver it to her personally. Ten-fold."

Riva stopped dead. "Are you saying you're coming *back* for her? That's *insane*. Once you're out of Cosio, you should never come back. Ev-er."

Gideon leveled a dead-on stare at her. "She's not going to get away with stealing my life from me," he said, his tone even, but the muscles in his jaw tense. "Sure, I'm going home. I'll sort out what home is and who I am. The second I reclaim my life, I'm coming back." He wiped his mouth with the back of his hand, like something foul tasting lingered on his lips. "I've been in the inner sanctum of the devil that's held this region down for years. There are good people who live here, Riva. Their lives have been destroyed because of that she-devil. What she's done to hostages has been horrific. Not to mention the evil created because of her drug trade.

"She's a fucking leech on mankind. She deserves to die. I deserve to be the one to do it for what she's done to me and to others. And then I'll rip what remains of the ANLF to shreds."

"Hell, Stark," she said, studying him. "Remind me not to piss you off." She gave him a half-smile that didn't reach her eyes. "Maybe I'll come back with you, to settle my own score."

He'd be damned if he'd drag her anywhere near the burning vortex of Satan.

Sidestepping the buttressed roots of a hundred-foot-tall kapok tree whose smooth gray trunk measured at least fifteen feet across, they gave a wide berth to several muru-muru palms with their twenty-foot-long fronds covered in protective spikes. Vincente, after a drunken night out, had returned to camp covered with painful gashes after falling into one of them.

Gideon had a healthy respect for the rain forest, but was glad this was his last walk through it. Massive biodiversity made seeing trees of the same species within the same area unlikely. In the last mile alone they'd probably passed at least a hundred types of trees. Cosio's rain forest would be a goldmine to any biotech or medical research facility.

Bright red epiphyte tree bromeliads flourished on the branches, looking like alien pineapples sprouting out of the branches. Purple and pink lobster claw-like Heliconia hid among lush ferns and big-leafed philodendrons. Stunningly vibrant, the colors of the flowers and plants broke up the myriads of greens.

What *wasn't* beautiful was the stink of putrefied flesh, which got progressively stronger.

"How do you feel about going home?" Riva adroitly avoided the four-foot-long, charcoal-gray tree boa hanging from a nearby similarly colored branch. Taking out a bandana, she tied it over her nose and mouth. After several minutes, as the smell got even more rank, Gideon was compelled to do the same.

"Oddly, I'll miss *this*." He indicated the surrounding vegetation and a flight of dozens of tiny iridescent orange butterflies that took off as they approached. "But not Cosio. And this," he indicated the bandana he'd tied to his face to muffle the unpleasant smell. "As for going home—I still don't remember where it is. It's only a name. There's no image, or solid memory, or feeling attached to it."

"Will you contact your brother?"

Why the interrogation? Friendly conversation or was she as curious about him as he was her? If she was, then maybe she cared more than she tried to pretend with her hard-ass attitude. He'd have to push at that a little bit more. For now, he wanted to know if she had someone to return home to. She never had answered that question. Perhaps, he told himself, because she considered that none of your damned business. Too bad, because when this was all over, it wouldn't *be* all over. "I'll find a lawyer first. Who knows what *those* circumstances we— *Shit*."

Three crumpled, mutilated bodies explained the stench. Swarming insect life covered them and showed they'd been killed within the last few hours.

He recognized the blond hair of one of the prisoners Riva had liberated from the ANLF camp. Three bodies. Five people had been freed. He pointed to what was left of the woman's head. "Shot, so at least it was quick. Did the others make it?"

She shook her head. "No. Nor is this a surprise, but I hoped somehow my visions were wrong."

"Have you had visions of events that in the end haven't actually happened?"

"Occasionally. When I have a vision, it doesn't show me what the variables are. Not always. So yes, what I see ends up changing on occasion. But that's more the exception than the rule. I knew when I freed the captives that they probably wouldn't make it. But I hoped that I was wrong. And damn it, look how close they were to real freedom. The road to Santa de Porres is just a couple of hours away. They would've made it on foot into the city."

Riva's coolness in the face of such hideous death of innocent victims made him wonder what else she'd seen in her life. How did she shut off and block out this horror, knowing that these people were only trying to get home? How was he supposed to do it when he'd done nothing to help them? That truth tore at his gut with thick, slashing talons. The hideous loss of innocent lives, the human suffering in which he'd played a part, strengthened his resolve to come back and wipe Mama and the ANLF off the face of the Earth so they couldn't do any more harm.

"I have a shitload of sins to atone for," Gideon said grimly. He'd have to find their families. Jesus Christ. He was not looking forward to *those*conversations.

With her bandana pressed to her face, Riva walked around the bodies. "Could have been either faction that killed them."

"Yeah. The ANLF uses this route to Santa de Porres. There's a poacher's track up from there, halfway up the mountain. Ironic that the SYP's camp was so close when we've spent months searching high and low for them." Not ironic. Unbelievable. Yeah, the jungle was dense, mountainous and thousands of hectares in size. But he'd had a small army of men, patrolling daily, searching the mountain and rain forests for months.

"It's more than ironic, don't you think?" Riva once again read his mind, which was a bit disconcerting. "Thanks," she said as he held a thick clump of vines aside for her to pass beneath them. "Your nemesis's camp is in an area any one of the ANLF could've passed countless times over the months."

"Yeah. Just what I thought when you gave me Maza's coordinates the other day."

She looked over at him as she removed something from the side-zipper compartment of her pack. A small earpiece. She placed it in her ear and made an adjustment. "You never said a word."

"Why would I?" Now that Riva was connected with her people, Gideon felt as though she'd put a physical wall between them. He didn't like it, and it pissed him off that he felt that way. "I didn't know who you were, or what your real agenda was."

"*Someone* kept you distracted. Someone was playing guess which cup it's under." She used her bandana to wipe perspiration off her face and neck. "Who was close enough to you to do that? Who had your trust and your ear? Andrés?"

Gideon turned to look at her.

"Crap. It was Andrés, right? Could he have been in cahoots with Maza?" Gideon started to walk again and Riva pressed on. "It makes sense. I wouldn't be surprised. He seemed shifty as hell to me. Shifty and weak. A man who could be bought pretty cheaply."

Gideon shrugged. "Possible. Hell, *probable*. He craved power, and status. Angélica kept him on a short leash. If Maza offered him some incentive, he would've betrayed her in a heartbeat."

"Betrayed you, too. He was supposed to be your friend."

"No one has friends in hell." He blew out a heavy breath. "I saw through that in short order. Took me longer than it should've, admittedly, but I was so doped, I wasn't really functioning on all cylinders until a few months ago." He thought back to all the fucking lies and bullshit Andrés told him. "We had someone in the SYP's camp. Guy called Loza. According to Andrés, this guy would only talk to him."

"Convenient."

"Yeah. If Loza is still in Maza's camp, he might recognize me."

"Another reason for you not t—"

Gideon gave her a dark look. "As far as I know, I've never met the guy."

"How about Escobar Maza? Are you a thousand percent positive you've never come face-to-face?"

"Not unless Andrés brought him around me pretending he was someone else and Mama didn't know what he looked like." He wiped the perspiration off his brow. "Hell, anything's possible. Bottom line, it doesn't matter if he's seen me before. I'll have to risk it. Because where you go, I go."

"As long as I get to kill Maza, I guess I'll have to risk it, too."

THIRTY-FOUR

The closer they got to Maza's camp, the more strongly Riva knew she had to ditch Gideon.

This feeling had stayed with her since it first grabbed her by the gut and heart. The memory of the vision had taken root inside her like a venomous snake coiled around her organs. The lethal bite was coming. Coming soon. And there'd be nothing she could do to stop it if she didn't change what was about to happen. But what in the hell was she supposed to change?

She hadn't *seen* it. Damn it, unlike every other vision she'd ever had, she hadn't formed a *picture*. Just felt the unbearable pain of loss. The blackness of hopelessness.

Gideon was the catalyst.

Tick. Tick. Tick.

She couldn't allow him to come with her. Could freaking *not*. But how to prevent him from sticking to her like damned glue? A week ago, she would've just incapacitated him and taken off. Could she do it now?

Of course she could. But knocking him out would leave him alone and vulnerable at Maza's front door. And what if *that* action was what precipitated in the culmination of that vision?

Not an option.

Hell, Rimaldi. Get a grip. Stop being such a damn girl. Do what T-FLAC trained you to do. If anyone got in the way of any important mission, she knew what she had to do. Yet she couldn't do it. Killing Gideon wasn't an option and she sure as hell didn't want to explore why. Another option. Knock him out cold and take him to the city, before backtracking and showing up in Maza's doorstep. Crap. No time for that.

Not an option.

Tick. Tick. Tick.

He was quick, and far from stupid. Besides, as confident as she was in her ability to overpower him, in reality it was unlikely she'd get the drop on him. Especially since she knew he expected just that. She read his damned body language. He was braced for danger from every side, including, hell, *especially,*from her. The countdown in her head sounded like Big Ben.

Sick to her stomach, she put one foot in front of the other. The residue of the last vision clung to the edges of her mind like a sticky, black tar.

Whatever she was going to do, she had about forty minutes to do it. From the sparser pattern of the trees, she knew the road was dead ahead.

Her earpiece crackled to life. Relief flooded her. The satellite had picked up her position. They weren't exactly alone. T-FLAC knew where they were and had eyes in the sky.

"Alpha." Control's voice was deep and even in her ear. "Four hundred yards to transpo. Northeast seventeen degrees."

The vehicle had been moved to a different location. A closer location. Riva adjusted the wrist GPS with the new coordinates. "Copy that."

"We have eyes. Target in cradle. I'm with you all the way. Try to maintain radio silence until you put the baby to bed."

"Copy that." The connection went dead. She looked over at Gideon. "Maza is in camp. The truck is less than a quarter of a mile that way." She was walking in the correct direction, but her feet felt weighted with lead.

Gideon put a light hand on her forearm. Easy to throw off. He wasn't restraining her, but his face said he was not opposed to exerting any strength necessary. "The answer to the burning question buzzing around in that clever mind of yours is *no*. You can't get the drop on me. I'll be extremely pissed if you attempt to tie me up and leave me on the side of the road, shoot me, or run me over. Forget trying to ditch me, Riva. You might have special training, but I can assure you that I, too, know what the fuck I'm doing. We're going in there together." He scanned her face. "We'll leave together. And then we'll deal with whatever this is between us."

"Nothing—"

"*Together*," he finished as if she hadn't interrupted. "No arguments."

She gave him an innocent look. "I was just wondering which of us should drive?"

Tick. Tick. Tick.

The road was packed red dirt, narrow, and riddled with potholes and tire tracks. "Poachers cleared this for easy access. Big bucks in exotic animals and of course parrots on the black markets, worldwide. Clearly the SYP use it now, as did we whenever we wanted to get into the city."

"Didn't you have a chopper?"

"Yeah. Only holds four. And since Maza's arrival, we didn't want to send up a flag showing our location. I was working on procuring several drones, but they hadn't been delivered yet. The SYP has several that patrolled, hence the netting over the ANLF camp. I'm guessing that huge mountain of vegetation is our vehicle?"

Transportation was a beat-up, green and white late eighties Ford pickup truck hidden in the trees and covered with foliage. Together they stripped off the vines and leaves that had camouflaged the vehicle. When it was clear, they saw the piles of mesh cages strapped down in the bed of the truck.

"Either it belonged to poachers, or it's an excellent cover. Your people know what they're doing," Gideon said, getting into the driver's side.

"Yes," Riva answered. "We do."

He found the key in the ignition.

The engine turned over with a purr, indicating it hadn't been a factory upgrade. T-FLAC's work.

After a moment, Riva went around the front, and climbed in. "Turn around and head north. We're an hour out."

He made a U-turn on the narrow road and headed up the mountain. The dry dirt kicked up in a cloud behind them. It had clearly been washed away, re-scraped, and washed away again. It wasn't a road from anywhere other than Maza's camp. There was nothing else up the side of the mountain.

"We stick as close to the truth as we can," Gideon told her, going onto the verge to avoid a large pothole. The tires bumped over scrub grass. "I'm your bodyguard, our chopper was shot down. We escaped death due to one of your visions, escaped from the ANLF with several of their captives, and walked out."

Smart. The three captives who were killed were excellent cover. "Where did we get the truck?" She let him weave the story. She had other things on her mind.

"Stole it from an old man and his son who'd gone off into the jungle to trap parrots."

Riva dragged in a deep breath. "Will you promise me something?"

"Depends."

"Please don't do anything heroic."

"*Querida,* I *am* your hero. Heroic is what I do. If you didn't want a hero, you should've hooked up with my brother."

"There are so many interesting observations in there, I don't know where to start. You know you just said something about your brother? So what is he? An antihero?"

He shook his head as if clearing it. "I have no idea. Don't know where that even came from. All I know is I have one and he left me in the jungle, but I sure as hell haven't seen him in the last few months."

"But you were found a thousand miles from here—"

"The world, Riva. I'd have found my brother anywhere in the fucking *world* if he went missing. And I wouldn't have stopped until I did." His determination was evident in the solid line of his jaw, and the pulse that throbbed at his temple. He glanced at her, and the hard glint in his eyes told her he wasn't bullshitting. "Or I'd have died trying. So do not ask me *not* to protect you. I might not remember much about my past, but I now know myself. I don't leave anyone alone or behind to fend for themselves. I've got your back. We're in this together and there is nothing you can do to get rid of me."

Yes, I know. I'm trying to figure out how to change that before it gets you killed.

Tick. Tick. Tick.

THIRTY-FIVE

Gideon knew, by the thickness and oppression of the air, that they were in for rain in the next hour. Then all traces of their passing would be obliterated.

Trees and lush vegetation crowded the dirt road, encroaching strategically, making it narrower and narrower as they approached Maza's camp. Shrubbery almost obliterated the path between foliage and boulder outcroppings. It was barely wide enough for the truck to pass. Branches snagged the side windows, ran scraping fingernails along the sides of the vehicle, and rattled the undercarriage. The tires shimmied over loose rocks. Thick red dust plumed behind them, showing exactly where they were.

Nothing subtle about being watched. For the last six miles, well-armed soldiers in camo stood every hundred feet along the way. Instead of a wide-open space so he could see his enemies approach, Maza had chosen to use the jungle to his advantage, and funnel visitors directly to his front door. No room to back up. No exit for a quick retreat.

According to Riva, her T-FLAC people now had them in view via satellite. "It's fucking all well and good, Riva, that your pals can see and communicate with you now, but we need to know if and how quickly they can reach you if..." he paused, changed his mind about saying when. "Hell breaks loose. No one is going to just stand around and let you walk up to Maza and take him down and then not retaliate."

"I have my orders," she said, not bothering to look at him.

"Can you clue me in, since I'm in this shitstorm with you?" His voice was controlled, but his anger battled with his worry that she was about to walk into an ambush.

"You were given the choice to opt out. You chose to ignore me. Just stick close to me. Be ready for anything." Now she did turn to look at him. "Or, get out of the truck now. It's your last chance to walk away."

Nice set of choices. He didn't bother responding. No need. She knew his answer and it fucking well wasn't going to change just because she kept asking the question. They rode in silence for a few more minutes.

So her pals could see them get their asses kicked and heads speared on the flagpole from their damn satellite pictures in the comfort of their cozy offices. Great. Front-row seat to their slaughter. What the hell good did that do? Did they have any operatives close enough to fucking show up for all the fun and games if it turned into a goatfuck?

He didn't need the memory of how she'd reacted to that last vision to make him hyperaware of everything around them as they drove. Maza's sentries stood with sniper rifles on outcroppings of rocks, and were perched strategically in treetops. And if those precautions weren't enough, a plate-sized drone, fitted with a small camera and what looked like an automatic machine gun, hovered right above them.

"Brilliant," Gideon observed as the road took them around an enormous outcropping of rocks, revealing armed guards watching their progress through the view-finders of what looked like an M47 Dragon missile launcher. "No one can turn around here either. One way and that's in."

Riva gave her KA-BAR another wipe, then returned it to the leg sheath. "I'm just glad Maza's in residence, and we don't have to go all over hell and gone to find him."

"You hope he is. All this might just be a power trip. Maza could be hell and gone to the city to personally oversee whatever chaos is supposed to go down."

She'd spent the last ten miles fieldstripping every weapon they had between them. The interior of the truck smelled strongly of gun oil and solvent as the sun, shining in, baked the plastic seats. Since she'd cleaned them all last night, doing so again was unnecessary. But he got it. She needed to keep her hands and mind busy. He did the same thing. Cleaning his weapons allowed his mind to roam. Only his mind had been on a fucking short leash for the last five months.

"You know it won't be a cakewalk getting out of here with all these men." He glanced over for a quick look at her face. Tense, but utterly calm. Stoic. Ready to face anything. Her skin gleamed with good health and a sheen of perspiration. The window, cracked a few inches, blew the loose strands of her hair around her face as she folded her clothes and put them neatly into her bag.

Pulling her braid over her shoulder, she unraveled the lengths of black silk until her glorious hair spread like a cape over her shoulders. "T-FLAC has us covered. I'm not worried."

"Damn, you're good. You managed to say that with a straight face."

"I'm not worried," she repeated, eyes front, not a muscle in her entire body relaxed that he could tell.

He eyed her loose hair. Glossy and wavy from being braided, silky soft as it spread around her to pool in the bends of her elbows. Gideon wanted to run his fingers through it. What he didn't want was Escobar fucking Maza looking at her when she appeared this sexy and vulnerable. "You're going in like that?" He hoped he was the only person who saw the vulnerability beneath her strength.

"My hair, you mean? I don't want anyone getting even a hint that I have an earpiece in. My hair covers that. Plus it gives the appearance I'm girlie, just like his psychic should be, don't you think? Not someone who'd knock a guy on his ass if he messed with me."

Gideon smiled. "No man in his right mind will mess with you." Not if he looked into her eyes first. *And not,* he promised her silently, *if I'm alive to prevent it.*

A horn honked. Incongruous in the middle of nowhere. Riva put her hand on his arm. "Slow down even more. Vehicle pulling out on the right."

Yeah, he'd seen the glint of sunlight off glass a dozen yards back. A late model black Expedition pulled out of the trees ahead and pulled into the road ahead of them. Gideon had to tap the brakes as it eased in front of the truck's bumper. Tinted windows gave no indication of the occupants. As the truck crawled past where the vehicle had intersected them, a second black SUV slid in directly behind them.

"Game on," Riva said dryly as they continued to drive sandwiched between the two vehicles. "I suspect they know who we are, and have for some time. And I suspect it wouldn't matter. I bet they treat all their guests like this."

Because the truck's windows, like the other two vehicles, were tinted, the drone that had followed them hadn't been able to take pictures. And because it was a truck procured and enhanced by T-FLAC, Riva had told him that no one could overhear their conversation. No one but the T-FLAC bug in her ear, that was.

The three vehicles rounded another corner as the road made an S. They passed high ground where more armed sentries with rocket launchers stood.

Five or six miles farther on, the convoy stopped at a ten-foot-high rusted, corrugated iron gate, guarded by four men carrying AKs. The gate looked deceptively weak and flimsy. "Bet that's reinforced with tungsten steel in back."

"No doubt."

Because of its extreme weight, the gate swung open slowly, and his suspicion of the reinforcement was confirmed. The small convoy passed through. A dozen more men were waiting for them inside.

Low-slung buildings, similar to the cement block barracks at the ANLF camp, lined the narrow street and were nestled between kapok and Brazilian nut trees, giving a nice thick canopy overhead. Painted camo, the buildings blended with the landscape, flat roofs sprouted shrubs and hanging vines. The enclave was well-disguised. And very similar to what they had at the ANLF camp.

"There's no way this was built in five months," Riva observed as they followed the SUV down the narrow road. "That's when Maza arrived on the scene in Cosio, right?"

"I was thinking the exact same damned thing. This place has been here for years, not mere months. Look at the vines on the walls. Several years." Things grew fast in the rain forest, but many of the vines covering the building were twelve inches around and more. That said years.

Ignoring Control's directive to maintain radio silence, Riva spoke quietly into her mic, "You seeing this?" After a few seconds, she said, "Shit. *That*many?" Listened, then said "Copy that." And continued staring straight ahead. "They estimate Maza has five thousand soldiers in this camp. Well-armed, and we already know well-trained. Restrain your macho, heroic tendencies. Let me do all the talking, and follow my lead. I am Graciela Estigarribia and you can be— Who would you like to be today?"

"Dante Cordero."

"Dante Cordero. Bodyguard." She was taut as a bowstring, vibrating with energy. He nodded. "I'm just the muscle, ma'am."

Riva huffed out a disbelieving laugh as the lead car slowed, then came to a stop in front of a vine-covered cement building that looked the same as all the others. "Showtime."

A couple of soldiers opened their respective doors. Riva slid out. "It's hot and I'm thirsty," she told the man near her, her voice deeper, and more coarse. "Inform *el jefe* that Graciela Estigarribia has come." Her Spanish was fluent, colloquial, and imperious. She indicated Gideon on the other side of the truck. "He's with me. Come."

Gideon presumed the order was for him, and went around the front of the truck to stand by her side.

The man between them glanced at her, then Gideon, and back to her. "You will both wait here, señorita."

Her gaze went beyond him. "No. I will not wait here in the hot sun with all of these men staring at me." Graciela was used to giving orders and having them instantly obeyed.

Gideon suppressed a smile. Jesus, she was good.

"I've come far. It has been a difficult journey. I'm an invited guest of Señor Maza. He will not be happy if you delay me any further or do not provide the courtesy of a cold drink, and shade. *Now*. You—" She raised her voice to get the attention of the soldier next to him. "Take us to Señor Maza. Immediately. He has waited long enough for the information he seeks."

"You have returned from the dead, to order my men around like a general, my dear Chela."

The man came up behind and around Gideon, and went to Riva, both hands outstretched. Sixties, well-preserved, slicked back black hair, silvering temples, slight, five seven, dressed in khaki chinos and a powder blue golf shirt. He read preppy, and not drug lord at all. Which was probably why the man was so successful. No one expected their golf buddy to pull out a Tondar submachine gun and blow their entire family away because of a drug deal gone bad. His teeth were very white, and liberally capped with gold. Other than a soul patch, he was clean-shaven.

A Beretta in a tooled leather holster was strapped low on one hip, on his other was clipped a cell phone.

Taking Maza's hands, Riva gave him a big smile in return, all traces of tears gone. "Escobar! I feared I would not make it to you. If not for my visions telling me that I would reach you, I don't know if I could have endured another day." She shook her head, tossing her hair back off her shoulders. "I have *much* to tell you."

"I thought you were dead, Chela." Soft spoken, and almost eerily smooth, he squeezed her hands, then leaned in to kiss her on each cheek. "I was told no one survived the helicopter crash, but I knew if anyone could, it would be you." He smiled. "Come. I will listen to what you have to tell me, and give you food and drink." Over his shoulder he motioned at the soldier standing beside Gideon.

"No." Riva tucked both hands into the bend of Maza's elbow. "Dante must stay with me." Lowering her voice to almost a whisper, "He is going to be your lucky charm, my dear. I will tell you."

Maza snapped his fingers for the soldier to bring Gideon along. A ballsy move from Riva, joining him to Maza's good fortune.

Brilliant. God, she was good

THIRTY-SIX

R iva accompanied Maza to one of the cement block buildings. It looked no different than all the others, with vine-covered cement and a door made from rusted metal. Reinforced, she suspected, like the front gate.

He stopped at the door. Surrounding them were half a dozen of his men, and Gideon. "My men will take your weapons, and that of your man before we enter my home, dear Chela. You have nothing to fear. Everyone here is trustworthy."

Riva put her palm over the SIG tucked into her belt, and put a stop–right-there palm up when one of the soldiers went for the KA-BAR strapped to her thigh. Her heart did a quickstep, but she didn't glance over to see how Gideon was faring. This was about power, and here and now she was the one who had to wield it.

"We will not give up our weapons. I'm sorry, Escobar. *You* I trust. But there are two of your men who are not trustworthy. Until such time as they die, we retain our weapons."

He gave her a shocked look. Hard to tell with the amount of Botox on his face. "Who—"

Riva placed two gentle fingers over his mouth, making sure her fingers brushed his lips intimately. "I will share that vision with you when we have more privacy," she whispered for his ears only. "Be patient."

Maza waved the men away. He trusted Graciela, she'd never lied to him. As far as T-FLAC knew. Opening the front door of heavy painted steel, he stepped inside, then held the door for her.

"Oh, my. This is unexpected," Riva said, inserting wonder and approval in the words as he led her into a large room that smelled faintly of mildew, and strongly of a powerful musky incense that made Riva sneeze twice in a row.

"*Salud.*"

The rustic, utilitarian exterior didn't match the overly accessorized interior. Predominantly royal blue velvet furniture, and a lot of it. Lampshades with bullion fringe and a gory, giant-sized oil painting of bullfighters in a heavy baroque gold frame. The floor was covered with a Turkish rug of blue and black with swirls of gold. Knickknacks—either rampaging bulls, or fighting cocks—in ceramic, bronze, and glass, and of varying sizes and every description covered every flat surface on numerous shiny brass and dusty glass shelving units.

These weren't collections amassed in months. These were well-loved collections gathered over many years. Had Maza been in Cosio all this time? And if so, why had he only popped up less than six months ago?

"It's so lovely and cool in here, such a treat after the hot, stifling jungle. You must have a very big generator," she said for the benefit of control listening in. Probably a 10kW for this building, which she suspected housed his personal space. A generator was always a fun thing to disable to disrupt things.

"What can I offer you to drink? *Limonada Peruana?* Pisco?"

"*Limonada*, please." She smiled, taking a seat at one end of a bright blue, deeply tufted velvet sofa with a serpentine back, the whole curving length topped with a gilded wood carving of an anaconda. "No alcohol for me until your project is complete."

"Yes, we must address that issue." He signaled one of the two men standing beside a door leading farther into the house. He was instantly replaced by another soldier dressed in the same fatigues as the others. The guy went off to, she presumed, get the drink. Gideon, standing between two soldiers armed with AKs behind the curved sofa, was offered nothing.

Maza came and sat right beside her, their knees almost touching. Unnecessary, since the damned sofa was ten feet long. He wore some pricey cologne smelling like vetiver and heavy on the patchouli. "But first. I will hear about this miracle that saved you from the helicopter crash. I thought I'd lost you forever, and my heart has been heavy. And what must you have encountered on your journey to reach me. I shake to think how you managed to survive the ANLF, as you must've passed through their territory, yes? The ANLF, animals... All the dangers of the rain forest, alone—"

"I wasn't alone, my dear. I had my faithful Dante with me." Riva cast an appreciative glance at Gideon, before returning her attention to Maza. "No one could ask for a more faithful, loyal bodyguard. If not for him, I would not be with you today."

Maza's appearance wasn't unexpected. She'd read his dossier in flight and was prepared for the odd, preppy look of him. Knowing who and what he was, his clean-cut persona was jarring. He looked as if he belonged to a country club, and had a blonde wife and two adorable children and a puppy in the suburbs. The reality was so far from who he really was that it was chilling.

His looks and her opinion didn't mean squat. As soon as she knew what he was going to do the next day in Santa de Porres, he'd be dead.

While she casually pretended to admire his décor, she checked out the entrances and exits of the room, counted weapons and types of weapons, tried not to spend too much time making eye contact with Gideon, and told Maza an abbreviated summary of the past week.

Her lemonade drink, in a Baccarat-looking crystal glass, was set before her on a red lacquered tray with a silver platter piled with small Ecuadorian*Postres* filled with fruit and dusted with powdered sugar.

Curling her leg under her, she pretended to sip her drink from the heavy glass. Real crystal from the weight. She didn't trust him not to slip something into her drink. Setting the glass down on the tray, she took a moment to assess the dangers in the room. Spatially aware of where everyone was situated, Riva kept her attention on Maza. Up close, she could tell that his black hair was colored, leaving silver at his temples. She already knew he was vain from her briefing.

"Surely God has blessed you to save your life. That is quite the hair-raising story," he said admiringly when she finished her tale with the theft of the truck from the poacher.

"What an adventure for you, and yet, you didn't have a vision of any of this?"

"As I've told you before." One of the tapes obtained of the conversations between Maza and the real Graciela came to mind. "One cannot change fate. And I do not see my *own* future. Escobar, you know this. I saw only that you and I would meet because I saw it in *your* future and that sustained me. I was fortunate that I made it to you alive."

"Yes. Indeed. I am most fortunate. What can you tell me of my new undertaking tomorrow? Success?"

Riva took his hand and squeezed his fingers. "I've seen that you should not do anything decisive for at *least* seventy-two hours, my dear. Nothing at all inflammatory. The perfect time to get everything you desire will be three days from now, at three thirty-three in the morning."

"*Impossible,*" his voice rose, and his skin darkened as he flung off her hand. "It must be tomorrow."

Riva held his gaze as she said quietly. "Then you will fail."

His hand shot out and he slapped her across the cheek, so hard her head bounced off the back of the butt-ugly sofa and her hair went flying. "You lie! Do it again. Look into my future again, damn you!"

Riva straightened, smoothing down her hair as she touched her palm to her hot cheek. Out of the corner of her eye, she saw the two men set to guard Gideon halt his forward lunge. Her cheek stung as if bitten by fire ants, and her eye watered, making Maza's angry face blur.

"Strike me again," she said coldly, getting to her feet, "and I will see no more visions for you. *Ever*. For all these years you have trusted me, and now, when I refuse to pretend the vision is what you want, you strike me?" *I want you deader than dead, you sick fuck.*

"It is only because I value your services so much that I strike you. Anyone else in my employ would have a bullet in their brain at such a comment."

He spoke conversationally. Riva had never seen brown eyes so dead, so cold. "Sit."

She held his gaze.

"You will sit down and you *will* have another vision. A more *favorable* vision."

Riva knew she was walking a fine line between getting killed and obtaining respect, but the tightrope was a deadly necessity. "Striking me is not conducive to me producing a clearer vision, Escobar. Just the opposite. If you strike me again, I will be less willing to help you. And the more distressed I am, the less able I'll be, as well. My mind must be clear, and trouble free, if not, I see nothing." *If only* that *was true.* "I hope I make myself clear."

"I brought you to me for the express purpose of ensuring that my next project go well. God spared your life for this exact purpose. You will not tell me what to do and you *will* have a new, advantageous vision. One that enables me to do exactly what I need to do."

No escape.

Anything she did at the moment would screw the mission, and get herself and Gideon killed.

Unacceptable.

Taking advantage of her hesitation, Maza grabbed her by the wrist and pulled her down beside him. She didn't fight him as she so desperately wanted to. Instead she resumed her seat, keeping her gaze flat, her features non-homicidal.

"You must give me the perfect time," he spoke through clenched teeth. "What is the perfect time. *Tomorrow?*"

He was so close she could see the lines around his eyes and mouth, and the striations in his flat brown eyes. Riva knew she could have the SIG in her hand in seconds, fire a shot a second later. And a second after that she'd be a bloody mess on his hideous carpet, too.

"Wait. Get what we need," control said unnecessarily in her ear.

No shit.

"Heed me, Escobar," She leaned in closer to him, keeping her eyes steady on his. "I cannot change what I see. I cannot change fate if you do not listen to me." She paused for maximum impact. "If you do not alter your course of action, *tomorrow* you will die. I cannot be more plain than that."

"Have another vision."

It doesn't work like that, asshole. "I will try, but I must know more about the variables. More about your alternatives. You need to talk to me, my friend. Tell me what you feel are the obstacles, and I will do my utmost see alternative courses of action for you. You have been my *patrón* for years now, and you know I always want to help you in any way I can. Please, do not doubt me now."

He sighed, and gave her a white-capped, gold-toothed smile. "Thank you, my dearest Chela. You have always been truthful with me. I have had hundreds of successful business dealings with you, and much success defeating my enemies. Surely this will be the same."

"I will attempt to have another vision. But, if I have the same result, you must believe me, my dear. I would be devastated should you die. I value our friendship so very much, and I can't imagine my life without both your friendship and your patronage."

He nodded. "Just so. I will let you enjoy your drink, perhaps one of these delicious pastries, and let you rest for half an hour." Getting to his feet, he snapped his fingers as if he'd just remembered something. "Before you go, I have a small gift for you, my dear. I'd be most honored if you'd accept it for all your years of loyalty to me." Going to a gold-leafed box on the other side of the wide coffee table, he returned with a blue Tiffany box with a white bow.

What was inside that box had never seen a jewelry store, much less Tiffany's. She knew it in her gut, and she knew it with utmost certainty by reading his microexpressions. His primary muscle movements were malice, triumph, and brilliantly disguised fury.

God, she wanted to pull the SIG and put a bullet right between his too close together eyes. Leaning forward, she picked up her glass as if it was a lifeline. Leaning back, she gave him a confident smile. "No gifts until I can assure you, you will have a long, healthy life." She forced a smile. "Keep that until your project is completed."

"No. I insist." Riva felt the return of her previous vision as a cold, dark red throbbing warning surrounded her.

"And *I* insist we wait." The vision crowded back, too damned vague to grasp other than extraordinary mental anguish. Nausea rose in the back of her throat and her mouth went dry. She brought the heavy glass to her lips with difficulty.

"I appreciate that you so generously bought me a gift, but in a few days we will have your triumph to celebrate." She couldn't drink, her limbs felt heavy and numb as the swirls of darkness surrounded her. "That would be a more appropriate time, don't you think?"

Pushing the tray out of the way, he sat opposite her on the wide marble coffee table and untied the glossy white bow. His tanned fingers were thin—skeletal, with big knuckles. Eyes fixated on his hands, Riva noticed his painful-looking hangnails, rough and red, and his ragged cuticles. Taking a bracelet out of the box, he dangled it between his fingers, a pendulum for her to admire. She knew looking at his hands was a hell of a lot safer than seeing what he was offering her.

Lifting her eyes, she forced herself to see what he held.

It swam into focus. Just a narrow band of dull silver. The sharp jolt of foreboding felt like a physical blow. It resonate in her bones and made her muscles feel water-weak.

There was so much evil in it Riva could barely force the air in and out of her constricted lungs.

Ohgodohgodohgod.

Every drop of moisture in her body seemed to dry up. If she didn't grip the sofa cushions she'd dry up and fly away. Mouth parched, lungs constricted, Riva had the sensation of drowning.

"Regulate your breathing," Control warned.

Yeah, she couldn't hide anything from her control in the sky. He was getting all her haywire vitals in real time.

"Thank you," she said, hoping like hell Maza didn't hear how breathless she was. "It's..." *Evil.* "Beautiful. But I don't like to wear jewelry when I have to concentrate. It interferes with the energy flow." She pressed her fingertips to her temples for emphasis.

Energy flow? Understatement. What was flowing through her was cauldrons of lava, pulsing red and burgundy with washes of black. The bracelet inspired a vision of fear and foreboding that was eating her alive. Dear God...

He swayed the bracelet in front of her. Paralyzed, she couldn't even flinch as he brought the dull circle closer and closer. "I insist, my dearest Graciela. I insist. Here, give me your pretty arm."

When Riva remained still, he grabbed her wrist, turning her skin white from the pressure of his fingers. Open, and hinged like a handcuff he snapped and locked it around her wrist. It wasn't tight, or restrictive, it didn't look like anything other than a rather plain piece of jewelry. His fingers felt hot on her icy skin. "There. We are joined inextricably forever."

She couldn't look at it. It wasn't an aggressive slap and it wasn't a threat of a bullet to her brain. It was much, much worse. He had one-upped her with lethal ramifications, because the smooth metal felt like putrid death on her wrist. The grim reaper's hook would feel no worse. She was so cold, goose bumps had formed on her skin.

"Your temp dropped six degrees," Control cautioned, his voice even in her ear. "And regulate your breathing, you're hyperventilating. Your BP is dropping."

Sure, as soon as she got this damn thing off her wrist. She had to inspect it carefully and report back to control, but right now she couldn't even abide by the fucking directive to even her breathing. She sucked in a ragged breath, too overwhelmed by the physical ramifications of the damn bracelet to process anything else.

"That's sweet of you. But you know eventually I must return home." God. She had to snap the hell out of this fugue state, and start being active instead of reactive. "I'm exhausted and need to rest if you require me to have another vision. Is there somewhere quiet I may lie down for a few hours?"

"Of course." He rose. "One of my men will take you to a room where you may rest and reflect. I'll return for you in an hour for a more favorable answer."

THIRTY-SEVEN

"Tell me how can I help you," Gideon demanded, closing the door after Maza's people escorted them to a windowless room so Riva could rest and have another fucking vision. As if she was a goddamned psychic hotline.

On Maza's orders, his men had stripped them of all their weapons.

The room was drug dealer chic with alien-style purple flower prints covering the bedspread, pillow shams, and swagged drapes over a nonexistent window made of mirror. The ghastly fabric even covered the lampshades. To break up the overpowering floral tribute, there was plenty of brass ornamentation and a variety of large, strategically placed, mirrors.

And plenty of places to hide cameras and microphones.

Maza could watch them in 3-D, and Gideon didn't think for a moment that he wasn't enjoying this particular show. The room was clearly designed for spectator sports.

Riva sank down on the edge of the king-sized bed with a heavy scrolled brass headboard. For bondage purposes, Gideon supposed, not missing the gold-veined mirrored ceiling.

"I'll get you some water." He went into the bathroom. It, too, was covered in mirrors and brass, with white faux marble, female crap all over. Found a glass, and filled it with tap water. Returning to the bedroom, he found Riva with her head on her knees.

Really bad fucking shit. "Do you want a sip of water? It's cold." He wanted a fast car, an Uzi—no, he wanted a missile and a clear shot. He'd settle for a fucking army so he could throw her over his shoulder and haul ass out of there. Away from Maza, the jungle, and Cosio.

"Give me a sec," her voice was muffled. "I think I might puke."

"That bad?" She looked up at him with glassy eyes. Yeah, that fucking bad. Her olive skin was dead pale, and she was sweating and shaking as if in the grips of a fever.

The comm was in her left ear. Could her control hear their convo? He hoped yes.

"Go for it. Nothing could make this room any less hideous. Being in here with all these mirrors makes me want to puke as well. Who'd want a bedroom without any windows, anyway?" He crouched down in front of her, hovering his hand over the thick fall of her hair, but not quite touching.

If T-FLAC could hear him, what the hell good was it knowing their circumstances? Unless they had a bulldozer right behind that wall?

Gideon didn't know what the fuck to do. He liked being in control. Hell, he'd run a multibillion-dollar corporation— A spear of pain ricocheted around the inside of his skull. Jesus, yeah. He *had* run a multibillion-dollar corporation. Was there anything in his past that could help him in his present? Because he fucking-well did not like seeing her undone and being powerless to fix it.

She was scaring the living crap out of him. Another vision from hell in less than twelve hours? There was some extremely bad shit coming down the pike. Did her buddies listening in realize how bad this was for her? Did they give a flying fuck, or was it all about the mission? If she failed, would they simply send another operative in her place? Was Riva's mortality simply a speed bump? Had they heard him?

Pressing her face to her knees, she held her hand over her head. *"Take it off."*

Take it off? The bracelet? That's what she was freaking out about? Taking her hand, he rotated her slender wrist. "Hang on, looking for a clasp—" Wasn't one. He'd observed as Maza opened it. So it had a hinge somewhere. He couldn't find it now. Nor could he find a fucking clasp. He'd got the damn thing on her, so there must be a way to get it off.

He'd seen the Tiffany box, in fact been surprised that he'd recognized it as such. This was one ugly-ass piece of jewelry. Plain, and a dull nonreflective material, no links, no jewels. One solid circle with a bicolored substance bisecting it as its only ornament.

Not Riva's style, and judging from Maza's home, not Escobar Maza's style either.

Gideon attempted to slip it over her hand. It wasn't big enough. Not tight, but not any room to slip a finger between the band and her skin. His heart beat uncomfortably as he looked at the thing more closely.

Twisting the solid band around her fragile wrist, his mouth went dry. He was no weapons expert, but this looked like something high-tech out of a James Bond movie. Something clever and lethal that Q would give Bond to use as a last resort deadly weapon. Farfetched? Gideon wasn't sure. Time and a loupe might tell him. But he was fuckall out of time, and there was nothing as bizarre as a jeweler's loupe around.

Had she known the second Maza offered it that there was something off about it? No wonder she'd immediately looked as if she was about to pass out. "Fuck."

"Can you be a little more specific?" she muttered from the depth of her lap as she took several slow unsteady breaths.

Gideon stroked a strand of hair off her sweaty cheek, swollen and pink from that motherfucker's hand. He'd kill him for that alone.

"I... Give m-me a minute here." She was talking to her control.

"Give me your comm," Gideon ordered softly, speaking close to her face, so that anyone's view was blocked. "Let me speak to them."

She fumbled through her long hair, then took it out of her ear and handed it over so that it looked as though she was merely touching his hand. "It's hot," she whispered. "G-go for it."

He took precious seconds to insert the damn thing into his left ear beneath his own hair. Beneath the circle of his fingers, her pulse beat too fast and too hard. "You hear me?" he said, stroking Riva's hair and hoping it looked as though he was talking to her, and not some invisible-fuck-ing *useless* guy in wherever the hell he was.

"You don't have to shout," a man's calm voice in-structed. "Tell me what we have?"

Head bent low over hers, Gideon said quietly, "Quarter-inch wide, quarter-inch thick steel, possibly titanium, band. Slightly smaller than one eighth of an inch glass channel running the full circumference, right down the center. One side contains yellow liquid, the other blue. Markings all the way around. Looks like some sort of timer."

"Detonator?"

Gideon rotated her wrist. Riva still had her head in her lap as she struggled to calm her breathing. "Don't see one. But fuck, that doesn't mean shit. I don't have a jeweler's loupe handy."

"It's detonated by remote."

Detonated? No. Just fucking no. "Maza's holding the other end?"

"What do you think?" Control's voice was even. "Rimaldi has to get her vitals under control. Respiration up. Heartbeat in panic mode. This isn't the norm for her. Do something."

"Right. Got my doctor's bag right fucking here, filled with everything I need."

Control was silent. Good. Neither of them was fucking amused.

Riva straightened, her face on a level with Gideon's. Even her lips were colorless, and she was still seeing or feeling whatever she'd seen or felt when Maza had snapped the bracelet on her wrist. She was struggling to maintain her calm, but her entire body still shook, and her glassy eyes were unfocused.

Getting to his feet, he reached over and took her upper arm gently. "Let's go and splash cold water on your face, okay?"

She obediently got to her feet, and allowed him to walk her into the bathroom.

"What happens if the comm gets wet?" he asked the man in his ear.

"You're good. Hot shower. Noise, steam. I'll hear you."

Under other circumstances that would be an issue. But it wasn't right now. Now he needed all the fucking guidance he could get. Cranking on the water in the glass box with its marble seat and multiple showerheads, Gideon kept hold of Riva's arm. As soon as the steam filled the shower stall, he walked inside it, both of them fully clothed. Cold water would probably be better under the circumstances. But steam gave them some measure of privacy.

She braced both hands on the back wall and let the hot water sluice over her.

"Okay. How do I get this off her?" Speaking a shitload more calmly than he felt, he held her loose hand, turning it this way and that, running the fingers of the other hand lightly over the surface of the bracelet as the water poured over her. "I don't feel a latch."

"There won't be one. Once the two liquids combine, it'll detonate. Hear me, Stark? A chemical reaction will take place when those two reactants interact. Bonds will form, atoms rearrange. Once those precipitates turn into a green solid..."

Riva, unable to hear the convo, pushed away from the wall and turned to look at him through spiky lashes. Thank God. She was back. Gideon reached through the water to cup her cheek, indicating he was listening. She nodded, and reached for the shampoo.

Hair piled on top of her head with frothy white foam, she pulled her T-shirt over her head, then reached behind her back to undo her bra. He didn't blame her for taking advantage of a steamy bathroom and soap. He just had bigger concerns than washing up. He pointed to her arm, and when she held it out, carefully soaped her skin from knuckles to elbow, then attempted to slide the device off. No go.

"He's not going to kill her before she assures him that whatever the fuck he's planning will go off without a hitch. So, since you're God in the fucking sky, exactly what is it that he's doing? And how fast can you get your operative the hell out of here, and a chemist, jeweler, and explosives expert standing by?"

"The answer is we're working on the situation blind. The BRICS summit convenes tomorrow, eight a.m. We've changed the location, have all delegates on security round the clock. That's our most likely target. But we aren't sure. We *need* Rimaldi.

So, to answer your question, Mr. Stark, not until she ascertains exactly what it is that Maza is about to rain down on the world. You can give the comm back to her now."

THIRTY-EIGHT

She'd never had such a powerful, freaking nebulous, *useless* vision before. *Colors* told Riva bugger-all. By the way the two visions had left her all but incapacitated, she knew it was *bad*. But what kind of bad? She didn't know.

The room had an enormous closet, and Maza had a vast array of various sized girlfriends. Too bad his taste ran to see-through, cut down to there, and up to here outfits. Finding something dry to wear was easy. Not looking like a cheap Cosian whore was another thing altogether. She'd found black crop pants and a black tank top. She wore her own wet bra and underwear, and her own wet boots. And the damned bracelet.

Gideon hadn't been as fortunate. He'd showered, washed himself fully clothed, and wore everything wet. Including his boots. He'd tied back his hair with an elastic band found in one of the bathroom drawers. The scruff on his jaw was turning into a full beard.

She'd like to see him clean-shaven one day. But for now, the beard was useful, because no one had seen him with one, so he was less likely to be recognized.

Now he looked even more like a dangerous desperado with his slicked back hair and hairy face. Sexy, dangerous, and Riva wanted to grab hold of him for just a few moments and feel that beard against her skin.

In the shower she'd seen the way his eyes devoured her when she was naked. She'd wanted him just as badly. But the steam hadn't lasted long, and she didn't plan on giving Maza a peep show.

Still, she did appreciate being clean.

"Glad you're feeling better." His hazel eyes met hers in the mirror, asking more than that. Riva nodded. With no residual effects of the last vision, she felt just fine, and ready to do battle.

She stood in front of the bathroom mirror, brushing out her wet hair, and looked at Gideon's reflection as he stood behind her. "That was a very powerful vision," she said for any listening devices.

Gideon curved his hands around her shoulders, and gave a little squeeze. "Will you be able to give Señor Maza what he asked for?"

Riva shrugged. "I need more information. Then yes, I think I can."

Moments later, the door to the bedroom opened without a knock and two soldiers walked through the bedroom to stand at the bathroom door. "*Jefe* is ready for you, *señorita.*"

"Great," Riva said with false cheer. "Lead the way."

They didn't return to the living room. Instead the men escorted them through a side door and outside, where a covered truck waited. "Where are we going?" she asked as a soldier opened the door for her. Gideon helped her up into the high front seat, then followed her in. A soldier pushed in beside him. It was a tight fit. Gideon's thigh pressed against hers, and his arm stroke hers.

"*Jefe* wants to show you a demonstration."

She and Gideon's eyes met. A demonstration didn't sound as if Maza was ready for a new vision. Unless it was a demo of what would happen to her if she didn't comply. The heavy truck bounced over ruts in the road between the buildings. It had started to rain, and the windshield wipers thumped unevenly back and forth, back and forth, making muddy red tears from the red dust on the windows, like rivulets of blood.

The growth of vegetation here was less dense, the large trees further apart, with swaths of grassy, open land. The soldiers, now standing in the pouring rain, were in the same formations, but this was not the way they'd come into the compound.

Her heart gave several hard knocks. This all felt...*off*. Did her subconscious know something from the visions that her conscious mind couldn't understand? Had Maza somehow discovered that she wasn't his precious Chela?

Did he know... *What?*

Neither of them had any weapons. Riva inspected the camo uniform of the man beside her. He wore a pistol, a knife in a sheath, and he'd placed an AK in back behind the seats. The beefy, aggressive looking soldier beside Gideon had the same.

They shared another look. They could take these two guys.

Too bad the truck bed, covered partially by canvas, was filled with twenty similarly clad men.

"This isn't the way we came in. Are we going far?"

"We have you, Alpha."

Thanks, Control. Nice to know. Not fricking helpful, but nice to know. That meant that, unlike the jungle surrounding the ANLF's camp, there was no satellite blocking over Maza's camp, and even under dense tree canopy, infrared would see them just fine.

The sky opened, and the deluge made visibility almost impossible. "Seems we're destined to always be wet," Riva told Gideon in English.

"Sweetheart, my fondest desire is to always keep you wet." He gave her a cocky smile that made her heart leap and a smile tug at her lips.

Sweetheart. That was a first. Too bad she didn't have a moment to treasure the first time in her life that anyone had called her that. It would've been nice to just sit in the shade of a leafy tree and let the pet name wash over her, since it might be the last time she heard anyone call her sweetheart, too. The damn bracelet locked and loaded to kill on her wrist, plus the dangerous mission to off Maza when he was surrounded by literally thousands of armed loyal soldiers, reduced her life expectancy to hours. She damn well deserved that moment, she thought, knowing she'd never get it as the truck pulled to a creaking stop in front of a small square building.

At the urging of their two personal guards, they exited the truck, and entered the building.

When this was over—if she was alive when this was over—she was going somewhere dry. Like the Sahara, maybe. She was sick of rain. Sick of being wet. Any more of this and she'd have webbed feet.

Not bothering to wring out her hair, or brush the water off her skimpy clothes, she followed soldier number one into what looked like a control room. Gideon stayed glued to her side. The second man stood just inside the door. She presumed the truck full of men was still outside, as she hadn't heard it drive away.

Glancing around, she let her gaze go over Maza, who stood before a console in his preppy golf outfit. The twelve by twelve room was dim, and air-conditioned. One wall held multiple, full-color monitor views of a rainy open space surrounded by jungle.

She and Gideon crossed to his side. ""What an impressive display of electronics, my dear," Riva kept her voice light as she looked over the eight-foot-wide console covered with intriguing buttons and switches.

Gideon stayed right beside her as she went up to give it a curious look. Fairly current technology. Maybe not state-of-the-art, but definitely brought here for some purpose. The wall above it held six large monitors, three over three.

"Looking at an empty field? I don't understand." Riva tucked her hand into the crook of Maza's elbow and leaned against him. God, she couldn't wait to kill the sick bastard.

"Did you have a clearer vision, my dear Chela?"
He stepped out of her hold.

Warning bells went off in Riva's head. What was he up to? Why was he stopping what he had planned to show off at this isolated building in the compound? If he was going to kill them, he'd had ample time to do it at his house. She doubted he was squeamish about a little blood.

Folding her arms at her waist, she kept her gaze steady as she studied his profile. Unnaturally calm. But seething beneath the placid exterior was a psychopath who would stop at nothing to get what he wanted.

His microexpressions were ones she'd seen on serial killers. He had no conscience, no feeling of guilt, no remorse for anything he said or did.

Damn it to hell, I want a weapon. Right now she'd settle for a goddamned nail file. Gideon had stepped back at the same time, and stood, partially concealed in the shadows nearby. She didn't need to read *his* microexpressions to know what he was thinking.

"I had an *incomplete* vision, but I really do need more information to conclude it. If you tell me what you have planned, maybe that will help me. In my new vision, I saw many important people gathered in Santa de Porres. Is your goal to disrupt this group? If so, tomorrow is definitely not the day to do so. As I told you earlier. In seventy-two hours—"

Maza turned his back to the monitors, bracing his hands on the edge of the console, and looked at her for several long seconds before he extended his arm. "You see, my dearest Chela? I like your bracelet so much I have one of my own."

It wasn't any prettier on his tanned, muscular arm. Not that she gave it more than a cursory glance. The microexpressions fleetingly stamping his features told her volumes. He was furiously angry. Frustrated. Vengeful. And had made a decision.

The son of a bitch had something unpleasant up the sleeve of his damned golf shirt. What was it?

Tell me, damn it. I can kill you even without a weapon. Although she could take his in a push, or relieve one of the soldiers at the door. But hell, at this point, her hands were itching to wrap around his neck and be done with it.

"So I see. But what does this have to do with your plans?" He hadn't confirmed that the summit was his goal, but then he hadn't said it wasn't. She'd like to shake him before she put a bullet in his brain.

"You will have to ensure that your vision is incorrect, my dear."

"Escobar," Riva let her annoyance creep into her voice. "I'm your psychic, I'm *incapable* of changing fate. My visions show me the truth."

"And your vision shows that if I attempt to do what I have to do tomorrow I will die?"

"Yes, there's no doubt."

He extended his arm. "If I die, so will you. If my heart stops for more than one minute, you will die."

His neck looked strong, muscular. She'd need leverage to strangle him. She trusted that Gideon would deal with the soldiers. Maza was hers. Man, she missed her KA-BAR. "Are you threatening me?" she asked dangerously.

"No." His eyes were cold as he straightened away from the wide metal console. Over his head, he snapped his fingers at the two men guarding the door, his attention not leaving Riva. "I make you a promise."

"How can I prevent you from dying if you refuse to *listen* to me?"

"This device monitors my vital signs," he said, talking over her. "If, for any reason my heart stops, the electrical signal will activate the liquids in *your* bracelet. A chain reaction will detonate. You, and anything, and anyone within a thousand feet of you will go—" He raised his hands like a fucking jazz singer. "*Bang.*"

While her flesh crawled knowing he'd strapped a bomb to her arm, she reminded herself that she was dealing with a psychopath here. Riva gave him a cool look, spreading her feet to center herself. "You'd kill me for being *right*? For telling you the truth? For trying to *protect* you?" Hell, yeah, he most certainly would.

"You will have to have a *new* vision."

"What's so important about tomorrow that it must happen then instead of in three days, Escobar? Perhaps if you give me more information on what your goal is, I can understand and interpret the vision another way." She sighed for effect, feeling more and more frustrated that she was getting nowhere with the asshole. "I can't change a vision for something I do not know or understand. Being secretive will get us both killed. If you won't give me the information I must have to make favorable sense of my vision, I'm done here. Have your men take us back to the house. If you won't listen to me, I have nothing more to say."

The door opened, letting in more light, and the pounding sound of the rain. "Excellent." He waved the three figures closer. "Bring her in. Oh, you may remove the tape from her mouth, but keep it close. I might require it be replaced. Come in, my Angel, let me look at you."

"Who the fuck are y— *Carlos*?" The woman's voice rose with outrage. "No. Impossible. It can't be you. You are dead!"

Holy crap! "Angélica Diaz," Riva whispered to control.

It was as if hell had just spewed up two devils.

"Did you just say Angélica Diaz?" Control demanded, at the same time Gideon grabbed her elbow and pulled her to one side of the darkened room. The TV monitors, the only source of light, showed a flickered view of the scene outside. Nothing but an empty field and pouring rain.

Not turning her gaze from the two main players in this little drama, Riva whispered, "Wait, did she just say *Carlos*?"

"Jesus," Gideon whispered in return. "Escobar Maza is Carlos Dias."

THIRTY-NINE

All hell was about to break loose.

Seeing Angélica restrained by Maza's soldiers didn't surprise Gideon, but having her in the same room with him and Riva sure as hell did. What a goatfuck. Any second now, when Angélica took a breath from her tirade, she'd look up to see them standing in the far corner.

It was unavoidable, inevitable, that she'd instantly recognize them and alert Maza. Because as pissed as she was with her husband, she was even more pissed with the man whom she'd planned to use as a stand-in for her dead son. The mystery was, how long had she thought the ruse could possibly last?

Dumb bitch. It obviously hadn't worked at all, since Maza had known the truth all along, thanks to Andrés.

Like Maza, Angélica was a psycho. Two psychopaths in a twelve-by-twelve box with only one door was a recipe for disaster.

The entire time Riva had been talking to Maza, Gideon had kept his mouth shut and his eyes moving. This was her gig. Her mission. But Angélica showing up changed things. Riva's mission was to kill Maza, but Gideon's goal was to kill Angélica. And if Maza laid a hand on Riva again, he'd gift her with his dead ass, too.

Gideon had already assessed the parameters of the room, the size of the large console with its lit-up buttons. He knew where the heavy-duty power cables ran into the raised floor. Raised to vent and hide all those Teflon-sheathed, and raceway enclosed, cables. Double-shielded, coaxial, dual coaxial cables indicated far more than a decade-old console and late model monitors. Somewhere in this room, under the false front of the giant console with its too regularly blinking lights, was a sophisticated, state-of-the-art data center.

Gideon bet Maza ran his entire business from right here in this shithole on the outskirts of Santa de Porres, buried in the jungle where no one had thought to look for this size and scope of an operation. From here he surely also managed the electrical net thrown over the entire area, denying the ANLF any Internet connection.

Genius.

Gideon's attention didn't stray from Angélica and Maza. The four guards two with Angélica, two in front of the door—would do nothing without Maza's say-so.

Body coiled, ready to intervene, Gideon didn't take his eyes off the two combatants as they growled and hissed like jungle cats circling one another for a fight to the death over territory.

He might not be trained to read microexpressions, but he knew *Riva*. He listened for any sign that the fucking vision would return to incapacitate her. So far, so good.

Bracing himself as the heated convo continued, Gideon mentally rehearsed each move he'd have to make to counteract someone else's, like a living game of chess. Then he replayed the match, adjusted, formulated the best plan of attack to ensure a win, just as he did in the boardroom when he anticipated an adversary's move.

In the boardroom it was a power play. Here, it was life and death.

This time, the thought—memory?—Didn't make pain knife through his brain.

The soldier to the left of Angélica, five nine, solid, weight-lifter arms, shaved head, had his weapon harness unfastened for quick release. He had one hand clamped on her thick upper arm to restrain her as she and Maza yelled at each other.

The guy to Angélica's right, a linebacker type with no neck, and arms and legs like tree trunks, had a tight grip on her upper arm. His other ham-sized fist covered his gun. Blocking the only door, the other two soldiers still held their Uzis in the shoot-you-dead position.

Maza had mobility, his wife didn't. Maza's voice was even, controlled but loud, and commanding. The man was fearless. His wife, probably the only person who dared to spit venom at him like a striking cobra, was restrained by his loyal soldiers. They were not giving her an inch, their fingers digging into her dirty skin, turning it white where they held her. She was on her toes, jerking and lunging, not getting anywhere. She distracted the soldiers, each of whom had a weapon-hand free. Gideon remained motion-less in the shadows.

Yeah. Doable.

Gideon calculated that it would take him two running steps to reach Weight Lifter. Elbow to face, knee to groin, slip weapon free. Commence shooting.

Angélica's eyes, full of hatred, were glued to Maza. Her loathing seemed to give her tunnel vision, which worked in Riva and Gideon's favor.

He wasn't a mind reader, but he suspected Riva, standing beside him, was calculating the same odds for the players on her side of the chessboard.

"...seven years." Maza's voice was ice over heat. "Seven fucking *years* to amass another fortune so that I can come back to my country, wrest back control, and restore everything you stole from me." His face was inches from Angélica's. His fury was drawn in every line of his body, yet the tone of his voice was composed. Even softly spoken he gave the impression of leashed screaming. It was chilling.

Reading what was in his eyes, Angélica pulled back her head, but otherwise couldn't move. The change of angle revealed a large dark bruise on her jaw. A jagged cut, thick with dried blood, was on her right temple. Her right eye was swollen almost shut. She'd had the crap beaten out of her, and Gideon was pretty damned sure Maza had ordered it with great pleasure.

"You built a *new* business," she snapped, tendons straining in her neck. Water from her wet clothing dripped on the floor around her boots. No sign of the Aitor Jungle King knife that was always shoved in her boot.

"Cosio is no longer your country, *cabron*," she sneered. "Nobody wants you here. Why return to a place where everybody hates you?"

Maza's smile, all gold and white, made the hair on the back of Gideon's head lift. Jesus, the guy was scary as shit as he said with soft malice, "I *will* take everything you hold dear away from you, you fucking bitch. Just like you took my business. My son."

Riva turned her head slightly, Gideon knew, so that the earbud picked up the conversation. "This is what he planned all along," she whispered, barely moving her lips. "Not the BRICS Summit. *This.* He's been orchestrating a coup to take over the ANLF all along."

Gideon wasn't so sure. There were elements that didn't quite gel here, but he couldn't put his finger on what that was.

Angélica struggled in the hold of the two bulked-up soldiers. Her black hair dripped water in her eyes and onto the rain and blood-soaked collar of her camo shirt. "You *and* that boy were useless."

Maza's icy control snapped, and he roared, "That boy was your *son!*" He backhanded her, the full force of his body behind the blow.

Gideon heard her neck snap back, as the two men holding her staggered under her weight. The smack of flesh against flesh and the crunch of bone reverberated in the confines of the cell-like control room. Other than a grunt, Angélica didn't utter a word. After a few seconds, she lifted her chin defiantly. Blood spurted from her nose to dribble down her shirt-front. She gave Maza a one-eyed glare of death-ray proportions.

For now, Angélica's profile was toward himself and Riva. Gideon hoped like hell Maza didn't start circling the bitch, causing her eyes to track him.

"Useless?" No indication that he'd just gone DEFCON 1 on her seconds ago, as he resumed his cold and absolutely steady tone of voice. "So you *killed* us? Is that how you solve your problems, Angélica? You murder your problems? Your family? An eighteen-year-old *boy*? The very people God gave you to love and cherish?" He enunciated each word inches from her face so that it dripped venom, making her flinch. There was nowhere for her to go, no way to back up.

"The money meant more to you than any loyalty?" Maza's voice rose several octaves, and even in the dim, flickering light, Gideon saw a vein throb in his forehead, and the high color in his cheeks. "Any *family*? You killed your own flesh and blood for *money*?"

Angélica stopped struggling, her pugnacious jaw rigid, as she glared at her husband. "Clearly rumors of your death were exaggerated, for here you stand,*mi amado esposo*," she mocked. "It was a business decision. You are weak. Your boy was like you."

"Holy crap," Riva whispered, horrified. "She killed her own son? No wonder she was delighted to have you as a stand-in for Sin. She'd been pretending he was alive for years."

"Murdering bitch." Maza rubbed his hands together, as though resisting striking her. The dull metal of his bracelet looked incongruous on his wrist, reminding Gideon that he had to find a way to get the damn thing off Riva's arm, and *soon*. Maza had enemies everywhere. He could be offed at any time, by fucking *anyone*.

In a compound of thousands, there must be people right *here* who hated the mother-fucker enough to kill him. People who wanted to take over, who'd be happy to do it over his dead body. Jesus. Until he figured out how to get the damn bracelet off Riva's wrist, he was now *Maza's* fucking bodyguard.

If T-FLAC ran out of options, if they no longer had a choice about keeping him alive, they *would* kill him. Riva would be collateral damage.

"An unnatural mother." Maza slid his hand into the front pockets of his chinos. It was a bizarrely casual, laid-back gesture. "You belittled him, *me*. You were hard. Unrelenting. Unforgiving."

"Yes." Angélica sneered. "Good qualities in a *leader*. But then you wouldn't know that, would you, *mi amor*?"

"Unbecoming traits in a *woman,*" Maza continued, as if she hadn't spoken. "If you learned nothing from our marriage, you should know from studying your enemy what I am now capable of."

"My people are strong." Her chin jerked up as if she was daring him to strike her. "Kill me, and they will avenge my death. It is the ANLF that owns Cosio. Your few thousand men can never take us."

"You think not? Who do you think Andrés Garzon works for, eh? How do you think I stayed hidden for so long, despite all your searching? I have hundreds of men on the payroll of the ANLF, reporting to *me*. Fighting for *me*. All of them in your organization. It is not ANLF who controls Cosio, it is I. You have merely been my puppet."

Gideon met Riva's quick glance. "Her right, on your word," she said under her breath.

He nodded. It was a given that they had to take Maza alive at all costs. The others they'd kill. Strategy planned, if only the first few dance steps. Coiled, he was as ready as he'd ever be.

"I tire of this game, Angélica," Maza informed her, pulling from his pocket a familiar bracelet.

Jesus, did this guy buy the things by the dozen?

Angélica tried to rear back, but was immobilized. "I want nothing from you."

"Hold out her arm," he instructed No Neck. Easier said than done. The woman moved lightning fast, and while the soldier fumbled to adjust his grip, she yanked her arm free and almost broke the guy's nose as she hit him with her palm.

Maza pulled back his arm, and punched her in the face so hard Gideon heard the crunch of cartilage and bone. Blood poured down her face as she shrieked at the top of her lungs. Not fear. Pure rage.

Maza jerked his head again to No Neck, who also had blood spurting from a broken nose. Yeah, there was going to be a shitload of blood involved before this was over.

No Neck wrestled her arm straight out, clamping it under his arm so she couldn't break free. Screaming bloody murder, Angélica writhed, and bucked, but the guards were stronger than the five-foot woman, and held her immobilized. "Hold her arm still." Maza pried open the hinge on the bracelet and snapped it around her wrist.

Angélica went ballistic, spitting, kicking, and attempting to wrench her arms to get free.

"Take her to the truck," Maza instructed, judging by his expression already bored. "Remain with her for further instructions."

The door closed. Maza, two soldiers.

Gideon met Riva's eyes, and saw the same relief that they hadn't been made, there. He mouthed, "Let's finish this."

She gave her head a slight shake. *Wait.*

For what, for fuck sake? The odds right now were good. Kill the soldiers, take Maza.

She shook her head again.

Fuck.

Maza came to the center of the room, and held his hand out to Riva. "Come, my dear Chela. Let me show you what this has all been about. Come here." He wiggled his fingers to entice her closer.

"I can see just fine from here, thanks," Riva told him evenly.

Maza probably knew that Gideon was the man Angélica had tried to pass off as Sin. But did he know that Riva wasn't Graciela Estigarribia?

Did Riva have a feeling about it? A vision that would tell her if she was relatively safe with this homicidal maniac or not? If Maza still believed she was his trusted psychic, she was safe until whatever happened...happened.

"I ask nicely, and you disobey me? This isn't the Chela I know and love. Come, my dear. This is important."

Ah, shit. He knew. Gideon's balls sucked up at the cold chill that raced through him. They were dead. And he didn't need Riva's vision to know it. There was fuck-all chance the eyes in the sky were going to magically show up and save the day.

"What is it?" Riva crossed the room to stand five feet away from him.

Maza dropped his hand. "Very we—" There was a knock at the door. He nodded to the soldiers and they opened it to allow a man inside, then shut it behind him.

Gideon was more focused on keeping a line of sight open to Riva than on observing the new arrival. Another soldier dressed in camo, and carrying an AK-47. Forties, Gideon noted out of the corner of his eye. Slight of build, nervous as hell. His gaze flickered over to Gideon, then dropped back to the floor.

"Ah, Loza." Maza gave him a thin smile.

Shit...

His Adam's apple bobbed. Eyes downcast, he asked, "What job do you have for me, *jefe*?"

Maza raised his pistol, and said conversationally, "You've done your job," and shot him straight through the eye.

The bullet went through the back of Loza's skull, slamming with a high-pitched screech into the metal door between the other two men as his head exploded like a ripe watermelon, splattering the entire wall and door behind him with brain matter and blood.

Everybody fucking flinched. Except Maza.

He depressed a small yellow square button on the console. "Come get Loza, I'm done with him." He turned to Riva, who had specks of blood on her arms and bare legs, and was looking at Maza as if he was the devil incarnate. Which he fucking-well was. "Now, where were we?"

Jesus. *Loza*. Andrés's informant.

Maza was cleaning house.

"Do you really think that any of this"—Riva waved a hand at the carnage—"is conducive to me having a vision that will help you?"

"No, my dear Chela, of course not." Her irony went right over his head, or he chose to ignore it. "But I do have something most persuasive that might help speed up the process. Yes, come." He raised his voice after a knock at the door.

"Hurry," he told the two men who hesitated at the doorway. "Take him away, and come back later to clean up. I dislike the sight of blood. Now where were we? Ah, yes." He indicated the monitors above the console.

"My dear Chela needs incentive." He glanced at her, eyebrow raised. "I think you will soon have all the incentive you need." Glancing up, he suddenly noticed Gideon standing right beside her.

Gideon gave Maza a lethal look. "My job is to protect Graciela at all costs."

They all looked as if they'd been in a bloody battle. The sharp metallic smell of fresh blood mixed with the stink of the urine Loza had pissed when he died.

Gideon removed his bandana, wet from its multiple soakings, from his back pocket and handed it to Riva. Brain matter dripped off the metal lip of the console, and in places slid down the blood-splattered walls. None of them had escaped the flying debris. It looked grotesquely incongruous paired with Maza's polo shirt and chinos.

"Is that right?" Maza quirked a brow. "At *all* costs?"

"There will be an attempt on your life tomorrow, Escobar." Riva wiped her blood-splattered face and neck, and handed the bandana back to Gideon, who did the same. Her attention did not leave Maza. "It will be *Dante* who saves your life when two of your men attempt to assassinate you. I suggest you treat him with kid gloves until then."

"Until then. Yes. Come closer and watch the monitors, my dear. All right," he told her when she didn't move. "You can see as well from there."

The army green truck with the canvas cover that they arrived in came into view, driving from left to right across the empty, rain-washed field.

Two men jumped from the back, lifted a large, overly gilded red velvet chair from the truck bed. It immediately darkened in the rain. Maza depressed a button on the console.

"Put it over there by the red flag."

The men carried it a hundred feet to a small red flag on a wire, stuck in the grass.

"Bring out the prisoner. Secure her in the chair. As you can see," he said, turning to Riva, "there are leather restraints for just this purpose. No!" he yelled at the men through a speaker out of sight of the camera. "Tighter, Bruno, tighter! Tighter still."

Angélica screamed and thrashed, making the chair jump and buck on the rain-flattened grass. They couldn't hear her, but the sound of Maza's voice sent her into a tailspin. One of the soldiers held down Angélica's wrist with one knee. She tried to bite him. He got her other wrist buckled, and looked up at a camera for approval.

"Good man. Bruno. You and Iván stay there and wait for my orders. The rest of you may go."

"Do you see," he told Riva conversationally, oblivious to the runnels of blood sliding down his face and neck, and his blood-speckled shirt and pants, "Bruno has been honored with the same bracelet that we wear." He depressed the yellow button. "Are you pleased with my gift, Bruno?"

"*Sí, jefe.*" At the sound of his boss's voice, Bruno's head shot up as he finished securing Angélica. "It is a great honor."

Pretty easy to lip-read, since Maza zoomed a camera in for a tight shot of the three people in play.

"Secure her feet—no. Never mind."

The poor guy just stood there patiently, the rain flattening his hair. He exchanged looks with Iván.

"I don't need a show-and-tell. Just a tell, my dear." Riva brought his attention back to her. "Why don't you fill me in so that I can interpret my visions and see when the optimal time is for you to... Is what you told Angélica *true*? Are you here to take back control of the ANLF? So far, Escobar, all my visions have shown me is you drenched in blood. This much is true and has already come to pass."

If that was the case, her job here was done, and Gideon would be happy as a pig in shit to watch her put a bullet between psycho Escobar Maza's fucking eyes.

After they figured out how to get the thing off her wrist.

Until then the fucker had to be allowed to live.

"That's what you wanted help with? Taking back the ANLF?"

Maza smiled, showing off unnaturally white teeth and glints of his gold caps. "You didn't have a vision about this scenario?"

"Honestly, no. No, I didn't." She frowned, as if perplexed.

"Good, because that is not my purpose for returning to Cosio."

"Is it something to do with the dozen men in business suits coming here from around the world?"

"My legacy is to make a big impact on Cosio. No one will *ever* forget my name."

"*Which* name?" Gideon asked. "Maza or Diaz?"

"We are one and the same. I was born Carlos Diaz, and the name will hold me in good stead. I will run the SYP as Escobar Maza and the ANLF as Carlos Diaz, returned from the dead. The two entities will be a massive, secret conglomerate, controlling sales and distribution of Demon's

Breath *and* cocaine worldwide. I will be my own competition, driving up prices, completely controlling the markets. *This* is my legacy.

"Ah." He glanced up at the monitors. "I've been looking forward to this. Watch my dear, Chela. Just watch. Iván? Shoot Bruno. In the chest will suffice."

Without hesitation the man lifted his AK and shot Bruno from a distance of five feet.

"What the fuck was the point of that?" Gideon demanded. Angélica was screaming her head off. Fortunately, they couldn't hear her.

"Wait for it. Wait for it... Ah."

The monitors lit up like the Fourth of July. The building shook. Gideon grabbed Riva's upper arm to steady her. The brilliant flash whited out the monitors. Moments later they all flickered back to life.

With a cruel smile, Maza looked at Riva. "One minute after Bruno died, the chemicals in her bracelet combined. The mixture detonated. Should I die—" He pointed to the monitor and the still smoking field, where there was no indication that three people, or a chair, had ever been.

The entire area was one giant, fucking crater.

"Should I die, my dear Chela, one minute after my vital signs stop, your lovely bracelet will detonate and take out not only you, but anyone foolish enough to be anywhere within a thousand-foot radius." Maza smiled, his gaze encompassing both Gideon and Riva. "Shall we go?"

"Go?" Riva asked. "Go where?" "To Santa de Porres, of course. My destiny awaits me."

FORTY

gnoring Gideon, Maza smiled at Riva. "You and I, my Chela, deserve a little relaxation. My work is done for now and you, of course"—his eyes softened, as much as Maza's cold eyes ever softened, as they settled on her—"must need to relax, too. You've spent a horrendous few days in the jungle."

He was fucking serious. Even though Riva was rarely surprised by the evil people in the world, this bizarre, sudden shift to pseudo-tenderness was jarring. After blowing up his wife, the mother of his child, and two loyal, dedicated soldiers with an easy push of a button, in addition to obliterating a man's head right in front of them all, he had the freakin' nerve to talk about relaxing. The man was a true sociopath.

Riva inhaled deeply, reminding herself she was Graciela. She was the woman who would take this monster out of the world, making it a safer place. She pasted a sad, tired, Graciela-like frown on her lips. She let her exhale sound like a sigh of longing for the relaxation he mentioned.

"A good meal, time to bathe at your leisure, a good night's sleep? Yes. I will take excellent care of you, my dearest Chela, never fear."

"It's hard to relax with this." She held out her arm.

"With the assurance of my safety and well-being, and once my project is complete, I will let you return that piece of jewelry to me." He turned his palms up in a show of surrender. Riva didn't believe he'd ever surrender anything. "We will continue our long-distance relationship with no ill feeling."

Riva imagined him lying in a pool of his own blood, releasing his last breath. Yes. It would feel so good to take him out. If not for the powerful incentive not to die herself, he'd be dead right now. Riva gave him a cool look. "Knowing that if you die, so will I, does not change your fate, Escobar. My visions tell me that if you go through with your plans tomorrow, you *will* die. That you have now inextricably joined our fates will have no bearing on the outcome." She paused to make sure her words connected. "We will *both* die."

"But your vision tells you that some of my own people will attempt to kill me and your Dante will keep me safe. Surely two opposing visions?"

"If you try to go through with your plans *tomorrow*. You will die, he can't help you there. If, however, you wait the three days that I've seen, and your plans are successful..." More time for her team to figure what the hell he had up his sleeve. She closed her eyes for effect, nodded her head firmly, and said, "Dante will save your life when the men against you try to take away what you have built. That is all I can tell you." *And I just made that up. Not a damn thing is going to save you, asshole. Not a damn thing.*

Maza glanced at Gideon. "You must join us for dinner this evening, Dante. When did you realize you were not my son, Sin?" He gave Gideon an assessing look. "I suspect you were intelligent enough to stop taking Angélica's drugs at some point. Am I right?"

"The only thing keeping you alive right now, old man, is that damned bracelet." Gideon made no pretense of hiding how he felt. Jaw tight, eyes glittering, he was a bomb about to explode.

"She *bought* you in Venezuela, is that correct? Intriguing, I'd love to hear more."

"What do you know about it?" Gideon demanded.

"I know *everything;* do you think I do not? Nothing has occurred in the past seven years in the ANLF that I did *not* know about. Am I to take it that you disposed of Andrés? Ah, I see that is so by your look of satisfaction. That boy was always competitive. He didn't have the balls to follow through on things, but he wanted Angélica's approval as well as mine. He played both ends against the middle, but he had his uses. Andrés Garzon was ordered to be your good friend. You trusted him."

"Until I didn't. I slit his throat."

Maza shrugged. "A small loss, but one I risked taking when I tasked him to bring you and my dear Graciela to me. So be it. In the end, you came to me on your own. God's master plan at work. You will join us for dinner. I'm sure yours is a fascinating story to tell. Ah, I hear the helicopter. We leave for Santa de Porres. We'll spend a pleasant evening in the city. I will take you to one of my favorite restaurants for dinner, and you may sleep in a comfortable bed for a change. Tomorrow I will change the world."

A grandiose statement that gave Riva a bad, bad feeling, because she believed him.

"You're really going through with this? This doesn't sound like the controlled, rational man, I've been advising for years. Why so impetuous on this project, my dear?" Riva asked, calmly.

"*Despite* bringing me all this way so that I may be with you for this big event, you're ignoring what I tell you, and doing exactly as you want? Why did you bring me here, Escobar? To what purpose? You could've ignored me via *telephone,* you didn't need to bring me all this way for nothing. I almost *died*out there. I fought my way to your side, and for that I'm rewarded with this?"

She thrust out her arm. "*This* is how you repay me for the years I've assisted you in making exactly the right choice at the right time? Money I've guided you to, the business dealings I've ensured happened as planned, with the right people? *This* is my payment?" She dropped her hand, as she watched his microexpressions.

Puzzlement. Smugness. Triumph.

"You are angry?" He gave her a puzzled look. "I don't understand why, my dear. Everything will be just fine, you'll see."

"I *did* see. It *won't* be fine. Your stubbornness will cause my death as well as your own."

"I don't need to be psychic to assure you, you will not die, my dear Chela. You will keep me safe as a baby in its mother's arms. Nothing will befall me when I have both you and your Dante at my side to ensure my continued good health. He might wish me dead, but he will not do anything to endanger *you.* Therefore I have two extra bodyguards who will protect me with their lives. You are my *talismán de buena suerte.* Is that not so, my dear?"

Crazy, yes, but Riva had to acknowledge that Maza was more brilliant than crazy. Whether he knew Gideon's true

identity remained a mystery. Whether he knew the circumstances of how Gideon and Riva had joined forces, Riva
couldn't tell. What Maza had figured out was that Gideon
was going to do everything in his power to protect her, even
if that meant protecting Maza. His ability to divine that
truth made the man fucking brilliant and made her shiver.

Maza didn't need a psychic. His own intuition was damn
good enough.

Maza's ten-million-dollar AgustaWestland helicopter
was a far cry from the beat-up, faux Red Cross Alouette
Riva had arrived in a lifetime ago. The state-of-the-art
chopper seated fifteen, with herself and Gideon buckled
into middle seats surrounded by Maza's men. He sat up
front with the pilot.

Thirty-four minutes after leaving his jungle compound,
they landed lightly on the rooftop of the twenty-story Hotel
El Loro Rojo in downtown Santa de Porres. The midafternoon sun baked the rooftop helipad enough that Riva felt
the scorch through the thick soles of her boots as they ran
across the roof, crouching to avoid the rotating blades overhead. A squad of Maza's men was waiting for them, armed
and watchful.

A cursory glance beyond the roof's edge showed a colorful, overcrowded city with a traffic problem. Splashes of
vivid green indicated tree-lined streets and a large park.
The sharp smell of gasoline from car exhausts and the
sweetly scented fumes from the hotel laundry vent nearby
mingled with the pungent odor of Jet A fuel.

Smelled good to Riva. Civilization.

The muted din of the street was silenced as they entered
through a door to the service area.

"Tac team in three," Control informed her.

"I will send someone for you at nine." Maza stopped outside the elevator bank. One of his men pressed the call button.

He'd combed his windblown hair and tucked in his blood-splattered shirt as soon as they were inside, and looked ready to go out on the golf course and play a few holes. Apart from the gore on his clothing, he didn't look anything like the psychopath he really was. They could be convention attendees, arranging a dinner date.

Wasn't he in for a surprise.

Riva caught Gideon's eye. No way to give him the same heads-up she'd just gotten. But she used her eyes to indicate he watch the elevator, and hoped he got it. If not, he'd know soon enough.

"That's a long time from now," Riva told Maza, tapping a quick code on her ear, seemingly absently, as she spoke. *Thirteen tangos. Dead center. Principle left three feet.*

What the hell was Maza up to? "I should be with you to advise you." *To protect your freaking ass.* That one-minute warning, should someone get to him, was not going to give her any time to kiss her ass good-bye.

She just hoped he didn't get killed in the crossfire. Still, she looked forward to the shitstorm they were about to unleash on his ass. "No need, my dear." Maza patted her forearm. The same forearm that still had blood splatter and hastily wiped streaks of blood, now dried to a smeared crust. "Have a nice rest, enjoy the hospitality of this fine hotel. I'll have someone come for you at eight fifty-fi—"

The elevator dinged, and the doors glided open.

All hell broke loose. Four T-FLAC operatives, dressed casually to blend with hotel guests, fanned out from the elevator cage, guns blazing.

Everyone knew to protect Maza at all costs.

"Two each," Riva yelled, as she liberated the closest soldier's AK from his hands. "You snooze, you lose, *amigo*." And shot him in the belly. He dropped at her feet in a pool of blood. Jumping over him, she took down two more of Maza's men in quick succession. Exhilarated to finally be doing what she was trained to do, she swung the AK at a soldier aiming for one of her men and hit him a glancing blow on the temple. He swung with a roundhouse kick, knocking her on her ass and sending the AK skittering across the floor.

Shit. Should've seen that one coming.

Fighting the slick, bloody floor, she tried to get her feet under her.

Lightning fast, Gideon's reflexes came into play as he grabbed a handgun from the man beside him, shooting him with his own weapon point-blank. "Fish in a barrel. Hardly sporting. Need help there, Rimaldi?"

"You have your own problems, Stark. On your left."

Focused, and not caught off guard as Maza and his men were, Gideon got that guy and two more as he squeezed off a round of answering fire. He kicked a weapon out of reach, and her way, as he spun to throw off a soldier who'd tried to grab him in a bear hug. Adroitly he came up, taking the man off his feet and flinging him across the small room. The guy crashed into the far wall and lay still. Neck broken.

"Nice one, Stark— *Dios*. Deacon! Maza's making a run for it!" Heading back to the roof and the chopper.

Deacon, an operative she knew vaguely, and closest to Maza, grabbed him from behind in a headlock, dragging him into the elevator as bullets flew around the small landing.

Maza's men, suddenly remembering that this wasn't about them, that they were there to *protect* his ass, opened fire, just as Deacon turned with their boss in a choke hold.

Riddled with bullets, Deacon's eyes rolled up and he let go of Maza to crumple to the floor of the elevator. Dead.

Maza dropped on top of the dead man with a gurgled shout. Out of the corner of her eyes, Riva saw with dread that he, too, had been hit with the hail of bullets from the soldiers' submachine guns.

She scissored her feet, causing her soldier to stagger to maintain his balance. Straddling her with legs like tree trunks beside her hips, he fought the clasp on his holster, trying to liberate his weapon. "Yeah, you do that, *amigo*." Riva slammed her palm up into his balls, putting her weight into it. He screamed like a girl and dropped, writhing in agony. An operative put him out of his misery as she staggered to her feet.

"Maza's hit!" Gideon yelled, jumping over two bodies to get inside the elevator. He pulled off his shirt, cramming it against the gushing blood on Maza's chest. "Don't you dare fucking die, asshole! We need a medic!"

"Right here." Kyle Wright crouched beside Maza on the floor.

Littered with bodies, the landing was liberally covered in blood, gore, and shell casings.

The massacre had taken less than two minutes.

In the end, all of Maza's men went down, they lost one operative, and Maza bled profusely all over his pastel-colored golf shirt and chinos as he lay on the floor of the descending elevator, wounded, but still, thank God, alive.

"Car's outside the sub-basement kitchen," Control said in everyone's ears. "Elevator disabled. It's a straight shot. Hit it. Hold the blood inside that guy, Doc. Keep Maza alive."

"Copy that." Riva recognized Kyle Wright from a previous op. He was an operative first, and a medical doctor when push came to shove. It was shoving hard now. Crouched on the floor over Maza, he felt his pulse. "Give me handful of those bandages, Ellis, and hurry." Dave Ellis, who'd been wearing a small backpack, already had it open and was digging into its contents.

Oh, God. Oh, God. Oh, God. "That's a lot of blood," she observed, trying to maintain her cool. Every beat of his heart sent out a fresh rush of bright red blood. If Maza went now, his freaky little bracelet would bring down not only her, Gideon, and the T-FLAC team, but also the entire freaking hotel.

Gideon, standing beside her, but not touching, said, sotto voce, "Almost over."

Yeah, but which way? She'd like to believe they'd get Maza to the safe house alive. Prayed they'd keep him that way until they got the device off her. And really. While she prayed that if she exploded, she wouldn't take out anyone else, who the hell would miss her if she disappeared from the face of the Earth? Operatives died in the line of duty all the time. Maybe some of her fellow T-FLAC operatives and handful of friends would miss her. Until the next op.

"I might be out of practice, but I'm an excellent doctor," he told her, staunching the flow of blood with the bandages. They were high-tech, engineered to control blood loss, and had saved countless lives on the battlefield. "Although I suggest we haul ass, *muy rápidamente.*"

FORTY-ONE

The safe house, a boxy, bright blue two-story, was nondescript, crammed as it was between hundreds of similarly brightly painted hill homes and up a winding alley. The beat-up-looking SUV, which hid a fine-tuned, souped-up engine, screamed to a halt in front. It was well-choreographed madness as everyone piled out.

Maza was carried inside almost before Gideon opened his car door. In the chaos, all he could think of was: Maza would die. And so would Riva.

With an arm around her waist, and surrounded by the rest of her team, he ran for the open front door behind the others. "Where's the fucking bomb squad?"

A guy met them just inside. "You're looking at it. Navarro," he said by way of introduction to Gideon, eyes fixed on Riva's upheld wrist. "This it? Come on, Rimaldi. I have a place set up for you in back." Navarro glanced at Gideon. "*You*. Stay put."

"*You*. Fuck off. Where she goes, I go."

"Suit yourself."

At least the guy didn't say "your funeral" Gideon thought, following Riva and Bomb Guy down a long narrow hallway and into a sunny, all yellow 1950s-style kitchen. A guy stood at the antiquated stove, stirring something in a large saucepan. Another leaned against the counter nearby drinking from a mug. The kitchen smelled of strong Colombian coffee and spicy *lomo saltado,* a beef stir-fry, heavy on the aji amarillo chilis. Gideon's stomach responded to the savory smell of food. Shit, how could he even think about food now, when potentially they were all going to end up in a crater the moment Maza's heart gave out?

"You two, out," Navarro ordered. "That goes for anyone else on-site who's unnecessary."

The guy at the stove wiped his hands on a flowered dish towel, and smiled as he removed the pan from the burner. "We're all necessary, Navarro. Hey, Rimaldi."

"Yeah. Good point. Just give everyone the heads-up. You two," he said, pointing at Riva and Gideon. "In here."

"In here" was a tiny room, which Gideon guessed was originally a pantry. Now, the walls, ceiling, and floor were thickly padded with what he presumed were bomb blankets, all covered with a thin black fabric similar to a wetsuit. A couple of ladder-backed kitchen chairs faced each other, and a large black toolbox took up a big chunk of the limited floor space.

"Change," he ordered Riva, indicating a limp black garment slung over the back of one of the chairs. A couple of bulky bomb suits, with helmets, were tossed on the floor nearby.

"I'll find LockOut for your friend, but for the record, I don't want him in here with us."

"For the record," Gideon told him tightly, "he doesn't give a flying fuck what you want."

Navarro gave him an assessing look. "Fair enough. Be right back."

A triangle of sunlight fell across the black floor. Annoyingly cheerful, all fucking things considered. Feeling caged, scared shitless, and hopeful, Gideon prowled the small room. Took all of thirty seconds. "You trust this guy?"

Riva sat on the chair to take off her boots. The light glinted sapphire and amber off the liquid beneath the glass on the wrist device as she placed one foot over her knee to undo the laces. "Rafe's one of our best bomb disposal guys."

Gideon wanted to know where their number one guy was. *He's* the one he wanted on the job right now. "Then he'll figure out how to get that thing off," he said with a shitload more conviction than he felt.

Riva tossed her boots through the open pantry door, onto the linoleum floor of the kitchen with a *thud thud.* "Here," she said, removing her earpiece and handing it to him. "You can hear what's happening in real time. I just want to concentrate on not getting blown to smithereens."

Gideon inserted the comm. "...multiple GSW. Lungs, colon—the bullets had a party in his cavities. Yeah, I hear it. Slap some of that Saran wrap on here. How do we get that device off Ri-Graciela, prickwad?" A man's unsympathetic voice was backed by several muted conversations, and the clink of instruments and the harsh hissing wheeze of labored breathing.

Suffer long, asshole. Know your death is coming. That you're going to hell, you son of a bitch. "You're not getting blown to smithereens," Gideon told Riva, distracted by what was going on with Maza. "Fucker is too fucking evil to die just yet. Your efficient buddy will remove that, then I'll go and finish the bastard off personally."

"You'll have to get in line." Navarro stood in the open doorway and handed him a black garment. "Come out here to put this on, not enough room to swing a cat in there. Almost ready, Rimaldi?"

"Just about."

"Adrenaline's keeping this guy alive. BP is crap. Heart rate's spiking. He's losing a lot of blood." The voice in Gideon's ear was remarkably calm.

Navarro pointed to the comm that was set in his ear and told Gideon, "That's our answer to a doctor on this op. Dr. Kyle Wright, meet Gideon Stark."

"Tech genius Gideon *Stark,* of ZAG fame, is the guy Rimaldi picked up on her travels? Thought you looked familiar back at the hotel. Holy fuck."

"Yeah, that one," he said dryly. "Get rid of the boots," Navarro instructed Gideon. "This can go over your clothes. It'll be a bit of a job to get into it, but the LockOut will protect you." He crossed the kitchen and held up the coffeepot. "Then get into the bomb suit."

Gideon was so hyped up already, he doubted the coffee would have any impact. "Yeah, thanks." It was more than a "bit of a job" getting into the skintight wetsuit-like onesie. He almost gave himself a hernia tugging and stretching it over his clothes.

"Now the bomb suit. You can leave off the mask for a bit."

Gideon pulled on the hundred-pound bomb suit, feeling exactly like a sausage in a too-tight casing. If he was this scared, how did Riva feel?

"Okay," Navarro said, handing him a large steaming mug when he was covered. He entered the pantry with the other. "Ready, Rimaldi?" He handed her the mug and pulled up the second chair.

Gideon shuffled in behind him, then closed the door. His heart pounded uncomfortably when he saw Riva sitting in the chair. She turned around so Navarro could fasten the heavily padded suit up the back.

He knew she was terrified, knew it, but couldn't see it. His girl had fucking nerves of steel. Her skin was a little sweaty, a little pale. But she wasn't shaking. Not on the out-side anyway, and her hands were steady.

Only when she sent him a quick glance, did he see fear and doubt reflected in her eyes.

He had enough fucking terror and doubt for both of them. His stomach was in a tight knot and his pulse trip-hammered as Navarro fastened his suit next. The T-FLAC operative pointed to the corner, out of his way. By all of three fucking steps. Jesus...

"No suit for you?" Gideon asked the other man, who only wore the black wetsuit.

"Nah. Nothing's gonna explode here today. I just like to make my potential bombees feel safe." He shot Riva a small, intimate smile, which she returned, as she drew in an unsteady breath.

She watched Navarro's hands as he slipped a thin piece of LockOut fabric between her wrist and the device, then picked up a handheld water saw. "I'm going to cut here, and here. " He told her, indicating the cuts, two inches apart. "Just enough room to slip your wrist free. Two cuts, Rimaldi, and you're golden."

Awesome, they were upbeat and confident, and relaxed enough to smile at each other. Gideon felt helpless. He chugged half his hot coffee. It burned like hell going down. Good. Gave him something concrete to focus on. "The cuts will break the circuit? Render the fucker inactive? Or just let her get her arm out before it detonates?"

Navarro didn't glance up at him. "Remains to be seen."

Great, just fucking great. Gideon's heart lodged in his throat and his eyes burned because he was damned if he'd miss anything.

"Where'd you put the big bomb, prickass?" the doctor demanded in Gideon's ear. "He says he's happy to die, Navarro. No? Then tell us how to get that demon piece of jewelry off Graciela. Tell us now. No? He says no, Navarro."

Navarro grunted his response to that as he rolled over a small, high table and Riva laid her arm across it. Then he opened the toolkit with a loud, metallic snap. "Okay, here's what we have. The room is well insulated with blast mitigation blankets, and an added layer of protection with LockOut. That's for everyone else in the house if this all turns to shit. Nothing is going to shit on my watch, got that, Rimaldi? The headgear's right here if we get the one-minute warning."

"Just get it over with so I can get out there and do my job."

"BP dropping. 110/75. 100 beats a minute. Stay with me prickamigo, stay with me."

"Quit sweet-talking him and let him know that if he dies we'll stick his ass on a machine to keep his body going long enough to get this off of her. So dying won't achieve anything."

Gideon heard Wright convey the message to Maza as Navarro picked up a jeweler's loupe visor and put it over his head, then leaned in to look at Riva's wrist up close and personal. "We have full tac teams out there, Rimaldi. Everyone with one goal. Figure out what Maza is up to. You've been benched until we liberate this pretty wrist. Sit back and enjoy your coffee. Let me do my job."

"Do not upchuck on m—" the medic warned. "Shit, yeah. Bring that bucket over here. Puking up blood, Navarro. What's your ultimate target, prickpuke? Save your soul and tell us or your ass will burn in hell for eternity."

If Maza died and if Riva, God help him, died and whatever the fuck Maza had planned happened, then what the hell good had the last few days been, Gideon wondered. He looked at the smooth, brave face of Riva and knew. Their time together had been short, but he had had the most amazing, sensuous, daring, fun woman in his life. And he'd be damned if she was taken from him.

"Talk me through it, Navarro." Riva's tone was light. And only someone who knew her well would be able to detect the faint undercurrent of fear.

Heart skipping beats, Gideon let his weight rest against the wall. Did she see what was going down in the next hour? See her own death? No. She'd said she didn't get visions for herself. But what of the two she'd had at Maza's camp? Were *those* looking at her own future? Was that why she'd seen colors, and had intense feelings, but not "seen" a vision of herself?

Gideon's blood moved like icy sludge through his veins.

"Bracelet made from a titanium alloy. Extremely high strength-to-weight ratio," Navarro told everyone listening, but directed the words at Riva. "The problem with a titanium alloy is that they're poor thermal conductors. Heat during cutting doesn't dissipate. Okay. It's tough to cut through it. Not impossible, but tough. I have tools. I've done this before, will do it again. But be warned, it's *slow* going."

He set the blade of a small micrograin carbide substrate blade saw against the bracelet. The sound was music to Gideon's ears.

"That's the good news." Riva sounded shockingly calm. "I trust you to save the day, Navarro."

Jesus, she had *cojones*. What Navarro did not add, though, was that cutting temperatures could get so high that titanium chips sometimes burst into flames. Gideon had no idea how he knew that, he just did.

If the wrong tool was used, instead of cutting, it would push and strain the material. Which would then increase the material's strength, so that cuts that were possible at the start would become progressively harder.

"Good enough," Navarro assured her. "Educated guess. Yellowish liquid right here is probably $974CH3$. Extremely sensitive. Blue over here could be LT9. Put the two to-gether, even in these tiny amounts—*Big bang*. Not that that's going to happen on my watch, Rimaldi. So relax. This fine particulate in between is a catalyst used to create a void to aid in the initiation of the detonator."

"BP dropping. Yeah, prickface, I know you're having a hard time breathing, we can hear your life-sucking chest wound loud and clear," the doctor told Maza, not a trace of sympathy in his voice. "That's why we slapped this plastic over the gaping hole. Temporary measure at best. Tell us what we need to know, and I'll call in a priest and he can pray your way into hell. Tell me how this thing comes off."

"Is sharing all the details really necessary?" Gideon snapped at Navarro, then said to Riva. "We already know the two chemicals mix and blow the hell up."

Shit. He shouldn't have lost his cool. Everyone else around him was under far more pressure than he was. Except to everyfuckingone else Riva was a colleague.

To him she was... *Everything*.

Gideon reached across the small space, picked up her free hand, and brought it to his lips. Her fingers felt like ice against his mouth. Still holding her hand, he looked directly into her eyes. "Not. Gonna. Fucking. Happen."

Her smile was strained as her fingers curled around his. "Okay." Pulling her hand free, she returned it to the table where Navarro was sawing, at agonizingly slow speed, due to the need for heavy, constant pressure on the blade. Sparks glittered and danced over her wrist.

"Got it," she said softly, her eyes searching his face. "Can you give me a sec alone with Navarro?"

Fuck fuck fuck. What did she want to tell Navarro? Her last will and testament? Her last wishes? Lock the door so he couldn't get back in to be there if... When.

"Heart rate going under forty, BP 70/50." The doctor was giving them a sort of countdown to detonation. He sounded cool under pressure as the noises of an ER pumped, buzzed, and beeped in the background. Gideon heard it all under the hard thrumming beat of his heart.

He willed Navarro to communicate with him, but the man was focused entirely on gently examining the device with various tools. His bent head blocked Gideon's view of what he was doing. "Whatever you have to say, can be said to me, too," he told Riva.

"No. Leave," she added urgently. She looked up at him, skin pale and clammy, eyes shadowed. "Please."

Gideon's chest ached. He could refuse her nothing. "I'll be right outside." He shambled out in the clumsy suit.

"Close the door." Almost a whisper, as their eyes met.

Jesus. He died a bit as he tried not to look scared to death.

"Please, Gideon."

With a nod, he shut the door. If push came to shove he'd kick the fucker in to get to her. Leaning against the kitchen counter he closed his eyes. "Please, God . . ."

"Tell me what you have planned, or I swear to God, I'll make your last few minutes so painfully *hideous* you'll spend your dying breath begging for fucking mercy," the doctor said in Gideon's ear. "Here's my plan, prickdick. If we don't have answers right fucking now, I'm going to slice off your goddamn hand. Slowly, with a dull blade, *lo entiendes*? Then I'll start peeling the skin off your dick."

"If I die," Maza's voice came through the comm. Wheezing, fighting for each breath, he pushed out, "you will never know my master plan. And Graciela dies with me."

"Not if the device is immediately placed on someone who's *alive*. You didn't think of that as a solution, did you? Here's a better plan, since you won't tell us what we want to know. How about I knock your ass out for a while until we solve the jewelry issue. Then we can talk again."

"All going to die any—" His breathing became more labored and uneven.

The sound of the bone saw caused the hair on the back of Gideon's neck to lift. It was the sound of nightmares, but at that moment it felt like a fucking relief to Gideon. Could putting the device on someone else really save Riva?

Maza gave a gurgled, agonizing scream as the sound of saw met flesh. He sobbed, gasping for air. "*Thermobaric.* A thermobaric bomb. Big enough to wipe out Cosio. People are bidding on one of their own now. You can't stop it unless you swear you'll give me the surgery. Save me, I'll tell you where."

"You'll tell me where *now*, prickface. Aw, shit on a shingle! He's crashing. Don't you dare die on me. We're losing him! ETA, Navarro?"

Blood on fire, heartbeat manic, Gideon jerked away from the counter and wrenched open the door to the pantry.

Navarro didn't pause as sparks flickered over Riva's wrist. "Five minutes."

"We don't *have* five minutes!"

"Figure it out. We're close here."

"I'm taking the fucker's hand. Now!"

"Headgear on," Navarro ordered, not looking up as he switched the saw for a handheld laser cutter.

Gideon had never moved so fast. He yanked Riva's headgear up off the floor. Their eyes met. Her fear was palpable now. "When this is over, room service and a big bed, Rimaldi. That's a promise." He maneuvered the heavy helmet over her head.

He looked at the second helmet. Navarro was trying to keep that thing from going off, if anyone needed the second bomb helmet, he was the one. He started to put it on the other man. Navarro batted it away. "Won't be able to see."

The high-pitched buzz of bone saw, heard through the comm, was followed by an unholy scream. Then throbbing silence, which seemed to go on for an hour.

"Talk to me," Navarro said grimly as the small saw sent up a shower of fine golden sparks. He'd made the first cut and was working on the second. The laser sealed the cut edge so liquid inside didn't ooze out while he worked.

"Fuckit, we're losing him. "

Incapable of blinking, Gideon's eyes burned. Every drop of saliva dried up. Tightening his hand on Riva's shoulder, he prayed like he'd never prayed before. His focus cleared at the sound of the saw much closer to home. Navarro's at-tempt to make a second cut through the metal.

"Maza's dead."

FORTY-TWO

Riva heard the voices of everyone speaking through the comm before she had the bomb helmet securely on her head. Only one was as crisp and clear as if it was in the room with her, like an executioner's death sentence.

"Maza's dead."

Her heartbeat stopped along with Maza's.

This was it.

Navarro, head bowed over the laser cutter, said quietly, "Start the countdown."

"I'll do it," Gideon said, before Control started. "T-minus sixty."

Riva's heart began its own countdown in a rapid triple-time for each tick. It felt as though it was leaping around her chest in heavy boots, threatening to kick through her ribs. *Thud. Thud. Thud.*

Didn't her heart remember she was a trained operative? She'd faced life-and-death situations before. *This is part of your job, Rimaldi.* All the intense training, and numerous ops, were forgotten.

She wanted to live, damn it.

She sucked in another breath. Let it out slowly. Another breath...

"Cellular respiration declining," Wright said. Calm. Professional.

Holy crap. *Hurry, Navarro. Do this. Don't let me die.*

"Fifty-eight seconds."

With her job, she'd never imagined any kind of future. Never allowed herself to imagine sharing her life with anyone. Now that she had only seconds to live, it was *all* she thought about. It didn't matter that Gideon wouldn't stick around. She suddenly realized that in her heart of hearts, she'd hoped they might have a chance. A slim, crazy, *small* chance. Hell, any chance.

It was gone now.

The reality of *them* working out should never have existed in the first place.

He'd changed that. In the last couple days, she'd come to understand that. It didn't matter that Gideon wouldn't stick around. Hope for such a future was foreign to her. At least it had been foreign, before him.

The frigging bomb made her see that, when it was about to splinter her, and everyone around her, into tiny fragments. The clarity came with a price, because the bomb also obliterated her vague, nebulous slice of hope.

Hell, reality? Never existed in the first place. She'd known that all along. Of course she had. *Gideon Stark* and Riva Rimaldi? Never happen. Her wildest dreams had *never* taken her so damn far out of the realm of possibility. She was pragmatic, sensible, and above all a realist.

"T-minus fifty-four."

Were the last two visions she'd had reflective of what was about to happen? She tried to see into her own future. But as usual, her needs didn't equate into seeing her own outcome. Was that what they'd been about? Swirls of jagged red. Massive emotional pain... Unbearable agony.

Shorthand for her own death? His?

Dying wouldn't give her unbearable pain. Emotional or physical. She'd be freaking *dead*. So, not her own death, then.

Then whose?

Gideon's death?

While she'd seen only violent and painful colors, that felt closer to the truth. *Dios, his* death *would* give her unimaginable pain. She'd rather die herself.

The device didn't cover the razor-thin white scars on her wrist. Maza had pulled off what she'd been too chicken to do herself all those years ago. But she'd lived life between then and now. She'd learned and grown. She'd known happiness, but never love.

The thought of not existing any longer had not crossed her mind in over twenty years. Now she was faced with that reality. But for different reasons.

"Navarro." Control's even tone indicated a tension Riva hadn't heard before. "Not to rush you, but we have the small matter of a thermobaric bomb out there to contend with."

Riva started to get up. A hard hand on her shoulder pressed her down, as tight fingers steadied her arm. Gideon. "What the fuck do you think you're doing?"

Turning her head, she looked at Gideon through the visor. "You saw the demo at Maza's compound. My piece of jewelry here is about to take down this house and every other building in a thousand-foot radius. Hundreds of people will die. But that's small potatoes compared to what a *thermobaric* bomb will do. Navarro has to *go*!"

"Sit your ass down, Rimaldi," Rafe Navarro said. "And that's an order. We're almost done here."

Since she'd barely lifted a cheek to get off the chair, Riva hesitated, then settled back. "You know I'm right."

"You know how damned good I am," Navarro informed her, eyes down, saw showering her arm with sparks like fireflies dancing on a hot summer's evening. "I'm excellent at multitasking. The team has to *find* the device before my team and I are called in. Let them do their jobs, and I'll spend the next few minutes doing mine."

Gideon's voice sounded calm and controlled as he continued the countdown. "T-minus fifty."

"Tell you what." Navarro's head was so close to her wrist, Riva saw golden fireworks reflected in the lenses of the loupe visor. "If we make it, due to my prowess, brilliance, and dexterity with all things that go BOOM, you owe me a hundred bucks."

She gave him a weak smile, which he couldn't see since she wore the helmet. "How will you pay me if *I* win, Navarro?"

"Don't you worry, Rimaldi. I never lose."

Dr. Wright butted in. "Crap. Here's a new wrinkle we didn't anticipate—"

Oh God. Now what? It couldn't get any worse than it already was.

"There's an integrated microscopic probe into a vein," Wright continued evenly. "Fiber microchannels relaying info. The device won't *work* on anyone else. This fucker is calculated to his blood type as well as his blood oxygenation levels." He said something to someone else in the room, his voice muffled. Then came back. "We're going through records of local operatives to see who's a match. Someone with small wrist like his."

"T-minus forty-seven..." *Dios*. Under a minute to kiss her ass good-bye. Desperately, she needed Gideon to hold her, tight. Needed the feel of his warm skin. Needed his mouth on hers. Needed...more damned *time*.

"Almost there." Gideon's voice was strained as he tried to assure her that it was almost done.

Riva didn't believe him. She wished she could see him, but he stood slightly behind her and she felt his presence. But then, maybe not seeing his face, not reading his fear was better. It was enough that she had to deal with her own.

"What's his blood type?" Gideon asked. "I'm O neg."

"No go," Wright told him. "Need someone B Rh positive. One in about twelve have it. We're looking—"

"I'm B Rh positive," Riva told everyone listening.

At the same time Control inserted, "Rimaldi's a match."

"My hands are small enough," she finished. "I could slip into his device while Navarro works on mine."

"T-minus forty-four. Where's the surgical room?" Gideon demanded. Riva wanted to reach for him. To grab his hand and promise him everything would be fine. These men working around her were the best at what they did. But right now her entire focus was on watching the sparks fly as Navarro attempted to liberate her from the device, hot on her right wrist.

"Minute. Less if we haul ass." Navarro took her by the forearm, and stopped sawing. "Up."

They all knew they no longer had a full minute.

"T-minus forty-two. Haul ass." Gideon yanked open the door. They ran through the kitchen and down the hall.

"This way," Navarro still held her arm, but the sparks had stopped while they ran.

"T-minus forty."

With Navarro in the lead, they slammed into what had been a dining room. Maza was stretched out on the table, arm strapped to a board. All Riva could see was blood. Blood, and people moving about the room in slow motion.

"T-minus thirty-eight," Gideon stood beside her as someone shoved an IV stand out of the way, then pushed her into a chair next to Maza's body. "T-minus thirty-seven seconds."

The helmet gave her limited visibility. Blood. Maza's hand. Blood. The blurred spin of the bone saw. Blood.

Thank God she couldn't smell anything beneath the helmet. At some point, someone had placed both her arms on a small table. She'd hadn't been aware of the action at all. Odd. She was there. But not. Peripherally she noticed Navarro, back to grinding and sawing at her device. The sparklers showed up against the black of his LockOut as he bent over her hand.

"T-minus thirty-one."

Watching a man's hand sawed off his body was grisly business. Riva wanted to look away. She'd seen people blown to bits, people decapitated, limbs lost—all in the line of duty. This was a hell of a lot more personal, and she couldn't look away.

Her life hung on every red liquid spin of the blade. It was easier to imagine she watched a movie through the small view finder, than know it was a human being chopped up inches from her face. Even if that human *was* Escobar Maza.

"T-minus twenty-eight seconds." Other than Gideon's calm voice in her comm, no one said a word.

Tangentially, people moved around the table. Orange sparks floated over her wrist. Someone shoved back the bomb suit sleeve and managed to shove the LockOut sleeve up her forearm, baring it. Large drops of blood scattered before the saw applied to Maza's wrist. Mouth dry, Riva felt the itch of a drop of sweat trickle down her temple. Felt the hard, rapid *thud-thud-thud* of her heartbeat, pounded in her ears. Felt the burn behind her unblinking eyes.

"T-minus fourteen." No longer calm, Gideon's voice sounded strained and tense.

Maza's hand, flaccid and bloody, dropped into a bucket with a dull *thump*.

"T-Minus three seconds."

Competent hands slid the device off the stub of Maza's arm, and efficiently slid the Titanium band over Riva's fingers. It was still warm, and wet with Maza's blood and slipped over her knuckles, then aided by quick hands, seated on her wrist. The small prick of the probe piercing her flesh went barely unnoticed.

"Two seconds to spare," Gideon murmured, voice thick.

Thud-thud-thud-thud. Riva closed her eyes. T-minus two seconds. T-minus one second.

Thud-pause-pause-thud-thud-thud.

"Done!" Navarro said, with surreal calm. "Trigger cut. Hot shit, you're free. I'm a fucking genius!"

The second the device was removed, her arm felt as though it was filled with helium. Light and insubstantial.

A hot numbness swept over her entire body. Sagging, she realized Gideon hadn't left her side. Even encumbered as he was in the bomb suit, his arms were wrapped tightly around her, holding her upright as someone gently removed Maza's device, swiping her skin with a disinfectant pad as the probe slid out.

Her burning eyes met Navarro's. "Thank you."

"You're just too good of an operative to go kablooie, Rimaldi."

"Navarro." Control's voice sounded far, far away. "Chopper waiting on roof. *Go. Go. Go.*"

"Gone. And Rimaldi? You owe me a hundred bucks." Navarro shot her a grin and disappeared from view.

Riva's scalp tingled as she tried to swallow, but her throat muscles didn't work. "Helmet!" she pushed out, as claustrophobia swamped her. Cool air brushed her face as the bomb helmet was removed. She gasped for breath like a fish out of water, allowing all the pungent and metallic smells of surgery and death to overwhelm her senses.

Bile rose hot and acidic in the back of her throat, and she gagged. Prickly heat blanketed her body as she started to shake.

Gideon held a glass of water to her lips, tilting it so she could sip. Someone poured water over her arms, washing away the blood. Water, cold, and crisp, hydrated her throat, and reactivated her laboring lungs.

"Need a shower." Somewhere small and private, away from the eyes of her fellow operatives. She just needed a few minutes to be a scared woman before she went back to being a kick-ass operative. Just a few minutes...

The glass disappeared, and strong arms scooped her up out of the chair.

"Upstairs." Whoever spoke sounded far away and muzzy. "Second door on the right."

Dropping her head to his padded shoulder, Riva shut her eyes and let Gideon play the hero and get her the hell out of there.

FORTY-THREE

The second Gideon kicked the bedroom door closed behind them, he grabbed her up in a tight hold, and said raggedly into her hair, "Jesus, woman! I aged twenty-years down there. I thought I was going to lose you."

Riva pulled his head down and kissed him as she'd been longing to do for what felt like freaking eternity.

Their hands tore at the bomb suits as their mouths fused, tongues greedy.

"Turn around!" Riva demanded, grabbing his arm. The suit was thick, hard to maneuver in, but he turned so she could attack the clasps in back. "Hurry, hurry, hurry."

She spun around, and let him open the back of her suit just as fast. "Oh, freaking hell." *LockOut.* "I know where the— Move your arm. Stop helping." Breathless, she laughed as their hands tangled in their haste. "Now. Stand still. Let *me* do it." There was a trick to getting a LockOut suit off, and she didn't have the time or patience to show him.

Finally, they ended up naked and fell onto the bed in a tangle of lips and limbs, Riva on the bottom. Grabbing a handful of hair at the back of his head, she jerked his head down, then kissed him as she wrapped her legs around his hips, locking her ankles at the base of his spine.

He positioned himself at her entrance.

They came together fast as he buried himself in her. The act of penetration, over and over again, shoved their bodies across the width of the bed. He groaned with the force of his effort. She braced her hands on the headboard as she lifted her hips to meet each of his thrusts, half-sighing, half-panting with delicious pleasure as he rode her, hard.

They were both breathless as they came.

Now on top, when she could move again, Riva framed his face with both hands. She smiled. "*Awesome* thank-God-we're-alive-sex, Mr. Stark."

He lifted her hand, held it tight, then pressed his lips against it. "Bears repeating. Thank. God. We're. Alive. And Navarro. And the team of T-FLAC operatives."

"And you," she whispered as his lips found hers.

"And *you*," he said, pulling away from the kiss.

Sliding her leg over his hip, she slipped from the bed. For a moment she turned to look out of the window, trying to contain the intensity of her feelings.

Dusk fell in a translucent apricot haze over the city. Arms braced on the sill, she looked out over the rooftops of Santa de Porres. Picture postcard pretty, the city spread below in stair steps of vibrant color with the peaks of Qhapaq rising commandingly in the distance as a hazy blue backdrop. From this vantage point, none of the poverty, squalor, and corruption was visible.

"Riva?"

She turned, her heart clutching at the sight of him. Naked, he stood on the other side of the bed. The gloom carved shadows on the planes of his face, and delineated the muscles of his chest and ripped belly. Her eyes lifted to his face. Mouth somber, his eyes swept over her taut body as she remained backlit by the sky.

The very air seemed to shimmer with sensual heat.

She padded across the carpet, holding his gaze. Stupid to waste a single moment with doubts and insecurities. "Now," she told him cheerfully. "A hot, hot, *hot* shower. Come along, sir. I want to wash all your tasty parts, and see if we can take a more leisurely tour." Riva tugged his hand until he smiled. Slapping him on the butt, she dragged him into the bathroom.

The three-piece bathroom, small, utilitarian, and windowless, was en suite. As Gideon turned on the shower, she ran her hands down the curve of his back. "You have a lot of scars for a pencil pusher." Many of which looked older than the length of time he'd spent in Cosio. Perhaps many of them had occurred in Venezuela before he'd been taken by Angélica? Would he ever find out all the pieces that had brought him to this point in his life? She reached up and back for her braid, undoing it with practiced ease.

"Clearly pencils weren't the only things I pushed." He gave her a little push into the shower. "In, woman."

The molded plastic stall was barely large enough for the two of them to squeeze in side by side. The glass door didn't close, and a sliver of cold air crept into the steamy shower. The water was hot and plentiful, and felt incredible as it pounded down on Riva's head.

She tilted back her head and let the water sluice through her thick hair and run down her back. Riva was careful not to look at the water as it went down the drain. She knew that some of it would be red, and she'd seen enough red to last her for a long, long time.

He reached for the liquid soap and poured too much into his hand. He washed himself efficiently and fast, not aided in any way by her marauding hands as she committed his body to memory. Gideon laughed when she moaned at how great the hot water felt pouring over her. "That good, huh?"

"Right now? *Aaalmost* as good as sex." Riva loved the way his nipple hardened as she stroked her hand over his chest. She lingered, fascinated by the streams of water snaking through the hair on his chest and dripping off his beard. "Of course, I can say that because we just *had* amazing sex."

IloveyouIloveyouIloveyou.

"And are about to again." Putting the bottle back on the little shelf, he said, "Turn around."

There was no way to avoid touching him, even if Riva wanted to, which she didn't; the shower was too confining. Maneuvering her feet, she faced the wall. The brush of his erect penis made her moan in anticipation. But mixed with her arousal was an unbearable pressure of loss welling inside her.

The adrenaline that had held her together for *days* seeped out of her, and there was nothing left to hold her emotions together. *I'm a goddamn T-FLAC operative. I will not cry. I. Will. Not. Freaking-well. Cry!*

She tried to force a vision. A dress rehearsal for her future. But nothing came. Just the residual ache of the swirling red and the death of she didn't know what. She didn't need a damned vision to tell her that there was no *them* ahead of her.

Gideon was alive and well, his heart beating with life and vitality. And they had this moment.

IloveyouIloveyouIloveyou.

Lifting her face, she let the hot water stream over her. It took several moments for her to feel confident that she could speak without breaking down. "You know, if we tried to do it in here, we'd both dislocate our assorted body parts or potentially break through the stall wall." She added just the right amount of humor to her voice. "What do you say we speed wash and go back to bed?"

"I never took you for a woman who'd give up so easily, Rimaldi." Rubbing soap on her crown, he used both hands to massage her scalp until Riva practically purred. Or cried. Or purred and cried.

God she was a mess. And Gideon was the last person she wanted to see her at her vulnerable worst. She'd never wanted anyone's good opinion more. She couldn't bear for him to think of her with pity.

He stroked her ass with the hard bar of his penis and she whimpered with need as too many sensations, too many unfamiliar emotions welled up inside her.

"No fair."

He piled her hair on top of her head, then bent to bite her nape. "You can retaliate later."

The scentless soap didn't foam, but felt slick and sensual between his hands as he washed her hair, then her breasts. "You have beautiful breasts. Firm. High. Perfect. I love the way your nipples bead when I touch them."

Riva braced her forearm against the wall, leaning her forehead on it as he caressed her, tweaking her nipples until they peaked to painful nubs of pleasure. Hair roughened, and hard with muscle, his thighs pressed against her legs. His muscular chest crowded against her back, as he glided his soapy hand down her belly and between her legs.

His foot shoved her legs apart as he washed her swollen folds intimately.

Her breathing was erratic. It wasn't lost on her that only half an hour earlier, she'd thought she'd taken her last breath. She shuddered and clenched as she pushed her hips hard against him. "Killing me."

Fumbling behind her, she wrapped her fingers around the length of him. Slick with soap, his penis bobbed as she slid her hand down to the base, then up again, feeling the veins running the length, and the ridge of his glans.

I love you. She wanted to taste him. To see him.

Then she couldn't do anything other than gasp as he pushed two fingers slowly inside her slick opening. She shuddered at the slow glide as he curved them deeply, then pressed his palm against her clit. Riva moaned, and her entire body shook.

Her climax came slowly, like ocean swells, getting larger and larger, blocking out everything but the sensuous pull and slide of his hand in and around her. She felt full, swollen, so aroused that every slip and slide of his fingers made her peak a little higher. And conversely, had to bite her lip as she fought back the tears.

"Don't break it, sweetheart," Gideon murmured against her throat as she came in hard, trembling spasms.

"Oh, God." Unclamping her hand, she unfurled her fingers. "Sorry."

"Don't be sorry." He sounded amused as he brushed a kiss between her shoulder blades, his beard rough on her sensitized skin. "Having your hands on me feels incredible. But let's finish up in here and take this to a bigger arena."

"Give me three minutes and I'll join you."

"Two, and it's a deal." He dropped a kiss on her shoulder, and pushed the door open. Cold air swirled around her warm body.

Facing the wall, Riva swallowed the tightness in her throat. Water poured down her face, and she made no noise as she washed, then rinsed the soap out of her hair. Drawing in a shaky breath, and straightening her shoulders she turned off the water and stepped out onto the cool linoleum floor.

Wrapping the only towel around her dripping hair, she walked into the bedroom to find Gideon lying on the bed, hands stacked under his head, eyes closed. The last of the late afternoon sun streamed through the window, bathing the hard ridges of muscle on his chest and arms, and delineating his body in bronze. The dark hair on his chest tapered to his penis, which was large and semierect. She drew in a deep breath.

He looked like a sexy Greek statue.

He was also clean-shaven. Had she been in the shower that long?

Sitting on the foot of the bed, she flipped her head and towel-dried her hair as best she could with the thin cloth. Tossing the towel aside, she turned around to find Gideon's green eyes watching her intently. "What can I do?"

Riva crawled up to the head of the bed, lay on top of him. He was hard. All over. Brushing his newly shaven jaw with the tips of her fingers, she asked softly, "Do? A number of interesting things come to mind."

Gideon took her wandering hand and brought her fingers to his lips. "You know what I mean. Let the other shoe drop. Let it drop and get it out. You've had one hell of a day, and even the strongest man would have a meltdown after what you've just been through."

Riva shifted off him, pulling a pillow over her lap as she sat up, curling her legs under her butt. Combing her fingers through her wet hair, she gave him a steady look, while her heart jumped around her chest like a damned Mexican jumping bean.

"I'm a trained operative. Yeah, sure, it was stressful when my life was being counted in seconds. But I'm over it." Or would be over it once she got some distance.

Tossing the pillow aside, Gideon took her hand and pulled her back over him. She made a small *oomph* as she collided with his chest. Wrapping his arms around her, he said unsteadily, "Then hold on to *me* for a while, will you?" He sighed. "You might be unaffected, but *I'm* coming down from that adrenaline high with a crash." His arms tightened around her, and he kissed her tenderly on the mouth.

He wasn't the one who needed comfort, and Riva loved him even more for pretending that he did. They made love slowly, bathed in dying sunlight and deepening shadows. Riva imprinted Gideon Stark into every cell in her body with each stroke of her fingers, with each brush of her mouth. She didn't close her eyes as she came, fixing his face in her mind, as her body brought his body pleasure and release.

She'd remember the scar on his eyebrow, and the ones on his shoulder. She'd remember the way his lips tilted when he was amused, and his eyes deepened when he came.

She'd remember every microexpression, and the way his dark hair brushed his shoulders and fell like silk between her fingers. She'd remember the shape of his mouth, and the taste of his skin.

IloveyouIloveyouIloveyou.

She'd remember Gideon Stark until the day she died.

FORTY-FOUR

A note had been stuck under the door while she and Gideon dozed for a couple of hours. It said that clothes and weapons had been left in the hallway for them. She'd heard the house come alive as operatives came and went. Riva knew the drill. Maza's body and the two wrist devices would be removed.

Escobar Maza's identity would be confirmed, the two devices would be analyzed, and the room where Maza had been held would be sanitized as if nothing had ever taken place there.

And while she hadn't actually been the one to kill Maza, her job in Cosio was done the moment he took his last breath. She was not part of the tac teams here to defuse subsequent bombs.

The house was now as silent and empty as she knew her soul would be without Gideon. She didn't need a vision for that. She looked at him, sleeping naked, loose-limbed and contented. She wasn't a woman who ever thought of what-ifs, but right now, she sure as hell wanted to.

Wrapping herself in a towel, she opened the door a crack to retrieve the clothes and handguns. Grateful to be armed, and armored, Riva dressed in jeans and a black T-shirt in the bathroom, feeling almost like her old self. She placed his clothes on the rickety table beside the bed where he'd see them when he woke up.

She looked at the lights spread out below like multicolored stars in the night sky. Cosian's living their lives, their daily existence, unaware of how their lives hung in the balance. One wrong call, one wrong move by Navarro and his team, and everything she saw before her would be nothing more than a giant hole in the ground.

For two hours, she'd been free of thoughts of the threat of the thermobaric bomb. T-FLAC. Leaving Cosio. Leaving Gideon. And as long as she remained in this room with him, none of that was pertinent. Yet all those things pressed in on her whether she wanted to acknowledge them or not.

Her fingers curled on the sill. God, how was it possible to hurt this badly without actually having a gaping hole in her chest? She'd almost died a couple of hours ago, and yet, knowing this was the last private time she'd share with Gideon felt worse.

This was why she avoided emotional entanglement at all costs. This was worse than she ever could have imagined. Those visions were spot-on. The pain *was* red-hot, pulsing with finality and loss. She didn't understand the visions, but she knew that much.

And that pain of loss was with Gideon in the room with her. How would this feel when the last good-bye was said? When there wasn't one more chance to touch him, to see his face?

The view blurred and her eyes burned with unshed tears. Throat clogged and lungs tight, she forced herself to take one breath after the other. No one had ever died of a broken heart. She wasn't going to be the exception. The sheets rustled as he got off the bed. She heard the soft pad of his feet as he crossed the carpet to come to her.

Sliding his arms around her waist, he nuzzled his lips against her temple. "You smell sexy as hell." He swept aside the thick curtain of her hair to kiss her earlobe.

Wanting to turn and cling to him, Riva instead tilted her head. "There's no smell to our soap, that part's your imagination."

Mouth gentle, breath warm, he trailed kisses up the side of her neck. "*Your* skin smells unique, like apricots, and turns me on like nothing else. I'd recognize you in a dark room filled with a hundred women."

She smiled. It hurt. "What would you be *doing* in a dark room filled with a hundred women, Stark?"

"Searching for you." Cupping her breast through the soft cotton of her shirt, he stroked the under curve with a lazy thumb. "You didn't sleep long."

Wrapping her arms over his, Riva maintained a smile, determined that he never see how much it was going to kill her to say good-bye.

His forearms were like steel bands around her, steel softened by dark hair. Riva's fingers lingered and stroked. "We have that in common. Overachievers with insomnia." *Where will you be sleeping tomorrow night? Will you remember an old flame and try to rekindle memories with her?*

She closed her eyes. *Don't foreshadow. Enjoy the fleeting moment while you can. It'll be over soon enough.* Their time together was ephemeral, but that didn't mean she couldn't enjoy every moment they had remaining.

Riva loved the strength of his arms around her. Loved the heat of his body. She loved the way his heartbeat syncopated with hers.

Wordlessly they stared out the window. What was he thinking? They had been given a couple of hours, but she knew she had to go downstairs soon and start the rest of her life. Knew *they* were over once they left this room. Her vision told her of her heartache, and her visions were never wrong.

Her chest ached, and her arms reflexively tightened over his. She knew she was putting off leaving the room. Leaving him. There was no reason for Gideon to linger. He had a life to get back to. Her job in Cosio was done. She'd return to her furnished room at T-FLAC HQ in Montana, attend a debriefing, then await orders for her next op.

"I imagined meeting my son here one day." His breath whispered warm against her temple.

Riva stroked the heated muscles of his forearm. He sounded melancholy. She knew the feeling. Was he trying to figure out a graceful way to say good-bye? She had to make it easier for him. He owed her nothing. Their time together had been nothing more than danger linked together by short, passionate interludes. Hot sex in the jungle. Nothing to build on.

She easily imagined this tough, alpha male with a child. He'd be a great father. Kind and affirming. He'd build instead of break down. He'd love his child unconditionally. "I'm sorry," she said, softly, meaning it. She should tell him there would be other children. But children required a woman he cared about, and Riva wasn't a masochist.

"Ironically, me, too." He rubbed his chin on her hair and his arms tightened around her waist. "Weird, since believing I had a son was an unpleasant reminder of what kind of man I believed I was. Rapist was just one more black mark against my soul. And yet—"

"And yet you already loved him." Riva knew she had to pull away. Had to stop torturing herself *right now*. Nothing good could come from spending a few extra minutes indulging herself, when she knew the outcome already. This was as torturous as ripping off a Band-Aid slowly.

Licking her dry lips, she managed to say evenly, "Angélica fabricated the story to cement the fiction she was weaving around you. Something else to hold over your head. But it backfired, because it made you want to do right by him. You're a good man, Gideon Stark."

"Am I? Was I? I don't remember much more of *that* life than I did five months ago."

"I know it matters to you that you don't remember." *But I'm in this life. Will you remember me?*

"Odd bits of memory have been slowly sifting to the surface recently. More every day. But it's not enough. I want my past life back."

"If you don't remember, you don't. Can you live with never knowing all of it? Because, Gideon, you may have to. You can't spend the rest of your life chasing your past." Riva knew. What an irony. He was searching for a past he didn't remember and she was trying to forget one she remembered too well.

"You're right. But I'll find out who I was so that I can adjust my course toward the future."

"Smart man." As much as she wanted to stay right where she was, secure in the shelter of his arms, she disengaged. "We'd better head downstairs. Duty calls."

"Isn't your job here done?"

Riva picked up the comm from the rickety wooden table beside the bed and inserted it as they left the room. "I have to debrief before I head home. I'm going downstairs."

"Hang on. I'll finish dressing and come with you." He pulled on jeans, a black T-shirt, and his own boots, as she'd done.

The quietness of the house pulsed around them, especially after the high-tension activities hours earlier. The place looked old and unmaintained, but it was a T-FLAC property, and as secure as Fort Knox. Everything was in tip-top condition beneath the peeling paint and cracked plaster. The wood stairs did not creak as expected. T-FLAC ran a well-oiled machine. Vehicles and safe houses were no exception.

"Anyone home?" she said into the comm as they descended the stairs.

"Control room," Control responded instantly. "Turn right at the foot of the stairs, head down the hall. Fourth door to right."

Riva took out the comm, sticking it in her hip pocket. "I get to meet Control. Be warned, I might kiss him on the mouth."

"No tongue. But yeah. Me, too."

The door snicked as they approached, indicating that Control was locked in and secure. That unseen cameras charted their progress was a given as the door was unlocked before they got to it.

FORTY-FIVE

The minute Gideon walked through the door, he felt at home. The windowless room was cool and dimly lit, most of it taken up by a bank of screens showing various operatives in action at several locations. Several high-powered computers hummed quietly.

A giant of a man in a wheelchair talked calmly into his comm. Waving them in, he continued, "Bravo one. Stairs, southwest corner. Four tangos at your three. Five bad guys coming *up* those stairs. Delta two, bad guy right on your ass— Yeah, got him good. Keep moving south. Charlie, intercept six tangos about to come out and play with Bravo. Bravo one, sending Charlie to you."

When he turned, Gideon saw the guy's smile was distorted by a jagged scar across his face so he appeared to be snarling. "Rimaldi." He held out a hand the size of a ham hock, and Riva's small hand disappeared inside it for a moment. "Good to see you in one piece."

He turned slightly in Gideon's general direction, hand still outstretched, eyes on his monitors. "Darius," he introduced himself and at the same time adjusted his view of three figures crouched over a device. "Navarro. Sit rep?" Pause. "Any special requests?" He paused again. "Copy that. No, you know that's not exactly her field of expertise, but we're working on it." Pause. "Yeah, copy that. I'm here if you need anything."

"Where do you want me?" Riva asked her control.

God, did she really want to go back into the field mere hours after facing death in real time? Yeah. Gideon supposed she did. She was fearless, his Riva.

Control changed the view on one of the monitors. "You're off the clock, Rimaldi. We have everything covered for now. We're just circling the wagons around our bomb techs at the moment. Plenty of bad guys to go around, and plenty enough operatives to do the job. I have you on a flight out tonight at twenty-three hundred."

Eleven p.m.

Gideon noticed the clocks above the screens. It was now eight p.m. Three hours. Too much happening. Too fucking much that still had to be said to Riva. His heart was already thumping as adrenaline coursed through him; now it picked up speed as it thudded hard against his rib cage. He shot a glance at Riva to see how she was taking the news.

She was glaring at the back of Darius's head. Darius might have sensed her displeasure, because it rippled off her like lava from a volcano. If he did, he gave no indication. His voice was cool and steady as he gave directions to his operatives.

"Wait!" She gripped the back of Darius's wheelchair. "*What?* I call bullshit. I'm not going to be here when we save the day? What kind of freaking punishment is *that*?"

Darius turned to her, his eyes steady. "Stark. Explain to her that going home isn't *punishment*. It's the reward for making it out alive, and in one piece, and bringing the head tango bagged and tagged to our doorstep to deal with. Go home. Take some R and R, regroup. Job well done."

"You don't know me, Control." Her voice was tight, her features set. "I don't take R and R, for crapsake, and

I *never* leave until my whole team leaves." Not giving him a chance to respond to that, she gestured to the complex on the monitors. "Not a bomb set to detonate and wipe out the BRICS Summit?"

"Correct. The conference was moved to a different location three days ago, just to be safe, however. Nope. Different location; sports arena. Bigger explosion, bigger target. As your buddy Maza stated under some duress, we're dealing with a complex, *thermobaric bomb.*"

"Holy crap," Riva whispered.

"Fuck." Gideon had only vaguely heard Maza's words, but he'd had a more immediate issue to deal with at the time.

Thermobaric. Jesus Christ. Escobar Maza hadn't given a shit about simultaneously running two of the largest drug cartels in the world, or a piss-willy little financial summit meeting tomorrow in Santa de Porres.

Fuck no.

Gideon realized that he'd been fucking around with a weapon of mass destruction that, if not disposed of, would blow Cosio, and every man, woman, child, and fucking goat, off the map for eternity.

No wonder terrorists around the world were bidding to own one. Just the threat of a thermobaric, of the size he was now looking at, must be making bad guys worldwide salivate. Owning this thing would give them a leg up—way up—in the terror game. Forget the off the charts billions Maza would have made. His power would've been off the charts had he lived to hold his auction. The power he would've had would've been staggering. Terrifyingly so.

Gideon rubbed his hand over his freshly shaven jaw. Shit. The thermobaric would first disperse a flammable mist of underoxidized fuel, which would ignite to create a gigantic explosion of immense destruction. The massive fireball would incinerate everything in its path. The ensuing pressure wave would rupture internal organs, reduce load-bearing walls to rubble, bringing down buildings, tunnels, and underground facilities. It would also suck all the oxygen out of the air.

Whichever way you looked at it, if this sucker went off, everyone, every living thing for thousands of miles, would be toast.

And how the fuck did he *know* all this? The tight, painful band around Gideon's head intensified. Fuck, not *now* for crapsake.

Something else undeniable. Navarro and his team had approximately thirteen hours to disable the bomb.

Now Gideon saw the importance of the countdown clock Darius had set above the monitors. Just as, Gideon suspected, he'd done when Riva's bomb was being removed earlier. The guy must have fucking nerves of steel.

Darius gestured to the monitor image of an empty stadium centered between the other screens. "Soccer stadium. Part of a giant complex. Seats close to eighty thousand souls. Set to detonate at thirteen hundred. An hour after the game starts tomorrow. Canceled of course, but the bad guys don't know that. Tricky bastards. So far chatter has nine countries eagerly waiting to see the outcome of the blast before they start bidding on it. By then the whole world will be watching, and scared shitless someone will try the same thing in their backyard." He held up a finger to address his teams.

"Bravo, five—no, six—tangos at your five. Keep your heads low." He angled his head to look at the two of them standing nearby. "It goes off and it'll take out Cosio and half of the mountain, and everyone in and around. Leaving a mile-deep crater, a hundred miles wide."

"And hundreds of thousands of innocent people dead." Gideon watched the action on screen. Maza had been a monster, destroying an entire country and its population as a show of strength. Why? For the glory? The fucking fame? The money? "Maza's dead—"

Darius was a master virtuoso as he directed his people, knowing everyone's location and responding to a dozen convos at once. "His boss isn't," Darius said flatly, his attention on one of the screens where half a dozen black-clad T-FLAC operatives ran in a crouch on a rooftop. "Stonefish was the brains of—" He adjusted the satellite feed for a closer look in night vision. It was dark, and the city lights in the background screwed with the images. Gideon presumed the stadium lights were off to let the operatives move about unnoticed.

Watching half a dozen action movies at the same time, on standard definition, instead of high def, TV screens, made Gideon itch to get his hands on the computers. More, he itched to get his eyes on the schematics for the bomb.

"Delta. Up rez rescans. Copy that. I have visual." Darius told his people in the field. "Nine tangos coming up on your six. *And* on *your* nine. Delta, do you copy? Head for the third floor. Use stairs."

Fascinated, Gideon stepped in closer to watch the action, even as his synapses tried to tie in what he was looking at with some nebulous piece of knowledge, stuffed somewhere inaccessible in his brain.

Pain radiated through and around his head. *Dammit. Not now. Stay sharp.*

Riva touched his back. "There's a first-aid kit some- where, let's get you some aspirin for that headache."

"I'm good." Realizing that he sounded short, when he was actually touched by her gesture, he brushed her cheek with his fingertips. "It'll dissipate in a few minutes. Thanks." He'd become excellent at hiding the headaches from Mama and Andrés, but Riva had read his microex- pressions even in the flickering semidarkness of the control room.

It took a moment to figure out where the T-FLAC oper- atives were, and where Maza's men were as they tried to intercept them. Thanks to Darius, it was a well-choreo- graphed dance. The bad guys were like ants running around. The area where Navarro and the other two bomb techs were located was a locker room in the bowels of the stadium.

So after all that shit, Maza had a boss, someone control- ling the players like chess pieces. Well fuck. The world kept turning and there was always some asshole ready to step in and be the ultimate bad guy. Different face, same agenda.

"Can you zoom in..." Gideon asked Control, leaning in. The view of the bomb fuzzed, then came in clear and sharp. He narrowed his eyes as he looked it over. *"Fuck.* Not good."

"Things are going to get a lot trickier," Darius told them. "I'd appreciate you grabbing me something to eat, and a pot of coffee, if you don't mind. This has been an action- packed day already, and it doesn't look as if it'll slow down anytime soon. Besides, near as I can gather, you two ha- ven't had a real meal in days. Fuel up, it's going to be a long night."

To confirm that, Gideon's stomach growled. "We'll fix you up. Riva? Staying or coming?"

"Coming. But let's make this fast. Things are changing here on a minute-by-minute basis."

When they went into the hallway, the door automatically locked behind them. Riva shot him a small smile. "Safe house precautions. We protect Control like bees protect their queen. He's our nerve center."

"Efficient guy," Gideon observed as they entered the kitchen. A glance at the open door to the pantry showed it exactly as they'd left it this afternoon. He wasn't going to forget those few minutes. Ever. "What's his story? Was he an operative?"

"Darius *is* an operative," Riva told him, opening the refrigerator and removing the giant pan Gideon had seen one of the operatives stirring earlier. There was still a generous portion of fragrant *lomo saltado.*

"Injured last year in the line of duty. I didn't realize he was still in the wheelchair. Word is he's had a dozen surgeries, they told him he'd never walk, but apparently he's just as cool, just as organized, as a Control. He flat out refuses to be on disability or even slow down, and he's determined to get out of that wheelchair. Everyone's money is on him to be back in the field sooner than later. I've never met him before this, but his name is legendary at HQ."

"No one seeing him in there would think of him as anything less than on the top of his game. Guy must have nerves of steel to do what he does." Gideon stood back as she slid the heavy pan onto the stove with both hands, then turned the burner on low to start reheating its contents.

She turned, looking around as if trying to figure out what to do with herself. Gideon could think of several things, most of them to be done upstairs. She'd bared essential parts of herself, and he knew she was trying to crawl back into her shell to protect her underbelly now. Too late. He *saw* her, and that would never go away. He knew this woman. Knew that she hated being seen as vulnerable.

"God, I'm famished." Crossing to the sink, she refolded a flowered dishtowel. "I don't remember when last we ate something that wasn't a protein bar. Go ahead and start a fresh pot of coffee, would you?" She was talking a little too fast.

The dark window gave him a perfect reflection of her face. Tense, beautiful, strained.

Gideon went to her, turning her in his arms. Tilting her chin up with crooked fingers, he tried to read what was going on. "Are you worried about your team?"

Riva placed her hand over his, holding his fingers to her face. Gideon cupped her cheek. Her skin was cold, but the temperature was comfortably warm in the house. "No, they're the best. If anyone can defuse the bomb, it's Navarro and his team."

Stroking her cheek with the edge of his thumb, he crowded her against the counter. "Do you want to be out there with them?"

She bit her lip, her gaze never leaving his face. What did she read there? His desire? His feeling for her? His hesitation? Gideon knew he couldn't hide anything from her, even if he wanted to.

"Of course," she said lightly, sliding her hands up his chest and looping her arms around his neck. "But Control is right. I'm depleted right now. My reflexes wouldn't be as sharp as they should be. I'd be a liability. Tomorrow...Tomorrow it'll all be over. Everyone heading out, rig—"

Fisting the heavy mass of her hair, he kissed her. Loving the press of her body against his, he stroked a hand down her slender back, cupping her jean-clad ass in one hand.

Suddenly Riva stiffened. Slipping from between the sink and his body, she reached to the small of her back for her weapon. "Someone's coming."

He believed her and turned to the door with a small frown. "I don't hear anythin—" The front door slammed open, hitting the wall with a bang.

Riva whipped out her SIG and aimed it two-handed at the doorway. So did Gideon as he stepped in front of her. What the fuck?

Moving to stand squarely at his side, she said quietly, "They had the entry code."

Yeah, Gideon got that. But something felt off about the loud arrival. Riva didn't relax her steady stance. Neither did he.

Several pairs of heavy footfalls raced down the hallway. A tall, dark-haired man wearing jeans and a brown leather bomber jacket stopped dead in his tracks in the open doorway.

Anguish, hope, joy lit his face as he saw Gideon. "*Gid—*

FORTY-SIX

id—"

"Stand down, Rimaldi," a tall, redheaded guy wearing LockOut said as he and two other similarly dressed operatives came into the kitchen behind the guy in the leather jacket. "This is Mr. Stark's brother, Zakary."

Gideon's heart locked. Zakary. Zak.

His brother strode across the kitchen and grabbed Gideon in a tight embrace as Riva stepped aside. "Jesus." They were the same height, face to familiar face. Zak held him away, hands on Gideon's shoulders, searching his features. His eyes were almost the same color Gideon saw on the rare occasions he'd looked at himself in the mirror over the last few months.

Memories tumbled like marbles down a staircase as Gideon remembered the adrenaline rush of scaling that office building in Dubai, Zak laughing his fool ass off as they got to midpoint and turned to check out the view from a thousand feet in the air. God, what a rush.

"This is a fucking miracle." His brother's eyes never left Gideon's face. "Look at you. My God, all I was told was that you were here, and that your memory's impaired. I don't give a shit about that. You're fucking *alive.* I came as fast as I could. Didn't believe it, until I saw you."

Gideon's anger dissipated as memories rushed into the void that had marked his days for the last five months. *Zak.* Impulsive. Fearless. Foolhardy as ever, falling out of his canoe and almost killing himself white-water river rafting in crazy Cagayan de Oro, in the Philippines that broiling summer five years ago... "Impaired is one way of putting it, yeah." Gideon kept a straight face with effort as sudden elation swamped him. "What's your name again?"

Zak's face fell. "Shit! You don't remember me?" Stepping back and shoving his hands into his pockets, his eyes became even more intense, as if his very will would restore Gideon's memories instantly. Typical Zak.

Gideon stepped into him, touching the scar on his brother's jaw with his fist. "Cagayan de Oro."

"Fuckit, you prick!" Zak grabbed him in another bone-crushing bear hug. "You *do* remember!"

"Bits and pieces." Now, he suddenly realized, sans the splitting headache. *Hallelujah.*

"No sweat," Zak told him, eyes shiny with the same emotion Gideon felt. "I remember everything for the two of us. I'll help you."

"Swakopund?"

"Sandboarding in Namibia." The brothers shared a grin. "Efua." Zak sighed, hand over his heart. "Tall, gorgeous, skin like Valrhona dark chocolate."

"And just as bitter as I recall," Gideon said, dryly. "Didn't she try to lop off your dick after she discovered you'd cheated on her?"

Zak shot him a devilish scowl. "A minor misunderstanding."

Gideon's smile widened. "My memory isn't as it was, but I know that was a pattern, not an exception. What happened to that hot blonde they kidnapped with us in Venezuela?"

"Acadia. Married her."

Gideon did a double take. "Married her? You put a ring on it? Holy shit. Who are you, and what have you done with my kid brother?"

"And we have a baby girl. Her name's Gideola in memory of you."

Laughing, Gideon punched his brother in the arm. "Christ, I hope only half of that's true."

"Zelda." Zak's face was glowing with love. "She'll be a warrior just like her uncle."

"Yeah, well, more on that at a later date. I want you to meet someone. Riva?"

Zak cocked a brow.

Gideon held out his hand to urge Riva forward. She didn't take his hand, but she extended it to Zak; in the other she held a plate piled high with stew and tortillas. "Riva Rimaldi." She shook his brother's hand. "You two have a lot to catch up on." Moving toward the door, she gave them a cool, professional look, and a polite smile. "I'm going back into the hub, see if Control needs me for anything." She glanced at the operatives who watched the interaction as if they were at a tennis match. "Don't you three have something to do? Give these guys some privacy. And Control wants some hot coffee and food. My hands are full; can one of you take care of that?"

"Geez, Rimaldi." The redhead, steaming mug of coffee in hand, inched closer to the stove. "Can we at least grab something to eat first?"

Knowing how erratic and infrequent sitting down to a meal was for Riva and her fellow operatives, Gideon took Zak's arm. "We'll go in another room."

"Not the dining room," the shorter of the three men told them. "Garbage isn't done in there yet. There's a maid's room or storeroom near the back door. Nobody will bug you in there."

"Walk with us," Gideon told Riva. *Stay with me. Be with me. I can give you the real me now.* Holy shit. He might not remember every detail of his prior life, but the memories he had were full and in brilliant technicolor. He was *back*.

Thank God. He. Was. Back.

They left the operatives to their meal and proceeded down the wide hallway together.

Zak looked from Riva to Gideon. "Care to fill me in?"

"We're in the middle of an op." Riva's voice was cool and short to the point of rudeness. "I have to talk to Control. Catch up with you later."

Gideon knew a brush-off when he heard one. But something important crashed into his brain with lightning speed, and literally stopped him in his tracks.

Holy fucking shit!

He and Zak had worked on a government project a few years ago. Tailoring a thermobaric weapon for use in the military targets tunneled in rock in Afghanistan. Gideon's heart leapt.

Hot shit. He remembered things.

Zak was here.

Their combined knowledge and expertise could help T-FLAC, and specifically Navarro, defuse the bomb set by Maza. "Principal bad guy, Escobar Maza, now deceased, set a thermobaric to detonate at tomorrow's soccer game," he said evenly, holding his brother's gaze. He saw the same leap of interest there as he felt himself. "Game's canceled, bomb still active."

Zak whistled. "Project L Seven, right? We know a bit about those. How big?"

"Big enough to take out Cosio and a good chunk of Peru with it."

"What are we doing just standing here? Presumably you're working on this with these people, right? Or don't they need your expertise?"

Gideon would have laughed if the situation hadn't been so dire. "They don't know I have any. Our involvement on that project was classified. Hell, *I* didn't remember DC until a nanosecond ago, myself."

"Are you saying they don't know about our familiarity with this particular weapon?"

The door to the hub clicked as Darius unlocked it from the inside. "Come in, gentlemen." His voice came through a small speaker above the door. "I believe you can both assist us."

Fascinated by this new development, Riva followed them into the hub. Turned out that one of numerous government contracts held by the Stark brothers was one of their inventions. A remote detonator for a thermobaric weapon. Go figure.

Riva stood back as Control gave the brothers a computer, access to the dark net and to whatever else they needed, including entrée to T-FLAC's servers and all the backup personnel they wanted.

Gideon and Zak worked alongside Darius, with a live feed directly to Navarro and his team, and to computer tech Honey Winston in Montana, already in contact with her husband, Navarro. It was one big party in the Hub.

There were enough operatives to protect the perimeter as the bomb techs worked. Riva was grounded. Not needed in the field, nor was she needed while Gideon and his brother saved the world.

She was redundant.

Picking up the plate of ignored food, she quietly exited the room, making a detour through the kitchen, then left via the front door so she could get a damned grip.

She'd had a vision in the hub. Of Gideon and his family at a barbeque in a pretty backyard in Seattle. His home, she knew. Warmth and love. Light and laughter. The vision was all things fluffy. Rainbows and puppies.

Dear God. She was carving out her own guts with a grapefruit spoon.

The door to the safe house shut quietly behind her. Allowing a few moments for her eyes to adjust to the darkness, she started walking. Long, purposeful strides that widened the space between Gideon and her real life.

Either she'd find a cab at this ungodly hour, or she'd damn well walk the sixteen miles to the Santa de Porres airport. She had plenty of time. A quarter moon hung in a starry sky, making it easy to navigate the black and white landscape of garbage cans, kids' toys, and the occasional cat darting in front of her. A distant dog howled. She knew how it felt. She wanted to howl, too. Fortunately, she was a trained operative, a pragmatic and sensible woman, and a realist.

This feeling would pass. She was sure these kinds of too-powerful emotions burned themselves out. Eventually. Her hate of her stepfather had eventually cooled to indifference, her pain to a dull throb of memory. This would pass, too.

All she had to do was hop a plane to Montana, get back to work, and not read a newspaper for about a year. She figured it would take that long for the sensation of Gideon Stark's return from the dead to die down.

Using her palm, Riva swiped at moisture on her face. "Out of sight, out of mind."

The warm evening air smelled not unpleasantly of various dinners and the sharp scent of marijuana. She lengthened her stride. The moonlight provided enough illumination to see by. Good thing, since the streetlights had all been shot out at some point. Only a few lights were still on in the houses lining the street as she headed down the hill, staying in the deeper shadows. A few riffs on a piano started out promisingly, but abruptly stopped.

The population of Santa de Porres slept, unaware that a team of crack T-FLAC operatives and the amazing Stark brothers were securing their futures as they dreamed of keeping the roof over their heads, and how to put food on their tables.

As she walked, tears fell. Her first instinct was to make herself stop. But she couldn't. What the hell. No one was there to see her weakness. The distant hum of light traffic almost masked a horrible, jarring raw cry. Riva stop dead in her tracks, trying to drag in a breath because she felt as though she was suffocating. Then she realized the sound of an animal crying out in agony was herself and it scared the crap out of her.

Bending from the waist, she braced her hands on her knees like a long-distance runner, trying to suck in more oxygen. *You're okay. You're okay. You're okay.*

Okay? Not even close.

This. This was her vision? Jagged red edged with black. Excruciating, unbearable pain.

Her pain? Her emotional death?

Damn it to hell. She still couldn't get a handle on the dark vision.

Was it her future? Black. Bleak.

Her chest hurt. Riva pressed her fingers to her eyelids as if that would staunch the tears. It was as though she stood outside herself, watching as she disintegrated emotionally.

Internal detonation.

Helpless despair.

She hadn't cried like this since she was a nine year old sitting on the closed toilet lid with a razor blade in her sticky red fingers.

This was worse. Paralyzed by the sharp shards of ripping emotions, Riva fell to her knees on the dirty sidewalk. Head to her knees, a raw keening wail ripped up through her chest. .

The intensity of her sobs tore her throat, shaking her entire body. After minutes, or hours, she whispered in a hoarse, broken voice, "Stop. Stop. Stop." But the Genie had been released from the bottle, and there was no stopping the flood of grief pouring from her very soul.

She had no idea how long she crouched there, curled into herself. Heart pounding frantically, she fought to catch her breath. "You're all right. You're all right. You're all right." The self-soothing didn't work anymore. "Please. Make it stop." She rubbed her hands over her face, wiping away the tears.

"Snap the hell out of it, Rimaldi." Her voice raw and shaky, she forced herself to straighten. Everything ached. Her muscles and sinews, her bones, her lungs, her heart. It all damn well fucking hurt as if she'd been beaten.

She *had* been beaten. Frequently. Had worse than beatings. Frequently. But this upped the level of her tolerance to pain a thousandfold.

Staggering to her feet, she resumed walking. Fast, long strides. "You know you're being an overly dramatic idiot, right, Rimaldi?" Pragmatic, sensible, dependable, Riva Rimaldi? *Dramatic?* Riva didn't know who she was anymore. She didn't like this woman. Weak. Fearful. Resigned. Jealous of a relationship Gideon had with his brother. They were a unit.

As ever, she was outside in the cold.

Her therapist would be bitterly disappointed to see that she'd regressed. Riva released a harsh, wobbly laugh.

She'd give herself three more minutes at her pity party, then she'd get back her spine, and go back and find herself something useful and constructive to do until she could say a mature, casual good-bye to Gideon.

A car screech to a stop behind her. The headlights bathed the trash-littered road in front of her in an unflattering spotlight which she saw through a blur of tears. Great, now she was going to be frigging-well mugged.

Someone grabbed her upper arm, yanking her to a stop. Numb, she apathetically barely reached back for her weapon as she lifted her tear-streaked face.

"Dear God." Gideon's voice cracked as he wrapped his arms around her with bruising strength. "Riva. Sweetheart. What happened? What's wrong? Where the fuck are you going alone in the middle of the night? If you wanted to come to the airport someone would've brought you here. You didn't have to fucking *walk*!"

The lure of his hard chest made her neck feel too weak to support her head, but she kept it upright. What she couldn't do was stop sobbing. Great, heaving, gut-wrenching sobs that ripped her apart.

"Riva. Fuck it. Talk to me."

"Go back to the-the house. You guys have a bomb to defuse."

"We did it. We're done. Everyone's on their way back. Zak just left with some of the guys to buy beer."

They were done? The bomb defused? She gave him a blank look, trying to compute defusing a thermobaric bomb, beer, and the microexpressions on Gideon's face through a watery veil "How's it possible you did all that in such a short time?"

"You've been gone for hours, sweetheart. Look you're almost at the airport." He used his shoulder to indicate the fence, and beyond that the rows of white runway lights and several gleaming white jets.

Pushing her hair off her face, he gave her a look so tender, so filled with love, the tears threatened again. "Where were you going, honey?"

God, all these endearments were freaking *killing* her. She tried to muscle his arms away, but he didn't budge.

"Home." Her voice sounded thick and pain-filled. "I'm going home to Montana."

"I don't get it. You told Darius you were staying until you left with your team."

She shrugged, willing the tears to stop damn-well falling. This was humiliating. Later she'd be ashamed that she was behaving like a lovesick schoolgirl, but right now she didn't give a shit. And even if she had, there wasn't a damn thing she could do about it. "I'm redundant h-here. Navarro has things covered out there. You and Zak are reunited. And I'm happy for you, Gideon, I really am. You guys will figure things out. He'll help you fill in the blanks—"

"I don't give a flying fuck right now about any of that." His strong hands came up to bracket her face. "I love you."

Her heart stopped beating. A moment. Two. Then started again fast and erratic. "We've barely known each other five minutes. You can't fall in love with someone in such a short time, you know you can't." She lied. She had.

"I have. I love you, Riva."

Oh, God... "Don't." Ragged and broken, her voice was a mere whisper. "Don't love me, I'll just disappoint you."

"How could you possibly disappoint me? You're... Everything."

"You want me? Sexually. Fine. We can figure out how to make that work."

"*No.* That's not enough. I want to spend the rest of my life with you. I love you, Riva Rimaldi. Love you, like you, am turned on by you. I want it all." He tilted her face so she had to look at him. "Don't overthink this. Tell me how you feel, here." He pressed his hand to her heart. Warm. Strong. Comforting.

"I'm sorry. I really am. It's me, not you. I'm terrible at relationships. I know I am. I've been working on myself for years. And, trust me, I'm not good at these kind of conversations. I can't be who you want, Gideon. Not who or what you want. That doesn't mean I don't have similar feelings."

"What feelings?"

She wasn't going to say it. Couldn't. Instead, she said brokenly, "I h-hate love." The tears had stopped, but she couldn't stop shaking. In response, his arms tightened around her

"No. You hate to trust," he said, hot breath warming the top of her head. "You hate to be disappointed. You deserve to have all the love in the world." He pulled back, cupping her face in his hands so she was forced to gaze into his eyes. "I love you, Riva. I'll love you forever."

"Don't." She tried again to wrench herself out of his hold, but Gideon held firm. Not letting her go. He would soon enough. Riva met his gaze head-on. He didn't get it. And as much as it killed her to reveal this part of herself, he deserved to know the truth.

"I'm good for a night or a weekend, maybe for a crazy dash through the jungle. But I don't do permanent."

"You won't know until you try it, will you? Open yourself to the possibility that you're lovable. Let me in."

She shook her head. "I've been afraid to let anyone in, to risk losing myself, to be trusting. Protecting myself is a habit."

He used his thumb to brush away a tear, and said with aching tenderness, "Maybe it's time to change your habits."

She couldn't stand seeing the look of love on his face, and squeezed her eyes shut. "Habits protect me."

He brushed a kiss to her lids. One, then the other. "Love is everything, and none of us can go on without it. I'll protect you, body and soul and heart."

"Who'll protect me from you?" It came out in the barest whisper.

"You don't need protection from me. Let go. Just let go of all those old habits and fears. Take a chance on me. Take a leap of faith."

As she looked in his eyes, it came to her, a blinding flash of insight. That dark, jagged vision was Gideon's life without her in it. It was *his* pain she'd felt.*His* loss of hope. Her heart leapt.

"Maybe you're right, maybe it is time for new habits." She shook her head. "I don't want to be without you for the next twenty years, or fifty, or however many there are. And I don't want to lie to you. I'm a kick-ass operative, but I'm a total screw-up emotionally. That's why I've been in therapy for years. Trust me, you don't know me, so you can't love me. And even if you did, I'm bound to make you miserable."

His microexpressions showed her his joy and his pain. Happiness and fear vying for supremacy in an ever-changing display of his deepest emotions. "Don't waste our time trying to talk me out of what I feel. What I know. You're brave, kick-ass, smart as hell, and I'd like to keep you naked in a room with just a bed, and room service." The look in his eyes pierced her heart. "You aren't the sum of your past. I'm sorry you had to endure what you did. But everything that happened to you, brought you to the here and now. To me. Don't use your past to deny all the amazing possibilities of your future."

Moonlight loved the angles and curves of his face. It tangled in the long dark strands of his hair, falling around the strong column of his throat, and limned his broad shoulders. "I love you. I love the way you tilt your head down and read through your lashes when you face-read. I love the way you bite your lip when you're trying to figure out what to do next. I love the way your eyes go misty when we make love. I love that you get wet just thinking about having sex with me. I love the smell of your skin." His tender smile filled her universe. "I know that you're honest. You're dogged. You're an excellent shot. You're fearless about everything but love."

He brushed away another tear she hadn't been aware of shedding. "I know that you're scared that I'll find you unlovable because of the lies told to you by people you should've been able to trust. I know all that. I don't love you *in spite of* all those things. I love you because of them. I love the way you've overcome so much in your life, with such bravery. And I love that I can't imagine spending the next fifty years of my life not waking up beside you every morning."

His tender smile pierced her aching heart. "That chopper crash was the best thing that ever happened to me. I do know you, Riva. And what I don't know, I'll have the rest of my life to find out."

It finally made sense. The muddled confusion of expressions crossing his face faster than lightning across a stormy sky in the jungle was love, in all its crazy, twisted glory. He loved her. Her heart pounded.

She thought of a million ways to argue with him, but he put a finger on her lips and shook his head. "Don't even try to talk me out of it."

She drew a deep breath. "It won't be easy. I'm going to have to work at this love thing really hard. I don't want to disappoint you."

"The only thing that would disappoint me is you not loving me. The rest we'll work on. Together. Forever, you and me, every day. Say it, Rimaldi."

She rose on her toes to bring their mouths closer. At long last, she had a vision of her future, and he was right in front of her. "I love you, Gideon Stark."

About Cherry Adair

Always an adventurer in life as well as writing, New York Times best-selling author Cherry Adair moved halfway across the globe from Cape Town, South Africa to the United States in her early years to become an interior designer. She started what eventually became a thriving interior design business. "I loved being a designer because it was varied and creative, and I enjoyed working with the public." A voracious reader when she was able to carve out the time, Cherry found her brain crowded with characters and stories of her own.

"Eventually," she says, "the stories demanded to be told." Now a resident of the Pacific Northwest she shares the award- winning adventures of her fictional T-FLAC counter terrorism operatives with her readers. When asked why she chooses to write romantic action adventure, she says, "Who says you can't have adventure and a great love life? Of course if you're talking about an adventurous love life, that's another thing altogether. I write romantic suspense coupled with heart-pounding adventure because I like to entertain, and nothing keeps readers happier than a rollercoaster read, followed by a happy ending."

Popular on the workshop circuit, Cherry gives lively classes on writing and the writing life. Pulling no punches when asked how to become a published writer, Cherry insists, "Sit your butt in the chair and write. There's no magic to it. Writing is hard work. It isn't for sissies or whiners."

Cherry loves to spend time at home. A corner desk keeps her focused on writing, but the windows behind her, with a panoramic view of the front gardens, are always calling her to come outside and play. Her office has nine-foot ceilings, a fireplace, a television and built-in bookcases houseapproximately 3,500 books.

"What can I say? My keeper shelf has been breeding in the middle of the night, rather like drycleaners' wire clothes hangers."

Where can we find out more about you CherryAdair?

On my website: www.cherryadair.com,

Twitter and my beloved Facebook. I love hearing from readers – wherever you may find me.

Look For These Thrilling eBooks in the Cherry Adair Online Bookstore.

http://www.shop.cherryadair.com

Lodestone Series

Hush - Book 1

Gideon - Book 2

T-FLAC/PSI

Edge of Danger Enhanced

Edge of Fear Enhanced

Edge of Darkness Enhanced

T-FLAC/WRIGHT FAMILY

Kiss and Tell Enhanced

Hide and Seek Enhanced

In Too Deep Enhanced

Out of Sight Enhanced

On Thin Ice Enhanced

T-FLAC/BLACK ROSE

Hot Ice Enhanced

White Heat Enhanced

Ice Cold

T-FLAC SHORT STORY

Ricochet

Cherry Adairs' Writers' Bible

Available Exclusively on the Cherry Adair Online Bookstore

We hope you enjoyed this Cherry Adair ebook. Connect with Cherry on CherryAdair.com for info on new releases, access to exclusive offers, and much more!

CPSIA information can be obtained at www.ICGtesting.com
Printed in the USA
LVOW04s2139300415

436833LV00013B/163/P